THE RED WYVERN

Voyager

THE
RED WYVERN

BOOK ONE OF
THE DRAGON MAGE

KATHARINE KERR

HarperCollins*Publishers*

F54,678

HarperCollinsPublishers
77–85 Fulham Palace Road
Hammersmith, London W6 8JB

£16·99

Published by HarperCollinsPublishers 1997
1 3 5 7 9 8 6 4 2

A catalogue record for this book is
available from the British Library

ISBN 0 00 224142 0 (hardback)
0 00 224351 2 (trade paperback)

Printed and bound in Great Britain by
Caledonian International Book Manufacturing Ltd, Glasgow

For Jo Clayton

AUTHOR'S NOTE

I must apologize to the faithful readers of this on-going project who have had to wait so long for the volume now in hand. I have been much distracted of late by legal matters, in particular the suits and counter-suits concerning a certain Elvish scholar of Elvish and his libellous attacks upon me. When Gwerbret Aberwyn ruled in our favour in malover, my publishers and I hoped that the matter had ended at last, but alas, our opponent saw fit to appeal to the High King himself. After an enervating journey by coach and barge on the part of myself and a representative of my publisher, we settled into a suite at a public guesthouse in Dun Deverry and filed our counter-suit. While we waited for our proceedings to be summoned, I once again applied myself to the craft for which I am better suited than legal wrangling, that of writing novels.

Some months later, we are still waiting. Let us hope that the High King's courts take up and dispose of this matter soon.

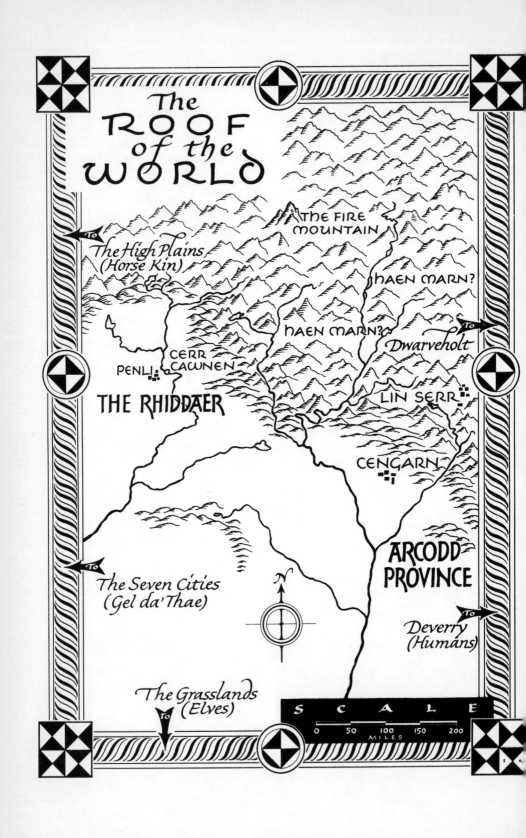

PROLOGUE

Winter, in a Far Distant Land

Some say that all the worlds of the many-splendoured universe lie nested one within the other like the layers of an onion. I say to you that they lie all braided and wound round and that no man nor woman either can map all the roads of their twisting.

The Secret Book of Cadwallon the Druid

Domnall Breich knew the hills around Loch Ness well enough to know himself lost. The hunting accident that had killed his horse and separated him from his companions had happened some two miles straight south, or at least, in that direction and at that distance as closely as he could reckon. By now he should have reached the frozen dirt road that led back to the village and safety. He stopped, peering through the rising mists at the snow-streaked valley, stippled here and there with pines. The gathering dark of the winter's shortest day shrouded Ben Bulben, the one landmark that might guide him through the mists. When he glanced at the sky, he realized that it was going to snow.

'Mother Mary, forgive my sins. Tonight I'll be seeing your son in his glory.'

They always said that freezing was as pleasant a death as any, more like falling asleep to wake to fire and sleet and then the candlelight that would guide you to the gates of Heaven or Hell. Domnall felt no fear, only surprise, that a man like him would die not in battle or bloodfeud but in the snow, lost like a lame sheep, but then the priests always said a man could never tell the end God had in store for him.

Ahead against the grey of clouds, the western sky gleamed dull red at the horizon. When he faced the glow and looked round, he saw off to his right, at the edge of his vision, a tall tree. He turned and sighted upon it. His last hope lay in keeping a straight course toward the north, the general direction of the loch, which ran southwest to northeast. If he reached the edge of that dark gash in the land, he could follow it and head for Old Malcolm's steading, which he just might, if Jesu favoured him, live to reach. Worth a try, and if he were doomed, he might as well die on his feet. He wrapped his plaid tight around him, pulled his cloak closed around it, and walked north.

The first thing he noticed about the tree was that it grew straight and remarkably tall. As the sunset faded into darkness, he noticed the second thing, that it was burning. Here was a bit of luck! If he could nourish a fire against the snow, it would keep him through the night.

As he drew close, he noticed the third thing, that although half of the tree blazed with fire, the other half grew green with new leaf. For a moment he could neither speak nor breathe while all the blood in his veins seemed to freeze like water spilled into snow. Was he already dead then?

'Jesu and the saints preserve,' he whispered. 'May God guide my soul.'

'It's a waste of your breath to call upon the man from Galilee,' the voice said. 'He doesn't do us any favours, and so we do none for him.'

Domnall spun around to find a young man standing nearby. In the light of the blazing tree he could see that the fellow was blond and pale, with lips as red as sour cherries and eyes the colour of the sea in summer. He'd wrapped himself in a huge cloak of solid blue wool with a hood.

'And are you one of the Seelie Host, then?' Domnall said.

'The men of your country would call me so. There's a great grammarie been woven at this spot, and it's not one of my doing, which vexes me. What are you doing here?'

'I got lost. I wish you no harm, nor would I rob you and yours.'

'Well-spoken, and for that you may live. Which you won't do if you stay out in this weather much longer. I need a messenger for a plan I'm weaving, and it's a long one with many strands. Tell me, do you want to live, or do you want to die in the snow?'

'To live, of course, if God be willing.'

'Splendid! Then tell me your name and the one thing you wish most in all the world.'

Domnall considered. The Seelie Host were a tricky bunch, and some priests said them no better than devils. Certainly you were never supposed to tell them your name. Something touched his face, something cold and wet. In the light from the blazing tree he could see snow falling in a scatter of first flakes.

'My name is Domnall Breich. I most desire an honourable death in battle, serving my liege lord.'

The spirit rolled his eyes.

'Oh come now, surely you can think of a better boon than that! Something that would please you and bring you joy.'

'Well, then, I love with all my heart the Lady Jehan, but I'm far beneath her notice.'

'That's a better wishing.' The fellow smiled in a lazy sort of way. 'Very well, Domnall Breich. You shall have the Lady Jehan for your own true wife. In return, I ask only this, that you tell no one of what you see here tonight except for your son, when he's reached thirteen winters of age.' The fellow suddenly frowned and drew his hands out from the folds of his cloak. For a moment he made a show of counting on his fingers. 'Well, thirteen will do. Numbers and time mean naught to the likes of me. Whenever you think him grown to a man, anyway, tell him what you will see here tonight, but tell no one else.'

'Good sir, I can promise you that with all my heart. No one but his own son would believe a man who told of things like this.'

'Done, then!' The fellow raised his hands and clapped them three times together. 'Turn your back on the tree, Domnall Breich, and tell me what you see.'

Domnall turned and peered through the thin fall of snow. Not far away stood a tangle of ordinary trees, dark against the greater dark of night, and beyond them a stretch of water, wrinkled and forbidding in the gleam of magical fire.

'The shore of the loch. Has it been here all this while, and I never saw it?'

'It hasn't. It's the shore of a loch, sure enough, but's not the one you were hoping to find. Do you see the rocks piled up, and one bigger than all the rest?'

'I do.'

'On top of the largest rock you'll find chained a silver horn. Take it and blow, and you'll have shelter against the night.'

'My thanks. And since I can't ask God to bless you, I'll wish you luck instead.'

'My thanks to you, then. Oh, wait. Face me again.'

When he did so, the fellow reached out a ringed hand and laid one finger on Domnall's lips.

'Till sunset tomorrow you'll speak and be understood and hear and understand among the folk of the isle, but after that, their way of speaking will mean naught to you. Now you'd best hurry. The snow's coming down.'

The fellow disappeared as suddenly as a blown candle flame. With a brief prayer to all the saints at once, Domnall hurried over to the edge of the loch – not Ness, sure enough, but a narrow finger of water that came right up to his feet rather than lying below at the foot of a steep climb down. By the light of the magical tree he found the scatter of boulders. The silver horn lay waiting, chained with silver as well. When he picked it up and blew, the sound seemed very small

and thin to bring safety through the rising storm, but after a few
minutes he heard someone shouting.

'Hola, hola! Where are you?'

'Here on the shore!' Domnall called back. 'Follow the light of the
fire.'

Out of the tendrilled snow shone a bobbing gleam, which proved
to be a lantern held aloft in someone's hand. The magical fire behind
cast just enough light for Domnall to see a long narrow boat, with its
wooden prow carved like the head of a dragon, coming toward him.
One man held the lantern while six others rowed, chanting to keep
time. As the boat drew near, the oars swung up and began backing
water, holding her steady as her side hove to.

'It's a cold night to ask you to wade out to us,' the lantern bearer
called, 'but we're afraid to run her ashore with the rocks and all in the
dark.'

'Better I freeze seeking safety than freeze standing here like a dolt.
I'm on my way.'

He hitched his plaid up around his waist and bundled the cloak
around it, then stepped into the lake. The cold water stole his breath
and drove claws into his legs, but it stood shallow enough for him to
reach the dragon boat, where hands of flesh and blood reached down
to pull him aboard.

'Swing around, lads! Let's get him to a fireside.'

Shivering and huddling in the dry part of his plaid, Domnall
crouched in the stern of the boat as they headed out from shore. In
the yellow pool of lantern light he could see the man who held it, a
fellow on the short side but stocky. He wore a hooded cloak, pinned
with a silver brooch in the shape of a dragon. In the uncertain light
Domnall could just make out his lined face and grizzled beard.

'Where are we going, if I may ask?' Domnall said.

'The isle of Haen Marn.'

'Ah.' Domnall had never heard of the place in his life, and he'd
spent all twenty years of it in this corner of Alban. 'My thanks.'

No one spoke to him again until they reached the dark island,
looming suddenly out of falling snow, a muffled but precipitous shape
against the night. A wooden jetty appeared as well, snow-shrouded in
the lantern light, and with a chant and yell from the oarsmen, the
boat turned to. One man rose, grabbed a hawser, and tossed it over
one of the bollards on the jetty to pull them in. With some help
Domnall managed to scramble out, but his feet and legs had gone

numb and clumsy. The man with the lantern hurried him along a gravelled path and up a slope, where he could see a broad, squarish manse. Around the cracks of door and shutter gleamed firelight.

'We'll get you warm soon enough,' the lantern-bearer said, then banged upon the door. 'Open up! We've got a guest, and all by Evandar's doing.'

'Evandar? Is that the man of the Seelie Host? You know him?'

'Better than I wish to, I'll tell you, far far better than that. Now come in, lad, and let's get you warm.'

The door was creaking open to flood them with firelight and the smell of resinous smoke. They brushed past the servant woman who'd opened it and hurried into a great hall where fires crackled in two hearths of slabbed stone, one on either side of the square room. The walls were made of massive oak planks, scrubbed down and polished smooth, then carved in one vast pattern of engraved lines rubbed with red earth. Looping vines, spirals, animals, interlace – they all tangled together in great swags across each wall, then swooped up at each corner to the rafters before plunging down again in a riot of carving . . .

Domnall followed his rescuers across the carpet of braided straw to the hearth at the far side. At a scatter of tables sat a scatter of men, all short and bearded, and in a carved chair right up near the fire a lady, wearing a pair of drab loose dresses and heavy with child. Like the men around her, she was not very tall, more like the grain-fed Sassenach far to the south in stature, and since her pale hair hung in a single braid, Sassenach is what he assumed her to be. Domnall knelt at her feet.

'My lady,' he said. 'My thanks and my blessing to you, for the saving of my life.'

'My men saved you, not me,' she said in a low, musical voice. 'But you're welcome in my hall.' She glanced round. 'Otho! Fetch him a tankard and some bread, will you?'

'As my lady Angmar commands.' One of the men, a bare four feet tall, and white of hair and beard, rose from a table. 'Sit in the straw by the hearth, lad, and spread that bit of cloth you're draped in out to dry.'

They had to be Sassenach, all of them, because they wore trousers and heavy shirts instead of proper plaids and tunics, but he wasn't about to hold their birth against them after the way they'd rescued him. Since the hearth was a good ten feet long, Domnall could move

a decorous distance away from the lady to sit near a brace of black
and tan hounds. He unwound his plaid, stretched it out on the straw
to dry, and sat in his tunic by the fire to struggle with the wet bindings of his boots. By the time he had them off, Otho had returned
with the promised tankard and a basket of bread.

'A thousand thanks,' Domnall said. 'So, this is Haen Marn, is it?
I've never seen your isle before.'

'Hah!' Otho snorted profoundly. 'And I wish I never had either.'

'Uncle!' A young man sprang up from his seat at a table. 'Hold your
tongue!'

'Shan't! I rue the day that ever we travelled to this cursed place. I
just get myself home and what happens? Hah! Wretched dweomer
and-'

'Uncle!' The young man hurried over. 'Hush!'

'You hold *your* tongue, young Mic, and show some respect for your
elders.'

The two glared at each other, hands set on hips. During all of this
Lady Angmar never moved or spoke, merely stared into the fire.
Behind her, shoved against the wall, stood another carved chair, fit
for a lord but empty. Domnall wondered if she'd been widowed; it
seemed a good guess if a sad one.

'Well, now,' Domnall said. 'Do you all hail from the southern
lands?'

'Who knows?' Otho snapped. 'It could have been any wretched
direction at all!'

'You'll forgive my uncle, good sir,' Mic said. 'He's getting old and a
bit daft.' He grabbed Otho's arm. 'Come and sit down.'

Muttering under his breath, Otho allowed himself to be dragged
away. Domnall had the uneasy feeling that the old man wasn't daft
in the least but speaking of grammarie. Yet his mind refused to take
that idea in. He found it easier to believe in a lady sent away by her
brothers after a husband's death, or perhaps even a lady in political
exile, allowed to take a small retinue away with her. The Sassenach
chiefs were always fighting among themselves, and he'd heard that
their women could do what they wished with their bride-price if their
husbands died. The welcome fire, the warm straw, the steamy reek
of his drying cloak and plaid, the taste of ale and bread – it all seemed
too solid, too normal to allow the presence of magic. As he found
himself yawning, he wondered if he'd merely imagined the man
named Evandar and the blazing tree. They might merely have been

the mad visions of a man come near death by cold.

At length Lady Angmar turned and considered him with eyes so sad they were painful to look upon.

'I can have the servants give you a chamber,' she said, 'or would you prefer to sleep here by the banked fire?'

'The fireside will do me well, my lady, and I'd not cause you any more trouble.'

Her mouth twitched in a ghost of a smile.

'There's been trouble enough, truly,' she said, then returned to watching the fire.

Angmar never spoke again. At length she rose and with her elderly maidservant left the hall. Young Mic brought Domnall a blanket; Otho banked up the fire; they took the lantern and left him with the dogs to curl up and sleep.

When he woke cold grey light edged the shutters. Otho was just letting the whining dogs out at the door. Stretching and yawning, Domnall sat up as the old man came stumping over, poker and tongs in hand, to mend up the fire.

'I'll get out of your way, good sir,' Domnall said.

'You're a well-spoken lad.'

'It becomes a Christian man to watch his speaking.'

Otho glanced puzzled at him.

'A what kind of man?' he said.

'A Christian man, one of Lord Jesu's followers.'

'Ah. Is this Yaysoo the overlord in these parts?'

'Er, well, you could say that.'

Otho hunkered down and began lifting the chunks of sod away from the coals. Domnall pulled on his boots, bound them tightly, then stood up to wrap and arrange his plaid.

'The Lady Angmar? Has she lost her husband then?'

'Lost him good and proper,' Otho said. 'No one knows where he may be or if he lives or lies dead, and here she is, heavy with his child.'

'That's a terrible sad thing.'

'It is, truly. If she knew he was dead, she could mourn him and get on with life, but as it is . . . '

'The poor lady, indeed.'

'It's just like him, though, to do something so thoughtless. An inconvenient man, he was, all the way round. Ah, but who knows why women choose the men they do? She's still wrapped in sorrow over her Rhodry Maelwaedd, no matter what we may say.'

That was doubly odd. What was a Sassenach woman doing married to some lord from Cymru? Or could this be the reason for her exile? Otho glared at the coals, then blew a bit of life into one of them and threw on a handful of tinder.

'Do you have a home near here, lad?'

'I do. I serve Lord Douglas and live in his hall.'

'Then let me give you some advice. Get out of here while you can and head home, or you may never see it again. The snow's stopped falling, and the boatmen will row you across.'

'I'll need to give the lady my thanks first.'

'She'll not come down till well past mid-day. Her grief rules her. Get out while you can, while the sunlight lasts, and that won't be long, this time of year. I warn you.' The old man glared up at him, his face red and sweaty as the fire leapt back to life. 'Haen Marn travels where it wills, and faster than spit freezes on a day like this.'

Grammarie. His memories of the night before, of Evandar and the burning tree, came back like a slap in the face. Domnall grabbed his cloak from the straw.

'Then I'll be off. Good day to you, Otho.'

The old man snorted and turned back to his work.

Outside Domnall found a day ice cold but clear, with the watery sun just rising – he'd slept late. At the door he paused, looking around him in the crisp day. Wind whined around walls and soughed in trees. He walked a few paces down the path, then turned back for a proper look at the place. In the sun the island seemed much larger than he'd thought the night past. The manse itself stood long and low, with behind it a rise of leafless trees, pale grey and shivering, and behind them a tall, squarish tower, perched on top of a little hill. He shaded his eyes and studied the tower for a moment; it sported three windows, one above the other, and a peaked roof covered in grey slates.

In the middle window someone was standing and looking down. From his distance he couldn't tell whether it was a man or a woman, but he suddenly knew that he was being watched, studied as intensely as he'd been studying the tower. There was no malice in the gaze, merely a shocking closeness, as if that person in the window had dropped down to stand in front of him. With a shudder he turned away. He could feel the gaze follow him until he started walking toward the lake. When he risked a quick glance back he found the tower window empty.

At the end of the gravelled path he saw the jetty and the dragon boat, riding high in the water. No one seemed to be about, but by the time he reached the jetty, the head boatman and his oarsmen came strolling down the shore to join him. Otho must have sent a servant down to rouse them, Domnall supposed.

'Ready to go back, lad?' the boatman said.

'I am, though I wish I'd had a chance to pay my thanks to Lady Angmar.'

'Ah, she won't be down for a good while yet.' The boatman shook his head. 'It's a sad thing.'

They all boarded, and when the oarsmen settled at their thwarts, Domnall sat in the stern, out of their way. Here in daylight he noticed a bronze gong, hanging in a wooden frame. The boatman saw him looking at it.

'That's for the beasts in the lake,' he announced. 'In this cold weather they sink to the bottom and sleep, or some such thing. Like bears do, you know, in caves. In the summer, they're a fair nuisance, but luckily they hate noise, and banging that gong keeps them off.'

'Beasts?' Domnall said.

'In the lake, truly. Huge they are, with long thin necks and mouths full of teeth. They can capsize a boat like this as easy as I can squash a bedbug.'

All the oarsmen nodded in solemn agreement.

'Ah,' Domnall said. 'This lake must feed into Ness, then. That gives me hope.'

'Here! You know of the beasts?'

'Well, of one. It lives in our lake, though you don't see it often.'

All the oarsmen glanced back and forth, nodding again, but in satisfaction this time.

'I think me,' their leader said, 'that our island may have returned home. Interesting, eh, lads?'

The crew nodded but never spoke. The boatswain raised his hand and called out. When he shouted 'three', they all fell to their oars.

Since sunlight brought safety, the oarsmen could pull the boat close enough in to the narrow strip of sandy beach for Domnall to leap ashore. Still, as a precaution he took off his boots. Better to land barefooted in damp sand and snow than try to walk in wet boots. He made it ashore safely, called out his final thanks with a wave as the boat shoved off, then sat on one of the boulders to put his boots back on. With quick hard strokes the dragon boat fled back across the water, so dark under a winter sky it looked black, toward the rise of the isle. As the sun touched the loch, mist steamed on the surface. All at once Haen Marn seemed very hard to see. Grammarie! It can be naught else, he told himself. The tall tree that had blazed with fire the night before had disappeared, but then, he'd expected no less.

Ahead lay trouble enough without worrying about magic. He'd had a safe night instead of a cold death, but he still needed to reach home if he were to live through another one. The sun would stay up only a few hours at best, and if the clouds and snow returned, the light would fade even faster. When he thought over his yesterday's misadventure, he could only assume that he hadn't gone far enough north before turning to search for the road. In the fresh fall of snow the countryside stretched around him like a place in a dream, featureless and forbidding. He commended his soul to the saints and headed out in the direction he hoped would lead him eventually to the road – if he could see it when he found it.

Yet in the event Lord Douglas himself, riding at the head of his men, found him and well before sunset. Domnall was just climbing a low rise when he heard the sound of horses and horns, blaring from the other side. He whooped, he yelled, he screamed out his lord's name, and sure enough, in a flurry of answering calls they crested the rise and pulled up, waiting for him to flounder through the snow and reach them.

'My lord!' Domnall called out. 'Never have I been so glad to see a man as you!'

With a toss of his head Lord Douglas laughed. A rider led forward a fresh horse and threw Domnall the reins. Calling out his thanks, Domnall mounted, then made a half-bow to his lord from the saddle. As the warband started off down the road, Douglas motioned him up to ride beside him.

'How did you live through the night?' Lord Douglas said.

To lie to his lord galled him, but breaking a sworn promise would have galled more.

'I hardly know. I prayed to every saint I could think of, and I found a hut of sorts. It stank of shepherd and sheep dung, but it was so small that I stayed warm. Well, warm enough.'

'Good. We give the saints and their priests enough in tithes. I'm glad to see they keep their side of the bargain.'

'My thanks for riding out after me, my lord. I thought you'd have given me up for dead.'

'I did, but you're one of my men, and damned if I'd leave you out here without so much as a hunt.' Douglas paused, considering something with an odd look on his face. 'Besides, Jehan would have sent me to Hell herself if I hadn't ridden out. You should have heard her, weeping and cursing and carrying on.'

'Your daughter, my lord?' Domnall felt himself blushing and stammering. 'But I never would have thought – I mean, uh er, my lord, I-'

'Hold your tongue, Domnall Breich. Her mother's a strong-minded woman, and so is she, and I've spent all I've a mind to on her sister's dowry. There's not much left for hers, but you'd not be asking for much, would you?'

'My lord, if she would have me, I'd ask for naught but her and count myself the richest man alive.'

'Good. Then if you can provide for her, you can have her. What about that, eh?'

'My father promised me a steading if I were to marry. It's not a great lord's lands, but we'll make do.'

'And I can spare you some milk cows and suchlike.' Lord Douglas considering, frowning. 'How long have the pair of you been hiding this secret?'

'My lord, I swear to you that I never knew she favoured me. I held her too far above me.'

'I believe you. She told me that she never knew she loved you until she thought you dead. It was my grief that made me see, she said.'

Remembering Evandar, Domnall found himself speechless. Had Jehan loved him at all until the night just past? But who was he to question this splendid miracle, this gift beyond hoping for?

'Then, my lord,' Domnall said, 'I'll count the night I just spent the luckiest of my life, for all that I thought I was a doomed man.'

When they rode back to the castle, the Lady Jehan stood waiting for them on the steps of the keep. As soon as Domnall dismounted, she rushed to him and flung herself into his arms. He held her tight, laid his face against her auburn hair, and thought himself the happiest man in God's world. Yet even in his joy he remembered the lady of Haen Marn, mourning her lost lord. That night he went into the chapel and prayed for her, that someday Lord Jesu might let her see her Rhodry Maelwaedd again.

PART ONE

The North Country

Autumn 1116

Ah, the beginnings of things! In another place have I discoursed upon the complexities that weave the origin of any event, whether great or small. Ponder this well, for if a magician would set a great ritual in motion, then he must guard every word he says and weigh each move he might make, down to the smallest gesture of one hand, for at the births of things their outcomes lie in danger, just as in its cradle an infant lies helpless and vulnerable to the malice of the world.

The Pseudo-Iamblichus Scroll

Loathing. Dallandra could put no other name to her feeling. Wrapped in a heavy wool cloak, she was standing on top of the wall that circled Gwerbret Cadmar's dun. Below and around her the town of Cengarn spread out over three hills, bound them with curving streets, choked them with round stone houses, roofed in filthy black thatch. Behind most of the houses stood pens for cows and chickens and of course, dung heaps. Out on the muddy streets she could pick out movement – townsfolk hurrying about their business or perhaps a pack of half-starved dogs. Here and there stood trees, dark and leafless under the grey sky.

The view behind her looked no better. Massive stone towers, joined together, formed the dark and brooding broch complex in the centre of the dun. The muddy ward of the enormous fort swarmed with dirty servants and warriors, cursing as they led their horses through a clutter of pigsties and sheep pens. A blacksmith was hammering at his forge; pages sang off-key or chivvied the serving wenches, who swore right back at them. In the crisp autumn air the stink rose high – human waste, animal waste, smoke, spoiled food – overpowering the pomander of Bardek cloves she held to her nose. You should be used to it by now, she told herself. She knew that she never would get used to it, no matter how long she lived among human beings.

'Dalla!' A man's voice hailed her from below. 'Care for a bit of company?'

Without waiting for her answer Rhodry Maelwaedd, who preferred to be known only as Rhodry from Aberwyn, began climbing the wooden ladder that led up the catwalk. A tall man, but oddly slender from shoulder to hip, he was handsome in his way with his dark blue eyes and ready smile. Despite the touches of silver in his raven-black hair and his weather-beaten skin, he looked young and moved fast and smoothly, too, like a young man. She knew, however, that he'd been born well over eighty winters ago. Although he shared her elven blood – his mother had been human, his father one of the Westfolk like Dallandra – he seemed to have distinctly human opinions about some things. He leaned on the parapet and grinned down at Cengarn.

'A fine sight, isn't it?' he said.

'Maybe to you. I hate being shut up like this.'

'Well, no doubt. But I mean, it's a fine thing to see the town standing and not some smoking heap of ruins.'

'Ah, now there I have to agree with you.'

But a few months before, Cengarn had stood in danger of being reduced to rubble, besieged as it was by a marauding army. Now the only threats hanging over the town were those faced by every city in Deverry each winter – disease, cold, and starvation. Dalla leaned on the parapet next to him, then stepped back. He smelled as bad as the rest of them.

'What's wrong?' Rhodry said.

'That stone is cold. Damp, too.'

'True enough.' But he stayed where he was. 'We should have snow soon.'

She nodded agreement and glanced at the lowering sky. A nice thick white blanket of snow – it would hide the dirt, she hoped, and freeze the offal and excrement hard enough to kill the stink.

'There's somewhat I've been meaning to ask you,' he said after a moment. 'I've been having some cursed strange dreams. Do you think they might mean dweomer at work?'

'I've no idea. Tell me about them.'

'Well, it's the Raven Woman, you see. She comes to me in my dreams and taunts me.'

'That *is* serious. Here, let's go somewhere warm, where we can sit and talk.'

They climbed down the ladder and picked their way across the mucky ward. As they passed, the various servants and riders out and about fell silent, turned to stare, and even, every now and then, crossed their fingers in the sign of warding against witchcraft. Dallandra ducked into a side door of the broch and out of sight of the crowded ward.

'Safe,' she whispered.

'What?' Rhodry said. 'Do you feel danger coming our way?'

'My apologies. It's the way everyone looks at me. I'm not used to being hated and feared.'

'Oh well, now, they don't do that.'

'Are you sure?'

'Why would they?'

'All the dweomer they've seen lately. Etheric battles, shapechangers, the way Alshandra would appear in the sky like a goddess – too many strange things, too many things they never should have seen. The Guardians live by their own laws, not those of the dweomer.'

Rhodry considered.

'True enough,' he said at last. 'We've all seen more than we can explain away.'

Her chamber lay at the very top of a side tower; her door shared a landing with heaps of bundled arrows and piles of stones, ammunition stored against another siege like the one so recently lifted. The chamber itself was a slice of the round floor plan set off from the storage area by wickerwork partitions. Straw covered the plank floor, and wooden shutters hung closed over the single window.

Rhodry perched on the wide windowsill and let her have the only chair. Before she sat down she heaped chunks and sticks of charcoal into a brass brazier, then snapped her fingers to summon the Wildfolk of Fire. When the charcoal glowed, she held her hands over the warmth.

'Aren't you cold there in the draughts?' Dallandra said.

'Not so I notice.'

She was always amazed at how little cold and other discomforts, even pain itself, bothered him; his dangerous life had turned his entire body into a weapon, hard as forged steel. Matters of magic, however, lay beyond his strength.

'These cursed dreams!' he snapped. 'I don't mind admitting that I'm half-afraid to sleep at night. You wouldn't have a talisman, would you, to drive them away?'

'Nothing so simple. Tell me about them.'

'I've been thinking a good bit about them. They have a sameness to them. I'll be walking somewhere I know well, this dun, say, or the town, or even Aberwyn. And all of a sudden, the air around me will turn thick, like, and a bluish colour, like looking into deep water, and there the bitch will be, stark naked and taunting me. She keeps saying she'll have my head on a pike one fine day and other little pleasantries.'

Dallandra swore at hearing her worst fear confirmed.

'You think it's dweomer, don't you?' He was grinning his twisted smile.

'I do. Whatever you do, don't go chasing after her. She's trying to draw your soul out of your body, you see.'

'And what then?'

'I don't know. If she were a master of the dark dweomer, she'd be able to kill you, but she's nothing of the sort. A poor little beginner, more like, who knows a few tricks and naught more.'

'A few tricks? Ye gods! She can turn herself into a blasted bird and fly, she can visit men in their dreams, and you call that tricks?'

'I do, because I've seen just enough of her to know that she doesn't understand how she does it. Her power is all Alshandra's doing, or it was. Now it's Evandar's wretched brother who's causing all the trouble.'

Rhodry laughed, a high-pitched chortle that made her wince.

'Tricks,' he said again. 'Well, if that's all they are, you wouldn't happen to have a few you could teach me, would you?'

'I don't, but I've got a few of my own. I'll scribe wards around you every night before you go to sleep.'

'Not so easy with me sleeping out in the barracks.'

'What? Is that where the chamberlain's put you? After all you did this summer in the gwerbret's service?'

'A silver dagger's welcome is a short one and his honour shorter still.'

'That's ridiculous! I'll speak with the chamberlain for you.' Dallandra hesitated, glancing around. 'Here, if you don't mind a bit of gossip, there's room enough in this chamber for both of us.'

'And why would a silver dagger mind gossip?' His smile had changed to something open and soft. 'It's your woman's honour that's at stake. But if there's no one up here to know-'

'No one wants to live next to a sorcerer. Which has its uses. No one's going to argue with me either, come to think of it. Why don't you just fetch your gear and suchlike?'

'I'll find young Jahdo and have him do it. He's been earning his keep as my page.'

'It's good of you to take the lad on like that.'

'Someone had to.' Rhodry stood up with a shrug. 'He's no trouble. I'm teaching him to read.'

'I keep forgetting you know how.'

'It comes as a surprise to most people, truly. But Jill made him a promise before she was killed, that she'd teach him, and so, well, I've taken on that promise with her other one, that she'd get him home again in the spring.'

Later that afternoon, with the chamberlain spoken to and Jahdo

found, Rhodry's gear got moved into a chamber next to Dallandra's
own. With the job done, Jahdo himself, a skinny dark-haired lad,
brought Dallandra a message.

'My lady, the Princess Carra did ask me to come fetch you, if it be
that you can come.'

'Is somewhat wrong?'

'It be the child, my lady, little Elessi.'

'Oh ye gods! Is she ill?'

'I know not. The princess, though, she be sore troubled.'

Dallandra found Carra – Princess Carramaena of the Westlands,
to give her proper title – in the women's hall, where she was sitting
close to the hearth with her baby in her arms. Out in the centre
of the half-round room, Lady Ocradda, the gwerbret's wife and the
mistress of Dun Cengarn, sat with her serving women around a
wooden frame and stitched on a vast embroidery in the elven style,
all looping vines and flowers. The women glanced at Dallandra, then
devoted themselves to their work as assiduously as if they feared the
evil eye. Carra, however, greeted her with a smile. She was a pretty
lass, with blonde hair and big blue eyes that dominated her heart-
shaped face, and young; seventeen winters as close as she could
remember.

'Dalla, I'm so glad you've come, but truly, the trouble seems to be
past, now.'

'Indeed?' Dallandra found a small stool and sat upon it near the
fire. 'Suppose you tell me about it anyway.'

'Well, it's the wraps. She hates to be wrapped, and it's so draughty
and chill now, but she screams and fights and flings her hands around
when I try to wrap her in a blanket. She won't have the swaddling
bands at all, of course.'

At the mention of swaddling, Lady Ocradda looked up and shot a
sour glance at the princess's back. The women of the dun had lost
that battle early in the baby's life. At the moment Elessario was lying
cradled in a blanket in Carra's arms and sound asleep, wearing naught
but her nappies and a little shirt made of old linen, soft and frayed.

'Most babies like to be warm,' Dallandra said.

'By the fire like this she's fine. But when I put her down in my bed,
it's so cold without the wraps, but she screams if I put them round
her.'

'It's odd of her, truly, but no doubt she'll get used to them in time.'

'I hope so.' Carra looked at her daughter with some doubt. 'She's awfully strong-willed, and here she was born just a month ago. You know, it seems so odd, remembering when she was born. It seems like she's been here forever.'

'You seem much happier for it.'

Carra laughed and looked up, grinning.

'I am, truly. You know, it was the strangest thing, and I feel like such an utter dolt now, but all the time I was carrying her, I was sure I was going to die in childbed. When I look back, ye gods, I was such a simpering dolt, always weeping, always sick, always carrying on over this and that.'

'Well, my dear child,' Ocradda joined in. 'Being heavy with child takes some women that way. No need to berate yourself.'

'But it was all because I was so afraid,' Carra said with a shake of her head. 'That's what I realized, just the other day. I was just as sure as sure that I was going to die, and it coloured everything. I'd wake up in the morning and look at the sunlight, and I'd wonder how many more days I'd live to see.'

'No doubt you were frightened as a child,' Ocradda said. 'Too many old women and midwives tell horrible tales about childbirth where young girls can hear them. I've known many a lass to be scared out of her wits.'

'I suppose so.' Carra considered for a moment. 'But it was absolutely awful, feeling that way.'

'No doubt,' Dallandra said. 'And I'm glad it's past.'

Carra shuddered, then began to tell her, in great detail, how much Elessi was nursing. Although she listened, Dallandra was thinking more about Carra's fear. Had she died in childbed to end her last life, perhaps? Such a thing might well carry over as an irrational fear – not, of course, that Carra's fear lacked basis. Human women did die in childbirth often enough. A reincarnating soul carried very little from life to life, but terror, like obsessive love, had a way of being remembered. As, of course, did a talent for the dweomer – she found herself wondering about the Raven Woman. It was possible that this mysterious shapechanger was remembering, dimly and imperfectly, magical training from her last life.

Later that night Dallandra learned more about her enemy. She was getting ready for bed when she heard a tap at her chamber door. Before she could call out a query, Evandar walked in, or more precisely, he walked through the shut and barred door and oozed into the room like a ghost. Dallandra yelped.

'I wish you wouldn't do things like that!' she snapped. 'You give me such a turn!'

'My apologies, my love. I did knock. I'm trying to learn the customs of this country.'

He took her into his arms and kissed her. His skin, the touch of his lips and hands, felt oddly cool and smooth, as if he were made of silk rather than flesh.

'It's been so long since I've seen you,' Dallandra said. 'I wish you could stay a while.'

'The dun's too full of iron, weapons and nails both, or I'd spend the night with you. When all this trouble is done, my love, we'll go back to my country, you and I.' He paused to kiss her. 'And we'll share our love again.'

'That will be splendid.' With a sigh she let go of him. 'From now on, can't we meet in the Gatelands? I'd rather spare you pain if I could.'

'My thanks, and the meadows of sleep will do us well enough for ordinary news. But something a bit more urgent brings me here tonight.' He paused for effect. 'I've tracked down the Raven Woman. She's sheltering in Cerr Cawnen.'

'Cerr Cawnen? Jahdo's city?'

'The very one. I found her when I was hunting my brother.'

'Shaetano?'

'The very one, and still working mischief. He's escaped me, but I think I know who let him out of the prison I made for him.'

'The Raven Woman.' Dallandra heard her own voice sag in sudden weariness.

'And once again, the very one, my love. Her name, by the by, is Raena. I did find that titbit for you. Now, you told me that you think her little skilled in dweomer, and I agree. Her magic's like one of those rain spouts that men make to carry water, and she's naught but the barrel underneath.'

'And Shaetano's willing to be the downpour, is he?'

'Just that. No doubt he's flattered to be worshipped as if he were one of the gods. He'll lend her power to make mischief, anyway, mischief being his own true calling. So I thought I'd tell you where I was bound. After all, you have good reason to hate him yourself.'

'Hate him? I don't, truly.'

'What? Why not? After the way he treated you – stealing you away, binding you, holding you up to mockery in that wretched wooden cage – how you can not hate him?'

He asked in all seriousness, and she considered with the seriousness that he deserved in his answer.

'Well, he frightens me, and when I think of the things he did, I'm
angry still, but it's not the same as hate. Does he truly understand the
evil he works, and why it's an evil thing?'

'I've no idea, and I care even less. He's crossed me and injured you,
and that's enough for me.'

'And so you'll be hunting him? If you can find him and stop him,
then Raena's dweomer should dry up and quickly, too.'

'Good. Let us hope. I'll find him, sooner or later, never you fear,
but I do have a few other errands to run as well.' Evandar turned away
and smiled, an oddly sly quirk of his mouth. 'I have a scheme afoot,
you see.'

'Oh ye gods, what now? Evandar, you know I love you, but those
schemes of yours! They always get out of hand, they always hurt
people, and I wish-'

'Hush!' He held up one hand flat for silence. 'I've been thinking.
Have I not learned from you, my love, about thinking and the passing of Time? Well, when Time passes, and my people are born into
the world of flesh and death, just as our Elessi's been born, won't they
need a place to go?'

'A what?'

'A place of their own, and I shall say no more about it.' He turned
back and grinned. 'It's a surprise and a riddle, and here's a clue: when
the moon rises again you'll see.'

Dallandra hesitated on the edge of snarling at him. Once he
defined something as a riddle, he would never tell the answer, no
matter how much she prodded or swore or wheedled.

'Oh very well,' she said with a sigh. 'And how soon will this moon
of yours rise?'

'I have no idea. I've been weaving this scheme for a long time, truly,
ever since I asked the man named Maddyn for his rose ring –
hundreds of your years ago now, isn't it?'

'It is. Wait – that's the ring Rhodry used to have, the one with the
dragon's name graved on it.'

'It is, but I'll speak no more about it now.' Evandar paused for a lazy
grin; he knew full well how his riddles irritated her. 'But to the matter
at hand, my love, Shaetano's clever, so that will take this strange
thing, Time, as well. He'll hide from me, but sooner or later, he'll have

to appear to his worshipper over in Cerr Cawnen. When he does, I'll be close by.' All at once he tossed his head in a spasm of pain. 'Iron! Wretched demon-spawn metal!'

Evandar took one step toward the window and disappeared. She saw nothing, not a fading or a trembling of him – one moment he was there; the next he was not. Dallandra shuddered once, but only once. She'd got used to him and his ways, over the years they'd been lovers, hundreds of years, in fact, as men reckon time.

The tiny room smelled of ancient smoke and recent dust. The fetid air hung cold and close around the two people standing, bundled in cloaks, with their backs to the wide crack between stones that served as its door.

'It be best not to light a candle or suchlike in here,' Verrarc whispered. 'Not enough air.'

'There's no need on us for one,' Raena said. 'Watch, my love. See what I did learn, this past year or two.'

He could hear her draw a deep breath; then she began to chant the same few words – he thought they might be Gel da 'Thae – over and over again. Up at the corner of the webby ceiling a silver light gleamed, then spread and brightened. Spiders dashed from her dweomer.

'Ye gods,' Verrarc whispered.

'Gods, indeed, my love. This be a gift from the gods I do serve, the true gods.' Raena turned, glancing around the room. 'What place be this? It must be old, truly old.'

'No one knows. When I was a boy, I did find all the secret places of Citadel. Some few I asked the elders about, but most, like this one, I did keep for my own.'

She nodded, looking round her. Near the ceiling and all round the room ran a line of triangles and circles, crudely carved into the stone. Verrarc had never seen it so clearly; when he had hidden in this half-buried chamber as a child, the only light had been a dim glow from the entrance.

'I feel despair here,' Raena spoke abruptly. 'And old fear.'

'Do you? We'd best be about our business. I don't want anyone wondering where we might be and come looking for us. What was this thing you were going to show me? Or is it the light?'

'Not just the light. Here.'

When she knelt on the dirty floor, he joined her. She flung both hands into the air and began a chant of different words, vibrated from deep in her throat and spat out like a challenge. In answer the silver light shrank and collected itself into a glowing sphere, about the size of an armload of hay, that hung above and before them. When Raena tossed her head, the hood of her cloak fell back. Her eyes were shut, sweat oozed down her face, and her long black hair seemed to gleam and flutter in the unnatural light. Verrarc felt himself turn cold as the sphere of light began to stretch itself in to a long cylinder.

Within the silvery pillar something – no, someone – was forming. At first it seemed only a trick of the light, a shape like a drift of smoke caught in a sunbeam, but gradually it solidified and turned mostly human. When the figure stepped free of the silver pillar, Verrarc could see that there was more than a touch of the fox about him. Red fur tufted his ears and ran in a brushy roach from his low forehead back over his skull and down his neck. Under their red-tufted brows, his eyes gleamed black and bright. Each of his fingers ended in a sharp black claw.

'I am the Lord of Havoc, ruler of the powers of strife and tumult.' His voice boomed and echoed so loudly that Verrarc feared someone in the town above would be hearing him. 'Why have you summoned me, O my priestess?'

'To beg my lord's favour,' Raena whispered. 'I have brought another who would worship thee.'

'Then you have summoned well, little one. I shall-'

All at once Lord Havoc hesitated, staring at something behind his two worshippers. When Verrarc twisted around to look, he saw nothing, but Havoc yelped. He flung himself backward into the pillar and disappeared, leaving behind him the stink of fox. The light that formed the pillar began to break up. Although Raena chanted to drive it back, the light stubbornly spread out and clung to the walls, as faded and torn as an old curtain. With a gasp for breath she fell silent.

'Rae, forgive me,' Verrarc said. 'But a doubt lies upon me that he be any sort of god at all. A fox spirit, more like, such as do live in the woods.'

'Animal spirits are weak little things!' She turned on him with a snarl. 'How could he nourish my dweomer if he were some woodland imp? I tell you, I've seen him do great things, Verro, truly great, and he does shower favour upon me.'

Verrarc got up, dusting off the heavy cloth wrappings round his legs.

'You saw the light, didn't you?' Raena snapped.

'I did.' He straightened up, then gave her his hand and helped her clamber to her feet. 'Here! You do be as pale as he was!'

She very nearly collapsed into his arms. He struggled with the folds of his cloak and hers, finally got a supporting arm around her, and helped her stand. All around them the silver light was fading.

'It be needful to get you back to the house,' Verrarc said.

He squeezed out of the room first to the dark tunnel beyond, then helped her through. The tunnel twisted and wound, the air grew fresher and colder, and about thirty feet along they came to its entrance, an opening in a stone wall. Beyond they could see snow and tumbled blocks of stone overgrown with leafless shrubs. Verrarc helped her climb out, then scrabbled after to the wan light of a dying day.

They were standing on the peak of Citadel, the sharp hill island that rose in the centre of Loc Vaed and the town of Cerr Cawnen. Between the trees that grew among and around the ruins of the old building, brought down in an earthquake centuries ago, Verrarc could see down the steep slope of the island, where public buildings and the houses of the few wealthy families clung to the rocks and the twisting streets. The blue-green lake itself, fed by volcanic springs, lay misted with steam in the icy air. Beyond, at the lake's edge, the town proper sprawled in the shallows – houses and shops built on pilings and crannogs in a welter of roofs and little boats. Beyond them, marking out the boundary of Cerr Cawnen, stood a circle of stone walls, built around timber supports to make them sway, not shatter, in the earth tremors that struck the town now and again.

They were looking roughly west, and the lazy sun was sinking into a haze of brilliant gold. Thanks to Loc Vaed's heat, Cerr Cawnen itself lay free of snow, but beyond the town the first fall of the season turned pink and gold in answer to the setting sun. Here and there in the distance stood a copse, dark against the snow, or a farmer's hut, barely visible in the drifts, with a feather of smoke rising from its chimney.

'It do be lovely up here, the long view,' Verrarc said.

'Someday soon, my love, I'll be showing you a view so long that all this,' Raena paused to wave a contemptuous hand 'will look like a dungheap.'

'Oh, will you now?'

'I will. The things that I have seen, my love, did stagger my mind and my heart, just from the seeing of them. The world be a grand place, when you get yourself beyond the Rhiddaer.'

'No doubt.' Verrarc hesitated. 'And just where have you been learning all these secrets?'

'You'll know in good time.' She shivered and drew the cloak more tightly about her. 'It be needful for me to consult with Lord Havoc, to see what I may be telling you.'

He looked at her sharply. Her mouth was set in a stubborn twist.

'Let's get back to the house,' he said. 'I want to see you warm, and I've got a few matters to attend to before the settling of the night.'

Dera had a rheum in her chest. Huddled in her cloak, she sat close to the hearth fire and sipped a mug of herb brew.

'Gwira left me a packet of botanicals,' Niffa said. 'I can make more.'

Her mother merely nodded. She was a small woman, short and thin, and now she looked as frail as a child, hunched over her mug. Her once-blonde hair hung mostly grey around her lined face.

'You be vexing yourself about our Jahdo, Mam. I can see it by the way you look at the fire.'

Dera nodded again. Niffa knelt down beside her and laid a hand on her arm.

'I do know it in my heart that he'll be coming home to us safe, Mam. Truly I do. I did see it, nay, I have seen it many a time in my true dreaming.'

'Hush. You mayn't speak about those things so plain, like.'

'There's naught here but us two.'

'Still, it frightens me. And what would our townsfolk do, if they began thinking you could dream true and see deaths, too, in their faces?'

'Well, true-spoken. I'll hold my tongue.'

Dera sighed, then coughed so hard she spasmed. Niffa grabbed a handful of straw from the floor and held it up for her mother to spit into, then tossed the wad into the fire.

'My thanks,' Dera whispered. 'And will I be here when our Jahdo comes home?'

It took Niffa a moment to understand what her mother was asking.

'You will. I did see that as well, you laughing with us all.'

'Good. I – here, what be making that noise?'

From outside the two women heard shouting, swearing, and a

peculiar sort of hollow bumping sound. Niffa got up and hurried to the door, opened it to a blast of cold air and peered out the crack. She could just see up the narrow steep alley that led from their door to the public street on the slope above. Panting and puffing, two men were struggling to get a four-foot-high barrel of ale down the rocky track without it escaping to crush the fellow at the bottom. The one at the top she recognized as Councilman Verrarc's servant, Harl.

'What are you doing?' she called out.

'Bringing you a gift,' Harl panted. 'From my master. For your wedding.'

'Less talk!' the other man snapped. 'Don't let it get away from you!'

With a grunt Harl steadied his grip on the barrel. Once they had it level with the entrance, getting the barrel over the doorstep and inside required a last round of curses and a lot of banging, but finally it stood on the straw-strewn floor. Harl and his helper – Niffa recognized him as one of the blacksmith's sons now that he was visible – wiped their sweaty faces on the sleeves of their baggy winter shirts, then stood panting for a moment.

'Ye gods,' Harl said. 'The stink of ferrets in this place be like to knock a man flat!'

The blacksmith's lad nodded his agreement. Dera wrapped the cloak tightly around her and walked over to survey the gift, almost as tall as she.

'It be a kind thing for the councilman to remember us,' Dera said. 'And so generously!'

'It be the best ale, too,' Harl said. 'My master was particular about that, he was, the best dark ale. He did send it this early so it could settle. He said to tell you to leave it be till the wedding day itself.'

'We will, then.' Dera shot Niffa a glance. 'And there be a need on you to go thank him.'

Niffa and her family, the town ratters, lived with their ferrets in two big rooms attached to the public granary, lodgings provided them in return for keeping the rats down. The big square building stood low on the Citadel hill, while Councilman Verrarc's fine house stood high, just below the mysterious ruins at the island's crest. To get there Niffa panted up the steep alley to the broader, cobbled path above, then followed it as it spiralled up the hill, past the white-washed fronts of family compounds and the occasional stone bench, provided for the weary. She dodged between the militia's armoury and a huge boulder to come out on the next street up. Here and there, twisted

little pine trees grew in patches of earth or shoved their way to the
sunlight from between rocks.

In the high white wall Councilman Verrarc's outer gate stood open.
Niffa walked into a square court, paved with flat reddish stones,
where huge pottery tubs stood clumped together to catch rainwater. A
pair of big black hounds, lying in a patch of sun, lifted their heads,
sniffed at her, then thumped lazy tails. The house itself stood beyond
them, a low white structure roofed in thatch. The front door sported
a big brass ring. Niffa banged it on the wood, then waited, shifting
from foot to foot, until it opened a bare crack. She could just see
Magpie, a girl of about her own age, staring back out. Magpie had a
pudgy round face, dark eyes, and a thin mouth that always hung a
little open.

'Let me in, Maggi,' Niffa said. 'There's a need on me to see the
councilman.'

Maggi considered, tilting her head a little.

'Come on now, you'd had the knowing of me since we were
children! Do let me in, and then fetch the councilman.'

When Magpie's eyes narrowed, Niffa realized she'd made a mistake by linking two different tasks together. It would take the poor girl
a while to sort that out, she supposed. Fortunately, a voice sounded
from inside the house, and old Korla, a bent and withered woman
who shuffled along in big sheepskin shoes, took over the door from
her grand-daughter.

'Ah,' Korla said to Niffa. 'So, you've come about that ale?'

'I have. I do wish to thank your master properly for so fine a gift.'

Giggling to herself, Magpie ran off. Korla led Niffa into the councilman's hall, a square room with a low beamed ceiling and a floor
covered with braided rushes. Below each shuttered window stood a
carved chest; in the middle of the room, a table with benches; at the
massive hearth, two carved wooden chairs with cushioned seats, and
against the wall, three other chairs – a fortune of furniture for a Cerr
Cawnen house. Here and there on mantel and table some small silver
oddment caught the firelight and glittered. Sitting in one of the
chairs, her feet up on a footstool, was Raena, dressed in fine blue
cloth and with her hair bound up like a great lady. She acknowledged
the servant with a small nod but said nothing to either her or Niffa.

'I'll be fetching the master,' Korla said and shuffled through a
side door.

Niffa walked close to the fire and held out her hands to the warmth. She could feel the older woman studying her, but when she looked up and arranged a smile, Raena looked away with a sneer. Perhaps she felt her shamed position – Niffa tried to think kindly about her. After all, Raena had been cast off by her husband for being unfaithful to him with Verrarc. She must have known that every woman in town gossiped about her.

On the hearth a log within the fire slipped, flashing with sparks and a long leap of flame. In the suddenly brighter light Niffa could see Raena's face clearly: pale, beaded with sweat, and under her eyes lay dark circles as livid as bruises.

'Be you well?' Niffa said. 'Should I be calling your maid to you?'

'My thanks but no. Tired, I be, not ill.' Her words slipped out one a time.

'Very well, then, but I –'

Niffa stopped in mid-sentence, caught by the way Raena was looking at her. The older woman's dark eyes glittered in the firelight, but her stare was cold, thorough, searching over Niffa as if she were hunting lice upon her cloak. All at once Niffa felt like screaming at her, like slapping her as well and yelling that she should take her filthy self out of Cerr Cawnen forever. She turned and hid her face in the shadows thrown by the fire, but she fancied that she could feel Raena's cold stare prying at her back.

'Well, a good day to you, Niffa!'

Verrarc strode in through the side door. He was tall, the councilman, blond and good-looking by most people's standards, but his blue eyes peered with a winter's cold, and to Niffa his smiles looked as painted as a wooden doll's.

'I trust your mam be well?' he went on.

'She does have a rheum, Councillor, though she fares better today than last. I did come in her place to thank you for that splendid gift.'

Briefly his smile turned warm.

'Most welcome you are to it, and your kin as well. Now, if your mother should need of somewhat, whether medicaments or food, please do ask me for it. I mean that from the bottom of my heart.'

He did, too – Niffa could tell even as she wondered why his very generosity irked her so. She managed a few more polite exchanges, then curtsied and made her glad escape.

As she picked her way down the icy steps that led to the granary and home, she was wondering why she hated Raena so much, and on sight, too. She'd never actually met the woman before that day.

Unless she was very badly wrong, Raena hated her as well.

But little could either of them know that their hatred went back hundreds of years to another life, when both of their souls had been closely linked indeed, as mother and daughter in a life so far removed from what they shared at the moment that it would seem to lie in another world – could they ever know of it. And less could they know that the man Raena hated as Rhodry Maelwaedd had been bound up with them in a knot of Wyrd, though he too had lived in another body and another life, back in those distant years.

PART TWO

Deverry, 849

The year 849. The spring brought terrible omens in the sky above the Holy City. A cloud shaped like a dragon flew overhead, and there was lightning. The sky turned the colour of copper, and a huge cloud like a spindle of black wool drew water from Lake Gwerconydd only to spit it out upon the land. So many refugees fled to Lughcarn that the city could not take them all in. High Priest Retyc gave them what food he could gather and sent them further east, where the farmlands had need of them.

The Holy Chronicles of Lughcarn

In the midst of a clamour, Lillorigga, daughter of the Boar clan, sat on a bench in the curve of the wall and wished that she were invisible. The King's great hall roiled with armed men, standing, talking, sitting, eating, calling out to one another and calling for ale. Spring had come and brought with it the annual muster of the King's loyal lords and their warbands, but in the two enormous hearths at either side the hall, fires blazed and sent wafts of smoke into the hazy room. The stone walls of the enormous round hall oozed cold, for the attacking sun never made more than a brief sally into the tangled complex of brochs and outbuildings that made up the royal palace of Dun Deverry.

Not that the hall looked particularly royal these days – a hundred long years of civil war had left the King poor in everything but men. Tapestries sagged threadbare and faded on the rough stone walls; straw and torn Bardek carpets lay together on the floor; the tables and benches listed and leaned, all cracked and pitted. The lords and the servants alike ate from wooden trenchers and drank from pottery stoups. Only the King's own table retained some semblance of royal splendour. From where she sat Lillorigga could just see a page spreading a much-mended and somewhat stained linen cloth over it while others stood by with silver dishes and pewter mugs. Behind the boys came the royal nursemaid with cushions to raise the seat of the royal chair; King Olaen had been born just five summers ago.

Lilli was the King's cousin – they shared a great-grandmother through the maternal line – and her uncle, Burcan of the Boar, stood as regent to his young highness. Her rank brought her bows and curtsies every time someone passed her bench or looked her way. She answered each one with a nod or a smile, but she hated the way the various lords looked her over, as if they were appraising a prize mare ready for market. Soon her mother would be arranging her betrothal to some son or another of one of the King's loyal men. She could only hope that when the time came, her husband would treat her decently.

Across the hall a herald called out for the men to make way. A procession of women was descending the huge stone staircase, with at their head Queen Abrwnna, who, older than her royal husband, was almost a woman, no longer a girl. Behind her came her retinue of maidservants and noble-born serving women, who included Lillorigga's mother, Merodda, a widow and sister to both Tibryn, Gwerbret Cantrae, and Regent Burcan. In the flickering dim light, Merodda looked no older than the young Queen. Her yellow hair lay smooth and oddly shiny, caught by a silver clasp at the nape of her neck. Her skin was the envy of every woman at court: smooth and rosy just like a lass, they said, and her with a marriageable daughter and all! She walked like a lass, too, and tossed her head and laughed with spirit. A marvel, everyone said, how beautiful she is still. If they only knew, Lilli thought bitterly. If they only knew – her and her potions!

At the bottom step Merodda paused, looking over the great hall, then turned to speak to a page before she rejoined the Queen's retinue at table. When Lilli realized that the page was heading for her, she rose, briefly considered bolting, then decided that if she angered her mother now, she'd only pay for it later. The page trotted over and made her a sketchy bow.

'Honoured Lillorigga,' he said, 'your mother says you're to come to her chambers when she's finished eating.'

Lilli felt fear clutch her with cold, wet hands.

'Very well.' She just managed to arrange a smile. 'Please tell her that I'll wait upon her as she wishes.'

With barely a glance her way he turned and trotted back to the Queen's table. Lilli saw him speak to Merodda, then take up his station for serving the meal. Lilli herself was supposed to eat at one of the tables reserved for unmarried women of noble birth. Instead she grabbed a chunk of bread from a serving basket as a page carried it by and left the press and clamour of the hall.

Outside the sun was setting, dragging cold shadow over the court-yard, one of the many among the warren of brochs and outbuildings. Lilli hurried past the cookhouse, dodged between storage sheds, and slipped out a small gate into a much bigger court, the next ward out, ringed round by high stone walls that guarded pigsties, stables, cow sheds, a smithy, a pair of deep water wells – everything the dun needed to withstand a siege.

At the gates of this ward someone was shouting. When Lilli saw servants hurry past with lit torches, she drifted after them, but she kept to the shadows. Down at the wall, the torchlight glittered on

chain mail and a confusion of men, arguing about who would do
what, a debate the captain of the watch finally ended – he ordered
his guards to man the winch that opened the enormous iron-bound
gates. They creaked open a bare six feet to let an exhausted rider
stumble through, leading a muddy horse.

'Messages for the King,' he croaked. 'From the Gwerbret of
Belgwergyr.'

Servants rushed to take his horse. Lilli trailed after the messenger
and the watch captain as they hurried up to the main broch.

'Good news, I hope,' said the captain.

'Bad,' the messenger said. 'His Grace the gwerbret's lost more
vassals to the false king.'

Lilli felt suddenly sick.

She trailed after the messenger and his escort as they hurried to
the great hall. By then all the important lords had gathered around
the King. On his cushions at the table's head Olaen, a pretty child
with thick pale hair, was eating bread and honey. At either side of him
Lilli's two uncles – Tibryn, Gwerbret Cantrae, and his younger
brother, Burcan, the Regent – sat as a matched pair between the King
and the rest of the gwerbretion and other such powerful lords who
dined at this table. Both of them were handsome men, tall and
warrior-straight, with the wide-set blue eyes they shared with their
sister, Merodda, but unlike her they showed their age in grey hair and
weather-beaten faces.

As the guards hurried up, everyone stopped eating and turned to
look. The messenger knelt before the King, then pulled a silver tube
out of his shirt and handed it to Olaen with a flourish. Burcan leaned
forward and snatched it, then gestured at the man to speak. The great
lords huddled around, narrow-eyed and grim. At the Queen's table
the women fell silent and turned, leaning to hear the news. From her
distance Lilli could hear nothing of what the messenger said, but a
rustle of talk broke out, first at the royal table, then spreading through
the great hall: more lords gone over to Cerrmor. With a curt nod,
Burcan dismissed the messenger. King Olaen was watching the
Regent with eyes full of tears.

Lilli saw her mother turn and leave the Queen's table, hurry up the
staircase, and disappear into the shadows at the top. With a wrench
of will, Lilli forced herself to follow. On the far side of the hall, near
the stairway, a page was seating the messenger while a serving lass
brought him ale. Lilli hesitated, then stopped beside the messenger,

who hastily swallowed his mouthful of ale and started to rise.

'Oh, do sit,' Lilli said. 'You must be exhausted. I just wanted to ask you if Tieryn Peddyc of Hendyr's gone over to the rebels.'

'Not him, my lady. He's steady as a stone.'

'I'm so glad. He's my foster-father.'

'Ah.' The rider smiled briefly. 'No wonder you wanted to know. He and the Lady Bevyan are in good health and as loyal as ever.'

'My thanks.'

Lilli hurried away and climbed the staircase. Maybe Bevyan would come to court, then, with her husband when he joined the muster. She hoped – no, she prayed so, as hard as she could to the Lady of the Moon. Merodda had sent her and her wet nurse to Bevyan when Lilli had been a few weeks old; until she'd seen twelve summers, Bevyan had been the only mother she'd known. If only I could have stayed with Bevva – her eyes threatened tears, but she squelched them and at the top of the stairs paused for a moment to catch her breath. The fear clutched at her heart again, but she had nowhere to run or hide. With one last gasp, she hurried down to her mother's chambers.

Merodda herself opened the door. She was carrying a long taper in a holder, and in the candlelight her face, her hands, glistened like wax.

'Good. You're prompt tonight.'

In a pool of candle-light near the chamber windows stood Brour, the man her mother called her scribe – a skinny little fellow, with an oversize head for his body and wispy blond hair, so that at times he looked like a child, especially since his full lips stuck out in a perennial pout. Merodda laid her hand on Lilli's shoulder and marched her down the length of the room. On the table in front of Brour, among the candles, stood a grinding stone, a chunk of something black that looked like charcoal, and a flagon of water. Apparently the scribe had been making ink, and a prodigious amount of it at that. He put a handful of powder ground from the ink block into a heavy silver bowl, then added water from a pitcher a little at a time, while he pounded and stirred with a pestle.

'Here she is,' Merodda said.

Brour put his tools down on the table, then considered Lilli so coldly that she took an involuntary step back. Her mother's hand tightened on her shoulder. In a hand black with dry ink Brour took the taper from Merodda and held it up to consider Lilli's face.

'No one's going to hurt you, lass,' Brour said at last. 'We've just got a new trick we'd like you to try.'

'You have strange gifts, my sweet,' Merodda said. 'And we have need of them again.'

For a moment Lilli's fear threatened to choke her. She wanted to blurt out a no, to pull free and run away, but her mother's cold stare had impaled her, or so she felt, like a long metal pin pushing into her very soul.

'Come now!' Merodda snapped. 'We women must do what we can to serve the King.'

'Of course, Mother. Of course I want to.'

'Of course? Don't lie to me.'

Lilli blushed and tore her gaze away.

'But I don't care if you do or not,' Merodda went on. 'Let's get started, shall we?'

Brour grunted and set the taper down among the others. On the table the candles danced and sent light glinting onto the black pool in the silver bowl. Lilli found herself watching the glints, staring at them, caught by them while her mother's hand slid from her shoulder to the back of her neck. She felt her head nodding forward, pressed down by the weight of a hand grown suddenly heavy. The ink pool seemed to surge and heave like waves on a black sea that swelled to fill her sight, to fill the room, it seemed, and then her world. As she sank down into the blackness, she heard Merodda's voice chanting, low and soft, but she could distinguish not a single word. The syllables clanged like brass and seemed to reverberate in her ears, foreign sounds linked into alien words.

In the blackness, a point of candlelight, dancing – Lilli swam toward it but felt her body turn to dead weight, as if she hauled it behind her when she moved. The point brightened, then dilated into a circle of light that she could look through, as if she'd pulled back a shutter from a round window and peered out at the sunny world beyond. From some great distance she heard Merodda's voice.

'What do you see, Lilli? Tell us what you see.'

She felt her mouth moving and words slip out like pebbles, falling into the black. In the window things appeared, creatures, vast creatures, all wing and long tails. Around them a bluish light formed and brightened, glinting on coppery scales, blood-red scales, a pair of beasts sleeping, curled next to one another. One of them stirred and stretched, lifting its wings to reveal two thick legs and clawed feet. A huge copper head lifted, the mouth gaped in a long yawn of fangs.

'Wyverns. I see red wyverns, and now they're flying.'

'Good, good.' Her mother's voice slid out like drops of oil. 'Where do you see them?'

'Over a grassy plain.'

Down from the mountains they swept, their massive wings slapping the air, and to Lilli it seemed that she flew with them while her voice babbled of its own accord. They circled round a meadow where a herd of swine fed, then suddenly stooped and plunged like hawks. Shrieking and cackling they struck. The blood-red wyvern rose, flapping hard, with a big grey boar clutched limp and bleeding in its talons.

In her vision Lilli flew too close. The wyvern's enormous head swung her way. The black eyes glittered, narrowed, and seemed to pierce the darkness and stare directly at her. Lilli screamed and broke the spell. She staggered, stumbling forward, knocking into the table. A candle tottered and fell with a hiss and a stench into the black ink.

'You clumsy little dolt!'

Merodda grabbed her by the hair and swung her round, then slapped her with her other hand. Lilli yelped and sank to her knees. Pain burned and crawled on her face.

'Stop it!' Brour snarled. 'She can't help it. She can't control the trance.'

Merodda stepped away, but Lilli could hear her panting in ebbing rage.

'She needs to be trained.' Brour's voice had turned calm again. 'I don't see why you won't let me-'

'We will not discuss this in front of her.' Merodda leaned down. 'Oh, do get up!'

Lilli scrambled to her feet.

'You may go to your chamber,' Merodda said. 'Leave us. And if you ever tell anyone what happened here-'

'Never, I promise. Never.' Lilli could hear her own voice swooping and trembling. 'I've never told before, have I?'

'You haven't, truly.' Merodda considered her for a long cold moment. 'You have some wits. Now go!'

Lilli gathered up her long skirts and raced from the chamber. She dashed down the hall, ran into her tiny chamber at the far end, and barred the door behind her. For a long moment she stood in the twilight grey and wept, leaning against the cold wall; then she flung herself down on her narrow bed and fell asleep, as suddenly as a stone dropped from a tower hits the ground.

That same spring evening, at the stillness before the sunset, Lady Bevyan of Hendyr stood at her bedchamber's narrow window and considered the ward of her husband's dun. Stone framed her view: the stone sides of the window slit when she looked through, the stone billow of the squat broch tower when she looked down, the stone walls of encircling fort when she looked toward the distant west and the silent gold of an ending day. All her life, stone had meant safety thanks to the civil wars, just as winter had meant peace, despite the snows, the storms, and the ever-present threat of hunger. Only lately had she come to think of stone as meaning imprisonment. Only lately had she come to wonder about a world in which summer, too, might mean peace.

Not that such a world coincided with her world, not yet at least. Below her, deep in shadow, the preparations of war filled the cobbled ward: extra horses, tethered out for want of room in the stables; provision carts, packed for the morrow's march. Her husband, Tieryn Peddyc of Hendyr, had called in his allies and vassals for the summer's fighting, defending the true king in Dun Deverry from the would-be usurpers gathering on the kingdom's southern borders. Or so her husband and his allies always called Maryn, Gwerbret Cerrmor, prince of distant Pyrdon – usurper, pretender, rebel. At times, when she wasn't watching her thoughts, Bevyan wondered about the truth of those names.

From behind her Bevyan heard a door opening and a soft voice.

'My lady?' Sarra, one of her serving women, stepped in the door. 'Are you unwell?'

'I'm not, dear.' Bevyan turned from the window. 'Just taking a moment's solitude. I'm trying to make up my mind about going to court. Tell me, do you want to go to Dun Deverry?'

Sarra hesitated, thinking. She'd come to Bevyan as an orphaned girl-child, long enough ago now that grey streaked her dark hair at the temples.

'Well,' Sarra said at last. 'Our place is at Queen Abrwnna's side, but oh, my lady, I shouldn't admit such a shameful thing, but I'm ever so frightened of being caught in a siege.'

'So am I. The Cerrmor men are nearly to our lands, aren't they? Sometimes I wonder what the summer will bring.'

Sarra laid a hand over her throat.

'But we mustn't give up hope yet.' Bevyan make her voice brisk. 'The gods will give us the Wyrd they choose, and there's not a thing we can do about it.'

'True spoken.'

'As for things we can do something about,' Bevyan paused for a sigh, 'I'm worried about little Lillorigga. She's the only reason I'll be going, frankly, if I do go. I keep asking for news of her, but no one ever sends me any.'

'Well, certainly her mother wouldn't bother.' Steel crept into Sarra's voice. 'Do you think we could persuade the Lady Merodda to let us bring her daughter back here? For the cleaner air and all. When you had the fostering of her, she thrived, poor child.'

'Merodda might well be glad to be rid of her. It's worth a try. I'll tell you what. Let's ride with my lord on the morrow, but there's no reason that we need to spend all summer in Dun Deverry. If things do look grim, the lords will be sending their womenfolk away, anyway.'

'That's true. Shall I tell the pages, then?'

'You should, indeed. We'll need them to get our palfreys ready, and we need to fill a chest to go into one of the carts. There. I feel better already, with the decision made.'

But Bevyan paused to glance out the window. The sun was setting in a haze that sent long banners of gold across the sky, as if they were the pennons of some approaching army. The traitorous thought returned full-force. What if Maryn's army ended the war this summer? He'd promised amnesty if he should conquer, promised full pardons even to the lords who'd fought most bitterly against him. What if next summer there would be no march to war?

'My lady?' Sarra said. 'You look so distant.'

'Do I, dear? Well, perhaps I've got a bit of the headache. Let's go down to the great hall and get somewhat to eat.'

In the great hall lords and riders gathered, standing more than sitting, drinking ale, talking in urgent voices, but they stood out of nerves, not for want of benches, and their voices seemed oddly quiet in the half-empty hall. Bevva ran a quick count of lords: a mere four of them, and each obliged to bring no more than forty men a-piece to augment her husband's eighty and the gwerbret's one-hundred-and-sixty. At the head of the table of honour sat her husband's overlord, Daeryc, Gwerbret Belgwergyr, while Tieryn Peddyc sat to his right and their last living son, Anasyn, stood behind His Grace to wait upon him like a page. No one who saw them together would ever have doubted that Anasyn was Peddyc's son. They shared a long face, long thin nose, and a pair of deep-set brown eyes, though Peddyc's hair had turned solidly grey and Anasyn's was still chestnut. When he saw his wife enter, Peddyc rose, swinging himself clear of the bench and smiling as he strode over to meet her.

'There you are,' he said. 'I'd wondered if you were ill.'

'Not ill, my love, merely thinking. I've decided I'd best ride with you when you go to Dun Deverry.'

'Good.' He let his smile disappear. 'You'll be safer there. I'm stripping the fort guard.'

Bevyan laid a hand on her throat. She wondered if she'd gone pale – her face felt so suddenly cold.

'Well, we've not lost yet.' Peddyc pitched his voice low. 'If the time comes for you and your women to leave Dun Deverry, I'll send you back with a full escort of men. Don't worry about that. You'll need to hold the gates long enough to negotiate a settlement with the Pretender.'

'I see.' Bevyan swallowed heavily and freed her voice. 'As my lord thinks best, of course.'

He smiled and touched her face with the side of his hand.

'Let's pray I don't need to do that kind of thinking, Bevva. Come entertain our gwerbret. You and I will ride to court together, at least, and after that, only the gods know.'

Peddyc looked up, and when Bevyan followed his glance she realized that he was looking at the row of cloth banners in gold and green cloth, faded and stained with age, that hung above the main hearth – the blazons of the Ram from time beyond remembering. She could only wonder if someday soon an enemy hand would rip them down.

'The omens?' Merodda said. 'The omens are hideous.'

'You sound frightened,' Burcan said.

'Of course I'm frightened. I suppose that makes me a poor weak woman and beneath contempt.'

'I wouldn't say that.' Burcan, second son of the Boar clan and Regent to the King, allowed himself a wry twist of a smile. 'I'd say it makes you sensible.'

Merodda sighed once and sharply.

Close to the mid-watch of the night they were sitting in her private chamber, she in a carved chair by the fire, he in another near the table. The candles burning there were freshly lit, and Brour and his bowl of black ink both had long since been tidied away.

'I wish I had better news to tell you,' she went on. 'But we have an enemy here at court.'

'I don't need omens to tell me that. Everyone envies our clan.'

'This is different. In the omen a red wyvern dropped out of the sky and slew a boar.'

'What? I wish you wouldn't speak in riddles.'

'I thought it was clear enough. The King's blazon is a green wyvern, and so someone close to but not of the royal family must be plotting to drop down upon us and supplant us.'

Burcan started to speak, then merely stroked his thick grey moustaches while he considered.

'You're right,' he said at last. 'It's perfectly clear, now that you've explained it. I don't know why, but I just can't seem to grasp things like omens.'

'You don't need to. You have me.'

They shared a smile. In the hearth the fire showered sparks as a log burned through and fell. Burcan rose, then strode over to take wood from the basket and lay it upon the flames. For a moment he stood watching it burn.

'Any idea of who this enemy might be?' he said.

'Not yet. You're right about the envy. There are a lot of clans with reason to hate us. I just hadn't realized how deep the hatred must run.'

'I'll think about it. A wyvern, was it? Someone with a touch of royal blood themselves, maybe.'

'There! You're beginning to puzzle this out.'

'Am I? Maybe so. Don't know if I like it, though. That so-called scribe of yours – are you sure we can trust him?'

'I don't know. He came to me for the coin, and if someone offered him more, I can't swear he wouldn't change his loyalties.'

'Thought so. I don't like the man.'

'Why?'

'He comes from the south coast, doesn't he?'

'Not truly. He's from the northern lands, though he did live for some years in Cerrmor.'

'Still! How do you know he isn't a Cerrmor spy?'

'I have ways to tell when someone's lying, as you know perfectly well. There's somewhat else, isn't there?'

Burcan scowled at the floor.

'I don't like the way he treats you,' he said at last.

'What? He's always courteous.'

Burcan raised his head and looked at her. His eyes searched her face, probing for some secret. Merodda stood with a little laugh.

'Don't tell me you're jealous of poor Brour.'

'I don't like the way he's always in your company.'

When Burcan rose to join her, she laid one hand flat on his chest and looked up, smiling at him. In a moment he laid his hand over hers.

'My dear brother,' she said. 'He's little and ugly. You've got no reason to vex yourself on his account.'

'Good. And the moment you think he might turn disloyal, tell me. I'll have the matter taken care of.'

Travelling with Gwerbret Daeryc's entourage, his attendant lords and their joined warbands, plus their servants and retainers, was no speedy thing, especially with carts along and a whole herd of horses. Rather than jounce around in a cart with the maidservants, Bevyan wore a pair of her son's old brigga under her dresses and rode her palfrey, as did Sarra. In the long line of march they travelled just behind the noble lords, although at times Peddyc would drop back and ride beside Bevyan for a few miles. It was pleasant, riding in the spring weather through the ripening winter wheat and the apple trees, heavy with blossoms, so pleasant that Bevyan found herself remembering the first days of her marriage, when she and Peddyc would ride together around his lands, alone except for a page trailing at a discreet distance. They had brought such a shock, those days, when she realized that she'd been married to a man that she would learn to love.

Now of course her lord, his hair streaked with grey, rode grim and silent, and behind them came what of an army he and his overlord could muster.

Along the way the entourage sheltered at the duns of various lords who owed men to either the tieryn or the gwerbret, or at least, they'd been planning to do so. Their first night, when they came to the dun of a certain Lord Daryl, they found the place empty. Not a chicken pecked out in the ward, not a servant stood in the broch. While Daeryc and the men waited out in the ward, Bevyan followed Peddyc through rooms stripped bare.

'They even took the furniture,' Bevyan said. 'Even the bedsteads. It'll be a long hard haul of it they'll have, getting those all the way to Cerrmor.'

Peddyc nodded, glancing around what had once been the lord and lady's bedchamber. All at once he smiled, stooped, and pulled something out of a crack between two planks.

'A silver piece,' he said, grinning. 'Well, I'll take that as tribute. Here's one bit of coin that won't buy a horse for the Usurper's army.'

Their second night on the road brought an even nastier surprise. Lord Ganedd's dun was shut against them, the gates barred from inside. Daeryc and Peddyc sat on their horses and yelled out Ganedd's name, but no voice ever answered. No one appeared on the walls, not even to insult the two lords. Yet the place felt alive and inhabited. In the long silences Bevyan heard the occasional dog bark or horse whinny. Once she thought she saw a face at a window, high up in the broch. When Peddyc and Daeryc rode back to their waiting entourage, they were red-faced and swearing.

'Are they neutral, then?' Anasyn asked. 'Or gone over to the Usurper?'

'How would I know, you young dolt?' Peddyc snarled. 'Oh, here, forgive me, Sanno. No use in taking this out on you.'

When the entourage camped, out in a grassy field stripped of its cows, Bevyan had the servants build a separate fire for the womenfolk. All evening, as they sat whispering gossip and fears, they would keep looking to the men's fire, some twenty feet away, where Peddyc and Daeryc paced back and forth, talking together with their heads bent.

The third evening, then, they rode up to Lord Camlyn's dun with dread as a member of their entourage, but the gates stood open, and Camlyn himself, a tall young man with a shock of red hair, came running out to the ward to greet them with four grey boarhounds barking after him. He yelled the dogs into silence, then grabbed the gwerbret's stirrup in a show of fealty and blurted, 'Your Grace, what greeting did you get at Ganedd's door?'

'A cursed poor one,' Daeryc said. 'I'm glad to see you held loyal to the true king. This autumn, when we ride against Ganedd, his lands are yours.'

At dinner that night the talk centred itself upon broken fealties – who had gone over to the Usurper, who was threatening neutrality, who was weaselling any way he could to get out of his obligations for

fighting men and the provisions to feed them. Since in the poverty of
Camlyn's hall stood but one honour table, Bevyan heard it all. She
shared a trencher with Camlyn's wife, Varylla, at the foot of the table.
In unspoken agreement the two women spoke little, merely listened.
By the time the page poured the men mead, Gwerbret Daeryc had
forgotten tact.

'It's the cursed Boar clan that's the trouble,' he snarled. 'Men would
rally to the King, but why should they rally to the Boar?'

'Just so,' Camlyn said. 'The wars have made them rich while the
rest of us – huh, we'll be out on the roads like beggars one fine day.'

The two men were looking at Peddyc and waiting.

'I've no love for Burcan or Tibryn,' he said. 'But if the King had
chosen them, I'd serve in their cause.'

'I like that if-' Daeryc paused for a careful bite of food; he could
chew only one side of his mouth, since most of his teeth were gone.
'I'd do the same. If-'

Peddyc glanced down the table and caught Bevyan's glance. She
answered the unspoken question with a small shrug. It seemed safe
enough to voice their long doubts here.

'Well,' Peddyc went on. 'They say that King Daen made Burcan
regent when he was dying. I wasn't there to hear him.'

'No more was I,' Camlyn snapped.

'Nor I either. And with Daen's widow such close kin to the Boar
. . .' Daeryc let his words trail off into a swallow of mead.

'Hogs root,' Camlyn said, seemingly absently. 'If you let hogs into
a field, they'll tear it up with tusk and trotter till the grass all dies.'

'There's only one thing to do in that case,' Peddyc said. 'And that's
turn them out of it.'

'Only the one, truly.' Daeryc hesitated for a long time. 'But you'd
best have a swineherd with well-trained dogs.'

The three men looked back and forth at one another while Bevyan
felt herself turn, very slowly, as cold as if a winter wind had blown
into the hall. She glanced at Varylla.

'I should so like to see the embroideries you've been making,'
Bevyan said. 'You do such lovely work.'

'My thanks, my lady.' Varylla allowed herself a shy smile. 'If you'll
come with me to my chambers?'

As they headed for the staircase up, Bevyan caught Peddyc's eye.
He winked at her in thanks, but his smile was forced. Why shouldn't
it be, she thought, if they'll be talking treason?

Late on the next day, with Lord Camlyn and his men as part of the army, Gwerbret Daeryc's entourage came to the city, which rose high on its four hills behind massive double rings of stone walls, ramparted and towered. A cobbled road led up to the main gates, ironbound and carved with the King's blazon of the wyvern rampant. To either side honour guards in thickly embroidered shirts stood, bowing as the gwerbret and his party rode through. Yet as soon as they came inside to the city itself, the impression of splendour vanished.

Ruins filled the space inside the walls – heaps of stone among rotting, charred timbers from the most recent siege; heaps of dirt covering stone razed long years past. Most of the remaining houses stood abandoned, with weed-choked yards and empty windows, the thatch blowing rotten through the streets. In the centre of the city, though, around and between the two main hills, Bevyan did see some tenanted homes, surrounded by kitchen gardens. A few children played in the muddy lanes; more often the people she saw were old, stooped as they tended their produce or sat on a bench at their front door to watch the gwerbret's army ride by. No one called out a greeting or a cheer. Bevyan turned in her saddle to look her husband's way.

'It's even worse this summer,' she remarked. 'The city I mean. It's so desolate.'

'Just so,' Peddyc said.'Everyone who could get out of here did.'

'Where did they go?'

'To kinsfolk, I suppose. The gods all know that there's plenty of farmland lying fallow these days. Hands to work it would be welcome enough.'

'It's so eerie, seeing all these empty houses. There can't be any militia left to help hold the city walls.'

'There's not, truly.' Peddyc looked abruptly away. 'If there's a siege this summer, we'll have to cede the Usurper the town and hold the dun.'

Or try to – Bevyan seemed to hear that thought hanging in the air like a rebel lord. All at once she realized that this summer could easily bring her husband's death. She had faced widowhood for so many years that the thought merely angered rather than frightened her.

The dun at least seemed in good repair. Through ring after ring of warding stone they rode, winding round on a spiral path to the top of the hill. A small village huddled around the final wall – the houses sheltering the King's important servants, the blacksmiths and the like. Inside the palace ward itself Bevyan saw plenty of armed men, and these did cheer when they saw Gwerbret Daeryc and his contingent. Outside the double doors to the great hall, pages and servants stood waiting to take horses and unload carts. Bevyan waited until Peddyc had dismounted, then allowed him to help her down.

'I have to attend upon the gwerbret,' Peddyc said.

'Of course, my love.' Bevyan patted his arm. 'I've been here often enough to take care of myself and my women.'

With a nod Peddyc strode off, yelling orders to his men. Anasyn followed his father without even a look back. Bevyan smiled – her son was growing up, all right, at home in the King's own dun.

'Bevva!'

Dashing like a dog greeting its master, Lillorigga raced across the ward and flung herself into her foster-mother's arms. Laughing, half on the edge of tears, Bevyan hugged her tight, then held her by the shoulders.

'Let me look at you, dear,' Bevyan said. 'Oh, you are so tall now! Oh, it's so good to see you!'

Lillorigga beamed. She was tall, yes, and far too thin, far too pale, with her long blonde hair hanging limp and dead around her face. Bevyan first suspected roundworms, always a problem in a winter dun, even the King's, but then she wondered, thinking of Lady Merodda. In the bustle of the open ward, with armed men trotting by, with servants flocking around, they could not talk openly, not even of matters of health.

'Come with me, dear,' Bevyan said. 'I've got to get our things into our chambers, and then we can talk.'

At the Queen's orders, or so the servant said, Lady Bevyan and her serving woman had been given a large suite in the King's own broch. While the servants hauled up chests and satchels, and Sarra fussed over each, Bevyan and Lilli stood by a window and looked down into the inner ward. This high up, sunlight could gain the walls and stream into the room. Lilli held her hands out to the warmth and laughed.

'It's been a hard winter, has it?' Bevyan said.

'It has, truly. I'm so glad of the spring, although . . .' Lilli let her voice trail away.

'Although it brings the wars again?'

'Just that. Oh Bevva, I'm so sick of being frightened.'

'Well, we all are, dear, but the gods will end it when they will and not before. There's so little that we womenfolk can do.'

Lilli turned to her with a look so furtive that Bevyan forgot what she'd been about to say.

'Lilli, is somewhat wrong?'

'Naught, naught.' Yet she laid a skinny hand on her pale throat.

'You've been ill, haven't you, dear?' Bevyan said.

'A bit. I'm fine now though, truly I am.' Lilli turned her back and looked out over the chamber. 'Sarra, there you are! Did you have a decent journey?'

And what was the child hiding? Soon enough, Bevva knew, she'd unburden herself of the secret. She could wait until Lilli was ready to tell her.

The dun, it seemed, held more than one trouble. At the evening meal in the great hall, Peddyc was seated at the King's table as a mark of honour, while Anasyn went with a pack of unmarried lords. Bevyan and Lilli sat together at one of the tables for the noble women and shared a trencher, though they talked more than ate. Although the young king came down early, escorted by Regent Burcan, the Queen made a much later appearance, sweeping into the hall in a crowd of young women. Queen Abrwnna was a pretty girl, about Lilli's age, with striking green eyes and coppery hair that in the uncertain fire-light shone with streaks of gold among the red. That evening it seemed the Queen had been weeping; her eyes were bloodshot and her full mouth screwed up into a most decidedly unpretty scowl. As the retinue walked by on their way to the table reserved for the royal womenfolk, Bevyan noticed that one of the Queen's serving women, also young and lovely, had a scowl of her own and a rising purple bruise on the side of her face.

'Oooh, that's nasty,' Lilli whispered. 'I take it Abrwnna found out about Galla and Lord Aedar.'

'Some sort of love affair?'

'Just that, and I'll wager Abrwnna's ever so jealous. There's a sort of fellowship of young lords devoted to her, you see – the Queen that is, not Galla. They all wear her token into battle, a bit of one of her old dresses I think it is. Anyway, she absolutely hates it when one of her serving women dallies with one of them – her sworn lords I mean.'

Bevyan laid her table dagger down and considered the Queen's retinue, settling itself at table.

'How interesting,' Bevyan said mildly. 'How many of these lords are there?'

'Only six. It's ever so great an honour to be taken among them.'

'No doubt. I do hope their devotion's an innocent one.'

Lilli blinked in some confusion.

'Well,' Bevyan went on. 'The King's wife absolutely has to be above suspicion. How else will men believe that she's carrying the true heir once she's with child?'

'Oh, that!' Lilli smiled, her confusion lifting. 'Well, the King's but five summers old, and he won't be getting her with child soon anyway.'

'Exactly.'

'Oh.' Lilli turned solemn. 'Oh, I do see what you mean.'

During the rest of the meal, Lilli pointed out the various lords of the Queen's Fellowship, all of whom were reasonably good-looking and generally wealthy. Bevyan told herself that she was turning into a small-minded old woman, but she couldn't help but wonder about the safety of this arrangement when she saw the various lords bowing over the Queen's hand and kissing it. Upon the virtue of the Queen rested the honour of the blood royal; not for her the small freedoms of other noblewomen. As the wife of a mere tieryn, Bevyan's own rank would hardly allow her to admonish the Queen. She did her best, therefore, to put the matter out of her mind.

Toward the end of the meal, Bevyan and Lilli were sharing dried apples when a page came trotting over. He bowed low to Bevyan, then turned to Lilli.

'Your mother wishes to see you,' he announced. 'In her chambers.'

Lilli turned dead-white.

'What's so wrong, dear?' Bevyan said softly.

'Oh, she'll want to talk about my marriage.' Lilli turned anguished eyes her way. 'I hate it when she does.'

Plausible, yes, but Bevyan had fostered too many children to miss a lie when she heard one. Lilli got up and ran across the great hall. As she watched her go, Bevyan was thanking the Goddess in her heart for her decision to come to Dun Deverry.

And yet, that evening Lilli had inadvertently spoken the truth. When she arrived at her mother's chamber, she found both her uncles waiting. For the occasion the table had been spread with a white cloth; candles gleamed and among them stood a dented silver flagon and pottery goblets. Burcan sat across from Merodda in a cushioned chair while Gwerbret Tibryn stood by the hearth, where a small fire burned to take off the chill.

'Come in, child.' Merodda pointed to a footstool placed near her chair. 'Sit down.'

With a curtsy to her uncles, Lilli did so. Both Burcan and Tibryn considered her for a long cold moment.

'It's time you married,' Merodda announced. 'You've been out of fosterage for what? Two winters now?'

'It's been that, Mother.'

'Very well, then. We've been discussing the matter. We need to determine how best your marriage could serve the clan, you see.'

They all seemed to be waiting for her to say something. Lilli pushed out a watery smile and clasped her hands tightly to hide their shaking. After a moment Merodda went on.

'Your uncle Tibryn wants to marry you to one of his allies in Cantrae, up in the Northlands. Tieryn Nantyn.'

'He's so old!' Lilli regretted the blurt the moment she'd said it and shrank back, expecting her mother to slap her.

Instead, Merodda laid a warning hand on her shoulder and squeezed, but not painfully hard. Tibryn glowered, his mouth set in a thin line under his heavy moustaches.

'Worse than that,' Burcan snarled. 'He's a brutal man who's already buried one wife.'

'So he did,' Tibryn said levelly. 'But who's to say he had somewhat to do with her dying? Or have you been listening to women's gossip?' His eyes flicked to his sister and then away again.

'And why shouldn't she listen?' Burcan snapped. 'Lilli's her only daughter.'

'Your Grace?' Merodda broke in. 'To have her only daughter sent so far away would grieve any woman in her old age.'

'Oh ye gods!' Tibryn rolled his eyes to heaven. 'You should have been a bard, Rhodi! The poor old woman and her daughter!'

'Don't be such a beast! I do want Lilli near court. You're my eld brother and the head of our clan, but surely I'm not forbidden to speak as a mother?'

'The gods could forbid it, and it wouldn't keep you quiet.' Tibryn allowed himself a short bark of a laugh. 'So why would you listen to a mere mortal man? Nantyn is important to me. So far all the northern lords have held loyal to us, but this talk of the Usurper's pardons is troubling a lot of hearts.'

'There are other ways to bind a man to his gwerbret,' Burcan said.

'There's that bit of land in dispute twixt him and me. I'll cede it if you think it necessary.'

Tibryn turned toward his younger brother, seemed to be about to speak, then hesitated. Burcan looked steadily back at him.

'If the matter vexes you as much as that,' Tibryn said at last, 'then very well.'

'My thanks, Your Grace.'

'And mine, too,' Merodda put in. She let Lilli's shoulder go and leaned back in her chair. 'My humble, humble thanks.'

Tibryn made a snorting sound, no doubt at the thought of Merodda being humble. Lilli realized that she'd been holding her breath and let it out with a small sigh.

'Who else, then?' the gwerbret said. 'If we're not to send her off to a northern lord, where's the best place for us to spend this coin?'

'I've been thinking,' Burcan said. 'Perhaps it would be best to keep it in the clan. All things considered. Do you want your niece and her child held hostage one day by someone who just went over to the Usurper? Turning Lilli over might be a good way for a new man to prove his loyalty.'

'True enough.' Tibryn paused to swear with a shake of his head. 'There's your lad Braemys.'

'Hmph, well,' Burcan said. 'I was thinking about one of the conjoint lords-'

'Why? If we're keeping her close to the clan's hearth, then let's do so. Some of our distant cousins would slit my throat gladly if it came to saving their own necks with the Usurper. They'd do the same for you.'

'I can't argue with that, but-'

'But what?' Tibryn waved the objection away. 'A cousin marriage is a grand way to keep land in a great clan, anyway. Lilli will bring her late father's land as a dowry, of course, since her brothers are dead, too. I'd like to see Braemys have it. The holding will be worth keeping in the Boar's hands.' He turned to Merodda. 'As the Regent's son, he and his wife will be living at court much of the time.'

'Just so, Your Grace.' Merodda favoured him with a brilliant smile. 'Brother? You look troubled.'

Actually, Lilli decided, Burcan looked furious enough to choke her; then the look vanished in a wry smile.

'It makes a man feel old, seeing his youngest son marry,' Burcan said and smoothly.

'Happened to me, too.' Tibryn nodded. 'Well, let's consider the matter settled. Rhodi, how about pouring some of that mead?'

'Of course.' Merodda got up from her chair and started toward the table, then glanced back. 'Lilli, you don't have any objections, do you?'

'None, Mother. I've always known I'd marry where the clan wished.'

'Good,' Tibryn said. 'Good child. Braemys is a well-favoured lad, anyway, and a good man with a horse.'

'And what about you?' Merodda turned to Burcan. 'Does this suit you well enough, brother?'

Burcan raised bland eyes.

'Well enough,' he said. 'We'd best start discussing the dowry and the bride-price.'

'Oh come now,' Tibryn said. 'The land she brings should be enough for any man, Burco!'

'Very true.' Merodda turned to Lilli. 'You may leave us now.'

Lilli rose, curtsied, and gladly fled. She hurried down the stone staircase to the first turn, then paused, looking out over the great hall, roaring with armed men in the firelight. Braemys had left Dun Deverry some days earlier, she knew, gone off to his father's lands to muster their allies, but then, his father would have to be the one to inform him of the betrothal, anyway. Perhaps Uncle Burcan would send him a messenger; more likely the matter would wait until her cousin returned to court. She wondered if he would be pleased instead of feeling merely relieved she wasn't someone else.

Lilli did however spot Lady Bevyan, standing by the royal table with two of Queen Abrwnna's serving women. Smiling, Lilli trotted down the steps and made her way over to her foster-mother, who greeted her by holding out one arm. Lilli slipped into that familiar embrace with a comfortable sigh. With nods and farewells, the serving women drifted away.

'My, you look pleased!' Bevyan said. 'The talk with your mother wasn't as bad as all that, then.'

'It wasn't. They've settled my betrothal, and it's not to one of Uncle Tibryn's awful vassals.'

'Good! I was afraid they'd be considering Nantyn.'

'They were, but Uncle Burcan spoke up for me. It was such an odd thing, Bevva! He even offered to cede Nantyn some land somewhere if Uncle Tibryn wanted to give the old sot that instead of me.'

'Well, may our goddess bless him for it!' Bevyan's voice sounded oddly wary. 'I wouldn't have thought he'd do such a thing, Burcan that is.'

'But he did, and now I'll be marrying Braemys, my cousin, you know?'

Bevyan's arm tightened fast and sharp around her shoulders, then released her. Lilli stepped away and looked at her foster-mother, whose face had gone as bland as her uncle's had, a few minutes before.

'Is somewhat wrong with him?' Lilli said.

'Not in the least. A decent young man and quite well-spoken, he is.' Her voice wavered ever so slightly. 'Well. I'll wager you're glad to have it settled, dear.'

'I am, truly. And this way I'll be staying at court, and I'll still be able to see you, now and again.'

'Just so, and that will be lovely.'

But the distant look in Bevva's eyes – it was fear, Lilli realized suddenly – bespoke thoughts that were far from lovely. She hovered, wondering what could be so wrong, until Bevyan broke the mood with a little laugh.

'It's so noisy here,' Bevva said. 'Shall we go up to my chambers? Sarra will want to hear all about your betrothal.'

With that, both Bevyan and the evening returned to their normal selves. Up in Bevva's suite various court ladies joined them for a long gossip. Lilli felt like a cat lying down for a good nap by a fire, all safe and warm at last. Here in the company of other women she could forget, for at least a little while, the black ink and its secrets.

In the morning Bevyan's suspicions woke with her. While she dressed, they seemed to sit on the edge of her bed, muttering in low voices, 'Could it be? Could it really be?' One never knew what Merodda might be thinking; she did, after all, lie as easily as a bard sang. Finally she could stand it no longer and went to Merodda's chambers, just to hear what she could hear, she told herself, just to prove herself wrong. When Merodda's maidservant let Bevyan in, she found the lady washing her face. In the corner of her bedroom stood a crockery basin on a wooden stand. Dressed in a plain white shift, Merodda was dabbling a thin cloth in strange-smelling water.

'I'll be with you in a moment, Bevyan. I shan't be able to talk while I'm doing this.'

'Of course. I'm in no hurry. Is it a herb bath, dear?'

Merodda gave her a brief smile for her only answer, then wrung out her cloth and began wiping her face with it. Every now and then she'd dip a corner of the rag back in the basin, but Bevyan noticed that she never let it get too wet and that she kept her lips tightly closed the while. No doubt the stuff tasted as bad as it smelled. When she finished, she laid the cloth at her windowsill to dry, then rinsed her hands with clean water from a crockery pitcher that stood on the floor.

'Now then,' Merodda said. 'What did you wish to speak with me about?'

'Lilli told me about her betrothal last night.'

'Ah, did she? What do you think of Braemys?'

'He's a very decent lad. A bit close kin, perhaps.'

'Oh, Burcan wanted a cousin marriage. It's the lands, of course. With my sons dead, my poor dear Geredd's lands came to Lilli. It's a nice holding.'

'It is, indeed, and worth the Boar's keeping.'

Merodda picked up a bone comb and began combing her hair, starkly gold in the sunlight. Another herb potion, or so Bevyan supposed, kept it that girlish colour.

'I did foster the lass,' Bevyan said. 'I'm not merely prying.'

'Of course not! And you did a fine job, I must say. Lilli's turned out to be a lovely child with very courtly ways.'

'My thanks. I'm so glad you're pleased.'

'And I am.' Merodda hesitated, glancing away. 'I did the best I could for her, with this marriage. I hope you believe me about that. I did the best I could.'

'What? Of course I believe you! No doubt your brothers did the real deciding, anyway. I'm just so glad that Tibryn didn't send her off to Nantyn to be beaten to death.'

'That was my worst fear.' Merodda looked at her again, and never had Bevyan seen a woman more sincere. 'It truly was.'

'Then we can both thank the Goddess – and Burcan – that it didn't happen.'

'Ah. Lilli told you about the way he intervened.'

'She did. It was very good of him.'

For a moment they considered each other.

'It was,' Merodda said at last. 'But Braemys is a decent lad. Lilli will be very well provided for, and I'll be able to keep her near me at court much of the time. She's my last child, after all, the last one these wars have left me. I know that you can understand how I feel.'

'Unfortunately, I can. You know, dear, I'd never do anything that would ever harm Lilli.'

Merodda nodded, then hesitated, studying Bevyan's face. It was a habit of hers, to peer at someone so intently you would have thought she was reading omens in their eyes. Bevyan had always assumed that she was nearsighted and nothing more, but this morning the scrutiny bothered her.

'I shouldn't take up more of your time,' Bevyan said.

'Oh, Bevva, don't be foolish! It's good to see you. In fact, may I ask you a favour?'

'Of course.'

'Come with me on an errand. I've got to consult with the heralds on an odd matter. Unless perhaps you know: is there a clan named the Red Wyvern among the Usurper's following?'

'I have no idea. I vaguely remember hearing the name once, years and years ago, but that's all.'

'Then let me dress, and we'll pay the heralds a visit.'

Merodda smiled; Bevyan smiled; the suspicions began their nattering again. And yet what was she to do, Bevva asked herself? Come right out and ask: Lilli is Burcan's child, isn't she? You're marrying her off to her own brother, aren't you?

In one of the side brochs the King's heralds lived and had their scriptorium, where they copied over and preserved the genealogies of the various clans and their intermarryings as well as the devices proper to each. When the two women arrived, a servant trotted off to fetch the chief herald himself, leaving them in the sunny room. A row of tables with slanted tops sat underneath the windows, while on the walls hung small shields, each about a foot high, the official record of each device. Merodda began circling the room and studying the shields, but what caught Bevyan's attention was a glass sphere filled with water that sat upon the window ledge. She was just puzzling over it when the chief herald himself, Dennyc, trotted in with low bows for the Regent's sister and her companion.

'Ah, there you are, good herald,' Merodda said. 'My thanks for attending upon us.'

'It's my honour, your ladyship. And what may I do for you?'

'I've a question,' Merodda said, pointing. 'On this shield here, whose device is this? The red wyvern, I mean.'

'Sadly, the clan that bore it is long gone.' Dennyc ambled over to join her. 'The last heir died before I was born, and so I know only what my predecessor told me. They held land off in the west and were related to the blood royal of both Deverry and Pyrdon. Just exactly how I don't remember, though I could of course look it up for you.'

'Oh, do spare yourself the effort. It doesn't matter.' Merodda suddenly laughed. 'Since they're long gone.'

Bevyan could only wonder why, but there was no doubt that Merodda looked profoundly relieved. Dennyc bowed again.

'I'd been hoping for a word with your ladyship,' the herald said. 'I understand that she's betrothed her daughter to Braemys of the Boar.'

'I have, indeed.'

'Ah, I was thinking, you see, being as I do study such things, your ladyship, the best to serve my king and all who serve him, that perhaps the marriage is a bit too much of a close one.'

For the briefest of moments Merodda went as a still as a rabbit in the bracken when it hears the hounds. Perhaps it was merely the bright light in the room, but she went a little pale around the mouth as well – again, for a brief moment. With what must have been an effort, she smiled.

'Cousin marriages are common in all the great clans,' Merodda said.

'Just so, my lady.' Dennyc bowed with the air of a man who wasn't quite sure of what else to do. 'But there have been so many first cousin marriages among the Boar that I thought perhaps it was my duty to warn her ladyship, merely warn her of course as the decision will always remain hers and her brothers, but,' he paused for a brief breath, 'perhaps if there were some other candidate who pleased her ladyship equally well-'

'There's not.' Merodda spoke firmly but politely. 'My thanks, good Dennyc. Lady Bevyan, shall we go?'

'As you wish, my lady.'

Bevyan and Merodda parted company at the door of the King's broch, but all that morning, as she walked in the gardens as part of the Queen's retinue, Bevyan found her worry gnawing at her. Apparently the news of Lady Lillorigga's marriage had reached royalty as well as the heralds. With a wave of one slender hand, Abrwnna motioned Bevyan up to walk beside her.

'I hear your foster-daughter is to marry Lord Braemys,' the Queen said.

'She is, Your Highness.'

'And here I was going to take him into my fellowship.' Abrwnna tossed her head with a ripple of red-gold hair in the sunlight. 'I'm glad now I didn't.'

'I see, Your Highness.'

They walked a bit further down a gravelled path to a wall where climbing roses were just beginning to bud. The Queen picked one and forced the tiny petals open with her thumb.

'I let your son know that he'd be welcome to join my fellowship. He declined. Did you know that?'

'I didn't, Your Highness. I hope you weren't offended.'

'Of course I was. But it's not your fault.'

Before Bevyan could think of a tactful comment, the Queen dismissed her again.

As Bevyan was entering the great hall for dinner with her women behind her, chance brought her face to face with Regent Burcan, followed by his own retinue. They smiled and exchanged pleasantries, but Bevyan found herself studying his broad face, the distinctive wide blue eyes, the thin mouth, both so like Lilli's – but like her mother's as well, she reminded herself.

'I must congratulate you, Regent,' Bevyan said at last. 'I hear you've made a good marriage for young Braemys.'

Burcan's expression changed; he kept smiling, but his entire face went tight from the effort of doing so.

'Lilli will make him a good wife,' Burcan said, and his voice was oddly tight as well. 'And she brings a nice parcel of land with her.'

'So she does. My congratulations to the lad.'

As Bevyan made their way through the tables to her own seat, she glanced back to find Burcan staring after her, his face set and unreadable. All at once she realized that letting him see her suspicions would be dangerous.

After the meal, there in the great hall before the assembled lords and the King himself Tibryn announced the betrothal of his niece to his nephew. Everyone cheered and called out their congratulations while Lilli smiled and blushed – everyone but the Queen, that is, who pouted. Bevyan could only hope that Lilli could keep her happiness safe from jealousy as well as death, that little bit of happiness allowed to a woman in the midst of the endless wars.

As always, the black ink seemed to rise out of the basin in a vast wave, catching her, pulling her under. This time the wave seemed so real that Lilli gagged and coughed, sure that she would drown. She could feel her mother's hand pressing on her neck and pushing her down into trance. All at once she floated in blackness, and the choking vanished.

'Tell us what you see.' The words swam after her, imploring. 'What do you see, Lilli?'

At first, nothing – then in the blackness the familiar circle of light appeared. Lilli floated through and found herself back in the dun, back in her mother's chambers, in fact, but a pale sunlight poured in through the open windows. 'Who's there, Lilli?' The voice sounded so strange, all syrupy and drawn out, that she could not tell if Brour or Merodda spoke. 'Who do you see?'

'No one. But there are things.'

A wooden chest stood open; dresses lay scattered on the floor; an empty silver flagon lay in the ashes on the hearth. In one corner sat a little doll, made of cloth scraps stuffed with hay. Lilli recognized it as something that had belonged to her years ago; Sarra had made it for her, and Bevyan had embroidered the little face. With a laugh she ran to it and picked it up, hugged it to her chest as she used to do, back in Hendyr.

'Can you leave the room?' The voice poured into her ears.

'There's no door to be seen.'

'Look into the chest.'

Still holding her doll, Lilli skipped across the chamber. She leaned over the chest and nearly screamed. Only her fear of her mother's slap kept her from screaming. Yet she must have made some sound, because the voice sounded urgent.

'What is it?'

'Brour's head, just his head, and the neck's all black with old blood.'

'Come back!' Her mother's voice said, and this time it was clearly her mother's. 'Come back now. Go through the window.'

Lilli found herself floating up and out, as light as a dandelion seed, up up into the blue sky and through the sky to candle flame. She found herself on her knees by the table in her mother's chamber. Merodda knelt in front of her, her waxy face sweaty-pale in the dancing candlelight.

'We've done enough for one night,' Merodda said. 'You need to rest.'

'Just so,' Brour said. 'Just so.'

With Merodda's help Lilli got to her feet. In a moment her head cleared enough for her to stand without help.

'Shall I go with you to your chamber?' Brour said. 'Will you get there safely?'

'I will, truly.' Lilli couldn't bear to look at him, not with the vision of his severed head still hanging behind her eyes. 'I'll be fine.'

Lilli hurried across the chamber and out, but as she closed the door she paused briefly and glanced back to see Brour and Merodda standing facing each other like a pair of swordsmen. She shut the door quietly and for a moment leaned against it to gather her strength. All at once she realized that she was – of course – no longer holding the doll. She would have wept, but she was learning that tears were merely her reaction to the scrying sessions and no true thing.

Yet all that evening and on into the night she found herself missing that doll. In her dreams she searched for it in strange chambers filled with armed men, who never noticed her as she crept along the walls and slipped through half-open doors. In the morning when she woke, she reached for the doll, which had always slept with her when she'd been a child.

'Of course it's not there, you dolt,' she told herself. 'You lost it when they brought you back here.'

What if somehow her mother had found and kept it? Perhaps it really was in that chamber, where she'd seen it in vision. Toward the middle of the morning, when she was sitting in the great hall, she saw her mother and Bevyan both in attendance upon the Queen. No doubt the three of them would go to the royal women's hall and be busy there for some long while. Although she felt foolish for doing so, Lilli hurried upstairs.

In her mother's chambers she found not the doll but Brour, sitting sideways by the window so that the sunlight could fall upon the pages of an enormous book, about as tall as a man's forearm and half-again as wide, that he'd laid upon the table. With his lower lip stuck out, and his big head bent in concentration, he looked more like a child than ever. When she walked in, he shut the book with some effort. She could smell ancient damp exhaling from its pages. Grey stains marred the dark leather of its bindings.

'I can't read, you know,' Lilli said. 'You don't have to worry about me seeing your secrets.'

'Well, that's true.' Brour smiled briefly. 'Are you looking for your mother, lass? She told me that she'd be waiting upon the Queen all day.'

'Ah, I thought so. I just wanted to see if I'd left a little thing here.'

'Look all you please.' Brour waved his hand vaguely at the chamber.

Feeling more foolish than ever Lilli walked around, glancing behind the furniture, opening the carved chests, which held nothing but her mother's clothes. Brour clasped his book in his arms and watched her.

'You don't see my head in there again, do you?' he said at last.

'I don't, and may the Goddess be thanked. That was truly horrible.'

'I didn't find the omen amusing, either.' His voice turned flat.

Lilli shut the last chest, then leaned in the curve of the wall to watch him watch her. His short thick fingers dug into the leather bindings of his book.

'It must have scared you,' she said.

'A fair bit, truly. What do you think the meaning was?'

'I've no idea. My mother never tells me how to interpret the things I see.'

'No doubt.' Brour made a little grunt of disgust. 'She treats you like an infant, doesn't she? You should be learning how to use your gifts.'

Lilli laid one hand at her throat.

'Does that frighten you?' Brour went on. 'A pity, if so.'

'I never asked for any of this. I hate doing it, I just hate it.'

Brour considered her for a moment, then laid his book on the table.

'You hate it because you don't understand it. If you understood it, you wouldn't hate it.' All at once he smiled at her. 'I'll make you a promise about that.'

Lilli hesitated, then glanced at the door. She could leave, she should just leave, and find some of the court women to keep her company.

'By all means, go if you want,' Brour said. 'But don't you even want to know what it is you're doing, when you scry at your mother's whim?'

'I'm seeing omens,' Lilli snapped. 'I know that much.'

'Ah, but where are you seeing them?'

The question caught her. She'd so often wondered just that.

'I don't know,' she said. 'Do you?'

'I do indeed.' Brour smiled again, and he seemed much kinder than she'd ever thought him to be. 'Come now, won't you sit down? Explaining where portents come from is no short matter.'

Lilli took a step toward the table, then stopped.

'If my mother finds out about this, she'll beat me.'

'Then we'd best make sure she knows nothing.' Brour pointed at the chair across from his. 'Haven't you ever wondered why Merodda doesn't want you to learn dweomer?'

'I have, truly.'

'She wants to use your powers for herself, that's why. When you learn about your gifts, you'll be able to use them for yourself, and she won't be able to force you to do what she wants.'

Lilli walked over and sat down. Brour smiled and opened his book.

'There's a picture in here that I want to show you,' he said. 'It shows what the universe looks like.'

Circles within circles, drawn in black ink – at the centre sat the Earth, or so Brour called it, and each circle around it bore a name.

'This is Greggyn lore,' Brour said. 'It came over with King Bran during the Great Migration. The sphere – that's what these circles represent, spheres – above and surrounding the sphere of the Earth belongs to the Moon. The next one belongs to the Sun. We'll learn about those higher ones when it's time. There's too much for you to remember all at once.'

'That's certainly true.' Lilli put her elbows on the table and leaned forward to study the picture. 'It gives me such an odd feeling, seeing this.'

'Ah, no doubt the knowledge is calling to you.'

In truth the feeling was more like terror, but she decided against telling him that. She listened carefully as he explained how the matter of each sphere interpenetrates the one below it.

'Only on the earthly world do all the others exist,' Brour finished up. 'Here they reach completion. And that means from here you can reach all the others. That's what you do when you go into trance. You leave your body and go to one of these other worlds.'

The terror stuck in her throat. That's what people do when they die, Lilli thought. They leave their bodies and go to the Otherlands.

'Now, omens of the future exist in the upper astral,' Brour pointed at a circle. 'That's where your mother sends you.'

'My mother sends me there? I thought you were the one who did that.'

'Not I, child. Your mother knows as much about these things as I do.' Abruptly he looked away.

In the hall, a noise – someone walking, several people, all talking at once. Lilli leapt to her feet. Brour shut the book. The sounds grew louder – and went on past. Lilli let out her breath in a long sigh and realized that Brour had lost the colour in his face.

'You're scared of her, too, aren't you?' she said.

'I can't deny it.'

Lilli stared. She'd never thought to see a man frightened of a woman, not anywhere in her world.

'I'd best go.' She got up. 'I don't dare have her find me here.'

'Just so. But come back when you can, and I'll tell you more.'

Lilli ran out of the chamber, slammed the door, and raced down the hall. At the staircase she paused to smooth her hair and catch her breath, then decorously descended to the great hall below. I'll never go back, she told herself. I'll never look at that book again.

At dinner that evening she sat next to Bevyan, whose warmth drove all thoughts of dangerous magic from her mind. They discussed Lilli's dower chest, which she'd started filling while she was still at Hendyr, although, as she admitted, she'd been lax of late.

'Well, dear, Sarra and I are here to help,' Bevyan said. 'The first thing we'll want to do is the wedding shirt for Braemys, and then the coverlet for your new bed.'

'We should have all summer,' Sarra put in. 'They won't be holding the wedding till the campaigning's over.'

'That's true.' Lilli felt oddly cold, and she rubbed her hands together. 'I hope naught ill happens to Braemys.'

'Ai!' Bevyan shook her head. 'You're a woman now truly, aren't you, dear? You've joined the rest of us in worrying about one man or another.'

That night, as she lay in bed and tried to sleep, Lilli was thinking about Braemys. She'd always liked her cousin, who had also been fostered out to Peddyc and Bevyan. Whether or not they married, she certainly didn't want him to die in the summer's fighting. And now, if he did die, whom would she be forced to marry in the autumn? Nantyn or some other old and drink-besotted northern lord like him. Uncle Tibryn would never allow his mind to be changed a second time; the miracle was that he'd allowed it once.

Her mind like a traitor turned up Brour's image, saying: you could use your gifts for yourself. What if she could read omens about Braemys's wyrd? What if she could know what was going to happen to her, instead of feeling like a twig floating on a river, twisting this way and that with the current beyond her power to break free? She sat up in bed and wrapped her arms around her knees. Through the window she could see a slender moon, rising between two towers, enjoying all the freedom of the sky.

In the morning, when Lady Merodda announced a hawking party, Lilli feigned a headache and stayed behind, moaning against her pillows like an invalid. As soon as she could be sure that they were well and truly gone, she got up, dressed, and hurried to Lady Bevyan's suite. She needed advice, even though she could never mention dweomer to Bevyan. Merely being around her foster-mother would help her think, Lilli decided. Bevyan would give her a kind of touchstone to judge the worth of these strange things. But Sarra met her at the door.

'Oh, Bevva's not here.' Sarra paused for a triumphant smile 'She was invited to go hawking with the Queen.'

'She was?'

'She truly was, and I'm ever so pleased. It's such an honour!'

Of course, but Lilli was wishing that Bevyan had been honoured on some other day. She went downstairs, hung around the great hall for a miserable while, then found herself thinking again and again of Brour's book and the secrets it held. At last, with a feeling of surrender, she returned to her mother's chambers.

Brour was sitting at the table by the window, but instead of his book, parchment and ink lay in front of him.

'Ah,' he said, grinning. 'You came back.'

'I did. Did you really mean what you said, about I could use my gifts for myself?'

'I did. I'll swear that by any god you like. Now, I'm just writing a message for your uncle, telling his son that you and he will marry. When I'm done, I'll take it back to Lord Burcan, and then we can look at my book again.'

Lilli sat down, elbows on the table, and watched him write, forming each black letter carefully on a parchment used so many times that it had been scraped as thin and flabby as cloth. The scribe who lived in Burcan's dun would be able to look at those marks and turn them into speech again – Lilli shuddered, but pleasurably. It seemed a dweomer of its own.

'My congratulations, by the by.' Brour paused to pick up a little pen knife. 'Or is the betrothal a bad one?'

'It's not, but one I'm well-pleased with.'

'Good.' He smiled, and it seemed to her that he was sincere. 'I'm glad of that. Some day you'll be able to use your gifts to help your husband, then, as well.'

'I'd like that. I just hope my mother doesn't find us out. She can always tell when I'm lying, you know. Is that dweomer?'

'It is, most certainly.'

Lilli caught her breath.

'Ah,' Brour went on, 'but what you don't understand is that dweomer can be countered with dweomer. I'll teach you how to defend yourself against your mother's prying.'

'Really?'

'Really. It's a beginner's sort of trick but a useful thing to know.'

Lilli smiled.

'I'm beginning to think I'll like these studies.'

'Oh,' Brour said, solemn-faced, 'I'm sure you will. I truly am.'

After a morning's desultory hunt, the Queen's party rode down to the grassy shore of Lake Gwerconydd for a meal. While the pages bustled around, spreading out a cloth and opening baskets of food, the women turned their horses over to the men of the Queen's guard and their hawks to the falconers. With Merodda and Bevyan in tow, the Queen ran down to the water's edge, where small waves lapped on clean sand. She threw herself down on her back in the thick grass and laughed up at the sky while Bevyan and Merodda sat more decorously beside her.

'It feels so good to be out of the dun,' the Queen said. 'Don't you think so, Lady Bevyan?'

'I do, Your Highness.' Bevyan paused for a hurried glance back – the men were all staring at the Queen. 'It's a lovely sunny day.'

'Perhaps Her Highness might sit up?' Merodda said, smiling. 'She has a great many men in her retinue, and dignity is never amiss.'

Abrwnna stuck out her tongue at Merodda, but she did sit, smoothing her white riding dresses down over her knees.

'I'm quite sure my guards know their duty,' the Queen said. 'And they're all very loyal to the King. Well, to your brother, my lady Merodda. He picked them, after all.'

'My brother acts purely in the King's interests,' Merodda said. 'Any loyalty paid to him is loyalty paid to our liege.'

'Oh please!' Abrwnna wrinkled her nose. 'You don't have to pretend around me. We all know who really rules the kingdom.'

A page was approaching. Bevyan laid a warning finger across her lips.

'Your Highness?' the boy said. 'The meal is ready.'

'Very well.' Abrwnna rose and nodded his way. 'Shall we go, my ladies?'

While they ate, with the pages hovering around in attendance, Abrwnna kept the conversation to court gossip. Her maidservants supplied her with every scrap of scandal in the dun, apparently, to augment what she gleaned herself. She ran through various love affairs or the possibility of them as if she were reciting the lists for a tournament.

'So you can see, Bevva,' Abrwnna finished up, 'all sorts of things happened this winter while you were gone.'

'Indeed,' Bevyan said. She reminded herself to tell Peddyc about this use of her nickname. 'Long winters do that to people, and with so many widows sheltering here under your protection, I suppose things might get a bit complicated.'

'Very, and I haven't told you the best bit yet. Lady Merodda's brother was the biggest prize of all. The Regent might as well be a nice fat partridge, for all the hawks that are set upon him.'

Merodda, who was buttering bread, smiled indulgently.

'Well, Your Highness,' Bevyan said. 'He has access to the King, and that does make a man attractive.'

'Just so. The worst thing happened though. It was right before the thaw. Two of the court ladies were fighting over Burcan, just like dogs fighting over scraps of meat. It was Varra and Caetha.'

'Caetha? I'd heard she left us for the Otherlands.'

'She did, and here's the thing. It looked like she was gaining the Regent's favour – everyone said he was much taken with her – when suddenly she died. Everyone said Varra poisoned her, it was so sudden. And then Varra left court and went home to her brother, which makes me think she really did do it.'

'Oh, my dear liege!' Merodda looked up with a little shake of her head. 'I doubt that very much. Here – it was at the bitter end of winter, and we all know what happens then to the food, even in a king's dun.' She glanced at Bevyan. 'The poor woman died after eating tainted meat. It was horrible.'

'But she's not the only one who ate it.' Abrwnna leaned forward. 'Merodda had some, too.'

'And, Your Highness, I was quite ill.' Merodda shuddered as if at the memory. 'Caetha wasn't strong enough to recover, I'm afraid. It happens.'

'Indeed, it does happen, and a sad sad thing,' Bevyan said. 'There's really no need to talk about poisoning people.'

And yet, despite her sensible words, Bevyan found herself wondering about Merodda's herbcraft. If she could wash her face with ill-smelling water and keep her skin as smooth as a lass's, what other lore did she know? No doubt the Queen had no idea that poor dead Caetha's real rival had been Lord Burcan's sister.

Since it was the Queen's pleasure to ride, the women returned to the dun late in the afternoon. Side by side Merodda and Bevyan walked into the great hall, where the men were already congregating for the evening meal. They watched the Queen and her maidservants flit through the crowd like chattering birds and chase each other, giggling, up the stone staircase. Bevyan could just see on the landing a handful of young lords, each marked as a member of the Queen's fellowship by a twist of green silk around their right sleeve. They bowed to the ladies and walked with them up the stairway and out of sight.

'Bevva?' Merodda said suddenly. 'You don't suppose Abrwnna has a lover, do you?'

'It's one of my fears, truly. She talks of little else.'

'Just so. Being married to a child is a difficult thing for a lass like her.'

They exchanged a grim glance, for that moment at least allies.

Later that evening, Bevyan remembered to ask Lilli about the lady Caetha in the privacy of her suite. Lilli repeated the story of the tainted meat and added that Caetha had died clutching her stomach in agony.

'How terrible!' Bevyan said. 'I take it that your mother was ill as well.'

'She was. She'd eaten from that same meat.' Lilli considered with a small frown. 'But she wasn't anywhere as ill as poor Caetha, though she threw up ever so much and told us all how much pain she was in.'

'That's an odd way of putting it, dear. Do you think she wasn't in pain?'

'Oh, my apologies. I didn't mean it to come out like that.' Lilli laid a pale hand at her throat. 'She was; of course she was. It was awful to hear her moan and not be able to do anything for it.'

'No doubt. You poor child! Well, I'm so sorry about poor Caetha.'

'Oh, indeed. We all were.'

Yet once again Bevyan wondered.

Often over the next few days Lilli found herself drawn back to her mother's chamber and Brour. She felt as if she were living the lives of two different girls. In the afternoons, she would sit and sew with Bevyan and the other women, talking over the news of the royal dun while the embroidery grew thick on the pieces of Braemys's wedding shirt. But in the morning, she would watch her mother to get some idea of Merodda's plans, and once they were established – a country ride, perhaps, or a session in the Queen's chambers – Lilli would slip upstairs for a lesson. Oddly enough, Brour always seemed to know that she was coming and would be waiting for her.

'Is that dweomer?' she demanded one morning. 'The way you know I'm coming?'

'It's not. I *am* your mother's scribe, after all. She tells me when she'll be occupied, and then I assume you'll be coming up here. Although, to tell you the truth, sometimes I worry about her laying a trap for us, like.'

'So do I. But today I know she's gone with the Queen to the temple down in the city, so she should be busy for a fair long while.'

'Good.' Brour considered, tapping his fingers on the closed book. 'I've got a thing of great import to tell you. Repeat back to me what I told you about the Wildfolk.'

'They are creatures of the Sphere of the Moon as we are of the Earth. They have eyes that see and ears that hear but not true wits. The dweomermaster can command them at will but should never trust them.'

'Excellent! And what of the Lords of the Elements?'

'They too are spirits, but of the Spheres of the Planets. They have the beginnings of true wits and thus are wily and hard to command.'

'Well done again. You have a fine mind, lass.'

Lilli blushed.

'What I'm thinking of doing,' Brour went on, 'is the evocation of one of the Lords of Earth. There's a thing I need to find, buried in the earth around this dun. I've asked here and there among the servants and the retainers, but no one knows where it lies.'

'What is it?'

'Haven't you ever thought it odd that this dun doesn't have a bolt-hole, a way out in case of siege?'

'You mean it doesn't?'

'Not so as anyone remembers. And yet I've looked over the chronicles of the kings, as the bards and the priests have kept them. This war's raged a long time, a hundred years and more, and as will happen in a war, the fortunes ebb and sway. There were times back in the early days when it looked black indeed for the true king here in Dun Deverry, times when one usurper or another had this city sieged. And each time the King disappeared from the dun and just like dweomer turned up in the Boar's own city of Cantrae, where he could rally his loyal men and ride back with an army to lift the siege.'

'Was it dweomer, then?'

'I doubt it very much.' Brour smiled briefly. 'I think there was a bolthole, some underground way out of this dun, and it must surface a fair distance from the city, too. Doubtless it was a well-kept secret, and it may have been too well-kept. It seems to have died with the last king to use it, and that was fifty years and more ago.'

'If you could find it again, then you'd have the King's favour for a certainty. I'll bet Uncle Burcan would be ever so pleased.'

'No doubt. So much so that I'm going to ask you to keep this a secret. Your uncle hates me, and I want to win him round, you see. I don't want someone else running to him first.'

'I'll keep it secret, I promise.'

'My thanks, lass. Now, let me tell you what we're going to be doing. The best time for this ritual is in the dark of night, but we'll need to practise it first.'

'I get to help?'

'You do indeed. You'll have to slip out and join me once I find a place where it's safe to study it. But pay attention now. There are many strange things you need to learn.'

'Well, I'm glad we've got a few moments to ourselves, love,' Peddyc said. 'When we're both awake.'

'So am I,' Bevyan said. 'I've stationed Sarra in the antechamber for a sentinel.'

He laughed and sat down in the chair opposite hers. The afternoon sunlight streamed through the windows and fell across them, a golden blanket. Peddyc yawned and stretched his legs out in front of him.

'You look weary,' she said.

'I am that. I've spent the afternoon with our Burcan. That's enough to weary any man. At least good news is coming in. None of the northern lords have gone over to the Usurper. They'll hold firm while the border holds.'

'And how long will that be?'

Peddyc shrugged.

'For this summer at least,' he said finally. 'Hendyr's become important. I find myself being courted.'

'Ah. That's interesting.'

'Well, ours is the last big dun on the border to the west of here. The King's forces have to hold it. If it falls to the enemy, then Prince Maryn can outflank us and start moving into the northlands.'

'Prince Maryn? I've never heard you call him that before.'

Peddyc winced.

'A foolish slip, my love. May the gods keep me from doing it in front of Burcan.' He hesitated for a long moment. 'Well, Maryn's a prince over his own lands, no matter what any of us think of his claim to the throne of Deverry.'

'Pyrdon – just so.'

They fell silent, considering each other, considering – Bevyan supposed – just how much it was safe to say aloud, even in the privacy of their chambers.

'I'd best get back.' Peddyc rose and glanced toward the window. 'The sun's getting low, and there's to be yet another council of war.'

'When will the army march?'

'I've no idea. Soon. It will have to be soon, or we'll find the Usurper at our gates.' He paused to rub his face with both hands. 'Gwerbret Daeryc brought that up this afternoon. Burcan said that he was waiting for more messages from the Northlands. One of the younger lords took offence for some reason, and everything turned into wrangling. A lot of pounding on the table and reminding each other of our rank.'

'That sounds awful.'

'Oh, it was. I'm of two minds, my love. You know how I feel about the Regent as a man, but he's the only leader we've got or are going to have. And without a leader, we're all-' He paused for a long moment. 'Well, I'd best be gone. No doubt I'll be back late tonight, but if you're awake, I'll tell you what decision we've reached.'

'My thanks. Queen Abrwnna has asked me to join her women tonight after the meal, so I may have gossip to tell you.'

'Good. It gladdens my heart to see you in her favour.'

'Is it her favour? Or are we being watched?'

Peddyc considered, his head tilted a bit to one side.

'Well,' Bevyan went on. 'You've just told me how important Hendyr is. I keep thinking of the dinner we had in Lord Camlyn's dun, and I wonder how skilled Daeryc is at hiding what his heart feels.'

'Not very.' Peddyc gave her an ironic smile. 'You speak very true, my love. I hadn't thought of that. There are times when Daeryc looks at the Regent, and the look on his face – you'd think he'd bitten into rotten meat.'

'Just so. I've seen it. And Daeryc is our overlord. If they suspect him, won't they suspect you?'

Peddyc nodded, thinking.

'My thanks for the warning,' he said at last. 'I need your sharp eyes. I'll do my best to act the loyal vassal around Burcan, then, and I just might have a private caution for His Grace Daeryc, too.'

Although Bevyan was undoubtedly rising in the Queen's favour, as yet she hadn't been invited to eat at the royal women's table. Her usual bench stood close enough to the Queen, however, for her to watch Abrwnna and her women as they sat giggling together over their meat and bread. Not far away, though at enough distance for propriety, the Queen's Fellowship shared a table while immediately behind them sat the sons of various high-ranking nobility, Anasyn among them. Bevyan enjoyed watching her son, grown so tall and strong, taken into the company of his peers. She had tried over the years to distance herself from him; she had mourned his brothers too bitterly to wish to repeat that particular grief. Yet she was proud of him and his courtly manners as well. Although the lords around him were drinking hard and laughing, Sanno watched his ale and spoke only quietly if at all.

Instead of ale, the young men of the Queen's Fellowship had been drinking mead, or so Bevyan heard later, and rather a lot of it. All at once one of them shouted, someone else swore, a third oath rang out and stilled the general clamour. Bevyan rose to look just as the Queen's men leapt up, knocking over benches, to rush the lords at Anasyn's table. Bevyan saw Anasyn jump free and grab a friend from behind just in time to keep the lad's sword in its sheath.

The fight devolved into shoving and cursing. A table went over with the crack of breaking pottery. Someone swung a punch, some-one else reeled back with a bloody nose, but the older lords were on

their feet and running, calling out to one another like hounds
coursing for game. They grabbed the combatants and dragged them
apart, then for good measure dragged them clear out of the great hall.

'And what was all that about?' Lilli said.

'Oh, who knows?' Bevyan said with a shrug. 'Men *will* take insult
and so easily, too.'

And yet she saw Anasyn, hurrying across to her through the
confusion and beckoning her to join him. With a gesture to Lilli to
stay put, Bevyan headed to the curve of the wall and a little space free
of gawkers, where he joined her. His right sleeve was soaked through
with mead, as if someone had thrown a goblet-full.

'There you are, Mother,' Anasyn said. 'Father said I should tell you
what happened.'

'Oh did he? It was more than some stupid insult, then.'

'Truly. Someone proposed a wager, you see, on how soon one of the
Queen's Fellowship would bed the Queen, and which one it would
be. Well, they overheard, and-'

'Oh ye gods! So the gossip's got as bad as all that? Who started it?'

Anasyn shrugged for an answer. Out in the great hall everyone was
sitting back down; a pair of pages were righting the overturned
benches and picking up trenchers from the straw while assorted dogs
wagged their tails and watched, hoping for another spill and sudden
meal.

'Your father was right to let me know,' Bevyan said. 'I'll have a word
with Merodda about this. As far as I can tell, she's the only one with
any influence over the lass.'

'So I've heard.'

'Which reminds me, dear. The Queen tells me you were offered a
place in her fellowship.'

'I turned it down.'

'So she said. I was just curious-'

'I've never wanted to be anyone's lap dog and run with a pack of
them. It's disgusting, watching them fawn over her.'

I see, Bevyan thought. So my lad's fallen in love! Aloud, she said,
'And quite right, too. Well, I'd best see how the poor lass fares.'

The Queen's hall in Dun Deverry occupied an entire floor of the
royal broch. Carved chairs, heaped with faded and torn cushions,
stood on threadbare Bardek carpets, while sagging tapestries covered
the walls between the windows. When Bevyan came in, she expected
to find the Queen in tears over this insult to her honour, but instead

Abrwnna was pacing back and forth in front of a cold hearth while
her maidservants cowered out of her way in the curve of the wall.
One of the girls was crying, and her messy hair, pulled every which
way in long strands, gave evidence of her royal mistress's bad temper.
Merodda, however, was calmly sitting on one of the wide windowsills
as if to take the air. None of the Queen's other serving women were in
evidence.

'There you are, Lady Bevyan,' the Queen said. 'I have need of your
counsel.'

'Indeed, Your Highness?' Bevyan made a curtsey in her general
direction, since she kept pacing.

'Indeed. Lady Merodda tells me I should disband my fellowship.'

'Ah. I fear me that I agree with her.'

'I don't want to!' Abrwnna swung round and threw one arm up, as
if she were thinking of slapping the older women down. 'They're mine
and I don't want to!'

'No one can force Your Highness,' Merodda put in. 'Bevyan, Her
Highness asked my opinion, and so I gave it.'

'As I have given mine,' Bevyan said. 'And there we'll let the matter
drop if Her Highness commands.'

'Well, I cursed well do!' With a deep breath Abrwnna caught
herself and lowered her hand. 'We do not wish to hear this matter
discussed in our presence.'

'Very well, Your Highness,' Bevyan said. 'So be it.'

In years past Dun Deverry had sheltered three times the men who
lived there now. In its tangle of wards and towers stood many an
empty building – sheds and stables, mostly, but in a small ward far
from the King's residence rose a deserted broch. Its lower floors
stored arrows, stones, and poles for pushing siege-ladders off walls,
but the top floor stood empty except for a stack of tanned hides, all
stiff and crumbling from age. These Lilli and Brour hung over the
windows until, after a lot of struggling and cursing, not a crack of
sunlight gleamed.

'Good,' Brour said. 'We don't want anyone seeing our lantern and
coming up here.'

'How did you find this place?'

'I've been searching for the bolthole for weeks, so I've been prying
into all sorts of deserted places. I remembered this one when I
decided to try a ritual.'

'Do you think anyone else comes up here?'

'There weren't any tracks in the dust.'

Lilli looked around the room – an ordinary sort of room for Dun Deverry, yet no one had been up here for years, if the dust and the cobwebs could be trusted.

'I hope my mother doesn't want me to scry this evening.'

'She won't,' Brour said. 'She told me she'd be attending upon the Queen again. Is somewhat wrong with Her Highness, do you know?'

'I don't, but I'll wager it's that fight in the great hall last night. Everyone is saying that the Queen's honour was insulted, and no doubt she's ever so upset.'

'No doubt. Well, that should keep your mother nicely occupied, then.'

'Truly.' Lilli paused for a sneeze. 'It's so dusty up here! Will the Lords of Earth like that?'

'I'll sweep up a bit before we start. Now you'd best run along before someone misses you. I'll go back later. We don't want anyone seeing us come in together.'

When Lilli returned to the royal broch, she found servants standing around gossiping about the insult to the Queen's Fellowship, if not the Queen herself. During their afternoon of sewing, Bevyan seemed worried about the incident as well.

'What's causing the trouble,' Bevyan said, 'is having all these young hotheads packed in together, waiting for the summer's fighting to start. The Regent needs to lead his men out soon.'

'I don't understand why he hasn't already,' Lilli said. 'Do you, Bevva?'

'Well, I don't truly know, but Peddyc's shared his guesses with me.' Bevyan hesitated, thinking something through. 'I'd say that the Regent doesn't have enough men to stand against the Usurper, and they're trying to round up more.'

'Oh. Oh, that means we're going to lose, doesn't it?'

Bevyan and Sarra both looked up from their sewing and stared at her. Lilli felt her face grow hot.

'I'm sorry,' Lilli stammered. 'I shouldn't have – oh gods! I always say the wrong thing – I'm sorry.'

'No need to apologize, dear,' Bevyan said. 'But it doesn't necessarily mean we're going to lose. The Regent thinks he can find the men we need, and Peddyc seems to agree with him. One good victory, and a lot of the lords who went over to the Usurper will swing back to the King's side.'

If, Lilli thought, if we can gain the victory in the first place.

'The waiting's just so awful,' she said aloud.

'Just so, dear, just so.'

Bevyan sighed and bent her head back to her work, but all at once she seemed old, and to Lilli's sight the streaks of grey in her pale hair suddenly spread and turned dead-white while her skin turned a cold dead grey to match it. Lilli nearly cried out. She's just weary! she told herself sharply. You're just seeing things again.

As soon as the evening meal was finished, Merodda and Bevyan went to wait upon the Queen, and Lilli could slip unnoticed from the great hall. In the abandoned tower she found Brour waiting for her. As she climbed the stairs, she saw a broom leaning against the wall on the landing, and the wooden floor inside had been swept clean. Brour himself was sitting in the middle of the circular room, while all around him huge shadows danced on the rough stone walls. He'd lit four lanterns and set them equidistant from one another.

'They sit at the four directions, as far as I can reckon them anyway.' Brour rose to greet her. 'East west, north south. It's in the pillar of light above each lantern that you're to imagine the great lords of the elements when the time comes.'

'Very well,' Lilli said. 'We're going to practise this a lot, aren't we?'

'Many times over, truly. It has to be done just precisely right. Tonight I'm merely going to tell you the different parts and what they mean. Oh, and I want to give you a lesson on hardening your aura.'

'My what?'

'It's like an egg of invisible light that surrounds every living person. It's the effect of the etheric plane interpenetrating the physical. When you throw a stone into a pond, the ripples spread. And what are the ripples? A pattern in the same water as fills the pond. Think of the aura as being somewhat like that.'

Lilli stared at the floor and tried to think.

'I don't understand,' she said at last.

'It's not an easy thing to understand.' Brour sounded amused. 'But spend some time thinking on it, and see what comes to your mind. But the point is, once you learn to control yours, your mother won't be able to pry into your mind again.'

'Splendid!' Lilli looked up and found him smiling. 'There's nothing I'd like more!'

'No doubt. Let's begin.'

'Braemys rode in this afternoon,' Burcan said. 'He's brought the news I've been waiting for.'

'Indeed?' Merodda said. 'Good or ill?'

'Good. The northern lords have agreed to strip their fort guards. We'll have a full army when we march.'

Merodda allowed herself a brief smile, which he returned. Late in the evening, they were sitting alone in her chamber by the light of a smoky fire. Outside, rain hammered against the walls, and every now and then the south wind lifted the leather hides hung at the windows.

'Have there been any omens?' Burcan said.

'I've not had Lilli scry this past few days. I was waiting to hear your news. You need to have some knowledge of how things are before you can interpret an omen, you see.'

'Very well, then. Huh, I'll have to remind Brae to have a word with her. About their betrothal, I mean.'

'If he's not too busy for a courtly gesture, of course.'

Her sarcasm earned her a sour smile. Burcan hesitated, studying her face. She knew what he wanted to know, what they all wanted to know, Bevva and that beastly little herald, too, and her women servants – they'd all suspected for years, after all, who her lover might be. She could see it in their narrowed eyes, hear it in the hesitations of their speech. In the hearth a log burned through and dropped in a gush of flame and a scatter of coals on stone.

'Rhodi?' His voice hesitated, stumbled. 'Do you really think this marriage is an, um, er, well, allowable thing?'

She smiled into the fire. On the hearthstone the coals were winking out, one at a time. She heard him move uneasily in his chair, then sigh.

'I'd best get on my way,' Burcan said. 'Daeryc and the other gwerbretion are waiting for me.'

'So late?'

'I promised I'd tell them when we'll march as soon as I'd spoken to the King. He was asleep when I stopped in there, but I spoke, anyway.' He smiled briefly. 'I didn't say I'd wait for his answer.'

'And when will you march?'

'As soon as the full northern contingents ride in. They're on their way.'

In the morning, when Lilli came down to the great hall, she found Braemys waiting for her near the foot of the staircase. He was a tall lad, as all the Boarsmen were, blond and blue-eyed and with the clan's squarish face as well. Since last they'd met, his upper lip had sprouted a line of hair that could be called a moustache for courtesy's sake if naught else. When he saw her, he strode over and bowed. She curtsied in return.

'My lady,' Braemys said. 'Does this betrothal please you?'

'It does. What about you, my lord?'

'Well enough.' He turned to look away – when she followed his glance, Lilli could see Uncle Burcan standing near the doorway. 'I'd best get myself to the council of war.'

He turned and strode off to join his father. Lilli watched them as they made their way through the crowded hall and out. Ah well, she reminded herself, he's ever so much better than Nantyn.

Over the next few days Lilli had scant time to worry about her betrothed. He was much involved with the councils of war, while she and Brour had their practising to do. Once as well, late of a rainy night, her mother called her to scry in the black ink. With Brour holding the long candle as usual, Lilli stared into the silver bowl, where shadows danced, black on a deeper black. She could hear the wind howling around the broch, and as the spell took her over, the sound transmuted into voices, screaming and crying out.

'Tears and rage.' It was the only thing Lilli could say about the wailing. 'I hear tears and terror.'

She could feel her mother's hand squeezing the back of her neck.

'Try to listen,' Merodda hissed. 'What are they saying?'

'No words. Weeping and fear.'

In the blackness images were beginning to form of headless riders on black horses, huge, towering over entire cities as they galloped through a stormy night. The wailing faded away, and Lilli heard her own voice start describing the omens. Swords that burned with blue fire formed a huge wall in front of Dun Deverry. An army all dressed in red threw itself against the wall but fell back, tattered and dying, only to regroup on a far hill.

'They're riding again,' Lilli said. 'I see them riding – wait. It's going away, it's all going away.'

In the basin the flaming swords winked out like sparks on a hearth stone. The images turned pale and watery, then faded in turn. For a moment, blackness – then lantern-light revealed a pleasant chamber with bright-coloured tapestries on the walls. In the middle of the chamber stood an elderly man with a shock of untidy white hair. He was leaning over a table and staring into a basin of water. All at once he looked up – looked right at her with ice-blue eyes that seemed to pierce her very soul.

'Well, here's a surprise!' He sounded amused, and his voice was oddly resonant for someone who looked so old. 'Who are you, lass? You'll hurt yourself spying on me like this, if you're not careful.'

Lilli started to answer but found she couldn't speak. All at once the vision broke. The image separated into pie-slice fragments like the design on a shattered plate – then disappeared. A white-faced Brour was shaking her by the shoulder.

'Are you back? Are you back?'

'I am, Brour. What's so wrong?'

'I'd rather like to know that myself,' Merodda said. 'Why did you stop her?'

'Because that old man is dangerous. He's the Usurper's personal advisor and a sorcerer of the greatest power.'

'I saw into Cerrmor?' Lilli said.

'You did.' Brour paused to wipe his sweaty face on his sleeve. 'Or Nevyn tricked you into revealing yourself.'

'Who?' Merodda broke in. 'No one? Don't talk in riddles.'

'I'm not. That's his name, *nev yn*, Nevyn, some miserable jest of his father's, it was, naming his son no one.'

Merodda was studying her scribe with her mouth caught in a sour twist. With a long sigh Brour composed himself.

'I studied under the man,' Brour said. 'I know him quite well.'

'He wasn't trying to trick me,' Lilli said. 'He was as surprised as I was.'

'Ah.' Brour considered this for a long moment. 'Still, you'd best not scry again tonight. He'll be looking for you. It's too dangerous.'

'What?' Merodda snapped. 'But the omens-'

'Will have to wait,' Brour said. 'It's too dangerous, my lady. Truly it is. I'll gladly explain.'

'Do so.' Merodda turned to Lilli. 'Leave us.'

When Lilli hesitated, Merodda raised a ringed hand. Lilli left and hurried down the corridor to her chamber. Once safely inside, she went to the window – the floor was soaked with rain, but outside the storm had ended. Overhead a pale moon seemed to race through the sky as torn clouds scudded past.

'He looked kind,' Lilli whispered. 'Truly kind. If he's the sort of man Cerrmor has on his side-'

She shook her head to drive the traitorous thoughts away.

Yet that night she dreamt about Cerrmor, or some dream image of it, at any rate, since she'd never been there, and of Nevyn, who seemed to be trying to find her in the middle of a vast maze of stone walls and hedgerows. When she woke to a flood of sunlight across her bed, the dream stayed with her. She dressed and was just thinking of looking for Brour when he knocked at her door.

'It's me,' he called out. 'Are you there, Lilli?'

'I am.' She unbarred the door. 'Come in. I've had the oddest dream.'

'I thought you might.'

Brour hurried in, then shut the door behind him. His round child's face was pale and stubbled, as if he'd waked all night.

'What's so wrong?' Lilli said.

'A number of small things that all add up to trouble. Nevyn spotting you, and then your dear mother's lack of sense. She refuses to stop this dangerous scrying.'

'Dangerous because of Nevyn?'

'Just so. If he makes a link with you, he'll be able to spy through your eyes.'

'Well, it's not as if I know very much about the King's plans.'

'You'd be surprised what you know without knowing you know it.' Brour smiled briefly. 'What troubles my heart is a selfish fear, though. I don't want Nevyn tracking me down.'

'Oh. Why not?'

Brour's eyes blinked rapidly; then he shrugged.

'I was a cursed poor student,' he said. 'And I left before I truly should have.'

Lilli hesitated, hearing pain in his voice. Something more than that had gone wrong, she suspected – something too shameful for Brour to admit.

'It was all a long time ago.' Brour paced over to the window, paced back again. 'But I've made up my mind. Once we work the ritual and find the bolthole, I'm leaving Dun Deverry.'

'Oh, don't go!'

'I'm sorry, but I can't stay here. Your mother and uncle have grown suspicious of me for some reason, and they'll kill me when the time seems ripe. You remember the omen of my head in a chest? Well, I'm sure it was quite true. I was hoping to win your uncle round by finding the bolthole, but now I think I'll just leave by it. Safer all round. Then once I'm gone, you can tell Burcan about it, and you'll get the gain and favour.'

'My thanks. But I wish you weren't going.'

'You could come with me.'

Lilli gasped and laid her hand at her throat.

'Just think about it,' Brour said. 'My offer is strictly honourable. I'll treat you like my daughter. Come with me and be my apprentice. And save your skin, too, when this miserable dun falls to the enemy.'

Lilli felt the blood pound in her throat.

'I've got to get back to your lady mother.' Brour looked as if he might spit at the mention of her name. 'But think on it, Lilli. I beg you.'

After he left, Lilli wandered over to the window. For a long time she stared out at the many-towered view without truly seeing it. She had a decision to make, and for the first time in her life, she couldn't go running to Bevva with it.

Over the past few days, Merodda had become more and more aware of Lady Bevyan's growing influence over the young Queen. Abrwnna included Bevyan in every royal progress through the town and every hawking party, visit to the temples, or special evening meal in the royal hall. At times, when Merodda went up to the women's quarters, she would find Bevyan there alone, listening to one of the Queen's rambling conversations.

'I was glad at first,' Merodda remarked to Brour. 'Abrwnna can be a tiresome little thing.'

'Indeed, my lady? But you're not pleased now?'

'Well, I don't want to see myself displaced in the Queen's favour.'

'Ah. That would be a great loss, truly.'

Merodda considered him for a long moment. His head bent over his work, he was writing out a proclamation of Lilli's betrothal for the heralds. She would regret his death when Burcan killed him, but Burcan's favour was the centre of her life, the one thing she desperately needed, far beyond even the favour of the Queen. If he wanted Brour gone, then gone he'd be. Brour stuck his reed pen into a hole in the side of his ink pot, then picked up a handful of sand from a tray behind him and sprinkled it over wet words.

'What do you think of Bevyan?' Merodda said.

'I rather like her, my lady, from what little I know of her, but I don't know much at all.'

'Well, true-spoken.' She hesitated, wondering what she wanted him to say. 'It's of no matter. Tonight I'll be in the Queen's quarters, attending upon Her Highness. If anyone else wishes to see me, they'll have to wait.'

'Very good, my lady.'

Brour picked up the sheet of parchment and tipped the sand back into its tray, then laid it down and got back to work.

That evening Merodda tried to reach the Queen's side early, but it seemed that the entire court was conspiring against her. As she made her way from the great hall, one person after another stopped her – servants asking for orders, lords hoping to wangle some favour from the Regent, ladies wanting to chat, a page with a message from Burcan. By the time she reached the women's hall Bevyan was there ahead of her, sitting at Abrwnna's side on a footstool while the Queen lounged in a cushioned chair. Her maidservants were laying a little fire in the hearth and lighting candles, while two serving women sang a song of love, trading off verses, and a third played a clumsy harp, all to keep the Queen amused.

In vain, that – Abrwnna was scowling. When Merodda came in, she turned her head to acknowledge her, then waved a hand at the music-makers.

'Oh don't!' Abrwnna snapped. 'I hate that song.'

The music stopped. The singers glanced at each other, then arranged smiles. The would-be harpist looked close to tears.

'This is all unbelievably tedious.' Abrwnna lay back with her head resting on the chair and stared at the ceiling. 'I think I'm going to die of boredom.'

'Well, Your Highness,' Bevyan said. 'We could play a game of carnoic or wooden wisdom.'

'I'm sick of games.'

'Your Highness?' the lass with the harp said. 'If your husband the King joined us, we could have a proper bard come in to entertain.'

'I don't want my beastly husband here. He sucks his thumb when he listens.'

All the women glanced sideways at each other. Merodda found an empty chair and sat down. Their tasks done, the maidservants scurried away.

'I want to go for a walk in the night air,' Abrwnna announced.

'Very well, Your Highness,' Bevyan said. 'We'll all have a nice stroll in the gardens.'

'I don't want anyone to come with me.'

'Your Highness!' Merodda broke in. 'That would be most unwise.'

'I don't care if it's unwise or not! I want to be alone.'

The serving women all began talking at once, but Bevyan rose, faced Abrwnna, and caught the lass's glance with hers.

'My poor dear child,' Bevyan said. 'I know how unbelievably dreadful this all is. My heart aches for you. I can hear in your voice just how tired and lonely and frightened you are.'

'Well, I am, and all of those things!' Abrwnna seemed on the edge of tears. 'When we were riding today, I just wanted to turn my horse and gallop away, just ride off somewhere and be lost. Anything would be better than another summer of this beastly war.'

Merodda felt a sudden chill – so! Bevyan had been riding with the Queen, while she'd been left behind.

'Well, we can all understand that.' Bevyan sat again, but she turned the footstool so the Queen could see her face. 'But you feel it much more keenly than any of us.'

'I'm just so tired,' Abrwnna whispered. 'It's just not fair.'

'It's not, truly,' Bevyan said. 'We did ride such a long way today. Shall I comb out your hair for you? And then perhaps you can sleep. The morning will bring the sun and better things.'

'I'd like that.' Abrwnna turned to one of her women. 'Fetch my combs for me.'

While Bevyan combed the Queen's hair, she kept up a flow of chatter in her soft, dark voice that soothed the Queen the way stroking will soothe a frightened cat. She allowed Bevva to lead her to her bedchamber, too, and tuck her in. When Merodda left the women's hall that night, she wondered if everyone she met could smell her fear – it seemed to trail behind her like smoke. To be supplanted this way! How could she possibly allow it?

Out in the deserted broch Lilli and Brour were ready at last to work the ritual of evocation. At each of the four directions stood a candle lantern which Brour lit from a fifth. In one curve of the wall lay a couple of cloth sacks – supplies, he said. On the floor he'd drawn a big circle with flour.

'It's a bit wobbly, isn't it?' Brour said, frowning at the mark. 'Well, the circle that really matters is the one I'll visualize, anyway.'

Lilli sat down cross-legged in the centre of the circle, facing their approximate east. Brour had brought a big pottery bowl for her scrying; they didn't dare risk Merodda noticing that the silver basin

had gone missing. He filled it with ink from a leather bottle and set it
down in front of her.

'Very well,' he said. 'Are you ready?'

'I am.' Lilli took a deep breath to steady her nerves. 'Let's begin.'

Brour stood directly in front of her, again facing east, and raised
his arms high above his head. For a moment he gathered breath; then
he began to chant in an odd vibrating growl of a voice. The words
themselves meant nothing to her; they were Greggyn, she supposed,
or some other ancient tongue. From his telling, however, she knew
that he was invoking the Light that dwelt beyond the gods and
drawing it down into himself to give power for the working.

He lowered his arms till they were straight out from his shoulders
and chanted again, waited, then let his arms drop. To Lilli it seemed
that the room had suddenly become larger – and crowded. Although
she could hear nothing but Brour's hard breathing, she felt that the
room buzzed with life and noise, like the great hall on some state
occasion. Brour held out one hand as if he were holding a sword and
began to chant again. As he growled out the sacred words, he slowly
turned, east to south to west to north and east again, drawing a circle
of blue light out on the astral plane – or so he'd told her. Again, she
could see nothing of this, but all at once she realized that the stone
walls of the broch shimmered in a faint silvery light, as if some
reflection of the magic had come through to her sight.

'I invoke thee!' Brour began to intone in Deverrian. 'I call unto
thee! O Great King of the Element of Earth, I invoke thee into my
presence! Show thyself and be known, in the names of the great sigils
of the elements and the Lords of Light!'

Brour turned toward the north, and Lilli twisted round so that she
could see. The candle lantern set there threw a mottled pillar of light
up the stone wall, at first no different than any of the others in the
room.

'I invoke thee! Lord of Earth and the North, home of the greatest
darkness, come to me and show thyself!'

The mottles of golden light on the wall suddenly swelled and ran
together to form a blazing pillar. Lilli gasped; as the light brightened,
it changed colour to glowing silver. Within the pillar of light a figure
was forming, man-shaped though strangely slender. It stayed cloudy,
shifting with the dancing of the light, yet it seemed far more sub-
stantial than a shadow. A faint greenish-grey light rippled across its
body, if one could call it a body, while a russet glow formed behind

its head. Its feet stood upon a sphere of polished black. Lilli heard words form in her mind and knew that this Other had sent them.

'What do you want of me, Child of Earth?'

'A question answered and one only, O Great Lord,' Brour spoke aloud. 'I know full well how honoured I am that thou hast answered my call.'

In the pillar the figure inclined its head. Lilli somehow felt that it was amused at Brour's presumption.

'What wish you to know, Child of Earth?'

'Deep within thy realm of earth and stone that lies under this dun and its outbuildings, there is a tunnel leading from the dun to somewhere beyond its walls and the walls of the city that surrounds it. We wish to know where it lies.'

The figure inclined its head toward Lilli.

'Look! Child of Aethyr, look into your basin!'

Lilli followed orders. On the black surface of the ink, pictures began forming: a gate in a wall, a narrow path between walls of stone, a broken tower standing in a cobbled ward. Behind that tower she saw wooden doors set into the earth.

'A root cellar?' She couldn't contain herself. 'It's in a root cellar? You're certain?'

Brour yelped in fear. She felt the King of Earth's laughter wash over her and looked up at the greenish-grey figure in his pillar of silver light. He did seem to be laughing, truly.

'We are certain, little one. You will find what you seek under those doors. Now fare thee well. Sorcerer! Release me!'

'I shall, Great King of Earth,' Brour said. 'And my thanks for thy aid in this matter.'

Brour flung his arms into the air and began to chant. With each alien word the silver light dimmed until at last nothing remained but the normal yellow light of a candle-flame dancing in a pierced lantern. With one hand raised to hold the astral sword, Brour turned toward the east. Chanting, he erased the circle of blue fire, then walked to the west and rubbed out part of the flour-marked circle with one foot.

'May all spirits bound by this ceremony go free!' Brour called out. 'It is over!'

He stamped thrice upon the floor. Suddenly Lilli felt the room regain its normal size and normal emptiness. Brour caught his breath in a long sigh and sat down quite abruptly upon the floor.

'Are you all right?' Lilli said.

'Tired. Thirsty. Bring me that waterskin, will you? You have some too. And there's cheese and bread in that bit of cloth.'

After the marvels she'd just seen Lilli found the idea of eating ridiculous – until she saw the food and realized how hungry she was. She and Brour sat in the middle of the broken ritual circle and gobbled, washing the food down with water that tasted as good as mead. When she had finished eating, she realized that the strange shimmer of light had faded from the walls. The view turned so magical had become mundane again.

'It's all gone,' she said wistfully. 'All the silver magic.'

'That's the point of eating,' Brour said, grinning. 'You can't go about your daily affairs in a state of trance. And besides, we've got one last marvel to view – our bolthole. We'd best take a look at it before we forget the vision, too.'

They blew out all the lanterns but one. Brour had brought extra candles as well as food; once the lanterns were cool enough, they packed them up and got on their way.

As soon as they were outside, Lilli recognized the path that the King of Earth had shown her. The little gate by the far wall seemed to shimmer, as if a trace of dweomer-light clung to the wooden door. They went through and found themselves in a narrow passageway between two high walls that led downhill to another door in a low one. That too was unbarred. On the other side stretched a big ward, ringed with high walls and scattered with ruins – a broken tower, tumbled heaps of stones, mounds of grassy earth that probably covered the remains of sheds and huts.

'It looks as though this place saw some fighting,' Brour said.

'So it does. It must have been an awfully long time ago. I've never heard anyone talk about it. There might have been a fire.'

'True spoken. And the King didn't rebuild in here because he wanted to keep the bolthole hidden, or so we can hope, anyway. No one would have any reason to come poking around in the ruins.'

In the event Brour's hope was justified. Around the back of the broken tower Lilli saw the stone lean-to of her vision and the pair of wooden doors, half-rotted but still closed. While she held the lantern Brour broke them open. Six steps of packed earth led down into an ordinary looking root cellar – ordinary except for the drifts of white mould and cobwebs.

'Oh ych!' Lilli said. 'It smells horrid.'

'Well, we're letting some fresh air in now,' Brour said. 'We don't dare linger out here. What if some watchman sees the lantern light?'

Lilli took a quick gulp of fresh air, then went down the steps. The floor was mostly muck from seepage, but someone had laid big flagstones across the middle. Although they were slippery, they held stable. Brour followed her, watching each step he took.

'How did anyone get horses down here?' Lilli said. 'For the King to ride away on?'

'Good question. I haven't the slightest idea.' Brour paused, looking around. 'Maybe it's not the right – oh! Look!'

A heavy door made of oak planks and hinged and bound in iron graced the far wall.

'Hah!' Brour said, grinning. 'You don't build a door like that to safeguard your turnips! Hold the lantern, lass. Let's see if I can get it open.'

Brour pulled, then tried pushing, shoved and grunted and shoved again. The door scraped inward by a bare inch. He set his back against it and began to walk backwards, driving hard with his legs. Sweat broke out on his face. He took a deep breath, then drove once more. With a screech like ravens the door scraped on stone and opened. Lilli held the lantern high and sent a beam of light into a tunnel, lined with worked stone blocks, about eight feet high and ten across, stretching into darkness beyond the lantern light's power to follow. Brour wiped his face on his sleeve and laughed, a bit breathlessly.

'Well, that looks promising,' he said. 'You could lead horses through it, sure enough, once you got them down here.'

'Are we going to follow it tonight?'

'Aren't you too tired?'

'I'm not! I want to see where it goes.'

'And so do I. Curiosity's a terrible thing.'

Though the root cellar was filthy enough, the tunnel was worse, stinking of old rot. Pools of mucky water lay across the uneven floor. Brour rolled up his brigga legs, but since Lilli couldn't carry a lantern and hold her skirts up at the same time, she had to let the hems fend for themselves. Fortunately she was wearing an old outer dress that she could give to a servant to keep her mother from asking about the stains.

'Do you think there are going to be rats?' Lilli said.

'Probably. They'll run from the light, though.'

As they walked on they did hear noises that sounded like small things skittering away in the darkness. As it ran forward, the tunnel sloped downhill, and a drainage channel appeared, lying along one side of the roughly paved floor.

'Good.' Brour pointed to it. 'We won't find a lake waiting for us at the bottom after all. I was beginning to worry, but they must have made some outlets for run-off somewhere.'

'That's probably how the rats get in and out, then.'

'Please stop worrying about rats, will you? I'm trying to forget about them myself.'

After what Lilli judged to be half a mile, the tunnel levelled out again and ran straight ahead, though after a few hundred yards or so it made an odd jog around an enormous pillar of worked stone.

'Know what that is?' Brour said. 'One of the foundations of the outer walls of the city. We're leaving Dun Deverry behind, all right.'

'Which way are we going?'

'I don't have the slightest idea.'

Whichever way it headed, the tunnel ran straight enough. Perhaps a mile on, Brour had to stop and put fresh candles in their lanterns. By the time the tunnel began to slope upward, those candles were burning down, too. Once they'd replaced it they walked forward for a long breathless climb up a slope. At the top the tunnel levelled out.

'Another door!' Brour crowed.

A door, bound and hinged in the exact same pattern of ironwork as the one back in Dun Deverry, stood across the passageway. This one, fortunately, opened outward and somewhat more easily, though Brour could shove it open a couple of feet and no more. They squeezed through into another cellar, though this one had lost its doors at the top of its steps. Fresh air, tinged with the damp of night, rushed in. Lilli breathed deep – no royal perfume had ever smelled better.

'It must open outside,' she whispered.

'If it's a root cellar, they usually do.' Brour stuck his head out. 'Ah, I see. This once lay under some kind of stone building, but it's been razed, and many years ago, too. Cursed good thing. I was afraid we'd come into some lord's great hall and have some explaining to do.'

When Lilli climbed out, all she could see were dark stone shapes, looming against a starry sky, but she could make out enough to guess that they were seeing the remains of an outer wall that once had circled a small dun. At their feet grass and weeds grew thick. Brour squinted up at the stars.

'We'd best get back. I don't want your mother sending a page first thing in the morning only to find me gone.'

On the trek back, Lilli suddenly realized that she was exhausted. Her excitement had kept her going on the way out; now she found herself yawning compulsively and shivering with cold. The long climb uphill under Dun Deverry left her gasping for breath.

By the time they emerged from the tunnel, the lanterns they'd left behind in the root cellar had long ago burned out. Brour flung open the doors overhead to reveal the first grey of dawn.

'You've got to get back,' he said. 'If you hurry, you should be able to get up to your chamber without anyone seeing you. And clean the muck off those dresses before your mother sees it, too.'

'I'll do that.' Lilli hesitated, thinking back to the Great King of Earth shining in his silver pillar. 'This has been splendid, Brour.'

He started to smile, then merely yawned.

'We'll talk later. Now hurry.'

Lilli did indeed manage to reach her chamber before the rest of the dun woke. She stripped off her dresses, hung them over a chair to let the mucky water dry – she could beat the worst of the mud off later – then fell into bed and deep sleep at what seemed to her the same moment.

'Have you seen Lilli?' Merodda said.

'I've not,' Bevyan said. 'I asked a page a while ago, and he told me she was still asleep.'

'Lazy little thing! Well, I'll find her later. Will you be attending upon the Queen this afternoon?'

'I won't. I've been asked to look in on Lord Arvan's wife. She's ever so ill, poor thing. She shouldn't have come to court this year at all, if you ask me.'

'She's never been strong.' Merodda considered her rival for a moment. 'If you do see Lilli, please tell her to find me.'

Here was a bit of luck! But it was late in the afternoon before Merodda got her chance to speak to the Queen alone, when Abrwnna's maids went down to the river to wash clothes and her serving women had gone off about their own business. Merodda and the Queen sat at a window in the high hall, where they could see the busy ward below, like a Bardek carpet scattered with children's toys.

'Look!' Abrwnna said, pointing. 'There goes Lord Belryc. Sometimes I think I like him best – the best of my fellowship, I mean.'

Merodda watched the young lord, sunny and blond, leading his horse toward the gates.

'Only sometimes, my liege?' Merodda said, smiling.

'Well, I like them all. Oh, it's so awful, wondering what people are saying! Rhodi, do you think I'm a slut?'

'Of course not, my liege! I have every faith that you understand how important your honour is. I know you'll act properly.'

'Well, it's just so unfair!' Abrwnna left off watching the ward and turned in her chair to face Merodda. 'Other ladies have lovers!'

'Those other ladies have given their lords legitimate heirs, my liege. Then they may –'

'But that's even worse! It'll be years before Olaen can – well, you know. If we even live that long! Oh gods, Rhodi, do people think I'm a dolt or suchlike? Don't you think I know I'm likely to spend my whole life in some ghastly temple, if Cerrmor doesn't have me strangled first?'

'My liege, you're just vexing yourself. The Regent's raised a decent army, and we're not defeated yet, not at all.'

Abrwnna tossed her head in her practised ripple of red-gold hair.

'Well, maybe not. But I don't want to die a virgin after being shut up for years and years. But I don't want people talking about me, either. Bevva says that honour's like water. Once you spill it, you can't get it back into the goblet, and it's all dirty anyway.'

'Lady Bevyan does take a strict view of such things.' Here was her chance!

'I do like her, though,' Abrwnna said. 'Don't you?'

'I do, indeed, my liege. In some ways we understand each other very well. We've both lost sons and lands to the wars.'

'That must be awful.'

'It is, truly.' Merodda looked away and allowed herself a small sigh. 'Women take it different ways. Some of us learn to seize every bit of joy our life offers, and others – well, they get strangely harsh.'

'Harsh?'

'When it comes to judging other women. Some do, you know, like – well, like our Bevyan.'

'Indeed?' Abrwnna leaned forward in her chair, her hands clasped. 'What do you mean, judging others?'

'Oh, that's very unfair of me, truly. It's just that she's led such an exemplary life herself. It must be a bit hard to understand that other people aren't as strong as she is.'

'She talks about being strong all the time.'

'She does, and she's quite right of course. In your position, my liege, you cannot be too careful. What the court thinks of you is very important and indeed, it could turn dangerous, if important lords like Tieryn Peddyc should begin to think ill of you. Which is why –'

Merodda hesitated, watching the young Queen's face.

'Why what?' Abrwnna snapped.

'Naught, my liege. Naught that need concern you.'

'Stop that! You were going to tell me somewhat, and I want to know what it is.'

'Very well. I wonder at times what Lady Bevyan might be saying to her lord.'

Abrwnna gasped, but it was an honest sound, not one of her rehearsed alarms.

'That's what I mean, Your Highness,' Merodda went on, 'when I say that you need to be very, very careful. You know the old saying: you can spoon the dead flies out of the honey, but it won't taste as sweet to those who saw them there. Your honour is all you have in life, and believe you me, there will be plenty of women who'll be judging how worthy of your position you are. The old ones are the worst. Sitting around and waiting for their betters to make a slip!'

Abrwnna leapt to her feet in a swirl of long dresses.

'What have they been saying about me?'

'Your Highness!' Merodda got up to join her. 'What makes you think anyone's been –'

'Oh don't! I'm not stupid. I can see what you're hinting at. What are they saying?'

Merodda hesitated, looking torn. Finally she sighed.

'Only what Her Highness might think,' Merodda said. 'It's the Fellowship of course. All those young men at your feet! Can't you imagine how jealous they all are, the other women? Especially those who aren't young any more.'

'I shan't disband my fellowship. I shan't shan't shan't!'

'Very well, Your Highness. Then you must be very careful about whom you take into your confidence.'

'I can't believe that Bevyan would betray me.'

'She hasn't.' Merodda hesitated again. 'Not that I know of, anyway. Not that anyone would dare repeat scurrilous gossip about you to me. But when the other women get to talking, it's so easy at times to go along with the drift, if you know what I mean. Especially if you really don't approve – I mean, especially if you're worried, and I know Bevva does worry, Your Highness, just as I do. We only want the best for you.'

With a toss of her head Abrwnna stalked to the window. When Merodda started to follow, she spun around. Tears streaked her face.

'Go away!' Abrwnna snapped. 'I need to think about this. Leave me alone!'

'Your Highness!' Merodda went cold with fear. 'I never meant to upset you so. Let me beg your pardon.'

'Oh, Rhodi, it's not you! It's just this – this – feeling betrayed. I need to think about Lady Bevyan.'

'Oh please, don't be angry with her! She really does mean well.'

'So they all do, everyone means well. The poor little queen, that's what they call me. Do you think I'm stupid, do you think I don't know? I'm supposed to be ever so honourable no matter how unhappy I am, and they all worry that I won't be, and I hate them all.' Abrwnna burst out sobbing. 'Go away! Get out!'

Merodda curtsied, then fled the chamber. As she hurried down the staircase, she was smiling to herself.

When she returned to her suite, Merodda called out for Brour, but there was no answer. She glanced into his sleeping room, found him gone, and considered sending a page to look for him. She was too tired to bother with scrying, she decided, and went down to the great hall instead, to watch from a distance the great lords at their mead and meat. Like the other women, she could only guess at the things they argued over so urgently.

That evening, watching the firelight play over their sweaty faces, she heard with a touch of dweomer the sound of ravens, screeching over a battle-feast. Fear sank long claws into her throat, and she knew with a dreadful certainty that the time would never come when that fear would leave her.

About two hours before dawn, Lilli met her tutor one last time in the deserted root cellar. Although he was wearing a wool travelling cloak, Brour carried only his book.

'You won't get very far without food and suchlike,' Lilli said.

'Oh, that's all waiting in the tunnel. I've been hiding things there, a bit at a time. Your mother spent most of the day with the Queen.'

Sure enough, when they shoved back the door Lilli saw a big pack on a wooden frame leaning against the wall. Brour lit a candle lantern by snapping his fingers over it, then shoved the door back but not closed.

'You won't get this open by yourself,' he remarked. 'We'll risk the odd chance of someone finding it.'

Brour rummaged in his pocket and handed her two candles for her journey back. He took off the cloak, rolled it and tied it to the frame. The book went into a leather sack and then into the pack. With a grunt of effort he swung the pack onto his back.

'I came to Dun Deverry as a peddlar, and I'll leave the same way. No doubt the King of Eldidd can use my services, so west I'll go.'

The very way he stressed the word 'west' made her wonder if he were lying to her.

'West, is it?' she said.

'It is.' Yet he couldn't look her in the eye. 'Ah well, bring that lantern, Lilli, and let's be off.'

Since carrying the pack took most of Brour's breath, they said little on the long trudge through the dust and slimy puddles to the door out. At the bottom of the steps Brour divested himself of the pack, then shoved open the door. Sunlight flowed down the stairs of the cellar. He heaved the pack out, then scrambled after. Lilli followed him out for the breath of fresh air. Here in the daylight she could see the ruins clearly – broken walls and burnt timbers such as decorated many a dead lord's dun. Black ravens flew through, shrieking as they dodged round a stump of broch.

'Come with me, Lilli,' Brour said. 'I fear for your life, I truly do.'

'I can't.'

'You're sure, lass? Ye gods, the whole city stinks of ruin! I swear to you, you'd be safe with me. I'd not lift a hand against you, but treat you like a daughter.'

'I know you would. It's not that.' Lilli hesitated, wondering why she did trust him so much – not that it mattered. 'But my place is here. I'm a woman of the Boar clan. I can't just run away. What would Bevva think of me?'

Brour sighed, rubbing his mouth with the back of his hand while he considered.

'Ah well,' he said at last. 'Mayhap you know best. It won't be safe out on the roads, anyway. My small dweomers will protect me well enough, but if some lord's warband took a fancy to your pretty face, I couldn't stop them. Now remember, give me a good long start, then tell your uncle about the bolthole. You'll rise high in his favour.'

'I will, then. And my thanks.'

Brour smiled, a twitch of his child's pouty mouth, and swung the pack onto his back. With one quick wave he set off, threading his way through the tumbled stone of the ruins. Lilli climbed onto a hunk of wall and looked around her, studying the terrain. Uncle Burcan would want to know where this treasure lay. At a distance toward the rising sun lay the Belaver, a gleaming silver road. In the opposite direction lay meadows and a deserted farm, a ruin of a house inside worn and grassy earth mounds that once had formed a wall. From her perch she could see Brour, striding down a dirt road with the rising sun at his back. Good luck, she thought after him. Good luck wherever you go!

She scrambled back down and returned to the tunnel. It was something of a struggle, but she managed to pull the door shut. Once she had a fresh candle in her lantern, she hurried back to Dun Deverry. All the long way, the question tormented her: what if someone had gone into the root cellar for some reason, seen the open door and, without thinking, shut it? She wanted to run, but if she did, the candle would blow out, leaving her in darkness. By the time she reached the safety of the filthy cellar she was nearly weeping.

Now all that remained was telling Uncle Burcan about the escape route. Since the weight of the pack would slow Brour down, she decided that she'd best wait two full days. She blew out the lantern and closed the door to the bolthole; then she climbed the steps to the ward. As she hurried back to the main broch, she kept an eye out for pages and suchlike who might tattle to Merodda. What was going to count now was avoiding her mother until she could clean the mud off her skirts.

She slipped into the great hall, then paused in surprise. Even though it was already mid-morning, the King's table was surrounded by angry lords, arguing furiously with Burcan while the young King cowered behind him. She saw Tieryn Peddyc standing to one side, his arms crossed over his chest, his lips white with rage. A servant girl saw her staring and hurried over.

'It's ever so nasty,' the girl whispered. 'The Queen has sent Lady Bevyan away from court.'

'What? Why? How could she?'

'I know not why, my lady. For not much of a reason at all, I'd wager. But oh! the shame of it!'

Lilli ran across the great hall and gained the staircase, got up it as fast as she could, then ran down the corridor to Bevyan's chambers.

She burst in without knocking to find Bevyan standing by the bed, calmly folding her bed sheets and laying them in a wooden chest for her journey, while Sarra sat weeping on a chair nearby.

'You've heard, have you, dear?' Bevyan said to Lilli. 'Now don't worry, it's not as bad as all that.'

'But it is! How could she? What a nasty rotten awful thing to do!'

'It is all of that, dear, but it's nothing that I can't bear. Oh, Sarra, come now! You need to get your things together, so do stop that bellowing!'

Sarra wiped her face on the trailing hem of one sleeve.

'That's better,' Bevyan said. 'Now why don't you fetch the pieces of Braemys's wedding shirt for Lilli? We don't want to pack them by mistake.'

With a nod and a hard swallow, Sarra did as she was told. Once she'd left the room, Lilli turned to her foster-mother.

'But why?' Lilli said. 'Why would she send you away?'

'She said that I'd angered her.' Bevyan actually smiled. 'No doubt I did, too, by pointing out a few truths. She's a silly child, and she's in a terrible position, one she doesn't have the strength for. But here, dear, help me pack these bedclothes. We're to leave today.'

'Today? Oh, that's not fair!'

'Life is very often not fair, dear. My lord has already sent his messengers to Lord Camlyn – that's where we'll stay tonight, you see.'

'You won't be safe out there!'

'Peddyc is giving us an escort of thirty men. They'll be our fort guard when we get home, too.'

Lilli picked up a blanket and began folding it in quarters.

'I saw the tieryn in the great hall,' Lilli said. 'He looked ever so angry.'

'No doubt. He demanded that Burcan intercede with your mother for me.'

'My mother?'

'The Queen mostly does what your mother says, you know.'

All at once Lilli felt as if her legs had lost all their strength. She sat down heavily on the edge of the stripped bed and rubbed her face with both hands, determined not to weep and distress Bevyan. She felt more like screaming in rage, anyway, that in the ·same day she'd lose the only two people in her life who'd ever cared about her welfare.

*

'And just why,' Burcan snarled. 'did you send the Lady Bevyan away from court?'

'I did no such thing,' Merodda said. 'Queen Abrwnna was the one –'

'Oh hold your tongue! The Queen does what you tell her.'

All at once Merodda realized that he was genuinely angry. A surprise, that. She put on her best soothing smile.

'It was a woman's matter, my lord. You needn't waste your time upon it.'

'If Tieryn Peddyc feels slighted . . .'

'Oh. Oh, I see. Well, Bevyan is wondering just who Lilli's father is. She made it clear that she knows enough to be suspicious of – of – us. I had to do something.'

Burcan considered. Slowly the blood-red rage ebbed from his face.

'You're afraid that Peddyc's wavering, are you?' Merodda said. 'Well, I suspect Bevyan of having somewhat to do with that. It's all very well for her to talk about peace and how splendid it would be to end the wars. She and her lord will get pardons from the Usurper should he win. We won't be granted such a pleasant boon.'

'Just so. But if you've sent her away, we won't be able to keep an eye on her. What if she's one of the ones you saw in your omens, the circle plotting against us?'

'Then perhaps she should be permanently disposed of.'

'Nonsense! I won't hear of it!'

'Why not? I don't trust her.' Merodda looked straight into his eyes. 'Besides, you're the one who's wondering if Peddyc is still loyal to our king. What if he went over to Cerrmor? How many men would he take with him?'

'Far too many, but ye gods! You don't keep a man's loyalty by murdering his wife. Have you gone daft?'

'Not at all. Come sit down and listen. I've got a plan.'

Burcan looked at her for a long moment, then shrugged. Very well,' he said. 'I don't know why I waste my time doubting you.'

Merodda smiled and allowed him to kiss her.

What with the wagon to be packed and the escort to be chosen, Bevyan left Dun Deverry just before noon. A smouldering Peddyc rode with her down to the city gates, then for another mile or so past them. When they reached the west-running road to Hendyr, he called for a halt, then leaned from his saddle to kiss her farewell.

'Now do watch yourself, my love,' Bevyan said. 'I've survived worse than this insult.'

'Indeed? Well, you'd best not have to survive suchlike again, or I'll –' With great difficulty Peddyc caught himself, glancing round at his men. 'Now then, set a good watch over my lady on the road, lads. The messenger should be well ahead of you by now, and so Lord Camlyn's lady will be expecting you.'

'Done, my lord.' Young Doryc, the temporary captain of her escort, bowed from his saddle. 'And we'll hold your dun until you return. Have no fears about that.'

Peddyc allowed himself one weary smile, then raised his hand and motioned them forward. Bevyan turned in her saddle for a last look back and saw him waiting at the crossroads. When she waved, he turned his horse's head and rode off toward Dun Deverry.

In the pleasant shade of the tree-lined road the horses ambled while Bevyan half-drowsed in her saddle. Her escort talked quietly among themselves; the cart coming along behind creaked while the harness jingled. Sarra began to sing one of the long songs the women traded back and forth to amuse themselves while they worked at various tasks. Bevyan started to join in, then realized what they were singing – the ballad of 'Brangwen and Gerraent'.

'Oh, not that song,' she snapped. 'Forgive me – I am a bit rattled, I suppose.'

'It's just that the ballad's one of your favourites.' Sarra glanced at her in surprise.

'I'd just rather sing somewhat else. Let's do the one about Lord Benoic. Here, I'll start.'

By the middle of the afternoon they'd finished so many ballads that they fell silent with sore voices. Bevyan was just thinking of calling a halt so they could water the horses and rest when ahead on the road someone shouted, a man's voice, incomprehensible but filled with danger.

'Hold!' Young Doryc threw up one hand. 'What's all this?'

The men halted, but their horses milled in sudden alarm. Bevyan heard horses pounding down the road fast, turned in her saddle to see a squad of armed men pouring out between the trees behind them. Sarra screamed, one high-pitched note, as another squad swarmed to the head of the line to cut the Rams' party off. The Rams' men were drawing swords and cursing as the strangers galloped straight for them. There would be no explanation, no parley. The enemies were carrying shields oval in shape and painted with three ships for a blazon.

'Cerrmor!' Doryc yelled.

The first wave of riders broke over the lad and knocked him from his horse. Shouting, slashing with their swords, the escort tried to form a ring around the two women, but the enemies mobbed in, two and three to a loyal rider. Bevyan had to fight to control her panicked horse, who reared and whinnied, kicking out randomly when it came down again. She heard Sarra screaming, heard the scream suddenly cut off, twisted in the saddle just in time to see her serving woman fall bleeding over her horse's neck. Bevyan yanked the palfrey's head around and kicked it hard. The horse leapt forward, darting toward the side of the road, but two riders swung round and cut her off. One raised a bloody sword, then stopped, half-frozen by shame when she stared him right in the face.

'Where's the glory in killing women?' she hissed. 'May the Goddess curse you all!'

He hesitated, mouth half-open, staring at her in agony. His companion swore, leaned forward, and stabbed. She saw and recognized the wide blue eyes beneath the edge of his helm.

'Burcan!'

The pain hit in a wave of fire that broke over her and dragged her tumbling down to the dust in the road. For a moment the world spun. Blackness claimed her with the hot smell of blood.

Rather than watch Bevyan ride away, Lilli hid in her chamber. Since she'd walked many miles through the escape tunnel and back, she fell asleep on her bed – only to wake suddenly. She sat bolt upright and listened, sure she'd heard a woman screaming, but the chamber lay silent around her. Through the narrow window the sunlight of late afternoon streamed in, flecked with dancing dust motes.

'That was Sarra's voice,' she said aloud. 'An awful sort of dream, I suppose.'

Dread, cold clammy irrational dread, wrapped her round so tightly that for a moment her breath caught, ragged in her chest. She got up, but the feeling kept hold of her, making her tremble. To get away from the silence she hurried down to the great hall, filling with people as time for the evening meal drew near. But she couldn't stand the noise, either, and went outside, wandering through the twilight wards and towers of the dun. The dread walked behind her and clutched her shoulders in cold fingers until she ached.

Finally, when the stars were coming out in a velvet sky, she fetched up near the main gate. The guard was changing, and weary men climbed down from the catwalks, calling out to one another and talking mostly about food. Just as the gates were closing, Lilli heard a silver horn on the road outside. Men shouted; she could hear hooves clattering in a trot and the jingle of tack. The guards threw their weight on the handle of the winch and stopped the gates, which halted, open just far enough for a single rider to pass by.

First through into the pool of torchlight inside the ward was Uncle Burcan. Lilli shrank back against the wall where no one would notice her and watched the Boarsmen ride their horses in. Some of them were wounded, she noticed; they must have run across a disloyal lord or Cerrmor raiders. At each saddle peak hung a shield, painted with the Boar blazon, but behind each saddle they carried a shield-shaped burden wrapped in old sacking – odd, she thought, and peered through the uncertain light for a better look. One sack had slipped to dangle down and expose the ship blazon of Cerrmor. Decidedly odd, and with that thought her dread threw its arms around her and clutched. Something was wrong, horribly wrong.

Lilli waited until the warband had long left the ward, then went back up the hill to the great hall. Inside, the Boarsmen had taken their places with the other riders at the long tables, but there was no sign of either Burcan or Merodda. Lilli hurried upstairs before anyone noticed her. If she never got a message from her mother, she couldn't be expected to wait upon her. Unfortunately Merodda had seen her go and followed her, calling out on the landing.

'Lilli, wait! I want a word with you.'

Lilli stopped and arranged a smile. Merodda hurried over, her mouth twisted in rage. Here was the crux, and Lilli visualized her aura growing hard and smooth around her, just as Brour had taught her.

'Where's Brour?' Merodda snapped. 'Do you know?'

'I don't, Mother. He's not in your chambers?'

Merodda cocked her head to one side and peered into Lilli's face. Lilli went on smiling and imagined her aura as a wall, turning to stone, a fortress around her.

'He's not,' Merodda said at last. 'He's not in the great hall, and the bards don't know where he is, either. How very odd!'

'There's some servant lass he fancies, isn't there? I heard gossip about it.'

'I never thought of that.' Merodda looked up with a startled little laugh. 'You might be right.'

Merodda turned and swept off, heading back to the great hall. Lilli walked decorously back to her chamber, but she felt like dancing in glee. It had worked! Brour's trick had worked! She need never fear her mother's ability to ferret out lies again. Yet once she was alone, watching the candle-thrown shadows on the stone, she remembered Bevyan, sent away from court into political exile, and all her pleasure in the dweomer vanished. She spent the evening hiding in her chamber, and mercifully, Merodda never sent a page to summon her. All night she had horrible dreams, in which a blonde woman, naked in moonlight, her mouth full of bloody fangs, ranged among the sheep like a mad dog, killing as she went.

At the noontide Lilli learned the meaning of her omens. She was sitting at her mother's table and trying to eat bread that seemed to stick in her exhausted throat. A ripple of excitement at the door caught her attention: a road-dusty messenger strode in. Although he bowed to king and regent, he hurried past them and flung himself down to kneel at Tieryn Peddyc's side. At that moment Lilli knew. She felt cold sweat run down her back and thought: Bevva's dead. Without thinking she rose, leaning flat-handed on the table to watch the rider talking urgently to the tieryn while Anasyn leaned over to listen. Peddyc's face turned white, then flushed scarlet, then whitened again. With a toss of his head he got up from his chair and headed for the royal table. Even from her distance she could see that Anasyn wept.

'Do sit down, Lilli!' Merodda snapped. 'What's so wrong?'

Lilli turned and looked at her mother, whose face was its usual bland and shiny mask.

'Somewhat's distressed young Lord Anasyn,' Lilli said.

'Ah.' Merodda looked across the hall. 'So it has. How odd.'

Yet Merodda was fighting to keep from smiling – Lilli could see it in the tightness of her lips, the forced wideness of her eyes. Lilli swung round and saw Burcan rising from his chair to speak to Peddyc. All around them silence spread through the hall like a wave from a stone dropped into a pond, as those close fell silent to listen first, then those farther on.

'Oh ye gods!' It was a girl's voice, squealing through the silence.

'They've murdered Lady Bevyan, and I sent her away, and it's all my fault!'

Shrieking, the Queen leapt up and rushed through the hall in a careening flight toward the stairway. Merodda rose and, cursing under her breath, hurried after as maidservants ran to do the same. All through the hall everyone began talking and yelling back and forth. Cerrmor raiders, they all said – Cerrmor raiders this far north and dishonourable enough to kill women on the road! Lilli stood by the table and tried to think. At first she had trouble identifying the feeling that flooded her, that made her burn and freeze in turn. At last she found its name: hatred. Her mother had killed Bevva somehow, she was sure of it – and Sarra as well. When she remembered the screams that had woken her the day before, she knew that Sarra lay dead without needing to be told.

'Cerrmor raiders, was it?' she whispered. 'And there were Uncle Burcan and his men, riding in with Cerrmor shields.'

In the uproar no one heard her. She watched as Peddyc and Anasyn left the great hall with the King and his escort, with both the Regent and the various gwerbretion in attendance, including Tibryn.

All afternoon Lilli hung around the great hall and fished for news. The rider who'd brought the message was one of Lord Camlyn's. When Lady Bevyan and her escort had failed to arrive, Camlyn's lady had sent out a search party, and they'd found the slaughter. Everyone was dead – every single man, even Bevyan's little page, as if the raiders had meant to leave no witnesses to their treachery, though carelessly enough, they'd left two dropped and broken shields behind. When she learned this, Lilli's certainty grew. Burcan wouldn't have dared let even the page escape, for fear someone had recognized him.

Toward evening she found a maidservant who'd overheard Tieryn Peddyc's plans. He'd got permission from the King to leave Dun Deverry in the morning with his men and go attend to the burying of his wife. He would then return and join the muster.

'And oh, how ever so angry he is!' the girl said, all wide-eyed. 'Swearing and carrying on and saying no Cerrmor man will ever have quarter from him again! I'll wager he kills ever so many this summer.'

'No doubt,' Lilli said. 'Tell me somewhat. Yesterday morn, did the Regent happen to go to my mother's chambers?'

'He did, truly. Why?'

'Oh, I asked her to ask him a favour for me. But it can wait, what with all this trouble.'

With a nod, the maidservant hurried off about her chores. All at once Lilli realized that she wanted to scream in rage at everyone over everything – and nothing at all. She fled the unwelcome sight of other people and hurried to her chamber. She barred the door, then leaned against it and looked at the pieces of Braemys's wedding shirt, lying on the wooden chest where she'd put them the day before. They were the last thing Bevva would ever give her.

'Why can't I cry?'

The hatred seemed to have dried all her tears. She lay down on her bed to watch the evening darken beyond her window. The worst thing was that no one would ever suspect Burcan of this crime, or Merodda, either, who had put him up to it. Lilli was sure of that. Brour had always told her that one day she could read the omens for her own purposes, and she understood now what her dreams had brought her.

'I know the truth, and I'll get revenge – oh don't be silly! What can I do?'

At that she did weep, sobbing into her pillow until she fell asleep. She dreamt, but this time of armed men and vengeance. She woke abruptly to find the chamber dark except for pale moonlight falling through her slit of a window. Once again the omens had come to her for the reading. She was smiling as she got up and left her chamber.

Tieryn Peddyc and Anasyn still slept in Bevyan's old suite. By the time Lilli reached it, her dream courage had faded like the moonlight. What if Peddyc refused to listen to her? What if her mother found out she'd been to see him? Silent, so silent in the corridor – Lilli crept terrified, certain that her breathing would bring every guard in Dun Deverry running. Four doors, five, and under the sixth a gleam of pale light – so, Peddyc did wake still.

She darted across the corridor and plastered herself against the wall beside the door. Dimly she could hear voices, masculine and unintelligible. She should knock on the door, but what if someone heard? In the dark corridor nothing moved, nothing made a sound. She forced herself to raise her fist, hesitated, felt sweat run down her back. She should turn away, run away, race back to the chamber before her mother found her gone. And what? Let Bevva lie unavenged? Lilli gulped once and slammed her fist against the wood.

The voices inside stopped, then one grew louder along with the sound of a bar scraping as someone lifted it. The door opened a bare crack to reveal Peddyc's face, pale and unshaven.

'Lillorigga!' he said. 'What's this, lass? Can't you sleep?'

'I can't,' she whispered. 'Please, let me in?'

Puzzled, he stepped back. She slipped inside, then stood listening to her heart pound while he dropped the bar across the door. Anasyn stood by the hearth, his face a mask, but his eyes were red and puffy. Lilli knew that she could wait not a heart beat more and still keep her nerve.

'It wasn't Cerrmor men,' she blurted. 'It was a trick. It was Boarsmen. My mother sent them with captured shields.'

Peddyc stared, his mouth open. By the hearth Anasyn grunted like a wounded man. Lilli knew she was trembling, and sweat ran down her back.

'I saw them,' she went on. 'My uncle and his men. They were riding back into the dun on tired horses, that night I mean, after Bevva was after she was slain. And they carried Cerrmor shields. There's a lot of them in the dun, captured from one battle or another.'

Anasyn threw up his head like a stag who smells dogs.

'I saw Boarsmen ride out,' he said. 'Do you remember, Da? I mentioned it to you, that some of the Boar's men were leaving the dun, and a cart followed them.'

Peddyc nodded. On his temple a vein throbbed.

'And this morning, when the news came, I watched my mother, and she smiled.' Lilli's courage came back with a rush. 'She tried not to, but she smiled. And I knew then she was behind it.'

Anasyn had gone an eerie pale in the lantern-light.

'By the gods,' Peddyc whispered. 'That stinking rat of a man! The Regent himself, was it? May every blessing in life be yours, lass, for bringing me this news.'

'Father.' Anasyn stepped forward. 'I want vengeance.'

'So do I, and if Merodda weren't Lilli's mother we'd go to her chamber and slit her lying throat before we went and did the same for Burcan. But she *is* Lilli's mother, and by the gods, cursed if I'll hang for avenging my wife! Let me think, just let me think for a moment here.'

Lilli sank to her knees, unsure of why she couldn't stand. Peddyc bent over and grabbed her hands.

'Come sit down,' he barked. 'Sanno, pour her a drop of mead. Here, here, lass, you're all to pieces, and who can blame you?'

In a flurry of murmurs Anasyn and a page sat her down in a carved chair, handed her mead, and brought a cushion for her back. All the while Tieryn Peddyc stood at the hearth and stared at the flames. Lilli took one sip of the drink, then realized her hands were shaking so hard that the pale gold liquor danced within the cup.

'I've got to get back.' She set it on the table. 'If she finds me gone, she'll kill me, too.'

'No doubt.' Peddyc turned from the hearth. 'And when me and my men don't come back when we've pledged, there's a good chance she'll kill you then, if she and her precious regent guess who told me the truth. You'd best ride with us on the morrow.'

'You'd take me away?' Lilli found that she could barely form the words.

'If you'll go, of course we will! You're my foster-daughter, aren't you? And even if you weren't, what kind of a man would I be, leaving you behind with that murdering bastard?'

Anasyn knelt beside her with a fluid motion and caught her hand in both of his.

'Come away with us, Lilli,' he said. 'We'll dress you in some of my clothes, and cut off your hair, and no one will notice another manservant or suchlike riding with us. And then you'll be safe, back at Hendyr if you like, or you can come with us to Cerrmor.'

'Cerrmor?' she whispered it like a dweomer spell. 'I could go to Cerrmor?'

'Cursed right, and welcome you'll be,' Peddyc said. 'The Boar's own niece, gone over to –' he hesitated, his eyes filling with tears. 'Gone over to the True King.'

For the last few hours of that night no one slept. While Anasyn stood watch at the door, Peddyc's old manservant cut off Lilli's hair, which she wrapped in a bit of old cloth, every scrap of it, to take with her lest her mother find it and use it to work dweomer against her. She rubbed ashes in the cropped remainder, too, and added a smear of the same along the line of her jaw and on one temple, as if she were a page, sleeping at the hearth. In the privacy of the bed-chamber she changed into the scruffiest clothes the men could find her. The three of them looked over the result and pronounced her well-hidden, but all she could do was nod and tremble.

Yet when the grey dawn's light finally broke, her terror vanished into a welcome numbness. When they left the chamber, she carried an armload of saddlebags and tried to swagger like a lad. No one noticed or spoke to her, not even Peddyc's captain when he joined the tieryn out in the ward, where the warband was assembling by the great gates. Lilli followed the manservant into the stables and helped him saddle Peddyc and Anasyn's horses.

'Hah, here's a mule for you, lad,' he said, pointing down the line of stalls. 'Put that saddle on him, and then we'll tie a load of grain sacks behind you, and you'll ride with me at the end of the line, like, and who's to cast a look your way?'

No one, in the event. Lilli rode out of Dun Deverry in a cloud of dust and a crowd of yawning men. Ahead lay the long parkland of the hill on which the dun stood. The road down twisted through a maze of baffles and walls, each one manned. They rode through gate after gate, but the gatekeepers never looked at her, nor did the sleepy guards, coming down from their night's watch on the walls. The last gate – out and safe! The old manservant caught Lilli's attention and grinned. As the warband made their slow way through the ruins of the city, she slouched in the saddle and leaned against the sacks of grain stowed behind her. No one ever looked her way.

Ahead the city gates stood open. Beyond them she could see green fields and a flash of silver river. As the warband plodded through, four abreast, she twisted in the saddle and looked back to the dun, rising towered and grey in the brightening light. What would her mother do when she found her gone? Use her dark dweomer and scry her out? The terror came back like a blow to her heart, and she gasped for breath while sweat beaded and ran.

'Hush, lass,' the manservant whispered. 'We're out now. You're free, and the good tieryn will keep you that way. Ye gods, I'd lay down my life to keep you safe myself, for bringing the truth of our lady's death.' His rheumy old eyes overflowed, and he turned away, wiping them on his sleeve.

'I'll pray you never have to,' Lilli said. 'From the bottom of my heart.'

While the sun climbed and the dawn turned into morning, the warband rode straight west, heading for Camlyn's dun and Lady Bevyan.

'Brour's gone!' Merodda snapped. 'I never had time to look yesterday, what with the uproar over Bevyan's death. But he's gone good and proper – his clothes, his book, everything!'

'Indeed?' Burcan said. 'Do you think he'll be heading back to Cerrmor to sell what he knows?'

'I don't. He left there in bad enough odour to never dare go back.

He's gone north, I'll wager. He comes from the far Northlands, and he's oft mentioned how he misses his kin and country.'

Burcan considered with a scowl. The morning light streamed through the windows of the reception chamber, and in the brightness his lined face sagged, all stubbled and pouchy-eyed.

'Lilli told me he might have a lass here in the dun,' Merodda went on. 'No doubt he lied to her – set up a ruse, perhaps.'

'Could she scry him out?'

'Now there's a thought! Wait here. I'll fetch her.'

When Merodda went to Lilli's chamber, she found it empty, though the bed had obviously been slept in. Swearing under her breath, she headed toward the great hall, but at the head of the stairs she found a page, returning from some errand.

'Go find my daughter and have her come to my chamber.'

'I will, my lady.' The page bowed and hurried off.

Merodda returned to her suite of rooms to find Burcan pacing back and forth by a window. She sat down in her chair by the hearth and watched him.

'Is your heart troubled?' she said at last. 'By killing Bevyan, I mean?'

'What makes you think that?' He paused to give her a puzzled look. 'I'm wondering about your scribe, and what he might be in a position to know and tell. A great deal, I should think.'

'Unfortunately, that's true.'

'Indeed.' Burcan flung himself down into the chair opposite her and stretched out his legs with a long sigh. 'Not much sleep last night.'

'I doubt if anyone in the dun did sleep well.'

While they waited for Lilli, Burcan drowsed, his head nodding against his chest. Merodda watched him, but she was remembering their father, all those years ago before she'd been married off to serve the clan. Father and Tibryn, his little namesake – a perfect pair they were, she thought. How I hated them! And I had naught, unless they threw a few scraps my way, not so much as a decent dress after Mother died. But once she'd made an ally out of her brother, seduced Burcan the only way she knew how, then things had improved for her. Only then, with a man to speak up for her, did they listen to what she wanted and even on occasion give it to her.

'My lady?' It was the page, standing in the doorway. 'I can't find Lillorigga anywhere.'

'Oh, she's probably moping around somewhere because of Lady

Bevyan. Never mind – I'll speak to her at dinner.'

In his chair Burcan had roused, yawning and stretching. He waited to speak until the page had left.

'Can't you do the scrying yourself?' he said.

'I can, at that. Wait here.'

Merodda hurried into her bedchamber and barred the door behind her. Under the bed lay a collection of small chests; she knelt and pulled one out. Inside lay two big leather bottles, their mouths plugged and tied shut, and a collection of small pottery jars. There was as well one small glass bottle, containing greyish-white crystals called Dwarven Salts – a gift from Brour, who had got it from the Northlands, or so he claimed – a dweomer potion indeed, because it worked both fair and foul. Mixed with liquid and drunk, it would poison the drinker; used as a face wash, it kept the skin young and radiant. Merodda held the bottle up to the light from the window; it was nearly full, but she felt a stab of worry. With Brour gone, she'd not be getting any more of these miraculous salts.

For a moment she allowed herself the luxury of wishing he'd escape. The man had dweomer, after all. She could lie to Burcan and say that Brour had hid himself with some magic spell and that she couldn't scry him out. But what if Burcan were angry with her? She could remember his anger all too well, the sudden way he turned on her, the slap from the back of his hand that flung her against the wall. Without thinking she laid her free hand on her face, as if she could feel the welt and broken skin there still. Over Aethan, that was. Oh ye gods! Aethan! She'd not thought of him in years, the one man she'd ever loved for himself alone – and Burcan had forced her to betray him.

'I feared he'd kill me. I truly did.'

Her sweaty hand tightened on the bottle so hard that it threatened to slip out of her fist. And who was she talking to, anyway, she asked herself? Aethan, perhaps, or perhaps the gods.

With a shake of her head, Merodda put the dweomer crystals away and took out the leather bottle of black ink, then found the silver basin, also cached beneath the bed, and emptied the ink into it. She sat cross-legged on the floor with the basin in her lap and stared into the pool of darkness. Although she lacked Lilli's natural talent for seeing omens, she had learned from her first teacher of dark things to scry out people she knew well. When she turned her mind to Brour, she murmured a chant, not magical in itself, but the memory

key that unlocked this particular power of her mind. The surface of
the ink seemed to swirl and tremble.

Merodda first saw flecks of sunlight, then a dusty road and Brour.
Carrying a pack like a peddlar, he was trudging along beside the river.
Ye gods! was he heading to Cerrmor after all? At that point she saw
trees and realized that the morning sun was casting clear shadows
toward the west, which lay at Brour's left hand. With a toss of her
head she broke the vision. The moment had come. Lie to Burcan or
tell him Brour's whereabouts? She could remember his face in a rage,
the purple veins throbbing on his temples. Carefully she set the basin
on the floor and rose, then left her chamber.

Burcan looked up at her with one eyebrow raised.

'I've seen him,' Merodda said. 'He's heading north, all right,
strolling along beside the river as happily as you please. He's got up
like a peddlar with a pack.'

'Good!' Burcan snarled. 'I'm going to take some of my men and ride
after him. If he's burdened he can't have gone far. If he gives us the
slip, I'll tell my vassals there's a price on his head. They'll bring it to
me soon enough.'

'Wonderful!' She forced herself to smile. 'And he's carrying a
treasure, too, a book.'

'A book?'

'It's filled with dweomer secrets, a big thing, bound in leather.'

'Very well. If you want it, it shall be yours.'

Burcan rode out around noon, and still Merodda had found no sign
of Lilli. The dinner hour arrived but brought no Lilli, either. Merodda
sent other servants to scour the dun, but they all returned without
the girl. She could scry her daughter out, and she was just heading
for the staircase to return to her chambers when a page came rushing
up to her.

'My lady, my lady!' He was near tears. 'The Queen just tried to kill
herself.'

'Oh ye gods!' The stupid little dolt! Merodda thought. Aloud she
said, 'Does she live?'

'She does, my lady. Her throat is ever so bruised, though. She tried
to hang herself.'

Everyone in the great hall was turning to look, to listen. In a ripple
of hushed noise the news spread out like a ripple in a pond.

'I'll attend upon her straightaway,' Merodda said.

She turned on her heel and hurried up the staircase, but at the landing she looked back to see the page mobbed by members of the Queen's Fellowship. The lad was talking and gesturing while the men listened, white-faced.

Merodda swept into the women's hall without knocking and found Abrwnna's maidservants huddled together and weeping. Merodda hurried through to the Queen's chamber on the far side. They'd laid Abrwnna on her bed with her copper-coloured hair spread out away from her face like a sunset over the white linen. Two of the royal chirurgeons were attending her; a young man held a flask of liquid to the Queen's bluish tinged lips and tried to force a few drops down. Old Grodyn stood nearby, leaning on the bedstead and frowning. Abrwnna lay so still that at first Merodda feared her dead; then the girl's eyes opened and flicked her way.

'Rhodi.' Her voice was a ghastly whisper, like the sound of a metal shovel scraping up coals from a dead hearth. 'Let me die.'

'Nonsense!' Merodda hurried to the bedside. 'My dearest liege!'

A welt of red and purple bruises circled her throat, with a fist-shaped bruise, bleeding from a scrape, just under one ear. Merodda felt herself turn cold all over, a sick kind of cold, as if she'd just vomited. Her hands shook with terror, but she could not force her gaze away until the chirurgeon spoke.

'It's a nasty sight, eh?' Grodyn said calmly. 'That's from the knot. They found her just in time. She didn't give herself enough of a drop, and so she was strangling in the noose.'

'Oh, ah, indeed.' Merodda had to force out the words. Deep in her heart she knew that it wasn't the sight that had sickened her, but some horrible omen – would she see the same mark on Burcan's neck one day?

'Are you all right, my lady?' Grodyn said.

'I'll be fine in a heart's beat or two. It's just so awful! Our poor queen!'

Abrwnna stared up at the ceiling and refused to look at either of them. Merodda caught the chirurgeon's attention and mouthed the words 'Will she live?' He shrugged and held both hands palm up.

'Her throat's all raw,' the young physician said. 'I'm trying to give her somewhat to soothe it.'

'Come now!' Merodda laid one hand on Abrwnna's face. 'Be a good lass and open your mouth, my liege. Just a few drops? Please? Do it for your Rhodi? No one blames you for our poor Bevyan's death. It was those fiends from Cerrmor.'

Abrwnna flicked her eyes Merodda's way, but she kept her lips pressed together.

'Just a little swallow,' Merodda went on. 'For the sake of the men in your fellowship. Why, just think: if you ask them, my liege, they'll swear an oath to avenge our Bevva's death.'

Abrwnna considered, then opened her lips and sipped the liquid.

'Just a bit at a time,' Grodyn said sharply. 'Don't choke her, lad.'

Merodda found a chair and watched the two men fuss over their royal patient. What if the Queen did die of her crushed throat? The King would have need of a new wife, then. What a pity that Tibryn had insisted on settling Lilli's betrothal already! Of course, betrothals had been broken before. Or would it be too obvious? Probably so, and she might find herself suspected. It was a good thing that Abrwnna had tried to hang herself, not eaten poison, what with all the nasty gossip about dear Caetha's death still very much alive. I should have known they'd suspect me, Merodda thought. But what if Caetha had taken Burcan's affections away? What place would I have then?

The sick cold swept over her again. Merodda laid a hand at her throat and sat shivering in the warm room.

The sun was well on its way towards setting when Tieryn Peddyc, his men, and Lilli arrived at Lord Camlyn's dun. Lady Varylla, with a black scarf thrown over her head, met them at the gates.

'Tieryn Peddyc —' Varylla started to speak, then merely wept.

Fortunately her old chamberlain, the only real servitor in the dun, had seen so much death and misery in his life that he kept his composure. While the servants and riders took the horses to the stables, old Gatto stood with Peddyc, Anasyn and Lilli in the ward and told them how he'd handled matters. The dead riders were all buried in a mass grave by the road along with the two common-born maidservants; the horses left alive had been rounded up; the bridles and saddles from the dead ones had been collected and were waiting for the tieryn to take with him. Lady Bevyan, Sarra and the young page, who was also of noble blood, had been laid out here in the dun.

'They're in the buttery, my lord,' Gatto finished. 'It's got a chill on it, even in summer. When your messenger got here today, round noon it was, my lady had all the servants comb the meadows for flowers, and we've piled them around her. Would you be wanting to see her?'

'I would, at that,' Peddyc said, and his voice sounded calm, even distant. 'And no doubt Sanno and Lilli will be coming with me.'

The buttery lay under Lord Camlyn's hall, reached from an outside door by steep stone stairs, dangerous with damp. Through the little stone room itself ran a trickle of water in a stone ditch, and the air was cold enough to make Lilli shiver. All the cheeses and suchlike had been moved to one side. At the other on trestle tables lay the three dead, mounded with wild roses and lilac, lavender and kitchen herbs, Bevyan to the outer side, as if in death she still protected those who had come to her in need of a home. Even with so many flowers a wisp of rot hung in the air. Holding two lanterns high, Gatto stood by the stairs and let the tieryn and his family pay their respects.

Peddyc and Anasyn stood shoulder-to-shoulder, and Lilli had never seen men turn so still, as if they'd willed themselves to stone. She herself could not stop shaking from the chill and grief both. Bevyan's face had gone a cold bluish-grey, and her dark eyes, so merry in life, had shrunk to a desiccated stare. All over her cheeks and on the hands that emerged from the flower mound lay white blisters. Very very slowly Peddyc reached out one hand and touched his wife's cheek with one finger. A blister split with a puff of stench.

'Vengeance, my love,' he whispered. 'I'd always thought that you would have the burying of me. Never did I dream that I'd be swearing vengeance at your grave. But swear it I will.' Peddyc turned slightly to look at Lilli and Anasyn. 'Leave me.'

Lilli had never been so glad to follow an order in her life.

That's not Bevva, she found herself thinking. And that's not Sarra, either. They're long gone, and those leavings aren't them at all. She kept repeating the thought, hoping that it would calm her, but Anasyn had to lift her up to the ground from the last step – she could not see through her tears.

It was a long while before Peddyc returned to join Lilli, Anasyn, and Varylla at the wobbly table of honour. By then servants were laying baskets of bread upon the table and pouring ale, which the tieryn's riders drank steadily and grimly across the hall.

'Very well, my lady,' Peddyc said to Varylla. 'You have my humble thanks from the bottom of my heart.'

'I only wish that this wasn't a favour that needed doing, my lord.'

Peddyc nodded, accepted a tankard, and drank a good bit off. He wiped his mouth on the back of his hand while he thought something through.

'My lady Varylla,' Peddyc said at last. 'I had a chance for a quick word with your lord as I was leaving Dun Deverry. He sent you a

message: I'll be coming home in a few days. Be ready to join me and
have anything you want to take with you packed in a cart. We'll be
heading to my cousin's down near Yvrodur. He'll shelter you while I
ride on south.'

Varylla went pale, her eyes wide, but she smiled when she nodded
her agreement. Torn with grief as she was, it took Lilli some effort to
grasp what Peddyc was telling Camlyn's lady. Bevyan would have the
best possible revenge: the fury over her death would lose the Boar
allies.

'And what about our gwerbret?' Varylla whispered.

'He won't be able to come over until the armies leave Dun Deverry.
But come over he will.'

Varylla nodded again, trembling a little, but her smile held firm.

'I'll pray to our goddess to get my lord home safely,' she said. 'My
thanks for the news.'

'Keep it as quiet as possible. You don't want some servant running
to the Boar with the news in exchange for a handful of coin.'

'True spoken. I'll talk up my fears. I'll have a dreadful bad dream.
I'll be loading the cart because the dream made me as sure as ever I
can be that all is lost, and the horrible Usurper will be upon us any
day.'

'Excellent!' With a firm nod Peddyc turned away. 'Lilli, Sanno – you
two get some sleep. We're burying our dead with the dawn, and then
we're riding out.'

All that evening visitors filed in and out of the Queen's bedchamber,
while Abrwnna lay dead-still, fighting to breathe, or so it seemed, and
truly, her throat must have burned with a thousand fires. Still,
Merodda decided, after some while it began to look as if the Queen
were enjoying this unusual reception. Her wan expressions, her little
moans, were entirely too graceful and even lovely; finally Merodda
caught her looking slantwise at a courtier to see the effect of some
gesture. At that point Merodda realized that indeed, the Queen
would live.

After dinner her husband arrived, carrying a wooden horse under
one arm. King Olaen climbed up on his Queen's bed and sat cross-
legged near the foot, watching Abrwnna solemnly while he cradled
the horse. He was, Merodda supposed, fond of the girl, as a boy
would be of his sister. With the King in attendance, the men of
Abrwnna's Fellowship could be allowed in without offending the

proprieties. Each knelt at her bedside and kissed a pale hand, extended to them with great effort. The Queen no doubt truly was exhausted, Merodda reminded herself. She had, after all, very nearly died.

'My liege?' Merodda murmured. 'May I leave you for a while?'

With her lords in attendance Abrwnna never noticed when her serving woman left the room.

With the problem of Lilli's whereabouts still on her mind, Merodda returned to her bedchamber. A servant had lit a small fire at the hearth, and from it she lit candles for the table. The silver basin still sat on the floor beside her bed. She fetched it out and set it among the glittering lights. When she turned her mind to her daughter, the image built up fast on the surface of the ink.

Her face drenched and raw with tears, Lilli stood beside a woman's corpse, laid on a trestle table and heaped with flowers. Of course! Lilli had crept out with Tieryn Peddyc to go say farewell to Bevyan. With a snap of her fingers Merodda banished the vision. Well, Peddyc would bring her back when he returned to the dun, then, and there was no need to worry. She couldn't blame the lass; Bevyan had been more of a mother to Lilli than she ever could have been. Eventually Lilli would learn, as Merodda had, that grief and mourning were luxuries beyond the reach of the women of the Boar Clan.

With a sigh Merodda leaned back in her chair. She could barely remember her own mother's face. She did, however, remember how her mother had died, slain by her husband for being unfaithful to him, cut down like a beast in the ward when she ran screaming for the gates. Merodda remembered weeping all night, and the way her brothers had tried to hush her, fearful that their father would kill her, too, if he heard her. No one had ever said a word against their father for the murder. It hadn't truly been a murder, she supposed, but his right as lord of the dun.

With a sigh Merodda rose. She wanted to sleep, but she knew that her place was at the Queen's side, lest some scheming courtier use her absence against her. She returned to the Queen's chambers to find the King curled up asleep at the foot of his wife's bed, while Abrwnna drowsed, propped up on cushions, under the anxious eyes of the chirurgeons.

Late on the morrow the muster began in earnest. Those lords whose lands lay nearest rode in, and each brought every man who owed him service or who could be bought or bribed. Behind each warband rolled provision carts, loaded with sacks of grain, wheels of cheese, and squealing pigs. Merodda stood on the walls with the other women in the dun and counted each contingent. The others laughed at how high the count climbed, but Merodda knew better. Burcan had begged and bullied an army of desperation into existence. If it failed to stop Maryn's advance this summer then nothing ever would stop the Usurper. The northern lords – no lord in the kingdom – would never risk so much two years' running.

Burcan himself returned on the day after, around noon. Merodda was in her chamber when a page came running with the news that the Regent and his personal warband had ridden in.

'And he's got ever so many lords and riders with him, my lady.'

'He must have joined up with them on the roads,' Merodda said. 'My thanks. I won't go down now, though. I'm sure he has important business to attend to.'

And yet Burcan came up to her chamber in a brief while. Dust from his ride streaked his clothes and hair, and he walked stiffly, more than a little tired, and he was laden with sacks, but he was grinning.

'I've brought you a pair of gifts,' he said and held out a leather hunting sack. 'I've got the book you asked about, and then, this.'

The sour stink of old blood hanging in the air warned her of what lay inside. She forced herself to smile as she opened it and peered in. Sure enough, Brour's head stared up at her, the stump of neck black with old blood, his flesh blue and rigid, his mouth half-open as if to cry out.

'Good,' Merodda said. 'We won't be worrying about him, then. My thanks, my love, my one and only true love.'

Burcan laughed in a burst of pleasure. She found herself remembering him as a lad, before either of them had married. He would find her the first violets of spring and bring them to her with just this sort of laugh. And they would eat them together, this first taste of fresh food, an omen of the summer to come.

Servants had dug graves for Bevyan and Sarra under an oak in the meadow behind Lord Camlyn's dun, but getting the bodies out of the cellar room took some doing. No one wanted to pick the remains up and carry them, but the stairs were too steep to use the trestles as a litter and carry them out that way. Servants dithered while Gatto swore until Peddyc bundled Bevyan up in a blanket and carried her out himself, shaming the servants into bringing Sarra and the page. This confusion nearly made Lilli retch. Even Anasyn looked pale and shaken.

Once the dead lay decently in their graves, the servants brought the wilted flowers to cover them. Since the nearest temple lay miles distant, no one sacrificed over the burial. Everyone stood for a moment, wondering what to do, until Peddyc turned to Gatto.

'Have them fill it in,' Peddyc said. 'We'd best be on the road.'

'Done, my lord. And may the gods bless you. Lady Bevyan was always so kind to me and mine.'

'That was her way, truly.' Peddyc turned to Lilli. 'If you get tired in the saddle, lass, we'll tie you on so you can sleep, but we're riding as fast and straight as we can.'

'Very well, father.' But Lilli hesitated, lingering by the grave – it was too horrible to just leave Bevyan like this without so much as a priest's blessing. Finally Anasyn caught her by the arm and half-dragged her away.

'Don't you think it aches my heart, too?' Anasyn said. 'But she'll have our vengeance to wrap her round, and that'll be better than a silk shroud.'

Since their horses had been well-rested, Tieryn Peddyc and his party reached Hendyr late on the second day after leaving Lord Camlyn's dun. By the time they saw the familiar tower rising on the horizon, Lilli understood Peddyc's remarks about exhaustion – she ached in every muscle. She had travelled back and forth to Hendyr so often that she knew all the small landmarks – the tall aspens nodding beside the road, Old Mori's farm, the view of the main broch from the final bend in the road. This time, however, Bevva wouldn't be waiting at the gates, nor would Lilli run up the stairs to the women's hall to find her.

When the warband clattered into the great ward, servants came running in a confusion of barking dogs.

'My lord, my lord!' Voryc, the chamberlain, cried out. 'Is all lost, then?'

'Not truly.' Peddyc leaned down from the saddle to clasp his outstretched hand. 'Only my heart and the light of my life's been lost. The kingdom still stands.'

Voryc stared up at him.

'Lady Bevyan's dead,' Peddyc said. 'Murdered upon the roads by the Boar clan.'

Voryc threw back his head and howled grief. When Lilli looked around, she saw all the servants weeping, too loudly, too coarsely, for their grief to have been feigned to please an overlord. She herself felt spent of all tears. When Anasyn helped her down from her saddle, he whispered one word to her: vengeance.

Dinner that night was a scratched together and cold meal. At their tables the weary warband ate in silence; at the head of the honour table, Peddyc had nothing to say, either, and Lilli and Anasyn followed his lead. But once the food was cleared away and ale poured all round, Peddyc told Voryc to call every servant into the great hall, whether cook or page or pig boy. They crowded in, standing among the tables where the warband sat.

Peddyc leapt onto the table of honour and raised his arms for silence.

'Listen, all of you,' he said. 'I've somewhat to tell you. Some of you already know the truth of my wife's death, how it was Lady Merodda of the Boar who had her murdered upon the roads.'

Not an oath, not a word – the men, the retainers, the very servants, all stared at him and waited, though here and there a few nodded, as if to say they'd suspected somewhat like that.

'My lady Lillorigga!' Peddyc called out. 'Stand up and tell the tale again.'

The servants listened to her tale with an attention more rapt than the King's best bard had ever received, while the warband listened again and as grimly as they'd taken the news the first time.

'And I beg you to forgive me,' she finished up. 'Oh please, forgive me? I didn't realize what she was planning until it was too late.'

At that she heard a few murmurs, saw a few kind nods or a grimace of pain as the men looked at her with pity in their eyes. When Peddyc raised his right arm, everyone turned toward him.

'Tomorrow at dawn I'm riding south,' he said, and as calmly as if he remarked upon the warmth of the evening. 'To join with the True King in Cerrmor. Who rides with me?'

His warband roared, they flung fists into the air, they cheered him while the tieryn threw back his head and howled, laughing like a berserker. At last the shouting died down and his mad laughter with it.

'All the rest of you,' Peddyc said, 'freeborn and bondman alike, either come with us or run for your lives. The Boarsmen will be taking Hendyr as soon as they hear the news.' He looked up at the row of faded, tattered banners. 'May my ancestors forgive me, but I can't hold the dun against them, not and serve my king.'

In the midst of the towers and walls of Dun Cerrmor stood a garden. Although it was an odd-shaped bit of ground and a mere thirty feet across, it sported a tiny stream with a wooden bridge, a rolling stretch of green grass, some rose bushes, and an ancient willow tree, all gnarled and drooping, that, or so some people said, had been planted by the ancient sorcerer who once had served King Glyn the First, back at the very beginning of the civil wars. Others dismissed the sorcerer as a bard's fancy, but they of course were wrong.

At the base of the willow tree Maddyn sat in the shade, tuning his harp. Although he considered himself a mere minstrel, everyone treated him these days as an important man, the sworn bard of the Prince's personal guard. Every now and then he would have to shake his head and laugh, when he considered just how long a road the silver daggers had ridden. Not many years before they'd been naught but a ragged troop of mercenaries without a scrap of honour; now they lived in what splendour Dun Cerrmor could offer, and all because their leader, Caradoc, could recognize an omen when he saw one.

As he worked, the Wildfolk gathered around him, sprites and gnomes, mostly, though occasionally an undine rose out of the stream to shake the water the from her long silver hair and listen for a moment. Close beside the bard sat his favourite blue sprite, a beautiful little thing until she smiled, revealing a mouthful of sharp fangs. Whenever some gnome would try to get too close to Maddyn, she would leap upon it, biting and scratching, until it fled and she had the privileged position to herself again. Once he'd finished tuning and began to play, they all sat solemnly on the grass and listened, sucking warty fingers or picking dirty fangs.

'Maddo! Ah, there you are.'

The Wildfolk leapt up and disappeared. Maddyn looked up to see the Prince's closest friend – in truth, perhaps his only friend – striding across the lawn toward him. He was an old man, Councillor Nevyn, with a shock of untidy white hair and skin as wrinkled as tree bark, but he strode along with all the vigour of a young warrior. It's his herbcraft that keeps him so strong, everyone said. After all, the Councillor had been a physician before he'd come to serve the Prince. Maddyn, however, reckoned that the old man's undoubted knowledge of the dweomer had more to do with it than any herbs or roots.

'I'm here, indeed,' Maddyn said. 'Do you need me for somewhat?'

'I do, as a witness. You can be the representative of the Prince's Guard at the council session.'

'What council session?'

'The one that's about to begin. Come along and you'll see.'

In the royal council chamber of Dun Cerrmor, the Prince himself was waiting with another pair of trusted advisers. Gavlyn, the grey and portly chief herald of the royal court, stood at a long oak table and unrolled three large parchments, which he snapped out like bed sheets, then lay down smooth with great ceremony. Councillor Oggyn, a barrel-chested man and egg-bald, leaned from the other side and considered them while he stroked his brindled grey and black beard.

Sunlight poured in through a narrow window and fell across the polished oak table to gleam on the Prince's honey-blond hair and glint on the enormous silver ring brooch that pinned his plaid at one shoulder. In the five years of his rule as Gwerbret Cerrmor and Marked Prince of what of Deverry he could hold, Maryn had aged ten, it seemed. He was a man, now, not that innocent laughing boy the silver daggers had sworn to serve so long ago. His grey eyes seemed to look at the world from a distance denied to ordinary men, and when he spoke, his low voice cracked with authority.

'Very well,' Maryn said. 'We're assembled. Let's get to the matter at hand.'

'It's a matter of choosing a new emblem for the future kingdom.' Councillor Oggyn nodded Maddyn's way.

'The question is legitimacy,' Nevyn put in. 'The stallion blazon will always mean a foreigner from Pyrdon to most people.'

'I suppose so.' Prince Maryn frowned at the spread parchments. 'These are the ancient clans, then?'

'They're clans upon which His Highness has some claim.' The chief herald, Gavlyn, stepped forward. 'As the learned councillor says, the crucial thing is legitimacy.'

From his seat in the corner of the council chambers, Maddyn sat quietly and merely watched the others. He felt too honoured at merely being present to speak up as the debate went on over the merits of one device or another. Finally Nevyn leaned forward to tap one long finger on a page.

'The Red Wyvern has possibilities,' Nevyn said. 'The false king's device is a green one, and I like the arrogance of appropriating it nearly whole.'

Maryn laughed, glancing round the circle.

'I like that as well,' he said. 'What do you think, Oggyn? Shall we filch their device like the usurper they call us?'

'And why should you not, Your Highness? This clan was very well-connected in its day.'

'Good herald, and what about you?'

'My liege, it seems a good choice,' Gavlyn said. 'I would suggest a wyvern rampant, in the same posture thus as the stallion of Pyrdon.'

All at once Maddyn was aware of distant shouting, realized in fact that he'd been hearing it for some little time. He got up and walked to the window, looked out to see dusty men and tired horses walking into the ward below while servants swarmed around them. Some ally arriving for the muster, then, but as one of the men dismounted, his shield swung free of his gear.

'The Ram!' Maddyn forgot himself and spoke aloud. 'By all the gods, the Rams of Hendyr have come over!'

'What?' Maryn swung round and grinned. 'Then truly the gods do favour us! This is a thing I'd never thought to see.'

'No more I, your highness,' Oggyn said. 'If I may be so forward and impertinent to suggest a thing, I'd suggest that your royal self would deign to welcome Tieryn Peddyc personally.'

'And so I shall, good councillor, so I shall.'

During the long journey south from Hendyr, Lilli had ridden at the head of the line with Peddyc and Anasyn, but she'd kept her boy's clothing. Now all three of them stood beside their horses and gawked at the clustered towers of Dun Cerrmor, built of pale limestone with dark slate roofs. Bright banners with the three ships blazon hung above the doorways, and white and blue pennants snapped in the rising sea wind. The doors to the main broch glittered with brass hinges. The well-fed servants and soldiers hurrying toward them wore clothes that were mostly new or barely patched.

'This is a splendid place,' she whispered to Anasyn.

'It is, but let's see what kind of man this prince is.'

In the growing crowd no one greeted them; everyone merely looked them over unsmiling. Lilli found herself remembering her first trip to Dun Deverry after her years in fosterage at Hendyr. She had stood beside her horse this same way, waiting while a page ran off to fetch her mother and tell her that Tieryn Peddyc and his foster-child had arrived. She had felt this same mixture of dread and eagerness then, wondering what her mother would look like and how generously she'd treat her returned daughter. In that instance, the dread had proved the more accurate omen.

From inside Dun Cerrmor a silver horn sounded; the doors were flung back. At the head of an armed guard, a tall and handsome man strode out; the plaid of Cerrmor flung over one shoulder and pinned with a huge silver brooch marked him as Maryn, prince and would-be king. Lilli stared. It seemed that the sunlight shone brighter around him than it did anywhere else, and that some private breeze lifted his blond hair. Where he stood the world seemed oddly larger. She found herself remembering the Great Lord of Earth and how the room had come alive when Brour chanted his invocation.

Without a word every man in the tieryn's army knelt, and Peddyc was the first to do so. Lilli and Anasyn sank to their knees beside their lord as the Prince strode over. His walk captivated her; he seemed to be holding back some enormous urge to run and leap like a boy. Behind him came guards in matching linen shirts, each with a grey dagger embroidered on one sleeve, and one old man, striding along like a warrior himself. Lilli recognized him instantly, and while Peddyc and the others watched the Prince, she was studying Nevyn's face. He did look kind, but she remembered Brour calling him dangerous and a sorcerer.

'So,' Maryn said. 'What brings you to me, Tieryn Peddyc?'

'I've come to beg a pardon for me and mine, Your Highness, for ever raising a sword against you.'

'I've never heard a request I was more minded to grant.' The Prince smiled and held out one hand. 'Rise, then. Come into my hall, and we'll drink mead together. I offered my pardon freely, and freely it shall be yours.'

It was so beautifully done, just like something out of an old saga, that Lilli felt her eyes fill with tears. Peddyc tried to speak, then merely wept. The Prince leaned down and with his own hands helped him rise. Lilli glanced at Anasyn, who seemed to be staring at a god, not a prince, just from the instant worship in his eyes. As everyone got to their feet, Peddyc's men broke out cheering. With a laugh the Prince acknowledged them.

'And are you ready to ride back to Dun Deverry?' he called out. 'With me?'

'We are!' The sound rang like bells around the ward. 'The King! the King!' One man started the chant, and the others joined in until Maryn flung up his hands for silence.

'Not yet a king,' he called out. 'I'll not claim that name until the high priest of Dun Deverry tells me that the gods have allowed it as my right.'

While he spoke, Lilli could have sworn that a beam of sunlight brighter than all the rest fell upon him. The men stood transfixed and listened.

'Many years ago,' Maryn went on, 'when I first rode to Cerrmor, I did fancy myself already King. But the priests came to me and told me that Great Bel demands humility from those he would favour. Until I won the brooch of kingship, they told me, I had no right to call myself High King. And so I did what the god asked of me and laid that name aside.'

The men nodded, wide-eyed and worshipful.

'And so,' Maryn said, grinning, 'we'd cursed well better get ourselves to Dun Deverry, hadn't we? Ride we shall, and soon enough. For now, come in and rest.'

They cheered again, one brief whoop of agreement. Laughing, the Prince summoned the waiting servants forward to take the horses and show the men to the barracks and suchlike. Peddyc wiped his eyes on his sleeve and recovered his voice.

'My liege,' he said to Maryn. 'May I present my son Anasyn and my foster-daughter, Lillorigga?'

'Indeed you may.' The Prince turned to Lilli in surprise and bowed with swift grace. 'My apologies, my lady, for thinking you a lad. You must be weary from all this travelling. I'll have one of the women escort you to my wife's hall, where I'm sure she'll make you welcome.'

'My thanks, my liege.' Lilli found it very hard to speak. 'You're very generous to such as I.'

'My liege?' Nevyn stepped forward. 'May I have the honour of escorting the lady? Oddly enough, we've met.'

Although the old man smiled pleasantly, Lilli felt herself begin to tremble. His ice blue eyes seemed to catch hers and bore into her very soul. When she tried hardening her aura, he raised one bushy eyebrow in surprise; then he looked away.

'You need to rest, my lady,' Nevyn said. 'And then we'll have a little chat.'

'Lilli?' Anasyn stepped forward. 'Will you be all right on your own?'

He glanced at Nevyn. 'We all owe my sister a great debt, my lord, and I'd see her well-treated.'

'It shall be so,' Prince Maryn said. 'I'll stand personal surety for it, Lord Anasyn.'

Anasyn bowed low. With a quick smile for his sake, Lilli allowed herself to be led off. Once again, she remembered those first hours in Dun Deverry, when it had seemed so huge and convoluted that she would never learn her way around on her own. And the people! Soon here too she would be meeting a flood of new people, who would all have to be sorted out and their ways learned. Now at least she was no longer the child who'd entered Dun Deverry all trust and good will; now at least she knew what being at court meant.

While they crossed the ward, Nevyn said nothing at all, and when they stepped into one of the side brochs, he merely remarked that the Princess's hall lay two flights up.

'I'm allowed in,' he said. 'Because of my great age, you see.'

'Very good, my lord,' was all she found to say in answer.

The Princess's hall turned out to be large and sunny, an entire half of one round floor of the broch. Bardek carpets in blue and green lay scattered across the polished planks, and new tapestries hung between all the windows, which sported wooden shutters carved with interlacements and ships. Scattered about were chairs and big floor cushions; on little tables stood glittering silver oddments – a dragon folding her wings, a spray of lavender so cunningly worked it seemed you could smell it, a silver casket engraved with a rose design. Under one table an elderly yellow cat was licking her stomach, propped up on front paws.

Sitting near a window was a young blonde woman, heavy with child, with a boy of about two sitting at her feet. Two other women in embroidered dresses sat near her, and a plain and plainly-dressed lass lounged on the floor nearby.

When Nevyn bowed to the woman in the chair, Lilli curtsied.

'Your Highness,' Nevyn said. 'May I present to you Lillorigga of the Ram, who comes to us seeking shelter as her menfolk have come to seek your husband's pardon.'

'Of course.' The Princess's voice was pleasant and lively. 'You're welcome in my hall, Lillorigga.'

'I thank you from the bottom of my heart, Your Highness.' Lilli curtsied again, as best she could wearing brigga. 'The Ram is truly my clan now, for they've taken me in when my own would cast me out.'

'Well and good, then.' The Princess glanced at Nevyn. 'You're supposed to tell her my name, you know. I'm trying to get all this courtesy stuff right for once.'

Everyone laughed, except Lilli, who kept herself to a smile.

'My apologies,' Nevyn said, grinning. 'Princess Bellyra, may I present to you Lillorigga of the Ram?'

'You may.' Bellyra returned his smile. 'But shall we call you Lilli?'

'I'd be honoured, Your Highness.'

'And this is Elyssa and Degwa,' the Princess waved at the two women, 'and my son, Casyl, and his nurse, Arda.'

Lilli smiled; everyone smiled in return. She realized that she was beginning to feel safe and wondered if it were a dangerous luxury, especially since Nevyn stood nearby, watching her with his gaze as sharp as any dagger.

'Have you proper clothing?' Bellyra said. 'If not, I've got lots, and you shall have some of mine.'

'Her Highness is too generous,' Lilli said. 'I'm afraid that I had to run for my life, and so I don't have anything but a couple of blankets and these clothes.'

'Very well, then.' The Princess turned to Degwa. 'The chest carved with the dragons has dresses in it that Lilli can have. I need to go speak with my husband. Arda, take Casso to the nursery, will you? Lady Degwa, if you'll take care of seeing Lilli settled?'

'Of course, Your Highness.' Degwa, stout and dark-haired, curtsied to the Princess, then turned to Lilli. Her dark eyes flicked this way and that, appraising her. 'I'll have the pages bring you up bath water.'

'Oh, thank you! There's nothing I'd like more!'

'Good,' Nevyn said briskly. 'I'll leave you to get settled among the women, my lady Lillorigga. But if you will do me the honour of allowing me to attend upon you this afternoon?'

'My thanks, my lord.' Lilli was thinking that she'd rather chat with vipers, but she would owe everything to these people's charity from now on. 'The honour will be mine.'

When Nevyn returned to the great hall, he found Maryn and his new allies sitting at table up on the royal dais. The Prince waved him up to the table with an expansive sweep of one arm.

'Tieryn Peddyc,' Maryn said. 'This is my most trusted councillor, Nevyn.'

'My lord.' Peddyc inclined his head Nevyn's way. 'I'm honoured.'

'And I in return.' Nevyn sat down with a nod at young Anasyn. 'The Princess herself is making your sister welcome, my lord.'

'My thanks,' Anasyn said. 'I'll owe her a debt forever.'

Nevyn's curiosity flared, but Maryn had matters of war on his mind.

'Peddyc's been telling me that he's bringing other allies with him,' Maryn went on. 'A certain Lord Camlyn and his men should arrive shortly, and Gwerbret Daeryc of Glasloc will try to make his escape when the Usurper's men march out.'

'Some of my lords already went over to the true prince,' Peddyc said. 'At least, when I rode their way to muster them, I found them not at home.'

'Daryl and Ganedd, my liege,' Nevyn put in. 'They sought your pardon a good month or so ago.' He turned to Peddyc. 'No doubt they'll be wondering what to say to you, my lord.'

'No doubt.' Peddyc stared down at the table and rubbed the back of his neck with a road-dirty hand. 'I wish I'd gone with them, now. But no man knows what tricks the gods are going to play on him, eh?'

Behind the dais were several doors; pages came through one of them with goblets and a flagon of mead. Since the Prince would wait to discuss grave matters till they were gone, Nevyn took his chance. He caught Peddyc's attention and Anasyn's as well.

'If you'll forgive my curiosity, my lords,' Nevyn said. 'Some great tragedy seems to be weighing upon you.'

'The Councillor has sharp eyes.' Peddyn smiled briefly. 'My wife was a jewel among women, good Nevyn. Lady Merodda of the Boar had her first dismissed from court, then murdered. It took us days to ride down here, and I've been trying to chew over why she'd do such a heinous thing. My foster-daughter tells me that Merodda was prob-ably jealous of my wife's influence over Queen Abrwnna. That's the only thing we could come up with, truly.'

'But the murder's not in doubt?'

'None, my lord,' Anasyn broke in. 'It would gladden my heart to tell you all the-'

'Not now, Sanno,' Peddyc said. 'The Prince has no time to waste on things like this.'

'But I'll gladly listen.' Nevyn nodded Anasyn's way. 'Perhaps we'll have the time later in the day.'

Carrying a cushion under one arm, Councillor Oggyn was approaching the dais. Nevyn felt his usual weariness at the sight of the man, a reaction that went back a hundred years – not of course that Oggyn would remember. In his last incarnation Oggyn had served another king in Cerrmor, Glyn the First, when Nevyn had been part of that court as well. Saddar, Oggyn's name had been then, although Nevyn had had to look it up in the court annals to make sure. Since at that time he was already well over two hundred years old, names had begun to escape his memory in an alarming manner.

'Tieryn Peddyc,' Oggyn said. 'Your men have been quartered, and the chamberlain has arranged a chamber for you and your son.'

'My thanks,' Peddyc said.

Oggyn bowed low to the Prince, then laid down his cushion and seated himself across the table from Nevyn and in a place that was one chair closer to Maryn than Nevyn's stood.

'I have heard, though,' Oggyn went on, 'a most interesting thing. Is it true that your foster-daughter is by blood a daughter of the Boar clan?'

Anasyn went white about the mouth. Peddyc laid a hand on his son's arm and addressed the councillor.

'She was, but she renounced them.' Peddyc glanced Nevyn's way. 'My wife had the fostering of her, and she was the only mother Lilli ever had.'

'Ah.' Oggyn rubbed his hands together. 'My liege the Prince, this is a most fortuitous hostage that the gods have brought us. We can bargain, perhaps, for-'

'Now here!' Anasyn slammed one hand flat on the table.

'Hush!' Peddyc snapped.

The men all turned to look at Maryn, who had been leaning back in his chair and listening.

'Lillorigga is my guest, not a hostage, Councillor Oggyn,' the Prince said. 'I made Lord Anasyn a promise, and keep it I shall.'

'Well, my dearest liege,' Oggyn said, 'never would I suggest that you dishonour yourself by breaking a promise, but-'

'Good.' Maryn flashed him a smile. 'Don't. Lord Anasyn, your sister shall be treated as my sister here.'

'My humble thanks, my prince.' Anasyn could hardly speak. 'We owe her so much.'

'Tieryn Peddyc, no doubt you and your son are weary. Oggyn, summon a page, will you? Have him take the men of the Ram to their new chambers.'

A simmering Oggyn rose and bowed. To make sure the peace got kept, Nevyn did the same. As Peddyc turned to leave, he touched Nevyn's arm.

'My lord?' Peddyc said. 'When will the Prince muster his full army?'

'The whole pack never will come to Cerrmor. The lords along the coast will be riding in with their men on the morrow. Once they've gathered, we'll head north, picking up lords and their warbands as we go. It spreads the cost of feeding everyone around.'

'And a good idea, that. But we'll ride out soon?'

'We will. You must be anxious to avenge your lady.'

'I am, truly.' But Peddyc looked so weary, so dreadfully, impossibly weary, that Nevyn wondered if he were longing not for vengeance but for death.

As the afternoon unrolled, Lilli felt as if she were dancing some complex figure to a tune she'd never heard before. At least in Dun Deverry, as a daughter of the Boar clan, she'd had a place and a rank, neatly defined. Here? She would have only what Princess Bellyra chose to give her. She did, however, have fewer personalities to sort out in Cerrmor than she had in her mother's circle. Since Maryn held most of southern Deverry loyal to him, and thus his vassals' lands lay safely behind the disputed border, there were surprisingly few home-less noblewomen living at court, and of those, only two seemed to be much in the Princess's confidence. Blonde, merry Elyssa was a widow and the daughter of Tieryn Elyc, regent in the dun when Bellyra was a child. Degwa, twice widowed, belonged to the dispossessed Wolf clan, who formerly had held lands that the Boar held now.

Once Lilli had had her bath and put on a pair of her hand-me-down dresses, she returned to the women's hall to find Degwa there alone. They chatted, while they waited for the Princess's return, about Degwa's young sons and daughters, living in fosterage in various safe duns on the coast.

'Someday,' Degwa remarked, 'I hope my children will have our lands back and restore my clan's name. My sons will go to their father's clan, of course, but my daughter knows her duty.'

'Um, I don't think I understand-'

'Of course! My apologies.' Degwa's voice turned cool. 'An outsider wouldn't know. The Wolf lands pass in the female line, you see. It was a ruling of Glyn the First of Cerrmor. My daughter's husband will be the Wolf.'

'How very interesting! And where are your lands, my lady?'

'Along the River Nerr, some miles south of Muir. Our village is named Blaeddbyr.'

'Ah. I've never been there.' Lilli was profoundly relieved – she'd been afraid that close kin of hers held those lands. 'But no doubt the Prince will grant them back to the Wolf when the times comes.'

Degwa smiled – oddly coldly, oddly thinly. Lilli tried to think of some conciliatory remark, but at that moment the Princess herself swept into the women's hall with maidservants behind her.

'The first peaches!' Bellyra announced. 'We can all gorge ourselves.'

A laughing maidservant set a big basket down on the table, and Elyssa pulled up a chair for the Princess. Degwa turned her cold stare away from Lilli and let it warm. Although all the other women, even the servants, dug into the basket, Lilli waited until Elyssa shoved it her direction.

'Do have one, Lilli!' Elyssa said.

'Thank you, I will. I wasn't sure-'

'Oh please!' Bellyra put in. 'Do you think I'd be mingy to an exile?'

'It happens, my lady,' Degwa said. 'Especially, or so I gather, among those around the false king.'

Lilli forced out a smile, then bit into her peach, wonderfully sweet and juicy. Summer comes earlier here, she thought. It seemed fitting, somehow. She reminded herself to tell Bevyan and Sarra this fancy – then remembered, of course, that she would never share a word with them again. She wiped her eyes on her sleeve and found the others watching her.

'Are you all right, Lilli?' Elyssa said.

'My apologies. I was just thinking of my foster-mother. She died just a fortnight past, you see.'

'Oh! That saddens my heart,' Bellyra said. 'No doubt it will take you some while to put your grief aside.'

'Her Highness is so kind.'

'I have my better moments, or so I've been told.' Bellyra smiled briefly, then turned to Degwa. 'I have a message for you. From your own true love.'

'Oh don't, your highness!' Degwa blushed furiously. 'He's such a bore!'

'One of my husband's councillors,' Bellyra explained. 'He thinks to better himself by marrying a noble-born widow.'

'Not Nevyn?' Lilli said.

'Alas, Degwa's not had the luck. Oggyn's his name. Nevyn would make an interesting husband, I should think.' The Princess turned to Degwa. 'But Oggyn most urgently requested you spare him a moment for some news he's had.'

Degwa raised her eyes heavenward. The maidservants giggled, watching her.

'Do go,' Elyssa said, grinning. 'Now I'm curious. Sacrifice yourself in our cause.'

'He said he'd be waiting near the door to the great hall,' Bellyra put in.

'Oh, very well.' Degwa rose with a dramatic sigh. 'I shall do my duty to Her Highness, then. No doubt he'll insist I walk with him a ways to earn my bit of news.'

A long walk, apparently – the women talked for some while before she returned. Bellyra and Elyssa took it upon themselves to tell Lilli the gossip of the dun: who might befriend her, who to keep at a safe distance. At first she merely listened, but a few words at a time she risked joining in to find her comments welcome. She had just begun to feel at ease with Degwa returned, striding into the chamber. With a furious glance Lilli's way, she stood at the Princess's chair.

'And what did Oggyn have to say?' Bellyra said. 'It must have been utterly dishonourable, from the look of you.'

'Not in the least, Your Highness. He told me that our guest was born a daughter of the Boar clan.'

Lilli felt herself turn cold all over. She laid a shaking hand on her throat.

'A Boar!' Degwa was near snarling. 'How can you treat her so well?'

'Oh, for the love of the Holy Moon!' Bellyra snapped back. 'She's had the good sense to desert them, hasn't she?'

'I don't care, Your Highness! She could be a spy and a traitor.' Degwa began pacing back and forth. 'All my life I've heard naught but ill about the Boar clan. Why should we trust this little stranger?'

'Hold your tongue, Decci!' Elyssa snapped. 'You're being wretchedly rude, and you know it.'

Degwa crossed her arms over her chest. The Princess sighed.

'Lillorigga of the Boar,' Bellyra said. 'Are you a traitor?'

'I'm not, Your Highness! Oh, please believe me! How could I be a spy anyway? When the Prince leads his army out, the Regent and his men can count them easier than I can, can't they?'

'Just so. And I can't see you murdering my husband by moonlight one night, either. He's quite a bit bigger than you.'

At this joke Degwa did snarl.

'Please don't,' Lilli said to Degwa. 'I'm not a Boar any more, anyway. I've no kin or clan except for Peddyc and Anasyn and the Rams of Hendyr.'

'I rather thought so.' Bellyra stood by pushing herself up on the chair arms, then heaving herself and the latest heir to her feet. 'Ye gods, I *am* pregnant, aren't I? Degwa, Lilli is no longer a Boar, and thus what you heard about them doesn't really apply, does it?'

'Whatever my princess commands me to believe,' Degwa said. 'I shall believe it.'

'It's not a question of believing in me like a goddess or suchlike. Nevyn's vouched for Lilli, you know.'

'Oh.' Degwa turned scarlet. 'Forgive me.'

The three women looked at Lilli, who sat fumbling for words. Nevyn again, and he'd vouched for her. Why? She could ask him, she knew. If she dared. Elyssa caught her arm.

'You've gone pale. Are you going to faint?'

'I'm not,' Lilli said. 'Everything's just so difficult.'

Degwa stared at the floor.

'It aches my heart,' Lilli said to her, 'that the Boars have brought you and yours the same kind of grief they've brought to me and mine.'

The silence grew. Lilli felt that she could hear her own breathing, ragged in her chest. At last Degwa looked up.

'I'd have peace between us,' Degwa said.

'And so would I.'

When Lilli held out her hand, Degwa took it in a limp clasp, briefly but long enough. Bellyra and Elyssa exchanged an approving nod.

'What I want to know,' the Princess said, 'is why Oggyn took it upon himself to tell you this.'

Degwa frowned, thinking it through.

'I don't know,' she said at last. 'But he thought she'd be better off locked up somewhere, so the King could bargain with her as a hostage.'

For a moment Lilli nearly did faint. She steadied herself, then slipped off her chair to kneel in front of the Princess.

'Please don't send me back.' She had to force out each word from a trembling throat. 'They'd kill me if you did.'

'Of course I won't, and I shan't let Maryn do any such thing, either.' Bellyra reached out one hand. 'Do get up. I hate it when people kneel to me. Come sit down again. Decci, can't you see? Oggyn's got one of his beastly schemes in mind, and he was using you to get at me.'

Degwa blushed scarlet; she tried to speak, then turned and ran out of the room. Lilli rose and flopped into a welcome chair.

'My humble thanks, Your Highness,' Lilli said.

Bellyra dismissed the thanks with a careless wave.

'When it comes to the Wolf clan, Decci never thinks,' Elyssa muttered. 'And that man plays her like a harp, I swear it.'

'He's the bald one with the beard?' Lilli said.

'He is. It always looks to me as if his hair slipped off his head and got caught under his chin.'

The Princess laughed, then smothered a sudden yawn.

'I've really got to lie down and nap,' Bellyra announced. 'I'm ever so tired. My ladies, please do as you wish.'

Both Elyssa and Lilli stood and curtsied, then stayed standing while the Princess and her servants left the hall.

'I have to go speak to the chief cook,' Elyssa said. 'If Nevyn's coming up to talk with you, you can just wait here for him.'

'My thanks.' Lilli curtsied to her as well. 'I shall.'

Nevyn arrived not long after, all good humour, but his smile struck her as dangerous. She considered feigning a headache to get out of this little conversation, but sooner or later, she knew, she would have to face him.

'And a good afternoon to you, Lilli,' Nevyn said.

'And the same to you, my lord. It's very kind of you to spare time for such as me.'

'Indeed?' He raised one bushy eyebrow. 'I was thinking you'd be dreading talking with me.'

Lilli forced a smile.

'Let's sit down. In the window seat, perhaps? After you, my lady.'

They walked together across the wide room. As Lilli passed it, sunlight fell across the silver casket on its little table nearby. It was a lovely thing, about a foot high, and its two sides rose in curves, so that the lid arched up to fit over them and sweep down again to close in front. All over this curve of silver, roses bloomed – engraved, of course, but so cunningly drawn that they seemed almost real. Only half-thinking Lilli reached out and ran her fingers over the pattern.

'Oh!' She pulled her hand back fast and rubbed her fingers. They felt as cold as if she'd clutched an icicle.

'What is it, Lilli?' Nevyn said. 'What's so wrong?'

'Naught.' Yet she could not stop the chill that ran down her back and made her tremble. 'I, uh, it must be the draughts.'

'Nonsense! What did you feel when you touched the casket?' Nevyn was watching her with such honest concern that Lilli could no longer think of him as a possible enemy.

'Somewhat evil,' she said. 'I don't know how to describe it, my lord, but somewhat evil and foul dwells inside that thing. The Princess should throw it into the sea and be rid of it. You must feel it, too. How can you let her keep it in here?'

'The Princess knows about the evil. She's chosen to guard it rather than let it fall into the hands of those who might use it to harm the Prince.'

With a long sigh Lilli sat down on the cushioned window seat. Nevyn sat at the other end and folded his hands across his stomach.

'I think me it's best we be honest with each other,' he said. 'About dweomer.'

Lilli laid a hand at her throat and turned to look out. Directly across, sunny towers rose at the far side of the ward. A few mare's tail clouds hung against the sky, and seabirds wheeled and called.

'I think me that you were born with a great talent for dweomer,' Nevyn said. 'And then someone taught you a few tricks about using it. I've always felt that there must be evil magic in Dun Deverry, but truly, there's none of that about you.'

'I should hope not, my lord. Never did I want to work anyone harm.'

'I can see that. When you were scrying – you must remember the night our paths crossed – when you were scrying, was someone else guiding you? Come now, lass, do tell me. It's important for your welfare, you know. My guess is that someone was riding your will like a horse. If so, it's dangerous and could have done you harm.'

'That's what he – what I was told.'

'He?' Nevyn sounded amused. 'Who's he? Your teacher? Was he the one controlling you?'

Lilli considered lies, but she was well and truly trapped.

'He wasn't,' she said. 'My mother did that.'

'Your mother? By the gods! Lady Merodda?'

'She is that, truly.'

'From what little I know of her, it seems like she's the sort of person who would exploit another's gifts that way. In fact, I've long suspected her of being the one who made the horrible thing,' he pointed at the casket, 'hidden under those roses.'

'It could well be, my lord. She bragged to me once that the Usurper could never win, because mighty dweomers were working against him.'

'The Usurper? But, of course, that's what you all would have called him. Do you think your mother wound the spell herself?'

'I don't. She told me that she'd found a man who could lay snares and traps, ones that the Usurper could never get free of.'

'I see. But she must know some magicks of her own.'

'She knows a lot of dweomer. She learned it from someone who came to her long before I was born. She talked of him now and again, and I think, my lord, that he was your evil man, from what the servants told me. They hated him, blood and bone, but I didn't know him at all. I was in fosterage, and he was my mother's retainer. Wait – I wonder if he were the one who laid those traps and snares?'

'It's a sound enough wager, I'd say. What happened to this man?'

'My uncle slew him before I got back from Bevyan's. It was in the Boar's hall one evening, and he was drunk, my mother said – her sorcerer, not Uncle Burcan – and he insulted my mother's honour somehow. So Burcan drew and killed him on the spot.'

Nevyn swore like one of the riders.

'My apologies,' he said. 'I forgot myself.'

'You look so upset, my lord. I should think you'd be glad he's dead.'

'Indeed? I have no idea of how to unwind that spell.' Nevyn gestured at the casket. 'I'd always hoped to catch the man who worked it and force him, one way or another, to tell me how. He won't be telling me anything now, will he?'

'Oh. Well, truly.'

'What puzzles me is the way you could sense the evil. I supervised the sealing of that casket. When we had done so, I couldn't sense dweomer upon it, not the slightest trace. And yet you touch it, just lay a finger upon it, and immediately you know there's somewhat wrong.'

'I don't know how I did it, though. I'd tell you if I did.'

'Oh, I believe you. Well, if your mother has somewhat to do with working the spell, maybe we can worm it out of her – if we ever see her again.' For a long moment Nevyn thought something through. 'Well, there's naught I can do about that now,' he said at last. 'So, then

– later your mother found herself another man who knew secret things?'

Here was the crux. Lilli refused to betray Brour, who'd been so good to her in his way. Yet, as she thought of Brour, she felt an omen growing in her throat, as if she'd swallowed something so hot that she must spit it out or choke to death.

'He's dead, anyway,' she said aloud. 'Brour. The one who taught me.' She felt tears gather and spill. 'He said he'd studied with you once.'

Nevyn made an odd sound – a grunt of pain.

'My mother must have had him caught and killed,' Lilli went on. 'He was trying to escape Dun Deverry.'

'Poor little Brour,' Nevyn said. 'Poor little talented dolt! It aches my heart to hear it, for all that he stole from me and ran.'

'That was your book? I mean-'

'I'll wager it was, if he had a book of dweomer secrets. A big thing, bound in leather, and full of Greggyn lore?'

'That's the one, truly. Just from things he said, I guessed he'd done somewhat shameful here.'

'I've never known a man who lusted after a lass as badly as Brour lusted after that book. So one night he took it, for all the good it did him.' Nevyn shook his head. 'Ah well, at least I know the end of his tale.'

Lilli wiped her eyes on her sleeve. I should be getting used to losing people, she thought.

'How much did Brour teach you?' Nevyn said.

'Not much. We were just starting. I have this – this knack for seeing omens. Not scrying things out, just seeing omens. I never knew what they meant, because my mother would interpret them, you see, but never in front of me.'

Nevyn blinked several times, rapidly.

'Try telling me a bit more about this,' he said. 'How do you see omens?'

'Well, sometimes they just come to me as words, and I'd blurt them out just like now, when I knew Brour was dead. So I'd blurt out somewhat about the war, and my mother would notice, and she'd ask me for details and suchlike. And then she and Brour made up a basin of black ink. I'd look in it and see things. It felt like I was dreaming, but I could hear my mother's voice when she asked me questions.'

'So, they were using you like a line of hooks to troll for fish, eh?

Very dangerous, that, very very dangerous.'

'I sometimes feared it would drive me mad.'

'That, too, but I was wondering: do you ever have trouble catching your breath?'

'Often, my lord.' Lilli paused, utterly startled. 'What does that have to do with seeing omens?'

'Rather a lot, actually, but it would take far more time than we have now to explain. Curse this war! It's always getting in the way.' Nevyn paused, thinking. 'In a few days I'll be riding north with the Prince. Until then I'll try to spare you what moments I can, but they won't be many. Lilli, when the summer's fighting is over, I'll want to talk about these matters with you. You've got a strange gift, all right, and you've got to learn to control it. If you don't, it could kill you.'

Lilli tried to speak, but she felt herself gaping like a half-wit.

'There, there,' Nevyn said. 'You're not in danger at the moment. You do look exhausted, though. I suggest you lie down and rest before dinner.'

'I will, my lord.' She found her voice at last. 'You've given me much to think on.'

For courtesy's sake she walked him to the door. When Nevyn opened it, Degwa nearly fell into the room. She started to speak, then blushed, running a nervous hand through her hair.

'My apologies,' Degwa stammered. 'I was just reaching for the door, and then it opened, and I'm afraid I was ever so startled.'

'The apologies are mine, then,' Nevyn said.

Degwa ran across the women's hall and hurried through the doorway that led to the sleeping quarters for the serving women and servants. Nevyn raised one bushy eyebrow at her retreat, then bowed to Lilli.

'We'll talk more,' he said. 'When it's private.'

After he left, Lilli stood in the doorway and listened to her heart pound. How much had Degwa heard of their strange talk, she wondered, and would she be running to Oggyn with it?

As Nevyn clattered down the staircase from the women's hall, he was thinking about Brour. Here he'd tried to train the lad right, and what did he do? Not just steal from his master, but endanger the very life of an innocent like Lilli! It's just as well he's dead, Nevyn thought. For his sake. If I'd got hold of him . . .

The long shadows of late afternoon were falling across the ward.

Servants hurried back and forth, carrying firewood and water to the cookhouse. At the gates guards shouted a greeting, and in a clatter of hooves the silver daggers rode in with their captain, Caradoc, at their head, and his second in command, Owaen, beside him. Caradoc's hair had gone mostly grey and his moustaches completely so, but his narrow dark eyes were as shrewd as ever.

'Nevyn!' Caradoc called out. 'A moment of your time, if you please?'

He dismounted; then oddly enough, like a servant he took the bridle of Owaen's black gelding, which was snorting and tossing its head. Owaen dismounted with a great deal of care, which he needed, since he was holding his left hand up and out from his body. His face was almost as pale as his ash-blond hair, but his ice-blue eyes showed no feeling at all. He looked briefly at Nevyn, then away.

'What's this?' Nevyn said. 'An accident?'

'Just that, my lord,' Caradoc said. 'And I've seen stupider ones but not very often.'

Owaen shot his captain a murderous glance. The little finger on his left hand stuck out at an impossible angle, and there was a blood-spotted bruise forming in the palm of his left hand.

'Looks very bad,' Nevyn said. 'Hold your paw out a little more, lad, so I can see it better.'

Behind them the rest of the men were dismounting; most were leading their horses away, but Branoic threw his reins to a friend and strolled over. He was enormous, Branoic, the tallest man in the silver daggers, broad-shouldered and a little fleshy at the moment after a winter of eating at the King's bounty.

'It's broken, isn't it?' Branoic said.

'You hold your leprous tongue,' Owaen said, 'or I'll cut off your black and crusted balls. Well, if you've got two, which I doubt.'

Branoic laughed, then set his hands on his hips and watched Nevyn study Owaen's injury.

'Broken it is,' Nevyn said. 'And badly so. How did it happen?'

Owaen glared at the cobbles as if he hoped to shatter them by sheer malice.

'His horse got a stone in its hoof,' Branoic said, grinning. 'And so he picked the hoof up with his left hand, but he didn't hold it very firmly, and so the horse took exception to the liberty he'd taken with its person.'

'I thought Owaen was going to slit the poor beast's throat,' Caradoc put in. 'But I stopped him. It's a good horse, except for its delicate temperament.'

'Give it to me,' Branoic said. 'I can handle it.'

Owaen turned on him like a striking snake, but in his rage he forgot his injury. All at once sweat beaded his face; he swore under his breath. Caradoc grabbed him by the elbow and steadied him.

'Branoic, that's enough!' Caradoc snarled. 'Get out of here and right now.'

'Captain.' Branoic ducked his head Caradoc's way and turned on his heel.

Nevyn watched him striding off across the ward to catch up with his fellows. Although he should have been used to it by then, at moments Nevyn still found himself amazed that the soul inhabiting that body had been for many incarnations a woman, and one he had loved. With a shake of his head he turned back to the immediate problem.

'Small injuries often hurt the worst,' Nevyn said to Owaen. 'The hand's not gone dead on you, at least. You need to get a chirurgeon to set it.'

Owaen let fly with a string of curses, ending with a sensible question.

'How long will it take to heal?'

'Weeks, and you won't be able to hold a shield, you know, with it bound up against the other fingers. You'll have to stay out of the fighting.'

'What? I can't do that.'

'Will you fight without a shield, then?'

Owaen started to answer, then merely glared at the offending finger.

'What if I have the chirurgeon just cut it off?' Owaen said at last. 'A clean cut should heal quicker than a break.'

'True, but ye gods! They don't grow back, you know.'

'I don't give a pile of horseshit about that. I can steady a shield with four fingers well enough. I want this god-cursed thing healed and done with before we reach the Holy City.'

'It's your choice.' Nevyn rolled his eyes heavenward. 'Tell Caudyr that I said he should let you have your way.'

Some while later, as he was sitting on the dais in the great hall with the Prince, Nevyn saw Owaen and Caradoc walking in. Sure enough,

Owaen's hand was bound with a linen bandage instead of splints. Maryn followed his gaze.

'Ah, that reminds me,' Maryn said. 'I wanted to ask you somewhat. It's about Caradoc. You know how much I value his advice. He's seen fighting in three different kingdoms, after all.'

'And he's been seeing it for years,' Nevyn said. 'Experience is always valuable.'

'Just so, but I worry. I'd hate to see him killed, but he insists on leading his men into battle.'

'Just so.' Nevyn considered for a moment. 'Have you talked to Caradoc about this?'

'I hinted, but he turned my words away. He's a proud man and a touchy one. I wanted your advice first.'

'Then I'll have a word with him.'

Down in the great hall, Caradoc was pulling out a bench and helping Owaen sit at one of the tables reserved for the silver daggers. The younger man's face glistened with sweat on pale skin. No doubt his hand hurt worse than he'd ever imagined it could.

'Owaen should be lying down,' Nevyn remarked. 'If my liege will excuse me, I'll tend to it.'

'Of course.'

By the time Nevyn reached them, Owaen was sipping ale from a tankard. He kept his left hand, a club of white linen, in his lap. Caradoc stood, leaning against the table, and watched him.

'I see you had the finger removed,' Nevyn said to Owaen.

'I did, my lord.' Owaen's voice sounded very small, like a child's. 'It went fast.'

'Indeed? You should be lying down, and don't argue with me. It's not a sign of weakness. I don't want you bleeding to death. The Prince needs you, and you've got to keep that wounded hand motionless.'

Owaen gulped ale.

'He's right,' Caradoc snapped. 'Will it take a direct order to make you do what Nevyn says?'

'It will.'

'Then I order you to go to the barracks and lie down.' Caradoc glanced around the hall. 'There's Maddyn and red-haired Trevyr. I'm now ordering you to let them help you.'

'As the captain commands, then.'

Caradoc made a snorting sound, then waved Maddyn and the other silver dagger over.

'Why do you always call him red-haired Trevyr?' Nevyn said.

'Because there used to be a black-haired Trevyr in the troop as well. He's been dead these four years, but somehow the name stuck, like.'

Nevyn gave Maddyn a few instructions on caring for Owaen and sent them off. Both he and Caradoc stood watching them leave the hall; Owaen was weaving a little but managing to walk on his own even though Trevyr Coch kept close to him.

'Stubborn little bastard,' Caradoc remarked.

'Well, some men show themselves less mercy than they'd show an enemy.'

'Owaen never shows anyone mercy. A consistent sort of lad.'

'He's always been that, truly.' Nevyn was thinking of the other lifetimes in which he'd known this soul. 'I suspect he'll get his wish, though, and the thing will be healed fairly well by the time he sees fighting.'

'Good, because there won't be any keeping him out of it. He'd feel shamed.'

'Well, some men are like that, truly. They won't stay out of a battle unless they're nearly dead already, and all for fear of what other men will think of them.'

'True enough, but you know, all a silver dagger's got in life is the fighting. Look at Maddyn, now. I told him to give it up, and he did, but that's because he's a bard. He has somewhat to live for, like, besides glory and honour. The rest of us don't.'

All at once it occurred to Nevyn that the captain remembered the Prince's hints perfectly well. Caradoc was watching him tight-lipped, as if squelching a smile.

'I'd say you have a lot to live for,' Nevyn said. 'The Prince's favour, for one thing.'

'Huh! And how can a man like me earn favour if he's not fighting?'

'Giving wise counsel, for one thing. And offering a different voice than Oggyn's for another.'

'Ah. Now that I hadn't thought of.' Caradoc spat reflectively into the straw on the floor. 'Can't stand the man. No more can you, I'd say.'

'You'd be right. He does understand questions of supply. I'll give Oggyn that. For some years he was the leader of the spearmen that Cerrmor owes the gwerbret, you see, and arming and feeding them was the hardest part of the job. So he knows how to provision an army and organize such things. But matters of strategy and suchlike? You could do the Prince a great service by joining his retinue.'

For a moment Caradoc was tempted. Nevyn could see it in the distant way he looked up at the dais, where the Prince sat, pretending to ignore both the captain and Nevyn. But all at once Caradoc shook his head.

'I couldn't live with myself,' he said. 'Sending my men into battle while I stayed safely behind.'

'Ah. Do you hold me a shamed man, then, for not fighting?'

'What? Of course I don't!'

'Why not?'

'Well, my lord, you're a scholar. You've got your medicines, you've got your dweomer lore and suchlike – how could the Prince risk losing you? Me – all I've ever known is battle.'

'And that knowledge is just as valuable in its own way. Here, how long have you been riding to war?'

'Most of my life. I was born with the turning of the hundred, my lord. My mother told me that, she did, and I've remembered it. I was born in the year the priests call 800, and so what does that make me now? Nearly half a hundred years.'

'Well, then, at your age there's no shame in retiring from the field.'

A blunder – Nevyn saw it instantly, but he couldn't call it back. Caradoc bristled.

'I'm not as old as all that!' the captain snapped. 'I can still swing a sword.'

'I never meant to imply otherwise. It's just that-'

'Just what? Are you trying to tell me I'm too blasted old to ride to war?'

'Naught of the sort! I was just trying to point out that your experience is long enough to be valuable, that's all.'

Caradoc set his hands on his hips and scowled.

'Ah well,' Nevyn said. 'Keep it in mind, will you, Captain? No doubt the Prince would like to speak with you about this later.'

'You can tell him my answer. I'm not decrepit yet, and cursed if I'll lead my men from behind.'

Nevyn left the matter there. Much later, when he had a chance to think about the conversation, the significance of Caradoc's birth date struck him. In those days, long before the priests began displaying the calendars in the temples for everyone to see, the dating of years meant nothing to most people. Only the oddity of his birth year's date had made Caradoc remember it at all, but to Nevyn it revealed an interesting secret. Glyn had died in 797 only to be reborn as Caradoc a scant three years later, far faster than usual. If Glyn had been so eager to return to his unfinished war, no wonder that he was refusing to play an onlooker's part now.

At dinner that evening, Lilli sat with Anasyn and Peddyc. In her current stage of pregnancy the Princess preferred to eat in her own hall, and generally her women stayed with her. Lilli came down because Anasyn wanted to hear in detail how she was being treated. When she told him that she had her own little chamber and two pair of nearly-new dresses from Bellyra herself, he seemed satisfied.

'But if you feel spurned, you come to me,' Peddyc put in. 'I'll not have my foster-daughter treated like a servant or suchlike. It would be an insult to our clan if naught else.'

'My thanks,' Lilli said. 'But so far the Princess has been wonderful to me.'

'Well, I've never known anyone as generous as our prince,' Peddyc said. 'It gladdens my heart that his wife's his match.'

At the end of the meal, a page came from the Prince to invite Anasyn and Peddyc to drink with him. Lilli decided to return to the women's hall rather than stay on display, as it were, among the men, some of whom were eyeing her with undisguised interest. She was particularly aware of a tall, beefy, blond lad, wearing the shirt and dagger of the Prince's guard. He'd watched her all through the meal, and now, when she rose to go, he got up with an exaggerated air of indifference and walked her way. When they met by this carefully arranged accident, he bowed to her with a small smile.

Lilli pretended not to notice and hurried past. Near the door she saw Elyssa, talking with a short man – exceptionally short, actually – with a grey beard and a mop of grey hair to match it. When Lilli joined them, the man gave her a sour glance, then ignored her.

'The Princess is doing well, Otho,' Elyssa was saying. 'The stairs tire her, is all.'

'Understandable, that. Well, you tell her to take care of herself.'

'I certainly will. Don't let it trouble your heart.' She glanced at Lilli. 'Lilli, this is Otho the silversmith.'

'How do you do?' Lilli said.

Otho looked at her, twitched his lips in what seemed to be a smile, then turned and stamped off.

'Manners our Otho lacks,' Elyssa said. 'But he's devoted to Princess

Bellyra. He made that lovely silver casket, the one with the roses graved upon it, for a wedding gift, and he makes her little trinkets now and again as well.'

If Otho had made the casket, then did he know about its evil secret? Lilli had no intention of asking outright, but as if thinking about dweomer might draw dweomer, Nevyn came strolling up to join the two women.

'Good evening,' he said. 'I was wondering if Lady Lillorigga might spare me a few moments for a little walk? The evening air is quite pleasant.'

Around back of the main broch complex Dun Cerrmor sported a large open garden as well as the secret one at its heart. A servant had hung candle lanterns here and there from the trees, and overhead a three-quarters moon was rising to match them. Since Lilli had never seen a formal flower garden before, she was enchanted. A long sweep of rose bushes were just coming into bloom, while in raised beds flowering herbs added their scent to the night air. Paths led among the glowing trees into mysterious darkness. From somewhere at the garden's heart came the sound of water, trickling over rock.

'This is lovely!' she said. 'What is it used for?'

'Naught. It's here to enjoy, and that's all.'

'I've never heard of such a thing. How wonderful!'

They walked down a gravelled path toward the sound of the water.

'I see you've met Otho,' Nevyn said. 'I suppose he was rude to you. He's rude to everyone, so please don't let it upset you.'

'So Lady Elyssa told me. It's odd, but he reminds me so much of Brour. Not that Brour was ever rude, I mean, and he was a young man to Otho's old. But there's somewhat about their faces that made me wonder if they were kin.'

'Distantly, they are. You have sharp eyes.'

'I've needed them.'

'No doubt. Otho made the casket that-'

'So Elyssa told me. Does he know about, well, about that *thing* inside?'

'He does.' Nevyn glanced around. 'Let's not discuss that matter, Lilli, until we can be sure no one will overhear.'

'Of course, my lord. My apologies.'

'I wanted to talk about you, anyway. I wasn't making some idle threat when I said that misusing dweomer could bring you harm. It's a question of the balance of the humours, you see. Using dweomer draws upon the fifth element, the aethyr, and its humours. Working magic drains, as it were, the aethyr from your body, and if you're not properly trained to restore it, you can become quite ill.'

'Aethyr? So that's what that word means! May I ask you about somewhat? A while back Brour and I worked a ritual, and we invoked this spirit. He called Brour a child of earth, but he said I was a child of aethyr. What does that mean?'

'Brour did what? Have you been trained to work invocations?'

'That was the first one, but we practised it a lot.'

Nevyn growled under his breath.

'Well, I'm so very glad he at least let you practise,' Nevyn said. 'We obviously have a great many things to discuss. Lilli, for your sake, I need to know everything you were taught and what Brour and your mother made you do.'

Lilli hesitated, wondering how much she should trust him, and he allowed her silence as they walked along. They reached a clearing among the trees. In the centre of the open ground stood a basin of cloudy white stone, touched with gold by the dim lantern-light. Water welled up inside it and overflowed in a graceful veil all round. Nevyn paused and dipped his hand into the water, then drew it out with a scatter of drops.

'There are four elements,' Nevyn said, 'fire, air, water, and earth. The aethyr is the fifth, their root and their unity, some say. Humans, people like you and me, partake of the nature of aethyr. People like Brour and Otho partake of the nature of earth. Far off to the west of Deverry there are others who partake of the nature of air, but I know not about water and fire.'

'People like them? They're different, somehow?'

'Somehow. I don't pretend to understand all of these things.' Nevyn suddenly smiled. 'Yet.'

Lilli laughed and looked into the heart of the fountain. As it rose up, the water seemed to form a crystal sphere that never changed form even as the individual drops passed through it. The crystal sphere glittered, then swelled, trapping her gaze. All at once she felt herself swooping through air and diving down toward the water.

'Stop it!' Nevyn grabbed her arm. 'Come back, Lilli! Stay here.'

Lilli staggered in sudden weakness. Nevyn hooked her arm through his and let her lean against him.

'So that's how you slip into trance, is it?' he said. 'That easily?'

'Is it easily? I wouldn't know.'

'You have an alarming ease when it comes to falling into a trance. I'll give you my solemn word on that.'

'Very well. I do have much to learn, truly.'

'Just so, but I'll wager you're very tired now.'

'I am. Looking into the black ink used to wear me out.'

'No doubt. Let's go back to the broch. You need to rest. But do you understand now why we absolutely have to discuss these things?'

'I begin to.'

'Good. We'll talk more on the morrow.'

High up in the broch, Lilli had been given a tiny sliver of a chamber, but the narrow bed was comfortable enough, and the view from her little window opened out wide. By standing on the wooden chest at the foot of the bed, she could see over the walls of the dun down to the town, which sloped gently away to a vast stretch of water, silver under the stars at the edge of the view. For a moment she wondered what river it might be; then she realized that she was seeing the ocean that stretched all the way to the edge of the world. She stood for a long time and gawked, imagining the distances, until exhaustion reminded her to sleep.

Once she woke in the morning, she returned to her perch. In the sunlight the ocean looked even larger and as wrinkled as a crone's neck. Those must be waves, she thought. I've heard about those. She was still staring at the ocean when a servant came to fetch her to the women's hall.

'There's ever so much work to do, my lady,' the girl said. 'The Prince has chosen a new device, and he wants new banners made, to take with the army, like, and they're leaving ever so soon.'

'It's a pity he didn't choose it months ago, then.'

'The Princess told him that, she did, right in front of everybody, too. He just laughed.'

In the women's hall a big table stood in the sunlight from the windows, and all the little ones had been shoved back against the wall. On the table lay fine red cloth, stretched out tight with weights to hold it down. Lilli had never seen such a beautiful red on cloth, a fine scarlet like roses. While the Princess supervised, a stout women with pale grey hair was marking out some kind of pattern with a chunk of chalk.

'Make the mouth bigger, Tidda,' Bellyra was saying. 'It should look fierce.'

'Just so, your highness.'

'And the tail should be lashing about, too.'

'Just so, Your Highness.'

Elyssa came up beside Lilli and greeted her with a smile.

'There's bread and fruit over there,' Elyssa murmured. 'If you want porridge, by all means go to the great hall.'

'My thanks, but bread will be fine for me. These are the devices for Prince's new banners, I take it?'

'They are. He's chosen a red wyvern.'

Lilli felt a dagger of cold run down her spine and back up it again.

'What's so wrong?' Elyssa said, still quietly.

'Naught. I think it's a splendid omen for him, that's all. He'll conquer in this sign.'

Elyssa was staring at her in concern, and one of the servant girls turned to look as well.

'I'd best get somewhat to eat,' Lilli said brightly. 'If you'll excuse me?'

Elyssa let the matter drop, much to Lilli's relief. Yet all morning, as the women sewed the cut-out wyvern to a heavy linen backing, Lilli could feel Elyssa watching her, just every now and then.

'A red wyvern, is it?' Branoic said. 'Now there's a grand idea!'

'Why?' Maddyn said. 'Have you been talking with Nevyn about it?'

'I've not.' Branoic cursed himself for blurting once again. 'Uh, er, it's just such a fierce beast, you know? And a poke in the eye for the false king, taking his wyvern.'

'That's true enough.'

Late in the afternoon the two silver daggers were sitting in the great hall. Down at the other end of their table a group of the lads were dicing for coppers to pass the time until dinner. With nothing particular to occupy him, Branoic had let his mind wander, and as it usually did in this situation, it had played a trick on him. Sometimes he saw things, mostly small creatures who skittered at the edge of his vision or appeared suddenly in a fire. Sometimes he heard things, mostly voices warning him of a future event. More often than not, when he heard one of these omens, it came true, and he knew in his heart that in the sign of the red wyvern, Prince Maryn would conquer – not that he'd be telling Maddo about his unwilling divinations. The bard's good favour meant too much to him for that.

'Quiet in the great hall today,' Branoic said instead. 'Where's Owaen and the captain?'

'I don't know about Caradoc, but Owaen's still in the barracks,' Maddyn said. 'The chirurgeons ordered him to stay in bed again today.'

'It's always pleasant to have Owaen elsewhere.'

'Oh ye gods! Aren't you two ever going to lay that feud aside? How many years has it been since-'

'I don't care! The little bastard shamed me and took my blazon, and he's ragged on me ever since besides. One of these days he'll go too far, and I'll wipe the cobbles clean with his ugly face.'

Maddyn made a growling sort of noise. Branoic sipped his ale and paid strict attention to the dice game. Soon they'd ride out, he reminded himself, and be free of the stinking boredom of a safe dun in winter.

'Speaking of Nevyn,' Maddyn said suddenly, 'there he is. I thought he was in council with the Prince.'

Branoic looked up to see Nevyn walking down the staircase with Lady Lillorigga of the Ram. At the sight of her he felt himself grinning. She was such a pretty lass with that boyish cut to her hair, and yet oddly frail, as if she needed a good man to stand between her and her troubles, that she'd caught his attention immediately. When he realized that she and Nevyn would walk right by, he swung himself free of the bench and stood up.

'Good day, my lord,' Branoic said, bowing. 'And a good day to you, my lady.'

Lilli smiled with a tremble of good humour on her soft, full lips, then looked down at the floor.

'And to you, lad,' Nevyn said, somewhat surprised. 'Maddo, how's Owaen?'

'Resting,' Maddyn said. 'But the chirurgeon says the wound's clean and on its way to healing.'

When Branoic risked a smile at the lady, she glanced up and seemed to be about to speak, but then Nevyn caught her arm and led her away. Branoic scowled after him.

'Well, well, well,' Maddyn said. 'Look who's nocking his arrow after some high-born game.'

'Oh hold your cursed tongue! There's naught wrong in being courteous, is there?' Branoic sat back down. 'The lady's suffered a great deal lately. She needs to see a friendly face now and again.'

'Indeed?'

'Indeed. Though I'll admit that she's a well-favoured lass. I wouldn't mind making her acquaintance, like.'

'And what would a noble-born woman want with the likes of you?'

'Well, she's an exile, isn't she? With no land or dowry to her name. After the fighting's over, a man of the Prince's Own might look pretty good to her.'

When Maddyn rolled his eyes skyward, Branoic threw a fake punch his way.

'Mock all you want,' Branoic said, grinning. 'But I'll make you a wager. Once the fighting's over, and we're all back here for the winter, I'll bet I can gain the Lady Lillorigga's favour. By midwinter, say.'

'You're on!' Maddyn said. 'One silver piece for me against your ten.'

'So! You're think I'm that far behind in the field, do you? Well, I've always wanted to be rich. One to ten it is!'

By working until their fingertips were sore from the needles, and by recruiting every lass of every rank in the dun to help, Bellyra and her women managed to finish four big banners and six pennants in three days. Since the red cloth had come all the way from Bardek and cost as much as two warhorses, they used every scrap of it. Some of the piece-work red wyverns were lumpy about the edges, and others had been shamelessly tacked down across their middles to keep them from bulging away from the backing, but as the Princess herself remarked, they'd be filthy soon enough anyway, and no one would notice the stitching.

'We'll have all summer to do a proper set,' Bellyra said. 'But I'm not going to start them right away. We've all done enough sewing for now.'

The women cheered her.

During this non-stop needlework, Lilli had been able to talk with Nevyn mostly in the evenings, when the light turned bad. They would stroll in the garden among the roses until the night chill drove them inside, where of course they could say nothing openly about dweomer. Even so, she'd learned enough about the meaning of her gift for seeing omens to understand his concern at the way that gift had been used.

'I won't say it would have killed you though it might have,' Nevyn remarked during that last evening's talk. 'But you would have found it more and more difficult to clear your mind after each working and return to ordinary consciousness. Tell me, have you ever had a dream so vivid that when you woke, you weren't sure if you were still dreaming or not?'

'I have, truly,' Lilli said, 'though not very often.'

'Can you imagine what it would be like to live that way? You'd never be sure if you woke or were entranced, or even if you were asleep and dreaming. Your mind would drift from omens to dream to ordinary life and back again without any barriers between them.'

'That's terrifying.' Lilli laid a cold hand on her throat.

'Good. I meant it as a warning.'

'Well, it worked. My lord Nevyn, I never wanted dweomer gifts, and now you're telling me they're dangerous! Isn't there some way you can just make them go away? I never want to use them again, I truly don't. I wish these wretched omens would just leave me alone!'

'It aches my heart, but I'm afraid there's naught I can do. A lot of people are born with odd talents, but they never use them, and eventually the gifts shrivel up and fall away, like an apple left on the tree too long. But you've already started using your gift, and studying dweomer too. You've set forces in motion, and there's no turning back now.'

'But it wasn't me! It was Brour and my mother.'

'So it was, and I'll tell you, I'm furious about it. The dweomer must be chosen freely, just because there's no turning back, and here they dragged you along the road without even telling you where you were going. That was a grave and ugly wrong they did you.'

Lilli risked a glance into the fountain. The water seemed ordinary water, but she looked away before a vision could trap her again. Around them the trees suddenly rustled; she started, then calmed herself. It was only a breeze, tinged with the sea, picking up as the evening turned cool.

'In a way I did choose,' Lilli said. 'I asked Brour to show me things. I wanted to know what the omens I was seeing meant, and how it all worked.'

'Ah, but Brour caught your interest with his hints and suchlike, and your mother of course had been exploiting your gifts for some while.'

'Perhaps so. It just makes me feel so helpless.'

'No doubt. I'm sorry, child, but at least you're free of them now. While I'm gone, please busy yourself with the daily life of the dun. I'll wager you find yourself tempted, when days pass without news, to try to scry us out. Don't! You need to let yourself build up strength.'

'Very well, my lord. I can't really scry anyway.'

'Ah. Well, this winter I'll teach you.' Nevyn hesitated, then suddenly frowned down at the ground beside her feet. 'Tell me somewhat, Lilli. When you were a child, did your foster-mother ever tell you stories about the Wildfolk?'

'Oh, of course. I loved them, too, the thought of all those little tiny people everywhere! I used to wish and wish that they were real.'

'Most children do, truly.' Nevyn smiled, but his eyes were narrow with some puzzlement. 'Well, I've got to pack my campaign chest and so on, and I know your foster-father wants a word with you. If we don't have a chance to speak again, fare you well, Lilli.'

'My thanks, my lord, and may you fare well, too.'

Lilli went to the great hall to look for Peddyc in a hall mobbed by the muster. The Prince's personal guard, the sworn warbands of Cerrmor itself, the soldiers who rode for Maryn's allies along the sea-coast – they all packed the huge room. Their talk and laughter mingled to such an incomprehensible roar that Lilli's ears buzzed and ached from it. Finally she found her foster-father, standing in the curve of a wall and talking with a lord she didn't recognize. At the sight of her Peddyc broke off the conversation and came to meet her. Together they walked out into the blessed silence of the ward. Above the gleaming towers of Dun Cerrmor, the rising moon turned cloud tendrils silver.

'Well,' Peddyc said, smiling. 'I hear our banners are done.'

'They are at that. May they bring you good luck.'

'I think our prince's Wyrd will bring us all the luck we'll need. Lilli, it's the regret of my life that I didn't go over earlier, when I first had the chance.'

'But none of us knew.'

'Just so, and it's too late to argue with the gods about our Wyrd. I've somewhat to say, so listen carefully. I've talked with Anasyn, too. It's time he married, but I want you to know that you'll always have a place in Hendyr. I'm hoping to get you a better settlement than that. Once the summer's fighting is over, one of us will see about making you a good marriage among our new allies.'

'Oh, Father, my thanks!'

'It looks like you'll be well taken care of here for the summer. You might listen to the gossip, see who's looking for a wife among the Prince's allies, that sort of thing.'

'I will. It's so good of you to think of me now.'

'And wouldn't our Bevva have wanted to see you settled?' Peddyc looked away, his dark eyes clouded ·with tears. 'The Prince has promised me we'll try to reclaim Hendyr this summer. If we do, then we'll go back there for the winter.'

Lilli hesitated, thinking of Nevyn. How could she study her dweomer if she went to Hendyr? Yet at the moment she wanted nothing more than to return to the place she'd always considered home, the one place where she'd ever felt safe, even though now it doubtless lay in the hands of enemies.

'I'll pray you can take the dun,' Lilli said. 'I – oh, what's this?'

A young page was trotting purposefully toward them.

'Tieryn Peddyc?' the boy said. 'One of your vassals is at our gates. Lord Cam-something and he said you'd go surety for him if we'd open up.'

'I will indeed, lad.' Peddyc gave Lilli's arm a quick pat. 'I'd best go greet him. As for you, foster-daughter of mine, take good care of yourself this summer, will you?'

'I will, Father, and my thanks.'

Lilli watched them hurrying across the ward. She felt sick with fear, wondering if he'd live to summon her to Hendyr in the autumn. She could perhaps find some omen – Nevyn's warning came back to her like a slap across the face.

'Ye gods,' she said aloud. 'They've not even left yet and already I'm tempted!'

With a shake of her head she strode back into the broch, where the sheer press of humanity made even thinking about dweomer impossible.

'And tomorrow we ride out for the summer's fighting,' Branoic said. 'You can call me daft for it, Maddo, but this is the night every year when I find myself remembering Aethan.'

'Oh, I do the same,' Maddyn said. 'You know, back when I first knew Aethan, years ago when he rode for the Boar and I was just a rider in an ally's warband, we'd not see each other all winter, of course. We'd always meet in Cantrae, when the Boar mustered his lords to lead them down to Dun Deverry. I suppose that's why I'm remembering him now.'

'Most like. Ah horseshit, we'll all die soon enough. But I wish he'd lived to see Prince Maryn come into his own.'

Maddyn sighed and raised his tankard.

'To our dead,' he called out.

At their long tables, the other silver daggers returned the toast.

They had honoured places, these days, right at the front of the hall.
Up on the dais itself, Caradoc was sitting at the foot of the Prince's
table, dining with the great lords, who had, over the years, come to
accept his presence there as a whim of the Prince's though not as the
captain's right. Tieryn Gauryc was the worst; he never spoke to
Caradoc directly if he could get a servant to relay his message, as if
his very words might be dirtied by the captain's hearing of them.
Maddyn watched him for a moment, a heavy-set lord, neither old nor
young, who wore his dark hair cropped off so close to his skull that it
stuck out at assorted ungainly angles.

'What's old Gauryc up to?' Branoic whispered.

'Naught that I can see. The man just annoys me, is all.'

All smiles and bobs of a subservient head, the tieryn was chatting
with Prince Maryn, while Councillor Oggyn looked on.

'Ah well,' Branoic said. 'He can swing a sword well enough.'

'True spoken, and that's all that counts.'

Yet later, oddly enough, Maddyn ended up having a word with
Tieryn Gauryc. He had just left the great hall to head back to barracks
when he heard an arrogant voice calling after him.

'Silver dagger, hold a moment! I want a word with you.'

Maddyn paused in a spill of light from the hall and let Gauryc
catch up with him. The lord was jingling coins in one hand, as if to
make sure Maddyn knew he held some.

'It's about these Rams,' Gauryc said. 'I understand that the lass
with them was born into the Boar clan.'

'She was, your grace,' Maddyn said.

'Our prince has a great heart for mercy,' Gauryc went on. 'Some of
us were born with colder natures. You're part of the Prince's guard,
and you hear what's to be heard, I'll wager. If you ever hear anything
suspicious about this tieryn and his son, there's coin in it for you if
you pass the word along to me or Councillor Oggyn.'

Gauryc held out his hand, the one with the coins. Maddyn shoved
his hands into his pockets.

'May I ask why, Your Grace?'

Gauryc nearly dropped his bribe into thin air, then caught himself
and the coins and stepped back.

'The Rams were very much in the Boar's favour. That's all.'

'Your Grace, you can rest assured that if I see Peddyc or anyone
else do anything that might be the least harmful to the Prince, I'll go
straight to him with the news.'

Gauryc froze for the briefest of moments, then forced out a thin smile.

'Of course, silver dagger. Of course.'

Maddyn bowed, then turned on his heel and strode away. At a good distance he risked a glance back to find Gauryc still staring after him. Ah by the hells! Maddyn thought. That's all I need – a well-born enemy! He decided that if Peddyc proved a decent lord, then he'd have a word with him and his son and warn them about Gauryc and his ilk. As a bard, after all, he could speak freely, whether the great lords liked it or not.

For five days, Prince Maryn's army crawled its safe if slow way north through the lands of the Prince's truly loyal vassals, the ones who'd backed him from the beginning. Once they reached the demesnes of those whose loyalties depended on the fortunes of war, they would have to travel more carefully. In the order of march Prince Maryn always rode at the head of the army with his silver daggers directly behind him. Alone of all the contingents, even in this safe country they travelled wearing mail and carried shields at their saddle peaks. Behind them came the noble-born and their warbands in order of rank. The spearmen marched at the rear, ready to guard the baggage train trailing along behind.

As the mood took him, Nevyn would ride at different places in the line, but he stayed toward the front to avoid the dust. Every night, he would scry out the terrain ahead of them. Although he felt stabs of guilt for twisting dweomer to such ends, he'd spent so many years using dweomer to put Maryn on his throne that a few more transgressions now weren't going to matter.

At every town or dun the army grew in size and slowed down just that more. Each lord they passed was obligated to bring so many riders, and with these warbands came spare mounts, servants, blacksmiths, chirurgeons, carts filled with provisions and other supplies, the carters to handle them, and from the larger demesnes contingents of free-born spearmen. By the time they reached Yvrodur, the army numbered over four thousand riders, a thousand spearmen, and a swarm of servants and skilled yeomen.

'A lot of extra mouths to feed,' Oggyn said dolefully. 'Still, we've got the first harvests coming in.'

'Oh come now,' Nevyn said, smiling. 'You're in your element, and you do a fine job of it, I must say.'

'Well, my thanks.' Oggyn tried to look humble and failed.

They were standing on a low rise and looking down at the encampment, which spread along the river bank just north of the town itself. Since the lowering sky promised rain, the men were pitching tents, blossoming like dirty flowers in the midst of a churning confusion of horses and men. In the middle of camp stood the Prince's white pavilion, hung with banners – the Pyrdon stallion, the three ships of Cerrmor, and the new red wyvern of Deverry.

'The greatest army Deverry's ever seen!' Oggyn rubbed his hands together. 'I'll wager the false king can't match our numbers.'

'Don't wager any such thing. Tieryn Peddyc tells us that Regent Burcan has persuaded his lords to strip their fort guards.'

'Oh.' Oggyn went very still. 'I hadn't heard that. Well, then. This is their last stand, then.'

'So we may hope. If we win.'

'Imph, well. Of course.' Oggyn swallowed heavily. 'Well, I'd best go down. Yvrodur owes us dried beef as well as spearmen, and I'd best claim it.'

'We ride out tomorrow,' Burcan said. 'The Usurper's army is on its way north.'

'Scouts have come in?' Merodda said.

'Just that. He's reached Yvrodur, and men are pouring in to the muster, or so they said.'

'Bad news, then.'

'Not so bad as all that. We match him, and we'll have position. He's going to have to come to us and fight on the ground I choose.'

Merodda merely nodded. Wrapped in cloaks against the damp of the night, they were walking along the battlements of the inner ward. She'd come up hoping for omens, and he had seen and joined her. She turned and leaned onto the wall to look over and down the hill, ringed with stone walls, black against the grey night. Overhead, rain clouds tore and scudded away south to let the great drift of the Snowy Road hang clear in the sky. Burcan sighed and leaned next to her, so close their shoulders touched.

'It's a pity that your daughter chose to desert to the enemy,' he said. 'We could use her peculiar gifts right about now.'

'Indeed. The little bitch!' Rage swelled and washed away any chance Merodda had of seeing dweomer-omens. 'I never thought – and Peddyc, too! Why? Why would he have gone over?'

'He might have seen through your little ruse.'

'Oh, my ruse, is it now? You agreed to it quick enough.'

When she felt him tense, she moved a little away, turning to peer at him. In the dim light from the ward below she could just see his face, an expressionless mask.

'So I did,' Burcan said at last. 'I shouldn't be blaming you. I suppose Lilli unravelled the truth and told Peddyc.'

'I suppose so. It's the only thing I can think of, with them both gone.'

'Doesn't much matter. What does matter is that he's gone, and his vassals with him, and ye gods, the grumbling the bastard's left behind! I'd not realized how many men looked up to him. If I had, I would have courted him more. Too late now.' Burcan shook his head. 'It's blasted cold up here for a spring night. I'm going in. Are you?'

'I'm not. In a bit.'

'Very well.' He ran his hand down her back and let it linger on her buttocks. 'I'll be waiting for you in your chambers.'

Once she was alone, Merodda looked up at the stars and focused her concentration. Against their glitter and light she could often see images of both present and future, but that night they refused to come to her. She tried thinking of Lilli, remembering Lilli's face, letting the memory slip over into scrying – the stars refused to blur into a dweomer-image. During Lilli's long traitorous ride south, Merodda had been able to scry her easily until she'd reached Cerrmor. Since then, nothing, and indeed, no matter how she tried, this night too her scrying failed.

Merodda found herself remembering Brour and the warning he'd given her about his old master in Cerrmor. Could he be hiding Lilli from her? Apparently so. She wondered just how powerful this sorcerer, this Nevyn, might be. With an involuntary shudder she left the stars to their own devices and went back to the dun.

When the Red Wyvern pulled out of Yvrodur, scouts rode ahead in squads of five men for safety's sake. Since they could travel twice as fast as the massive army, they would leave the river road at intervals and turn down the cross-running lanes through the fields. In the southern river valley the land stretched out flat. A man on horseback who found the slightest rise had a good view.

The first morning out of Yvrodur, Caradoc put Branoic in charge of a squad. The five silver daggers would ride in a loose cluster, ready to break up at the first sign of real danger and head back to the army.

'Remember, lads,' Caradoc said. 'No heroics. What counts is warning the rest of us. You can't do that dead.'

'Just so, captain,' Branoic said. 'Come on, lads! Let's get down the road.'

For a few miles they jogged their horses to put some distance between themselves and the army, then slowed to a steady walk. Off to their right the river flowed past silently; to their left lay a field of grain, pale green and nodding in a light breeze. In the hot summer sun staying alert took some doing. Unfortunately, none of the men who'd drawn scout duty with him were the talkative sort. Branoic's mind wandered, and as it did so it peopled the world around him with little creatures. He was sure he saw Wildfolk splashing in the river eddies; now and again faces peered out at him from the grass beside the road; once he distinctly heard a voice calling his name. The angrier he grew with himself for giving into these childhood fancies, the more distinct the wretched things became. Grimly he did his best to look only at the road, but even there warty grey gnomes appeared, waving to him pleasantly as the squad ambled past.

At length, when the sun was climbing toward noon, a real distraction presented itself. Where the river curved to the east and the road followed, the squad left both to cut straight across on a narrow track between two fields. Far ahead of them Branoic spotted a smudge on the horizon.

'Dust!' he called out. 'Hold up, lads!'

The squad jingled to a halt behind him. Branoic rose in his stirrups and shaded his eyes with his free hand. A lot of dust, it was, and moving purposefully down the road toward them.

'Trevyr! Head back to the Prince and tell him riders are coming, a good-sized contingent but no army.'

'Done, then.' With a wave red-haired Trevyr guided his horse out of line and turned it around. 'Do you want more men up here?'

'I don't, but you'd best get back here straightaway yourself.'

Trevyr trotted off down the lane, and Branoic went back to his watching. The dust cloud came along leisurely, finally resolving itself into a column of mounted men followed by what seemed to be a pair of carts – an ally, most like, joining the muster. Branoic sent another man off with this news, but just in case the column meant trouble, he led his remaining two men back to the main road. By the time they reached it the column had come close enough for him to see the blazons on shields – a blue circle with a line of darker blue knotwork around it, and nothing that Branoic recognized.

'We'd best get out of here,' he said.

The other two silver daggers nodded their agreement, turned their horses in the road, and jogged off fast. Branoic lingered a moment to estimate the contingent's size, about six twenties, he figured. None of them were wearing their mail, and their shields hung from their saddle bows. Just as Branoic was gathering his reins to gallop away, the lord at the head of the column called out to him.

'Are you a Cerrmor man?'

Branoic hesitated, but he had plenty of room to outrun them, and his own army would have closed much of the gap between him and it by now.

'I am.' Branoic called back. 'Friend or foe?'

'Friend! Do you think I'd head toward an army of thousands otherwise?'

Branoic laughed and paused his horse to sit easy in the saddle while the lord and his men travelled the last fifty yards or so between them. When the lord waved him up, Branoic fell in beside him. The lord had a ruddy face, which collapsed toward his chin; he'd lost most of his teeth, whether to age or a blow to the face Branoic couldn't tell.

'I've not had the honour of meeting you, my lord,' Branoic said.

'No doubt. My name is Daeryc of Glasloc.'

'Oh ye gods! Er, my apologies, Your Grace.'

'A bit startled, are you? I don't blame you, lad. If someone had told me last year that I'd change allegiance, I'd have had him hanged from my walls!' Daeryc sighed with a quick puff of breath. 'Cursed wars! A man can't know his own mind any more, eh?'

Branoic smiled politely.

'And who are you?' Daeryc said.

'Just a man of the Prince's guard,' Branoic said. 'Look ahead there, my lord. You can see the dust of the army coming. I've got to stay out on point, so I'll wish you luck and farewell.'

When the army paused at noon to rest the horses, Nevyn joined the Prince, who was standing near his mount and eating a chunk of bread out of hand like one of his men. A servant, however, was unsaddling his horse to let it roll and would doubtless take it to water, too.

'Nevyn!' Maryn hailed him. 'Did you see Daeryc of Glasloc ride in?'

'I did indeed, Your Highness. Tieryn Peddyc and his son were quite glad to see him.'

'No doubt. If you're going to change sides of a springtime, it's a grand thing to bring your overlord with you. Shall we see what His Grace has to say for himself?'

They found Daeryc not far away, talking with Peddyc while Anasyn tended all three horses. At the sight of the Prince, Daeryc sank to his knees. Nevyn hung back and allowed his vision to slip into the dweomer sight. He studied Daeryc's aura the entire time the lord talked and saw not a trace of treachery. If Maryn had had to depend on ordinary councillors to judge his new allies' worth, he'd not have been able to be so generous with his pardons.

'You may rise, Your Grace,' Maryn said. 'Tieryn Peddyc here has already stood surety for you.'

'Well, my thanks then, eh?' The gwerbret rose, smiling all round in an oddly tight-lipped manner – his lack of teeth, Nevyn supposed. 'Your Highness, I'll speak straight with you. Never did I think I'd come over to your side, but the real king in Dun Deverry is Regent Burcan, and that's too bitter a truth for me to swallow.'

'So I've heard from many a lord,' Maryn said. 'The Boar must be a hard man.'

'Hard? Huh!' Daeryc spat, as if in thought. 'Rotten to his kidneys, I'd say.'

'Tell me somewhat,' Maryn said. 'Here you are, riding to join us as free as bird, but they must be finishing the muster up in Dun Deverry.'

'They finished it some days ago, Your Highness. But once Burcan realized that our Peddyc here wasn't coming back from his wife's burying, he remembered Dun Hendyr. I'm Peddyc's overlord, and so he sent me and some of his own men to take the dun. When we got there, the place was empty. So I left Burcan's loyal men there on fort guard and rode out south.' Daeryc paused for effect. 'There's naught like sending a fox to guard a henhouse, eh?'

Maryn allowed himself a good laugh while Daeryc stood grinning at his own joke.

'Well, then,' Maryn said. 'The Regent must be riding our way.'

'True and twice true, Your Highness,' Daeryc said. 'I'm just cursed glad I got here before he did.'

When the battle came, it came on ground of the Boar's choosing. An army as large as Maryn's needed a prodigious amount of water, and that need pinned them to the river road. About two miles south of

Camrydd Bridge, the river curved toward the east before curving back straight north. In the embrace of water lay long green meadows. Burcan left his camp a few miles behind and disposed his men to block the road to Dun Deverry.

Nevyn scried them out and brought the news to Prince Maryn not long after dawn. While the riders pulled on mail and helm, the baggage train prepared to defend itself. During battles Oggyn commanded the camp; he knew the job well and performed it better – not that anyone but Nevyn gave him much glory for it. In a storm of oaths and shouting, the carters drove the loaded carts into a circle. Whips cracked and more oaths flew as they tried to back their teams into a close formation. Yelling back and forth, the servants carried supplies into the middle and the ostlers brought the extra horses, dancing and snorting with excitement, inside as well. On the outside of this improvised wall, the spearmen drew up in close ranks, leaning on their spears and yawning in pretended indifference.

Off to one side the chirurgeons had commandeered a few of the waggons, then unhitched their teams and sent them back to the circle. On the relatively clean waggon gates they could lay patients. Nevyn joined them there as they readied their supplies of water and the firewood to heat it with. After so many years of watching Death feast, Nevyn could no longer bear the sight of battle. He did however keep his horse saddled and ready, in case the Prince should need either his dweomer or his healing arts – the Wildfolk would come tell him if his own intuition should fail. When he tied the gelding to a waggon tree, Caudyr, the silver daggers' chirurgeon, came limping over to meet him. He had a club foot, Caudyr, which as he aged pained him more and more.

'Are you ready?' Nevyn said.

'As ready as any one can be,' Caudyr said. 'Which means not very.'

The camp fell silent to watch the riders mount up, making the meadow roil with horses and plume with dust. Horns rang out as the various lords tried to collect their men into some semblance of order. They would have to ride in a spread formation; Burcan could send his men charging into a column broadside and earn himself a cheap victory otherwise. Up at the head of this swarm the Red Wyvern banners bobbed along, dipping now and again as their bearers settled themselves on horseback. The Prince Nevyn couldn't see at all.

Horns shrieked; the lords screamed a last few orders; men shouted in answer. The front of the army lurched forward. The men in the first ranks set off, while those in the middle began jockeying for position, and those in the rear simply waited for a chance to move. It took a long time for all of them to be gone. For a while more Nevyn could see the dust cloud that marked their going and hear the jingling tack and shouting. Slowly the dust settled and the silence with it. Oggyn, wearing a hauberk and carrying a spear in one hand, came striding over to him.

'Well, let's pray for the best, eh?' Oggyn said.

'Just that,' Nevyn said. 'Not much more we can do now.'

Oggyn nodded with a decisive wag of his beard and went back to his men. The waiting stretched on while the sun climbed with the promise of a hot day. All at once Nevyn heard birds cawing and looked up to see ravens flying overhead, heading fast toward the battlefield.

'Ah,' Nevyn said to Caudyr. 'It's begun.'

As part of the Prince's guard, Branoic and the other silver daggers rode to keep Maryn safe, not to join the general fighting. If Maryn had had his way, he would have led every charge and been long since dead, his cause failed and the Boars or their candidates invested as High Kings of all Deverry. Over the years Nevyn had persuaded him to live and conquer. Even now he grumbled, but he did stick with his guards and let Caradoc's orders protect him. Not that they escaped the fighting – sooner or later the enemy would find the Prince on the field, close in, and try to kill him.

In this flat country, and under the dust, the armies soon devolved into a blind mob, in which the enemy shrank to the nearest man with a blazon you didn't recognize. The warcries, the shouts, the screams of the men and the whinnying of the horses – they blended with the clang and thwack of weapons on mail or shields into a roar that drowned any sound but the most strident of horns. Riding at the Prince's right flank, Branoic could see even less of the overall battle than the average rider. He kept twisting in his saddle and looking for enemies heading toward them from the rear, but he could see no more than twenty feet away at the best of times and ten at the usual.

The sheer press of bodies, horse and human, around them became frightening. In this mob an enemy could slip in from the rear and attack the Prince's horse without much warning. Since he carried his sword in one hand and his shield in the other, Branoic guided his horse mostly with his knees, and turning completely around for a good look was impossible. He could only curse and pray and swear while he swung his body back and forth in the saddle like a dancer. The sweat soaked through his shirt immediately, and not long after through the padding under his mail.

On and on it went. Although he never had a moment to look at the sky and see how the day fared, he felt the sun growing hotter still on his back. His horse began to foam, but he could do nothing for the poor beast. In all that time, they had travelled perhaps a hundred yards across the field, borne along by the fighting as the Regent's army fell back and the Red Wyvern pressed forward. The centre of the Regent's line suddenly gave way. Branoic had just time to think 'trap' when he heard the shouting behind him that confirmed it.

'They're here!' he shrieked.

As he struggled to turn his horse in the mob, he saw the silver dagger behind him go down over his horse's neck. The mount reared in panic, giving Branoic just the time he needed. He managed to lower his shield, grab his reins, and yank his horse's head around just as the first Boarsman broke through the Prince's men to the rear. Someone killed him for his trouble, but more men with the slavering grey boar on their shields took his place.

Screaming orders at the top of his lungs, Caradoc was turning the squad to face this thrust. Branoic parried more than swung to kill and held the Boarsmen up, trapped behind their own front men, until Owaen pushed through the mob and joined him. As always in a fight, Owaen stayed dead-silent, barely breathing hard, it seemed, as he slashed into the Boar riders. Warcries sounded behind them from familiar voices as a living wall formed around the Prince. Branoic killed one man, catching him off-guard and smacking him so hard across the face the nasal on his own helmet drew blood; another smack, and down he went into the maelstrom of iron-clad hooves.

As fast as they had appeared, the squad of Boarsmen pulled off and retreated, fighting past the clot of silver daggers. Suddenly the field began thinning; Branoic swung his horse around easily and realized that he could see a good way ahead.

'The bastards are retreating!' Caradoc howled out. 'But steady on, lads! Stay with the Prince!'

Branoic glanced at the sky and saw that the sun had just reached its zenith.

'Huh,' Owaen grunted. 'Not much of a fight.'

'They were just testing our strength, maybe.'

'Oh, now you've turned into a cadvridoc, have you? Reading the minds of the enemy like old Nevyn, are you?'

Owaen doubtless didn't realize how close he came to dying in that moment. Branoic felt his sword swing up as if some demon had grabbed the hilt and guided it.

'Hold!' Caradoc forced his way in between them. 'Owaen, get to the front of the squad!'

With an oath Owaen followed orders. Branoic lowered his sword and felt himself panting for breath.

'My thanks, captain,' he said. 'And a thousand apologies.'

'For a change it's Owaen that owes the apologies, but cursed if I want him dead. Understand me?'

'I do, captain.'

'Good.' Caradoc rose in the stirrups to look out over the battlefield. 'Ah horseshit! They're retreating in good order. And here I had hopes of a rout.'

'Let's not give ourselves airs,' Maryn said. 'We won that battle because nobody knew how to fight it. The two biggest armies Deverry's ever seen – ye gods! That wasn't a battle!'

'Well, truly, Your Highness,' Caradoc said. 'Reminded me of a fight in a crowded tavern. That's why you generally go outside if you're in the mood, like, for a brawl.'

'Just so. I've never fielded this many men.'

'Neither has Burcan.'

The Prince nodded. Long after the lords and their men both had gone to their blankets, Caradoc and Maryn were sitting at the dying council fire. Yawning on the edge of sleep, Nevyn sat with them. He'd been on his feet since the first of the wounded began coming in, those who could stay on a horse long enough to reach the camp, until but a few moments past, when he'd given up hope for the last of the dying.

'Interesting little problem,' Caradoc went on. 'I remember our first summer in Cerrmor. We would have given an arm apiece for more men. We only fought the battles we couldn't get out of fighting, and you won those by being fast and clever. Now we've got the men-'

'And we're as slow as toads on cold stone, truly,' Maryn said. 'Nevyn, what do you think?'

'Imph?' Nevyn shook himself awake. 'My apologies, Your Highness.'

'Nah nah nah, I'm the one who should be apologizing to you. You're exhausted. Get some sleep.'

'I will, my thanks. Humph. I must be getting old.'

It seemed that Regent Burcan was considering tactics as well. For two days the Boarsmen retreated north and the Red Wyvern followed. The closer they drew to the Holy City, the more the land rose, until by the third day they reached the South Downs, where the land swelled like waves far out to sea. When scouts rode out, they could see a long way ahead. They returned on the evening of that third day to report that Burcan's army had ensconced itself on a low rise some five miles north, blocking the road again but this time from high ground.

It was not good news. The Prince called for a council of war at his fire that night, and after the noble-born had wrangled among themselves for a while, Maryn turned as usual to Caradoc.

'Clever of them,' Caradoc remarked. 'We'll have a lovely little fight of it, trying to charge uphill.'

'Just so,' Maryn said. 'If we ride, they'll kill our horses as fast as we crest the ridge.'

'Fight unhorsed, my liege?' Tieryn Gauryc snarled. 'Surely you don't suggest that?'

Most of the noble-born jumped to their feet and began muttering. Maryn got up and shouted. 'Hear me out!'

The lords fell silent. Nevyn noticed Tieryn Peddyc soothing Daeryc with a friendly hand on his overlord's arm.

'If we try to fight on foot,' Maryn went on, 'they'll only ride us down. I know that as well as you do. So what do you suggest, my lords? With this big an army, we can't simply outflank them and ride around their position.'

The lords considered. No one spoke.

'With the river to one side of us,' Maryn said, 'we can't split our force and encircle them, either. Burcan's picked a nice spot for a fight.'

'Imph, well,' Tieryn Peddyc said. 'If we only had some way to drive them off that hill . . .'

'Good idea, my lord,' Caradoc said.

Nevyn suddenly realized that the captain was looking straight at him. He crossed his arms over his chest and glowered for an answer; he wanted no direct part in the fighting. As if Caradoc could read his thoughts, he smiled and strolled over.

'Let's have a chat, you and me,' Caradoc said. 'Away from the wrangling, like.'

Caradoc slipped an arm through Nevyn's and firmly guided him into the darkened camp, well out of earshot of the noble-born. With a scowl Nevyn pulled his arm free.

'Cursed if I'll take any part in a battle!' Nevyn snarled. 'May I ask just what you think I could do?'

'Well, when we were bringing the Prince to Cerrmor, like,' Caradoc said. 'There was a little matter of a battle, the one in which Aethan died. And if I remember rightly, all at once the enemy horses started panicking, didn't they? Like they could see somewhat that we men couldn't.'

Nevyn growled under his breath.

'I see I remember rightly,' Caradoc said, grinning. 'Well, my lord, couldn't you do the same again?'

'Burcan has too many men. I can't summon enough spirits to cause the same panic.'

Caradoc swore.

'Although-' Nevyn was struck by a sudden thought. 'I don't know if I can drive them off, but I'll wager I can make them cursed uncomfortable and in no mood to fight.'

'I'll take that, my lord. Gladly.'

'I think I can even justify it to my delicate conscience. After all, the fewer the men that fight, the fewer that will die.' Nevyn rubbed his hands together. 'Now let me just think for a bit.'

Now that he was recognized as a bard, Maddyn no longer rode to battle with the silver daggers. Besides composing praise songs and death songs, he acted as the troop's champion in quarrels with chamberlains, provisioners, and other such servitors who might skimp on their food and quartering. Early on the morning of the battle, Maddyn was complaining to Oggyn about the oats issued for the troop's mounts when Nevyn came strolling up to them, leading his horse.

'Feel like riding with me, Maddo?' Nevyn said. 'Those weevils can wait till the battle's over.'

'What's this, my lord?' Maddyn said. 'Don't tell me you're going to join the fighting.'

'Not precisely. Go get your horse.'

When the army rode out, Maddyn and Nevyn rode a little way

behind them. They'd gone no more than a mile when Nevyn gestured to Maddyn to follow, then took out cross-country. They jogged across a pasture, ducked down a narrow lane between fallow fields, then walked their horses up a long low rise where beech trees grew at the crest. From this shelter they could look out across the rolling downs.

'I spotted this ridge while I was scrying,' Nevyn said. 'It's more of a proper hill, and we'll have a good view.'

They stood indeed on ground a good bit higher than the farther rise where Burcan's army waited. From this distance the army seemed to be one solid mass, glittering with metal, as if an enormous snake lay stretched out on the crest, or so Maddyn remarked, to sun itself.

'Indeed,' Nevyn said, grinning. 'It's a lovely day, isn't it? Not a cloud in the sky.'

'It is.'

'Does it look to you as if it's going to rain?'

'It doesn't.'

'No chance of a sudden freak storm in this country?'

'There's not. Uh, here, my lord, what-'

'You'll see.' Nevyn was wearing one of his slyest smiles. 'Now, I'm about to go into a trance, and I'll need you to guard my body. That's why I asked you come along, just in case some enemy should find me by accident. We'd best slack the horses' bits and let them rest. This will take a while.'

'Oh ye gods!' the Prince snarled. 'Burcan's got his spearmen up there!'

'So he does,' Caradoc said. 'Clever fellow, isn't he?'

'Clever?' Gwerbret Daeryc snorted. 'Impious, that's what I call it. Battle's for the noble-born, not a pack of shoemakers' sons!'

Daeryc shook his fist in the general direction of the Regent, then peeled out of line and trotted off to join his warband. In the fallow fields below the rise, the army was in the long process of halting and spreading out behind the Prince and his silver daggers. From where they sat on horseback, Caradoc and Maryn could look up the long slope and see Burcan's position clearly. Branoic, riding as usual at the Prince's right flank, shaded his eyes with one hand and tried to estimate the distance.

The slope stretched maybe as much as a quarter of a mile to rise some hundred yards above the flat, not steep, no, but any charge to the top would arrive on winded horses. At the centre of the regent's line, directly across the disputed road, stood a shield-wall – a double line of spearmen standing so close that one man's shield protected half the man next to him as well as his own left side. To either flank stood contingents of mounted men, ready to close like a pair of jaws if the Red Wyvern sent a wedge to try to break the wall.

'I'd wager that Burcan has a good reserve,' the Prince was saying, 'behind that shield wall.'

'He'd be a fool if he didn't, Your Highness,' Caradoc said. 'And I've never seen him play the fool.'

'So then. We hold our position here and wait. Send a couple of your men along the line and pass the word to the noble-born, captain.'

Wait? Branoic shifted in the saddle and glanced at Owaen, who looked just as surprised as he was. Caradoc, however, was grinning – a good sign that the Prince had some clever dodge in mind. When the messengers trotted off, Branoic hooked his shield over the saddle peak to follow orders about that waiting. When Owaen did the same, Branoic caught a glimpse of his four-fingered hand. The scar from the amputation had broken open, and blood oozed; Owaen seemed not to notice.

The sun climbed and grew hot. Flies gathered. All up and down the Prince's line, both men and horses flicked them away and moved uneasily in place. The men muttered as well, turning in their saddles to ask questions of other men who knew no more than they did. Some of the noble-born began grumbling a little louder. The Prince and the captain ignored them all and sat easy in their saddles. Every now and then Caradoc would glance at the sky.

Up on their ridge Burcan's army began to turn restless. Branoic could see movement among the riders, as impatient horses danced and men leaned forward to pat their necks and calm them. The shield wall stood immobile; this wait in the hot sun must have been worse for them, Branoic realized, and he wondered if perhaps the Prince was hoping to wear them down before he charged.

'What?' Owaen suddenly hissed under his breath. 'What by all the hells?'

Branoic looked up and saw a cloud forming over the Regent's army, a small, rather ordinary cloud like a puff of fog from the harbour down in Cerrmor, but the sea lay over a hundred miles away. The white cloud drifted for a moment, then began enlarging and spreading out in long tendrils as it grew. Other clouds appeared near it so suddenly that it seemed some invisible hand had thrown them there.

They too enlarged themselves, joining and melding until at last storm clouds loomed high and grey in the sky, swirling over the Regent's army and stretching out north behind their position toward Dun Deverry.

At the southern edge of this storm the Prince and his men still waited in bright sun even though a shadow lay dark across their enemies. All at once lightning cracked; thunder boomed from a clear sky. With a slap of wind rain poured down upon the crest of the rise, a perfectly normal rain, it seemed, except of course the edge of the storm fell, sharp and clean, about half-way down the slope. Nevyn! Branoic thought. He's the one behind this! The Prince's men began cheering and laughing, as if they'd had the same thought themselves. Prince Maryn grabbed his silver horn and blew the alert. As the signal spread down the line, the laughter stopped. Men grabbed shields and settled them, then drew their javelins from the sheaths under their right legs.

Up on the rise the Regent's army was beginning to break. Horses were rearing and milling about; the shield wall was disintegrating. They were hardened men, used to marching and fighting in the rain, but this display of dweomer was another matter entirely. Over the past few years they'd heard a flood of rumours and omens about the coming of the one true king. For all they knew, some god or other had brought about this unnatural storm and was cursing them for resisting Maryn's advance. Lightning cracked again, and again the thunder boomed. Branoic could hear the sound of horns drifting down from the ridge – desperate horns, trying to rally men who were on the point of desertion.

Maryn drew his sword and held it high while he stared uphill at the enemy line. The Prince was grinning like a berserker with his entire concentration bent on judging the moment. Up on the ridge the Regent's left flank suddenly crumbled. Men were turning their horses; the noise of horns and shouts doubled. All at once the spearmen began to scatter, peeling out of position and running. Some shamelessly threw their shields; others held them over their heads to ward off the evil magicks in the sky.

'Now!' Maryn screamed. 'Now!'

Just as the front line leapt forward and charged, the rain stopped. Under the shadow of clouds they galloped forward. About half-way up the slope they hurled javelins, a metal rain that showered down upon the unarmoured backs of the fleeing spearmen. In a welter of screams men fell and sprawled. Their long shields caught the wind and flew under the hooves of the retreating cavalry. Horses reared in panic, then slipped on the wet ground and went down, throwing their riders and rolling on those who couldn't scramble out of the way.

Branoic broke out laughing and stopped just as suddenly when he saw that the Regent was rallying his men. Branoic saw the Green Wyvern banner and then the Boar, flapping in the wind. Riders gathered round them as the centre of the line suddenly steadied itself. Worse yet: Branoic glanced around and realized that the Prince and a handful of silver daggers had ridden free of their own charging army.

'Halt!' he screamed. 'Caradoc, get back!'

Branoic kicked his horse and caught up with them just as the Ram's men came charging up to join the Prince's guard. He could hear Tieryn Peddyc screaming orders as the Boarsmen galloped across the flat of the ridge. Branoic had just enough time to manoeuvre his horse up to guard the Prince's flank when they hit. Horses kicked out and bit; men swore; the two groups locked together on the field with no room to ride.

Impossible to count numbers, impossible to care – Branoic bent his will to the enemies in front of him, Boarsmen all. He ducked, parried, dodged more than swung. What counted now was staying alive long enough to keep himself between the Prince and the enemies pressing in. Over the general screaming and battle noise he could pick out Caradoc's voice, yelling 'to the Prince!' over and over again. The Boarsman directly in front of him leaned in too far; Branoic whacked his sword arm hard with a swing from underneath. Cursing, the Boarsman dropped his sword and had to try to back his horse out of the melee. With a wrench of his body and a hard nudge from one knee, Branoic got his own horse to dance a few steps to one side, so that he could use the trapped Boarsman's horse as something of an extra shield.

Yet another wedge of riders pressed in from the rear. Branoic swung both sword and shield while he swore in a steady mutter under his breath. Keep them off. He could allow himself no other thought but this. Keep them off the Prince. All at once he heard a warcry he didn't know from directly behind him. No time to turn and look, but he fully expected to die until the rider at last managed to fall in next to him. Branoic risked a glance and saw a Ram shield, one trimmed with silver.

'I'll guard your right!' Lord Anasyn called out. 'Owaen's directly behind the Prince.'

'Splendid!' Branoic called back. 'You bastard!'

This last was for the trapped Boarsman who in desperation had grabbed a javelin, his last weapon, and was trying to couch it in one arm like a spear. Branoic slapped the point hard and flipped it away from him, then leaned in and stabbed. Just in time the Boarsman flung up his shield, but Branoic's blow cracked the wood. Branoic slashed back at him and caught the shield again. Half of it fell away. When the Boarsman wrenched his horse's head around, Branoic's next blow caught him across the back. With a grunt he slumped forward, but his horse kept moving, shoving itself toward safety as other Boarsmen opened their line, and safety engulfed him. Branoic had to let him go.

Once again the Boars' line surged forward. Branoic returned to the hard rhythm of defence. Keep them off, keep them back – no room to manoeuvre, no glory for him – just the endless parry and dodge, duck and strike to drive away, not kill. As long as he lived, they'd never reach the Prince. Horns were sounding, but whose he neither knew nor cared. The Boarsmen fell back a little and were gathering for another surge when a squad with the blue shields of Glasloc slammed into them from the side. Cackling with laughter, Gwerbret Daeryc was slashing as he rode, and his men were screaming warcries as they struck. The Boars' line fell back, but only briefly. When Branoic risked a glance around, he saw the Regent's own guard riding to the Boar's aid. He knew them by the green wyverns on their shields.

'Hold, hold!' Caradoc was shouting. 'silver daggers, to me!'

From across the field silver daggers answered. Branoic could hear voices he recognized screaming warcries as they tried to cut their way to the Prince. The fighting went on while the last of the dweomer-clouds broke up and blew away in a rising wind.

From his position among the beeches, Maddyn had a distant view of the battle. Nevyn had lain himself down on his back in the grass, with a folded-up cloak for a pillow, but his restful pose had proved an illusion. As soon as he'd fallen into a deep trance, he began to move. At first he merely twitched, and his lips worked as if he were talking in his sleep. All at once he flung one arm straight up into the air. His head flopped from side to side. Maddyn crouched next to him and wondered what he should do. Since Nevyn was smiling, it seemed that he was safe enough, but suddenly he jerked his legs and let his arm flop down to the grass.

For a long while he lay so still that Maddyn risked getting up and looking around. In the valley below the Regent's position, he could see the Prince's army spreading out. Maddyn felt a twist of fear. A charge up that slope would cost a heavy price in lives. He stood shading his eyes with one hand and watching until the Red Wyvern army came to a halt. They had formed up in ragged lines five riders deep.

Behind him Nevyn suddenly spoke in a loud and ringing voice.

'Lords of Air, hear my plea!'

Maddyn spun around to find Nevyn spread-eagled on the grass, still in his trance. He knelt beside him just as the old man sat up, called out an incomprehensible word, and flopped down onto his back again. After a long moment, he fell motionless in a sleep that seemed nearer death. He could have warned me, Maddyn thought with some bitterness. Curiosity bit too hard for him to stay at Nevyn's side. He got up to look at the battlefield in time to see the unnatural storm forming over Regent Burcan's army. A wind slammed into the beeches and made them rustle as it tore past, heading across the valley to the ridge.

'Lords of Air, indeed!' Maddyn said aloud.

He stood watching as the clouds thickened and the thunder boomed in the sky. The air around him, far away though he was, seemed charged with some strange force or power, as if the very elements themselves quivered with excitement. When he rubbed a hand on his wool brigga, little blue sparks snapped and tingled. He wondered if the same were happening to Burcan and his men. When the rains started, he felt a small stab of pity for the enemy, trapped between the Prince's army and dweomer as they were, but the pity vanished when the Prince charged. Without thinking he yelled aloud to cheer them on.

From his distance Maddyn saw embattled armies whole for the first time, as if they were entities that had life and identity. Thanks to the wet ground, no dust cloud rose over the fighting. It was a greater marvel even than the dweomer storm to see in the clear what had so often trapped and overwhelmed him. He watched fascinated as the Red Wyvern rushed uphill to leap upon the Green, which broke apart and seemed ready to shatter, only to recover itself and counter-charge. Off to the flanks of the battle he could see fragments of the Green army running away. A few turned back to rejoin the fighting, but most eventually passed out of sight behind the sheltering downs.

'They're on their own,' Nevyn remarked from behind him.

Maddyn yelped, then collected himself. 'Ye gods, but you startled me! I've been cursed near entranced, watching.'

'My apologies. I could clear the ridge for them, but the Prince will have to win the actual battle. It's quite a sight, isn't it?'

'It is. I just wish my friends weren't in the middle of it.'

'That does take the bloom off.'

For a long while they stood together, watching the battle sway this way and that along the crest of the ridge. Over it the dweomer clouds broke up and dissipated as quickly as they'd formed. When Maddyn glanced at the sky he realized that the day stood well past noon.

By then the entire Red Wyvern army had advanced up the slope from the flat and taken the crest. The fighting spread to the north as the Prince's men drove the Regent's from the high ground and scattered them down the other side. More and more riders fled the field in a disorganized scatter.

'Maryn is going to claim the victory here,' Maddyn said at last.

'So it seems,' Nevyn said. 'We'd best get back to camp. I need to get ready for the wounded.'

The sun hung well past its zenith by the time that the last of the Regent's forces broke and fled. By then the brunt of the fighting had shifted away from the Prince. As his allies from the rear lines forced their way onto the crest, their fresher warbands drove the exhausted units in Burcan's army away from Maryn and the banners of the Red Wyvern. In this lull Branoic lowered his shield and allowed himself to pant for breath. Beside him, Lord Anasyn was doing the same. A flower of red blood bloomed on the lord's cheek and a bruise was swelling around it.

'Naught serious,' Anasyn gasped when Branoic pointed. 'Just a flick of a blade.'

Branoic nodded, then returned to watching the field. Around them the battle had broken up into little clots of fighting between the victorious Red Wyvern forces and men who could neither flee nor hold their position. Branoic rose in the stirrups and with his height got a good look round. Most of the Regent's army was retreating with the Boars falling in to guard its rear. Not far from the silver daggers' position, though, one Boarsman rode slowly alone, lurching back and forth in the saddle. When his horse stumbled, he dropped his shield; silver trim caught the sunlight and flashed.

'Oho!' Branoic said as he pointed him out. 'I think that's some lord of the Boars.'

'Some lord?' Anasyn snapped. 'By the hells, it's Gwerbret Tibryn himself.'

They exchanged a glance, grinned, then kicked their tired horses to a lope and charged after the gwerbret. Anasyn rode round in front to guard while Branoic grabbed Tibryn's horse's reins. Tibryn had lost his helm, and blood sheeted down the side of his face from a wound that had half-torn his scalp off. A flap of hair and flesh hung grotesquely over one ear. He stared at them both as if he had no idea who they were or where they all might be.

'Let's get him back,' Anasyn said. 'Before they come after us.'

At his voice, Tibryn clutched his saddle peak with both hands to steady himself and peered at the Ram shield.

'Traitor,' was the only word he spoke.

By the time Nevyn and Maddyn rode into camp, the battle had long since ended. Exhausted men led exhausted horses out to tether; others carried wounded friends to the chirurgeons; those who'd come through unscathed were heading for the carts to fetch food for the rest. Down at the river's edge men and horses alike waded out into the cleansing water to drink their fill after the thirst of battle. Nevyn rose in the stirrups to look around for the Prince, but a servant came running up to him.

'My lord! Caudyr sent me to you. They've got a prize, and they're trying to keep him alive.'

Nevyn dismounted, flung his reins to Maddyn, and hurried off after the servant. At Caudyr's station Branoic stood watching while Caudyr himself stitched a wound in the right thigh of a man lying on the wagon gate. Caudyr had already wrapped the fellow's head tightly with bandages, but blood was oozing through. Their prize lay mercifully unconscious, a middle-aged man with a broad face that seemed familiar.

'That's not Burcan, is it?' Nevyn said.

'It's not, my lord,' Branoic said. 'His brother.'

Nevyn washed his hands in the bucket of water Caudyr had ready nearby, then took a place on the other side of the gate.

'It looks as if you've done what you can for him,' Nevyn said.

'No doubt.' Caudyr looked up, then paused to wipe the sweat from his arm on his shirt sleeve. 'I mostly wanted your opinion. Think he'll live?'

'How much blood has he lost?'

'A hellish amount. And this wound here goes deep. A javelin caught him just below the skirt of his mail, I'd say, and then he probably pulled it out himself.'

'What about that head wound?'

'He must have lost his helm and been thrown to the ground. It looks to me like a glancing kick from a shod horse tore part of his scalp off.'

Nevyn winced.

He leaned down and listened to Tibryn's breathing: shallow and ragged. When he laid a hand on his face, he found the gwerbret's skin clammy and cold.

'Fetch a blanket, Branno!' Nevyn snapped. 'He's lost all his fiery humours with the blood, and the imbalance will kill him if we don't keep him warm.'

With his wounds tended, and him wrapped in blankets and laid near a fire for good measure, Tibryn fought for his life all that afternoon. Whenever he drifted into consciousness, Nevyn got him to drink as much water as he could take and a few sips of herbal medications as well, but he could see how little good they were doing. Tibryn's face stayed hideously pale, and his lips were bluish, as were the quicks of his fingernails. The pain of his torn scalp at times made him moan; it seemed to drain what little strength he had.

Not long after sundown Nevyn realized that the gwerbret was about to die. He knelt down beside him and laid a hand on his face – as cold and clammy as an eel. Tibryn's breathing came in big gulping gasps. Briefly he woke, opening his eyes and staring at Nevyn.

'Braemys,' he whispered.

'Who's that, my lord? Your son?'

Tibryn closed his eyes and drew a long hard breath.

'Tell Burcan,' he whispered. 'Tell him Braemys lives. I sent him home with fifty.' Again a long pause. 'Tell him-'

He choked once, spasmed, and died. Nevyn closed Tibryn's eyes and drew the blanket over his face, then rose to find Anasyn standing nearby.

'Braemys is Burcan's son,' Anasyn said. 'Tibryn's nephew.'

'I see,' Nevyn said. 'And what do you think he means, sent him home with fifty?'

'Fifty men, most like. Sent him back to Cantrae for some reason.' Anasyn considered, frowning. 'Well, if Tibryn even knew what he was saying.'

'I think he did, though it seems he thought he was among friends. Here, has anyone tended that cut on your face?'

'It's naught.'

'If I can see it by firelight, it's somewhat. Come along, lad. I want to wash that out, and then we'll take Tibryn's last words to the Prince.'

In the morning, just after dawn when the astral currents had steadied down, Nevyn scried out their enemies from the etheric. He found the Green Wyvern's army camped about five miles north of the battlefield. With his etheric sight, he saw not their bodies but their auras, egg-shaped clouds of light, most a grim reddish colour, some so dark and small that Nevyn knew they'd not live out the day. Counting them was next to impossible, but Nevyn could tell that the Regent's army had shrunk far more than its casualties would account for. When he returned to the camp, he brought the Prince the news straightaway.

'Desertions, my liege,' Nevyn said. 'I'd wager that a good many lords have pulled out and taken their men with them.'

'Good. Here's hoping Burcan's got a dispirited army on his hands.'

'He's got a battered one. I'll vouch for that.'

'Are they staying in their camp, then? They'll need to lick their wounds.'

'No doubt, Your Highness, but they're moving out anyway. I suspect they're running for their dun like rats for a hole.'

Maryn nodded, considering.

'Maybe that explains about Braemys,' the Prince said at last. 'If Tibryn was in his right mind, that is. Tibryn might have seen the desertions and wanted Braemys safe so he could rally the lords later.'

'That's a good guess, Your Highness. No doubt we'll find out all in good time.'

'No doubt.' Maryn allowed himself a wry smile. 'But we won't worry about it until the gods dump it in to our laps. We need to ride out fast if we're going to catch Burcan on the road.'

'Just so. We're only a bare score of miles from Dun Deverry.'

But moving quickly proved impossible. The Red Wyvern army had taken its own losses and suffered its own wounds. None of the warbands except the silver daggers had got itself ready to ride. With

Caradoc, Nevyn, and Oggyn in tow, Prince Maryn walked through the camp to find lord after lord, then persuade them get their sound men mounted and ready to chase the Regent's army.

'I should have held the council of war last night,' Maryn said. 'I don't care how tired we all were. Every now and then I have this dishonourable wish, Nevyn. I wish I could just give an order and have them all obey me without our having to discuss every cursed word I say.'

'It's a hard thing, being a cadvridoc,' Nevyn said. 'But if your lords take offence and ride out–'

'Oh, true enough, but ye gods, I don't have to relish it.' There was something of a snarl in his voice. 'Oggyn, I'm leaving you in charge of the camp. Get it packed up and ready to move out, but stay here until I send a messenger back.'

By the time the men who'd suffered no significant injuries were ready to travel, a good three thousand of them, the sun sat at zenith, and Burcan had a long start. When they reached Burcan's old camp, they found that he'd left his wounded behind, but with chirurgeons to tend them and supplies of food at their disposal. When Maryn stopped to parley with the captain of the camp, he surrendered willingly enough and promised to give the Prince no trouble.

'There's only about twenty of us who can ride at all,' the Boarsman said. 'You'll not be needing to worry about us attacking your rearguard.' He hesitated for a moment, then went on. 'Your Highness, could you deign to tell us if the Boar still lives, or do you hold him prisoner?'

'Tibryn?' Maryn said. 'He's dead. I'm sorry. We tried to save him.'

The captain nodded and wiped tears from his eyes with the back of his hand.

Maryn sent messengers back to Oggyn with orders to bring the camp along and take over Burcan's wounded, then led his army out. Through a long summer's afternoon they pushed on northwards, but when the sun was lying low in the west, they were still ten miles from Dun Deverry with Burcan far ahead. Nevyn joined the Prince and the captain to consider what they should do with the last of the daylight.

'If we press on now, Your Highness,' Caradoc said, 'we might catch them just at dark, but there's no guaranteeing the result of a scrap like that.'

'Just so, and we'll be too far from our baggage train,' Maryn said. 'If we turn back now, we can reach camp by twilight.'

'That sounds wise to me, Your Highness,' Nevyn said. 'Since Burcan knows where he's going, he can travel in the dark. We can't. I fear me we'll have to concede them the siege.'

It was late on the following day that the Red Wyvern finally reached the Holy City. The fleeing Boarsmen had left the gates to the city itself standing open, but just outside the Prince called a halt. He rose in his stirrups and peered through the opening, then sat back in his saddle. Riding just behind him, Branoic could see little but a dusty road leading into burnt-out ruins.

'I fear a trap,' the Prince said. 'What about you, captain?'

'A rearguard at least,' Caradoc said. 'A few picked men to harry us all the way to the gates of the dun. But in this rubble, my liege, you could hide half an army.'

'We'd best send in scouts, then. I'll wager the townsfolk are long gone.'

Although Branoic volunteered to scout, the captain turned him down because of his all-too-noticeable size. Twelve men, all short and on the skinny side, went in on foot, three at each gate. The army pulled back about a quarter of a mile and let the slower-moving baggage train catch up while they waited. Not long before sunset, the twelve brought back similar reports.

'There's not a soul living in the ruins, Your Highness, not that we could see. We got all the way up to the outer ring of the dun, and all the gates are shut, all right. We saw plenty of guards up on the outer wall, patrolling, like. It's blasted long, that wall. Must run a good three miles round the hill.'

'Well and good, then,' Prince Maryn said at the last. 'My lady's father was the last man to take this city, some twenty years ago now, but the siege held and he withdrew. I'll pray to every god that this time things are different.'

'I will, too, Your Highness,' Caradoc said. 'But the gods won't mind if we lay a few plans of our own. Three miles long, is it? Huh, interesting. You know, I think I'll just take a stroll up there myself.'

When the captain returned, the Prince called a council of war. Branoic learned its decision late, when the captain returned to the silver daggers' campsite. After they secured the city, Maryn wanted to seize the outermost ring of the dun fortifications in one swift move.

'The Ram told us all how the dun lies,' Caradoc said. 'There are five circles. The first three enclose empty land and not much else.

Inside the fourth one – counting from the bottom of the hill, that is – there's a village, where all the false king's servants live, and they've got cattle and pigs in there, or so Peddyc said. Inside the fifth ring is the king's dun proper, and by all the ice in the hells, we're going to have a cursed lovely time taking it. Lots of little walls and wards and towers, his lordship tells me.'

'Ah horseshit,' Owaen said. 'Ah well, first things first.'

'Just so.' Caradoc glanced at the silver daggers, pressing close around him. 'And one ring at a time. I've walked round the dun now, and I'm wagering Burcan doesn't have the men to hold that outer wall. After that, well, we'll see. We've been in sieges before, lads, but this one is going to give our bard plenty to sing about.'

In the morning the army packed up its camp and prepared to move into Dun Deverry. To a chorus of silver horns the banners of the Red Wyvern led the army to the open gates. As he rode through, Prince Maryn raised his sword high. Branoic could see his face, as wide-eyed as a child seeing his first tourney, head turning as if he wanted to look in all directions at once. We're here, Branoic thought. This is what we've fought for all these long years. Ahead of them the city spread out in row after row of broken houses, roofless walls, and piles of ruins where you couldn't tell wall from roof. How many times had the city been set on fire by design or accident? Plenty, Branoic figured. That's what sheltering an army did to a town.

Just inside the gates a broad street ran round under the walls, large enough and clear enough for the army to ride in behind them; contingents split off to approach the dun from different directions. The Prince and the main body waited to give them a solid head start. Branoic looked up at the dun itself, towering above the town, its dark towers grim against the glittering sky. He could just pick out the final ring of stone walls that encircled the hill crest below the brochs.

Distantly horns called from off to the west and east. Maryn raised his sword again.

'Forward!' he called out. 'For Deverry and glory!'

The army cheered him as they set off, heading up the long deserted streets to the dun's south gate. Close to the dun Branoic saw houses that seemed to have been inhabited until a few days past. Some still had kitchen gardens out in front, welcome patches of green in the destruction. The only living creatures he saw, though, were a pack of half-starved dogs that barked at the army's passing.

The outermost wall of the fortress itself stood a good forty feet

high, a rough rise of stone topped with merlons. Over the gate no
banners hung, and no pennants flew from the wall. Guards, however,
stood along the catwalks on the far side. Branoic could see them
moving between the merlons, and occasionally he heard them calling
out to one another as well. Since the fortifications marched up the
side of a fairly steep hill, he could see the upper walls, dark rings of
stone against grass. The third wall carried the banners and flew the
pennants, though at this distance Branoic couldn't see the device. He
caught the captain's attention and pointed them out.

'Good for you, lad,' Caradoc said. 'And your young eyes. I think me
the Regent knows what he can defend.'

For two days the army camped in the ruins and held a precarious
investment while they readied themselves for an assault on the outer
wall. The Prince had brought two rams, each the trunk of a young
tree equipped with iron handles and a heavy iron sheath at one
pointed end. Twelve men each would run them up against the gates
while others climbed the siege ladders and tried to overwhelm the
guards. Although they'd brought some ladders with them, they
needed a good many more now that they'd had a look at the extent of
the dun's outer wall. Squads searched through the ruins and stripped
timbers from the abandoned houses.

The morning of the third day dawned cloudy with ordinary
weather, a mackerel sky slipping in from the southwest with no help
from Nevyn's dweomer. The army split itself into four unequal parts.
The two larger assembled at the north and south gates, where the
rams would set to work; the two smaller, at the east and west to
prevent Burcan's men from sallying. While the rams attacked the
gates, half the Red Wyvern men, unmounted of course, would raise
ladders and try to scale the walls. It was not a job that Branoic would
have relished. He found himself thanking the gods of war that had
made him a member of the Prince's guard instead. After the gates
went down, picked men would charge to gain the ground inside. With
his usual guards the Prince would follow the wedge, while his allies
led their men in after – provided, of course, the gates did go down.

By mid-morning, everyone had taken their positions, with the
Prince and his guard at the south gate. While the trained assault men
readied the 'turtle shells,' hides stretched over wooden frames to
protect the ram bearers from rocks and garbage thrown down from
the walls, Caradoc picked men for the wedge that would charge the
broken gates on foot. Up on the high walls, the regent's men were

walking back and forth in full mail. Branoic could see them between the merlons as they paused, looking down at the enemy preparations, waiting for the assault.

The protected ram waited ready to charge when, at last, a messenger came from the contingent at the North Gate.

'We're ready, Your Highness.'

'So are we,' Maryn said. 'Captain, blow the signal.'

When Caradoc's horn rang out, the Red Wyvern army shouted aloud. The men with the ladders raced for the walls, and the ram crew took off running for the gate. The heavy iron head slammed hard into the wood and bounced back. Up on the walls the Regent's men screamed out warcries and threw down stones in a hard rain. A few had bows, but their short hunting arrows glanced harmlessly off mail. Since Branoic had been expecting javelins, he was surprised until he remembered that the dun had four more walls to defend and a limited number of weapons for the job.

When the ladders went up against the wall, the defenders wielded long poles and shoved them off again. At the gates the ram retreated, then charged once more. The men with the ladders spread out and rushed the walls a second time. Behind them the lords rode back and forth, shouting orders and encouragement. This time some of the ladders held long enough for men to start climbing, but defenders heaved them off again, men and all. The shouting grew louder still as a third assault formed and hit, then another, until the attack turned into a series of waves beating against stone. Here and there a few of the Prince's men gained the top like a few drops of deadly water splashing from the wave, only to be mobbed and killed.

Yet as the fighting continued, every man there could see that the defenders were spread too thin. They were running back and forth on the wall; no one could pick a position and hold it, everyone had to scurry this way and that. The ladders kept coming; the rams kept pounding. Messengers rode in to tell the Prince that the assault on the north gate was going well. He sent others back to say the same about the south.

In the long stretches of wall between the gates, the scaling ladders were winning handily. From his position on horseback Branoic could see a sudden burst of attackers gain the wall off to the west. Fighting spread along the top of the wall itself. At the gate the Prince's men suddenly cheered. The ram smashed through the thick wood and shattered one plank. Again the ram charged; another plank tore away;

they aimed lower and with their next blow snapped off the remnant
of the first. Branoic could see the defenders on the wall turning and
suddenly disappearing from his view as they climbed down to hold
the breach.

With that, the men on the scaling ladders took control. Like the
wave reaching high tide they climbed up and over to race along the
wall. Screaming for reinforcements, squads of defenders rushed to
meet them, but the attackers held. Down below, the ram charged
again and smashed through wood so hard that it stuck. When a mob
of Prince's men swarmed to its aid, some of the Regent's men charged
outside the wall to fight them off. From inside the dun horns sounded
in a frantic cacophony.

'Ready and arm!' Caradoc screamed out. 'Silver daggers, to the
Prince!'

Ahead the picked men of the wedge charged forward on foot to
take the breach. Branoic drew his sword and readied his shield.
Under him his horse shifted uneasily at the danger ahead. Still more
men climbed the unguarded walls, then disappeared as they hurried
down to attack the gates from within. All at once, the smashed
remnant of gates began creaking open.

'We've got the winch!' Prince Maryn crowded. 'Steady, men!
Steady, steady – now!'

With a scream of warcries the horsemen charged the open gates.
Men on foot scattered as they plunged through in to chaos. At the far
wall the Regent's men – Green Wyverns and Boars – were fighting a
rearguard action at those inner gates. Burcan's men were climbing
down the catwalks, leaping the last few feet to the ground, then
running for the gates and safety. From round the other side of the hill
mounted men galloped to meet the Prince – Glasloc shields, Ram
shields, the twined ivy blazon of Yvrodur. The north gate too lay
shattered and open.

Screaming like a madman, the Prince spurred his horse and
galloped along his line with silver daggers streaming after him.

'Open the east gate!' he was yelling. 'Let our men in! We can take
the second ring! Hurry, run! Open the west!'

The Regent's men had abandoned the winches. Men with Cerrmor
blazons took them over and began cranking. Mounted men poured
through all four gates like water through a broken sea-dyke. Silver
horns were blaring; captains and lords were yelling at the tops of their
lungs. The last of the Regent's men mobbed around the gates in the

second, inner wall, yelling and screaming as they tried to push through to safety.

'Speed, men!' the Prince cried out. 'If we rush them, we can take those gates!'

The Prince turned his horse so hard that his guards rode right past him. Swearing they swung out in an arc to turn and ride back. The dust of the retreat hung like smoke, but Branoic could see the Prince charging straight for the gates of the second ring at the head of a straggle of riders.

'My liege!' Branoic screamed. 'Wait! Stop!'

Cursing a steady stream, Caradoc went charging right after Maryn with the rest of the silver daggers close behind. Branoic pulled out of line and yelled at every familiar shield he saw.

'Inside, get inside! The Prince! He's inside the second ring! To the Prince!'

Whether they could hear or not, they seemed to understand. Half a hundred men at first, then more, galloped through the open gates of the second ring. Still yelling for reinforcements, Branoic followed. He rode through to see silver daggers riding down the Regent's men who manned the winch at the second ring's east gate. Prince Maryn himself slashed down to kill the Boarsman at the handle. The Regent's men were running so hard for the safety of the third ring that they never noticed the royal prize to their rear.

'We've got the west gate too!' a Cerrmor man was shouting. 'Daeryc's leading the charge there.'

The Red Wyvern army poured into the second grassy ring. Up at the third wall the Regent's men were running hard out for the gates, which slowly and inexorably creaked closed. One last unit squeaked through, but a couple of stragglers flung themselves against the iron-bound wood in vain. They spun around, backs against the gates, and waited to die as a Red Wyvern squad rode for them with swords flashing.

'Stop!' Maryn screamed. 'They're defenceless!'

Just in time the swords swung up and missed the men's faces by a hand's-breadth. The two stragglers fell to their knees as the squad swung their horses' heads around and thundered by.

Up above the gate the Green Wyvern men flung down ropes. The Prince called his men off and kept them off while the two stragglers climbed up. In the screaming confusion of battle, a little pool of silence spread around the Prince and the men he'd allowed to escape, as if everyone were holding their breaths, half-expecting Maryn to have them pulled down and slain at the last moment. But they reached the top at last, and their fellows yanked them over to safety. One of the two turned and called down unthinkingly, 'My thanks!'

'Be welcome!' Maryn shouted back. 'And remember the pardons I'm offering to lord and rider!'

For a moment the scene held, the Prince on horseback down below, the men on top of the wall transfixed. All at once someone on the Regent's side of the second wall started yelling orders. Maryn bowed from the saddle, turned his horse, and rode back to his own men. Open-mouthed with awe, Branoic watched him and wondered if it were a wrong thing to love another man the way he loved Prince Maryn.

By the middle of the afternoon the two armies had sorted out their respective positions. Prince Maryn's men held the two outermost walls, Burcan held the third, and that left the grassy stretch betwixt the second and third walls belonging to nobody. The Prince's men who were trained in siegecraft got straight to work; they tore down the catwalks on the inside of the first wall so that they could build them a-new on their side of the second. From there they could pull up and claim the wooden structures on Burcan's side of that wall to ensure that it stayed theirs.

In the stretch between the outermost and the second walls, Maryn ordered Oggyn to set up the camp. Predictably enough, a good many of the noble-born grumbled at this decision when they met for the council of war.

'My apologies and all, Your Highness,' Daeryc said, 'but I hope that these walls don't turn into a trap instead of a safeguard.'

'True spoken,' Tieryn Gauryc put in. 'With all due respect, my liege, we're wondering if any good can come of this.'

Maryn looked round the council, catching the glance of each lord in turn.

'I remember a book my learned tutor once gave me to read.' Maryn nodded Nevyn's way. 'In the Dawntime a great leader of our people, Gwersinnoryc, made the same mistake Burcan is making now. Hwl Caisyr, the Rhwman, besieged Gwersinnoryc in his dun, and when Caisyr built a wall around his own men, our Gwersinnoryc let him do it. In the end it saved the Rhwmanes when Gwersinnoryc's allies came to lift the seige.' He smiled briefly. 'Let's not forget Braemys of the Boar and the lords who deserted. If they rally and try to ride to the Regent's aid, they'll not be trampling our camp and killing our horses, whether Burcan sallies or not.'

'Don't you understand?' Burcan snarled. 'I didn't cede them the ring! We don't have the men to hold it. What with the battles and the desertions, we've been bled white. Why lose more men trying to defend an impossible position?'

Tieryn Nantyn crossed his arms tightly over his chest and scowled. All around them the great hall fell silent as men and women alike turned to listen. At the head of the royal table King Olaen was shredding a bit of bread between his fingers, head down while the men argued. Merodda, sitting nearby, slewed round on the bench for a better look. Burcan's face was a dangerous red.

'Too late to argue the point now.' Lord Belryc rose to join them. 'They've got it, and that's that.'

'True enough,' Burcan said. 'But I'll have it known that there were reasons for my decision.'

Nantyn stayed silent, glaring at him with ice-blue eyes. Belryc walked over and laid a friendly hand on his arm. Without looking his way the old man struck him such a hard blow backhanded that Belryc reeled with a bloody lip and nose.

'Don't you try to soothe me! I'm no fractious woman, you young cub,' Nantyn said in an oddly level voice. 'Listen, Regent! I never doubted you had reasons. I'm saying they're cursed bad ones.'

Belryc sat down in his place and turned his back on the dispute. Burcan considered Nantyn for a long moment.

'Stick to your opinion, then,' Burcan said at last. 'And I'll stick to mine.'

This manoeuvre took Nantyn utterly off-guard. For a moment he stood gaping like a fish; then with a sullen shrug he turned and strode out of the great hall. Burcan winked at Merodda and sat down to pick up his table dagger. As he resumed eating, it seemed that every man within earshot let out his breath at once, as if the great hall itself sighed in relief.

Since Merodda could do no more than pick at her food, she excused herself from the queen's presence long before the meal ended. Her dread seemed palpable, as if a small animal clung to her back and sank in claws to weigh her down. Ever since Tibryn's death, Burcan had fought off one challenge to his authority after another. Neither she nor Burcan, perhaps, had realized how much they depended on their elder brother's position to solidify their own. Tibryn's young son by a second marriage was the Boar now; he and his mother both were off in Cantrae, where perhaps they were safe, perhaps not.

Not that it matters, Merodda thought. Not that it will matter to anyone once this summer's past!

Up in the blessed silence of her chambers she lit candles from the banked hearth, then brought out her scrying basin and the bottle of ink. Most likely Prince Maryn's sorcerer had accompanied him to war, too far away from Lilli to hide her.

This time, indeed, when she thought of Lilli the images danced on the black surface. She could see her daughter sitting at table with three other women, all wearing dresses of some soft cloth in bright colours, yellow for Lilli. Although Merodda could hear nothing, they all seemed to be talking and laughing as they ate from trenchers heaped with meat and bread. She could just see a silver bowl piled high with fresh peaches as well. So there was Lilli, safe and pampered, while she herself trembled with fear in a siege that would doubtless end in starvation! Merodda's rage hit her like a blow. The images vanished, and she straightened up, barely able to breathe.

Someone walked up behind her. Merodda screamed and spun around – the room stood empty, the bar still lay across the door.

'Ah, Goddess!' she exhaled the words more than spoke them. 'May Aranrhodda protect me!'

The feeling of being watched persisted, grew stronger, until she wondered if she were going mad. Or was the feeling a warning that Brour's old master in the dweomer was spying upon her? She gathered herself with a couple of deep breaths, then drew in the air a pentagram with great sweeps of her right arm. Once the image held steady in her mind, she set its image blazing with blue fire.

'Begone!' she called out.

The sensation of being watched vanished. With a small tight smile, Merodda returned to the basin and her scrying.

'Well, that was clumsy of me,' Nevyn said. 'I never should have let her know I was spying on her. She's handier with her magicks than we thought.'

His audience, a fat yellow gnome, plopped itself down on his campaign chest and began to pick its fangs with a long claw. Although Merodda's clumsy banishment had affected neither Nevyn or the gnome, Nevyn had brought them back to the physical plane at the instant she drew her sigil.

Let her deem herself the stronger – and grow careless.

In the morning the Prince sent heralds to the gates in the third wall. From the newly-built catwalks on their side of the second, Nevyn, the Prince, and Oggyn watched their progress up the grassy slope. Each herald carried a long staff wound round with many-coloured ribands, a symbol that Regent Burcan and his men still respected, apparently, because no one slung a stone or an insult their way. Instead the gates opened a bare gap to let the two men slip inside. They'd barely closed, it seemed, before they opened again.

The heralds returned fast, shaking their heads, and strode through the gates in the second wall to the camp.

'Let's go down to meet them,' Maryn said.

As Nevyn followed him down from the catwalks, he was predicting to himself what they were going to say, and he didn't need dweomer to do it. The heralds knelt before the Prince.

'No parley, my liege,' Gavlyn said. 'The Regent ordered us to withdraw from his city and his dun, and that was an end to it.'

'His city? His dun?' Maryn snapped. 'Is the King dead, then?'

'He's not, my liege, but I doubt me if that matters one way or the other.' Gavlyn glanced at his companion, who shook his head in an agreeing no. 'I suspect the phrasing was an unfortunate slip of the truth.'

With the Prince gone on campaign, Bellyra ruled Dun Cerrmor as his regent. Every morning she sat at the head of the honour table on the dais with her women around her while the servitors came up to receive her orders concerning the daily life of the dun. Often enough she had to settle some squabble or legal matter as well, though any major dispute, especially those involving the noble-born, would have to wait until Maryn returned in the autumn. He was still gwerbret of this rhan and thus the only person entitled to hold full malover. During these sessions Lilli merely listened and watched, though the other women put in plenty of opinions.

'Once he's truly the King of all Deverry,' Bellyra said one morning, 'he'll have to elevate one of his loyal lords to the gwerbretrhyn of Cerrmor. He's not looking forward to sorting that out, I tell you.'

'No matter who he chooses,' Elyssa said, 'the others will grumble.'

'That's true enough,' Degwa put in. 'A lot of jealous children, that's what they are.'

'Oh now, please!' Bellyra tried to look stern and failed. 'After all, there's a lot of coin at stake too. It's not all hurt feelings.'

'Just so, but-' Degwa hesitated. 'Who's that at the door?'

Escorted by pages two armed men, dusty and road-stained, were striding into the great hall. One of them carried a silver message tube in one hand.

'From my lord, I'll wager.' Bellyra's voice caught. 'May it be good news.'

As if he'd heard her, the messenger raised the tube and shouted across the hall.

'Good news, Your Highness, the best! The Prince your husband has taken the Holy City and invested the dun itself.'

Bellyra whooped with laughter and rose, tossing her arms in the air as if she were going to dance a few steps. When Elyssa scowled, the Princess recovered herself and managed to arrange a solemn face. As the messenger mounted the steps, Lilli watched him, wondering if she felt glee or dread, then realized that the truth mixed both.

The tube held several long letters, tightly furled. While the Princess waited for the royal scribe, the news of their arrival spread and the great hall filled. Every servant and man on fort guard crowded in to hear the tale. When the scribe took the letters and snapped them out to smooth them, the crowd pressed close to the foot of the dais.

'Get up on the table, Maen,' Bellyra said. 'So everyone can hear.'

Obligingly Maen climbed, then read in his best public voice. As Lilli listened, she felt her soul split in half. One Lilli gloated over every victory; the other grieved for the young king in Dun Deverry and for all the lords whom she'd known there. Every now and then the letters would mention some lord slain or grievously injured; a fair number of Deverry lords had been captured and were being held for ransom. Although they described Tibryn's death in some detail, Lilli found that she couldn't squeeze out a tear for him, uncle or not.

Never did the letters mention Burcan or Braemys, but Lilli could assume that such meant they were safe. Surely such an important prize as the Regent or his son would be worthy of mention, if they'd been slain or taken. She was aware suddenly of Degwa, unsmiling, one eyebrow raised, watching her. Lilli looked away out to the great hall, where the crowd grinned as it heard the news.

'The Prince sends his best wishes to his wife,' Maen finished. 'Tieryn Peddyc and his son send their greetings to their daughter and sister, Lillorigga.'

So Peddyc and Anasyn lived, no matter who else might have died. At that moment the two Lillis reunited and laughed in sheer relief.

Maen climbed down from the table. As he was rolling up the letters, some of the servant lasses in the dun pressed up against the dais, asking him in low voices if such and such a man had been mentioned as living or dead, but of course, no one had thought to list the deaths of common-born soldiers.

'Maen?' Bellyra said. 'Can't you write down the names of the men they're asking about and send the list with the letters back? Surely someone can spare the time to find out how they fared. The beastly siege is going to drag on all summer, after all, and through the winter, too, unless the gods take a hand.'

'Of course, Your Highness,' Maen said. 'Wait here, all of you. I'll fetch ink and pen.'

The women huddled at the dais looked up at the Princess and murmured thanks. Some wept in unspeaking gratitude.

'Well, true spoken,' Elyssa murmured. 'About the siege, I mean. I'll hope and pray that the dun surrenders soon.'

'It depends on the provisioning, I suppose,' Degwa said.

Lilli suddenly realized that the Princess and her two women were all looking at her.

'It's awfully well-stocked, the dun,' Lilli said. 'It's huge, and they keep cattle and pigs right inside the walls.'

'A long, long siege, then.' Degwa looked away, chewing on her lower lip. 'Well, there's naught to do but pray.'

But of course, Lilli realized suddenly, she herself held the end of the seige in her hands like a trinket to drop or treasure. She could betray her kin and clan, betray the child – her own cousin – she once had honoured as the King, and hand Maryn the victory. If she dared. If such a thing would be right and not unspeakable treachery. She felt her soul split again like ripping cloth.

'Lilli?' Bellyra leaned forward. 'You look unwell.'

'I am unwell, Your Highness. I feel torn in half.'

'No doubt! Well, the outcome lies in the laps of the gods. There's naught we can do about it anyway, like Degwa says.'

Lilli nodded for an answer, not trusting her voice.

All that day Lilli fought with herself. She went to her chamber, then walked in the gardens of Dun Cerrmor alone. No one came near her; she assumed that the Princess had told the other women to allow her privacy. In so many ways Bellyra had treated her more generously than any exile could hope for, and Maryn was the true-born king and meant by the gods to rule. If she held back, wouldn't she be going against the will of the gods? As for her old friends, well, wouldn't everyone in the royal dun suffer if they starved through a winter? Maryn would pardon almost everyone – but not the Boar lords.

If she betrayed the dun, her clan would be wiped out, her surviving uncle hanged like a criminal. And what would she say to her mother, when they were sending Merodda off to some temple to be shut up all her days? She found herself thinking of Bevyan and weeping; for some ghastly reason, the image of the white blisters on her face had stuck in her memory beyond the dislodging. It would be vengeance for Bevva and Sarra, to betray the Boars. She wished that she could consult with Nevyn, but she knew what he would say. Nevyn was the Prince's man, heart and soul.

'And what am I, then? One of the Prince's people, or still a Boar? If I went back, would they take me in?'

Lilli knew at that moment what she would do. She left the gardens, but as she was stepping into a side door to the main broch, she looked back at the sky, framed in stone, and the new red wyvern banners that hung from the towers. She remembered then the omens she had seen in the black ink. So, she'd chosen wisely. The gods had ordained the death of the Boar, and there was naught that she, a mortal woman, could do against that Wyrd.

Lilli found Bellyra in the women's hall, alone except for little Casso. She was sitting at a table, sideways to allow for her pregnancy, while the child knelt on a chair, padded with cushions. They had between them a big wooden bowl of Bardek glass beads, which Bellyra was showing him how to sort by their colour and size while he laughed, staring at the pretties. In the afternoon sun their blonde heads, bent toward each other, gleamed as if they'd been gilded. Cerrmor was so immensely rich, Lilli found herself thinking, that they could use a bowl of treasures as a child's toy! Real glass beads, heaped up as casually as if they were pebbles from the seashore!

At that point Bellyra looked up, smiling in welcome.

'Your Highness.' Lilli made a quick bob of a curtsey. 'I've come to tell you somewhat. I know the way into Dun Deverry.'

Bellyra stared, her full lips slightly parted.

'There's a bolthole, I mean,' Lilli went on. 'It leads from a ruined dun outside the city right into the inner ward.'

'Oh ye gods,' Bellyra whispered. 'Some of our men could open the gates.'

'Just so, Your Highness.'

Bellyra grinned, then wiped the expression away.

'It must have cost you horribly,' the Princess said. 'Telling me this.'

'It did.' Lilli turned away. All at once it seemed hard to breathe, yet she couldn't say why. 'I couldn't just blurt it out. I had to think about it for a long time.'

'No doubt, what with your kin. But truly, Lilli, Maryn means it when he says he'll pardon anyone who asks. Really he will.'

'I believe it, Your Highness. It's just that most of them won't ask. They'd be dishonoured if they begged.'

For a long moment the two women stared at each other, while the sun streamed into the bowl of beads and touched them with fire, and a laughing Casyl ran his hands through them. Bellyra looked away first.

'Lilli? Find some pages, will you? We need to talk to the captain of the fort guard about getting you up to the siege.'

'Me? I–'

'Well, they'll need to know everything you do, where the tunnel leads, and what lies inside the dun between it and the gates.'

Lilli nodded, gasping a little for breath. Bellyra got up and walked over, holding out one hand.

'Come sit down. You're pale as death.'

'Am I?' Lilli sank onto a chair. 'Please, tell me somewhat. He really is the true-born king, isn't he? Maryn I mean. Oh ye gods, if he's not, then what have I done?'

'But he is. I know it in the very marrow of my heart and soul.' Suddenly Bellyra knelt, as if she were the commoner and Lilli the princess, and caught her hands. 'Help us, Lilli! Please? I'll send Maryn a letter with my seal upon it, begging him to spare your kin for your sake. But tell him what you know, all of it.'

'Your Highness, do get up! Oh, don't kneel like that! Of course I will. The Boars aren't my clan any more, anyway. They'd never take me back, would they? All I have is Peddyc and Anasyn and the Rams, and they're prince's men now.'

'That's true.' Bellyra did rise, dusting off her skirts with both hands. 'My heart aches for you, though. But Maryn will spare your mother. I can't imagine him harming a woman, I just can't.'

'No more can I. But will he force her into a temple?'

'Not if you beg him not to. He's going to owe you a lot, isn't he?' Bellyra smiled, then glanced at Casso. 'Oh, you little beast! Get those out of your mouth!'

At the sound of the Princess's raised voice, Arda came rushing in from the adjoining chamber. Lilli left them to fuss over Casyl and wandered across the room to look out the window. Between the towers of Dun Cerrmor she could just see a distant stripe of ocean, blazing with sunset. To her dweomer sight the water seemed to burn, and in that fire it seemed she heard men screaming in rage.

'Look – the moon's past full again,' Maryn said. 'She looked just like that when we invested the dun. So far they don't seem to be surrendering. I wonder why they're so slow about it?'

Nevyn allowed himself a brief smile at the Prince's jest. They were standing outside the royal pavilion, a large white affair with a peaked roof hung with the banner of the Red Wyvern. In the pale dawn light the gibbous moon lingered at the western horizon. Since he was hungry, Nevyn found himself thinking that she looked like a spectral cheese with one good slice nicked off. All through the scattered camp the army was waking. From cooking fires thin tendrils of smoke began to rise, as ghostly as the moon. Maryn yawned with a toss of his head.

'I wonder how my lady fares. Well, the messengers should ride in today, don't you think?'

'There's been more than enough time for them to reach Cerrmor and ride back, truly,' Nevyn said. 'But I doubt me if Bellyra will have given birth yet. Another turn of the moon, most likely.'

'Well, when her time comes, the messengers will know where to find me, sure enough.'

Messengers arrived that very afternoon, and with them aid for the Prince's cause beyond any Nevyn would have hoped for. He was helping the chirurgeons change bandages when he heard shouting in the direction of the main gates. Some while later, just as he was finishing up, a manservant trotted up to fetch him.

'The Prince says there's urgent news, my lord. Somewhat of a surprise.'

A surprise it was – when Nevyn ducked into the Prince's pavilion, he saw Lilli and two servant lasses, Lilli perched on a stool, the lasses sitting cross-legged on the ground – all of them wearing road-dirty brigga under their dresses. For a moment he goggled while Maryn laughed at him.

'I felt just the same, good councillor,' Maryn said. 'Lady Lillorigga of the Ram has brought us a boon beyond wishing for.'

'Indeed?' Nevyn bowed to her.

'Indeed. She knows the location of the bolthole out of the dun. And needless to say, what leads out also leads in.'

Lilli nodded and tried to smile, but she seemed nearer tears. All at once Nevyn remembered that she had blood-kin trapped inside the fortress.

'You look weary, my lady,' Nevyn said. 'We'd best work out where you and your women can safely shelter. Of course, with your foster-father here to protect you, you should have naught to worry about.'

'Just so.' Maryn glanced around and saw a page standing at the door. 'Go find Tieryn Peddyc and tell him his foster-daughter's here.' He turned to Nevyn. 'I'll have the herald announce it to the camp, that any man who gives her women the least bit of trouble will be publicly flogged.'

'That should take care of it, truly.' Nevyn allowed himself a wry smile. 'Lilli, will you and your lasses shelter near me? I have a large tent, which you three can have, and I'll commandeer myself a little one to put outside its door.'

'My humble thanks, Nevyn.' Lilli glanced at the girls, who of course agreed in murmurs. 'There's much I need to talk over with you.'

'No doubt. It's a grave thing you've done, but I honour you for it.'

Along with Lilli and her two lasses, Clodda and Nalla, Princess Bellyra had sent a cart with a royal amount of gear – mattresses, blankets, a little half-round chair for Lilli, a chest of clothes and oddments, even an old, faded Bardek carpet for the floor. Once all these furnishings were set up in Nevyn's tent, the place looked quite comfortable, as Nevyn remarked.

'Still,' the old man continued, 'I wonder about the wisdom of your being here. I don't like thinking about what might happen if the Regent's men sally.'

'We should be safe enough for now, my lord,' Lilli said. 'Here between the outer walls.'

'True. Still – I'd like you sent home to Cerrmor as soon as possible.'

Together they left the tent and walked outside. In the sun of a cloudless day Dun Deverry loomed at the top of the view, still seemingly safe behind its inner rings and baffles. Somewhere in those towers, Lilli thought, was her mother, perhaps looking down at the enemy camp so far below while her daughter looked up at her.

'Nevyn?' Lilli said. 'Do you think I'm doing the right thing?'

'Absolutely.'

'Even though I'm betraying my kin and clan?'

'Even so. Do you know how these wars started?'

'I don't, truly. I mean, I must have heard the tale at some time or other. I just can't remember it.'

'Very few people remember, it's been so long since, and fewer still care. War is all they've ever known. And that's why your betrayal is no betrayal, but an act of honour, because it will end the long war and let the people remember peace.'

'I hope you're right, I truly do.'

'So do I. I've staked my own Wyrd on it.'

She turned to see him smiling, but ruefully.

'Very well,' she said. 'Then I'll serve the Prince in any way that I can.'

Yet round her heart she felt as cold and hard as the stone towers, so dark against the sky. She stood looking up at them until a familiar voice called her name: Peddyc. She turned to see the men of the Ram trotting toward her.

'Lilli!' Anasyn threw an arm around her shoulder. 'The page told us about the bolthole. How splendid of you!'

Tight in his brotherly embrace she could laugh; she felt safe, she realized, for the first time in weeks. Peddyc stood watching, smiling a little, his eyes, set so deep in his lean face, weary from the soul.

'Bevva would be proud of you,' he said. 'You're a daughter of the Ram, sure enough.'

'Well, there! You see?' Oggyn said. 'Our little Boarswoman has found a way to get herself to the battle.'

'What?' Nevyn snarled. 'What could she possibly-'

'Who knows? But I think she should be placed under close guard.'

'Like a criminal? After she's risked so much to help the Prince's cause?'

'The matter could be presented as a move to protect her.'

Nevyn stopped himself from snarling again. Oggyn's moist mouth smiled inside his beard, as if at a victory.

'And how will Tieryn Peddyc and his men take that?' Nevyn said.

'Or his overlord, for that matter?'

Oggyn's smile disappeared. He turned on his heel and marched off, leaving Nevyn fuming behind him. Caradoc, who'd been watching from a little distance, strolled over.

'What a generous nature he has,' the captain remarked. 'So mindful of the niceties of honour.'

Nevyn relieved his feelings with a string of oaths. Caradoc laughed.

'I just don't understand why he's so suspicious of the lass,' Nevyn said. 'There's naught she can do that would injure Maryn's cause.'

'It's not the lass, my lord. It's you. You've got more influence over the Prince than any man alive. Oggyn's jealous. Needs to feel like he's bested you in somewhat, even a little thing that should be beneath his notice.'

Nevyn opened his mouth to speak, then shut it again.

'Him and that Tieryn Gauryc,' Caradoc went on. 'I see him and Oggyn with their heads together now and again.'

'Indeed? Interesting. You're right, of course, about Oggyn. He'd love to have more of the Prince's favour, and that means I need to have less. But Gauryc?'

'I don't know what's griping his soul so badly. I could ask around.'

'Would you? I should be most grateful.'

Nevyn had servants set him up a small tent some few feet in front of the door into Lilli's, so that he'd see anyone entering and leaving there. He'd just finished moving his things into it when Caradoc returned, bearing news. They walked a little away from the camp down toward the outer wall to get some privacy.

'Here's the gossip, my lord,' Caradoc said. 'And men who sneer at women for being gossips should sew up the rip in their own brigga first – I've seen a lot of bare bum today. Gossip about this, gossip about that! Ye gods! But the rumour that matters to us wins the tourney, like. When Maryn's High King, it runs, he'll bestow the Cerrmor gwerbretrhyn upon you. Gauryc rather fancies that rhan for himself or his eldest son.'

'That's ridiculous! I'm much too old, and I don't have heirs. I'm not likely to get any, either.'

'Oh here, my lord! If you were Gwerbret Cerrmor, would your age matter one whit to a noble-born lass? For that matter, here's young Lilli, an exile with no dowry. She can't afford to be fussy, like, and they've all seen her walking with you in the gardens back home.'

'Ye gods! They think I'm courting her? Well, that would indeed give our Gauryc somewhat to worry over.'

'Like a terrier with a rat.'

'My thanks, captain. I'll do some thinking and see if I can lay their minds to rest.'

'Why? Let them chew on it a-while. It'll keep them out of trouble, like. A terrier that's got a rat won't go killing chickens.'

Nevyn laughed while Caradoc stood grinning, his hands shoved in his brigga pockets.

'And speaking of the Lady Lillorigga,' Caradoc went on. 'The Prince wants to talk with her as soon as she's rested. He'd like you to escort her.'

'I will, of course. Huh. That'll give our terriers another nice juicy rat. Freshly killed.'

That night, in front of his pavilion Maryn held a council of war. Off to one side he had the servants lay a small fire and tend it to provide light without too much heat, while he sat in a chair with Oggyn and Nevyn standing behind him and the gwerbretion and Caradoc as well sitting on the ground in front of him. At the Prince's request, Nevyn summarized what Lilli had told them earlier.

'So there's a bolthole, sure enough,' Nevyn finished up. 'But it doesn't open anywhere as convenient as the King's bed chambers. It's a long walk from that side ward she described to the main gates, and between the main gates and us lie two rings of open ground as well.'

'It would be better, then,' Maryn said, 'if we took the next ring uphill before we used the bolthole. I doubt if they'll fight hard for it. It just encloses empty land.'

'That's a good point, Your Highness,' Caradoc put in. 'I've been doing some thinking. This dun was built as much for show as for defence. Why, by the hells! It would take ten thousand men to man these walls all proper, like.'

Maryn nodded a grim agreement. The noble-born sat quietly for a moment, digesting the news; then Tieryn Gauryc rose to speak.

'My prince? I'm wondering if perhaps we should just hold our siege and let hunger do the fighting.'

'A good point, my lord,' Maryn said, 'but starving them out means starving half the countryside with them. How are we going to provision this army all winter long? Not without stripping every farm for miles around. I have no intention of ruling a kingdom of ghosts.'

'Ghosts don't provision great courts, either,' Oggyn added. 'If I may be so bold as to speak, my prince?'

'By all means.'

'My thanks, Your Highness. By my reckoning, we've confiscated all we can from the farms without stripping their seed corn or starving the men who'll plant it. If there's no winter wheat to ripen in the spring, what will the army be eating then?'

For the first time since he'd met him, Nevyn felt that Oggyn was an excellent fellow. The noble-born began to talk among themselves, but in a few brief words of what seemed to be agreement.

'And another thing, my liege,' Oggyn went on. 'From what the men of the Ram tell me, the majority of the Usurper's provisions and stores lie in the next to the last ring. If we capture those, then the situation of the royal compound becomes even more precarious.'

'An excellent point,' Nevyn said. 'I recommend it to Your Highness.'

Oggyn smiled and bowed in his direction.

'Now here!' Gwerbret Daeryc scrambled up. 'Are we all cooks and chamberlains, to stand around discussing bins of grain and jugs of milk?'

'Of course not, Your Grace!' Peddyc rose and stepped forward to calm his overlord down. 'What truly counts, my prince and liege, is the honour of the thing.'

'Indeed, Tieryn Peddyc?' Maryn said. 'And what may that be?'

'That we're warriors born and bred, not gatekeepers!' Daeryc interrupted.

'That's true, Your Grace.' Peddyc smiled with a rueful twist of his mouth. 'And since there's a way in to the dun, I say we take it-'

'-and flush the bastards out of cover!' Daeryc broke in.

Maryn tossed back his head and laughed.

'It seems to me, then, that the chamberlain and the warrior agree.' Maryn looked round at the semi-circle of lords. 'What do you say, men?'

'Attack! Red wyvern! Red wyvern!'

Their cheers rang out like brass bells on the evening wind.

'They're up to something!' Burcan snarled. 'Listen to that!'

From a great distance the sound of cheering drifted to the dun on the night wind. The sound turned Merodda omen-cold.

'They are at that,' she said.

'Rhodi, are you well?' Burcan caught her arm. 'You sound as if you're going to faint.'

'My apologies. Let's go inside. The air out here's turned so cold.'

With his other hand Burcan held up the lantern he was carrying and peered into her face.

'It's quite warm, as a matter of fact,' he said at last. 'Let's get you to your chamber so you can rest.'

Yet after he'd left her, Merodda got out her scrying basin. Every time she thought of Lilli, she felt torn twixt joy that her only daughter was safe and bitter envy. That night she scried for Lilli in the same spirit as she'd poke a bruise to ensure it still pained her. When she thought of Lilli, nothing came. The surface of the black ink stayed black without the slightest trace of an image upon it.

When Merodda tried to pour the ink back into its leather bottle, her hands shook so badly that she let it be. This could only mean one thing, that Lilli was here at the siege where Nevyn could protect her. But why? Peddyc and the Rams knew the dun better than she did, after all. What did she know that she could bring to the Usurper, a traitor's gift? Or was it – Merodda's hands turned so cold that she tucked them into her armpits. No doubt this Nevyn knew of the child's gift with omens. No doubt he wished to use it for himself, just as she had.

Her own daughter had become a knife, laid against the heart of the dun.

On the morrow morning, Lilli escorted the Prince to the opening of the bolthole. As soon as she'd described the ruins to Peddyc, he'd recognized them, and now he led the Prince there, along with the Ram warband and the entire troop of silver daggers. For good measure Nevyn tagged along as well.

The sky hung heavy with clouds, promising summer rain. When they rode up to the broken wall and the stump of a broch, the oppressive air muffled sound. Even the cawing of the ravens seemed far away.

'This broch's been deserted for many a long year now,' Peddyc said. 'It's supposed to be haunted.'

'Of course,' Nevyn said, grinning. 'Aren't they all?'

Peddyc laughed, but uneasily. Everyone dismounted. The Ramsmen took over the horses while the prince, Nevyn, Lilli, and a few silver daggers, Branoic among them, walked into the waist-high weeds flourishing in the old ward. For a moment, seeing the place from a new angle, Lilli felt disoriented, but she recognized a spray of fallen stones.

'Around here, Your Highness,' she said. 'If you'll follow me?'

'Gladly, my lady,' Maryn said, bowing. 'But we'll send one of my men ahead, just in case someone desperate's found the shelter.'

Without incident, though, everyone trooped round the side of the broken broch. The gaping entrance to the stone steps lay just where Lilli expected it.

'Down there, Your Highness. There's a cellar and then a heavy door.'

'Splendid!' Maryn started forward, but Nevyn caught his arm.

'My liege, please.' The old man sounded weary. 'Do let your guards precede you.'

While the Prince and five of the silver daggers poked around in the cellar, Nevyn and Lilli sat down on a hunk of broken wall to wait. Overhead the skies were growing darker; the ravens had fallen silent and flown off to hide from the coming rain. Lilli felt sweat trickling down her back. She wiped her face on the long sleeve of her riding dress.

'Ugly sort of day,' Nevyn remarked.

'It is, my lord. I keep thinking of Brour. The last time I saw him was just there, heading off west with a peddlar's pack.'

'And now he's dead. A sad thing, truly.'

All at once it struck Lilli that Nevyn had never doubted her dweomer-produced knowledge that Brour was dead. Her mother would have probed like a judge.

'I wish she hadn't had him chased down and killed,' Lilli said. 'My mother, I mean. All he wanted was to get away.'

'I assume she was afraid of what he knew about her. I-' Nevyn hesitated.

From the cellar came a most unroyal whoop of triumph. With muck and dust all over his shirt, Prince Maryn emerged into the ruined ward. A cobweb gleamed in his golden hair.

'Cursed heavy door,' the Prince said, grinning. 'How did you get it open, Lilli?'

Hearing him use her nickname made Lilli blush, though she couldn't say why.

'I didn't, Your Highness. My tutor did that.'

'Ah, I see.'

'My liege?' Nevyn said. 'Where are your guards?'

'Following the tunnel down a-ways. Caradoc's as grim as you are,

Nevyn. He wouldn't let me come along.' Maryn glanced around, saw
a chunk of fallen stone, and sat upon it. 'I told him not to go too far.
Here, Lilli, you don't think anyone else knows this secret?'

'I don't, Your Highness.'

'Why?'

'My liege,' Nevyn broke in, 'there was considerable dweomer
involved in its finding.'

Maryn started to speak, then merely stared at Lilli, his lips half-
parted in sudden awe. She felt her face burning again, cursed it, and
looked down at the ground. Bevyan always said you should lower your
eyes if royalty looked straight at you, anyway.

'Well, then,' Maryn said at last. 'No doubt the secret's safe enough.
When we get back to camp, you can tell us where this opens out.
Could you draw a map in the earth?'

'I'll be glad to try, Your Highness.'

'You know,' Nevyn broke in again. 'Peddyc and Daeryc and all the
Rams and suchlike know Dun Deverry quite well. They can tell us
what we need. I think Lilli should return to Cerrmor.'

'But is it safe?' Maryn said. 'Even on a river barge? There are
marauders all around, Nevyn, all those deserter warbands, and
some of them have lost their lords, most likely, and turned into
brigands.'

'Huh.' Nevyn considered this for a long moment. 'True enough. I'd
forgotten about that.'

Lilli looked back and forth between them, struck by how casually
they spoke when there were no noble-born around to hear them. She
wondered if Nevyn was of royal blood himself, to speak to the Prince
so boldly.

'What do you say, Lilli?' Nevyn said. 'There's grave danger either
way, to stay or go home.'

'As long as my prince has need of me, I'll stay.'

Maryn smiled at her, and it seemed that the day turned bright. For
a moment she felt that she might slip into trance, as if his magical
power and grace blended to drug her senses. All at once she realized
that Nevyn was watching her with grim eyes. She looked away,
fumbling for something to say, but the silver daggers saved her by
appearing at the top of the steps.

'My liege?' Caradoc said. 'It never does turn narrow. We can get a
good lot of men down here if we want to.'

'Splendid!' Maryn jumped up with a toss of his golden head. 'Let's get back to camp and do some scheming.'

Lilli hung back and let him stride off in the company of his men. Nevyn slipped an arm through hers as they walked after.

'Some beautiful things are dangerous,' he remarked.

'Do you mean the Prince, my lord?'

'I don't. I mean the Princess.'

Their eyes met, and he raised one bushy eyebrow.

'I understand,' Lilli said quickly. 'Truly I do.'

And yet for the long ride home she felt half-sick with grief, no matter how hard she tried to pretend she cared nothing for Prince Maryn's favour.

On the way back to camp, the rain came with a boom of thunder and soaked everyone in the Prince's party before they could finish complaining about it. As they rode up to the city gates, Nevyn spotted another wet group of travellers there ahead them. Five riders led the way; then came a cart with wickerwork sides, drawn by a single horse, and behind that two men on foot. All of them, riders and walkers alike, wore plain tunics that left their legs bare.

'Priests!' Maryn said. 'What are they doing here?'

'I don't know, my liege,' Nevyn said. 'But I can hope.'

Maryn turned in the saddle to give him a puzzled glance. Nevyn laughed and clucked to his horse.

'Let's get back to camp, Your Highness. If the priests wish to speak to you, they'll know where to find you.'

That very night, indeed, the priests arrived at Prince Maryn's pavilion. During all the many sieges of Dun Deverry, the priests of Bel had held neutral, safe on their holy hill where no sane man would spill blood. This time, however, with the omens running as a high as a spring tide and an enormous army camped round the dun, the head priest Gwaevyr sent a pair of neophytes to Maryn, would-be king of all Deverry.

It was just after sunset when a servant pulled aside the tent-flap and ushered in two young men with shaved heads and golden torcs around their necks. Although they both bowed to the Prince, neither knelt. The only lord they paid fealty to was Bel himself. Maryn returned their bow.

'And what brings you to me?' the Prince said. 'Though the gods themselves know that the vassals of the gods are always welcome here.'

'My thanks.' The elder had a dry little voice. 'The High Priest himself, his holiness Gwaevyr of Dun Deverry, sent us to summon you to the altars of the god.'

'Did he say why?'

'He didn't.'

The priests bowed, turned, and strode out of the tent, leaving Maryn staring after them.

'Oho!' Nevyn said. 'I think me we'd best go, my liege. This could well be to your advantage.'

'It's not a summons I'd ignore, anyway. Very well. I'll take a pair of guards.'

'Please do, and I think we'd best take your council of lords as well. For witnesses.'

By then the rain had stopped, and stars showed in the rifts between the sailing clouds above. The temple complex perched on the top of the second highest hill in Dun Deverry, though unlike the royal complex it sported only two circles of outer walls. When the prince's party rode up to the first gate, they found the two messengers there to let them in. The elder raised a candle-lantern and peered at them in its light.

'His Holiness is waiting for you in the temple.' The younger turned to Nevyn. 'High Priest Retyc of Lughcarn is here.'

Nevyn felt cold excitement run through his blood. The time had indeed come.

Escorted by the two priests, they rode on through a strip of mead-owland, then through the second gate and into the complex proper. Priests' houses, a cow barn, vegetable gardens, outbuildings, sheds – a small village spread out inside the complex. Other priests stood waiting to take their horses, but no one said a word to them, merely watched the Prince with unreadable eyes.

In a grove of old oaks stood the round temple, a simple building made of white-washed wood and covered by a thatched roof, as if it were some country shrine. Inside, under a smoke hole in the roof, stood a stone altar at the centre of the round room. At the edge, under the eaves, stood a ring of wooden statues, each carved from a single tree-trunk, all huge and roughly man-shaped. Some had faces so beautifully carved you'd swear they were about to speak; others displayed rough-chiselled eyes and a single gash for a mouth. On all of them the arms were crudely cut, still attached to the body along the inside, but each broad-knuckled hand held a human skull.

In the Dawntime, Nevyn knew, those skulls would have been severed heads, tribute from the enemies of the tribe that supported this shrine. Now they were mementoes of the priests who had served at this temple over the past few hundred years – a last tribute to their god on earth as they went to join him in the Otherlands. At the altar stood a man so old and thin that his face seemed a mere stretch of skin over yet another skull, but his eyes were bright with life. As Nevyn, the Prince, and his lords approached the altar from the front door, a back door opened and more priests filed in, each dressed in plain linen tunics, each with a golden sickle at their belts, each carrying a candle-lantern. One at a time they took places in front of the statues until each wooden Bel had a living man to represent him, and the temple filled with dancing light.

'Welcome!' the High Priest's voice boomed, startlingly loud for one so frail. 'Is this the man men call Prince Maryn of Cerrmor?'

'I am, Your Holiness.' Maryn stepped forward with a respectful bob of his head. 'I've come in answer to your summons.'

Nevyn and the noble-born waited near the door while the Prince walked forward alone. On the altar lay a small casket, once silver, now green with age. Gwaevyr laid one hand upon it.

'Prince Maryn, the god shows me many omens. At night in the darkest hour I come alone to this temple and pray, listening for his voice, looking for a vision for my eyes. He has spoken to me. He has shown me. You are the rightful owner of what lies within this silver box.'

'Blessed be the name of the god,' Maryn whispered. 'I'll gladly take whatever he would give me.'

'Done, then. The false kings have come to me, now and again over the past many years. Where is the brooch? they said. Where is the ring brooch that marks the one true king of all Deverry? But never have I told any man until now.' He gestured at one of the priests. 'Retyc of Lughcarn has kept it hidden in his temple, lest any impious lord attack my temple and try to take it by force. Now the god has told me to give it to his chosen prince.'

Maryn sank to his knees before the altar. At Nevyn's bidding the Wildfolk of Air and Aethyr rushed to his side. All at once the temple seemed to grow in size and brighten with a silvery light that put the candle flames to shame. The noble-born gasped audibly; the priests stood unmoving. Gwaevyr pried at the lock until at last it broke off clean in his fingers. Nevyn swore to himself – he had wanted the omens to show clear and clean without any fumbling. The old priest's withered fingers shook as he opened the lid of the casket to reveal scraps of ancient silk, still bright red from their long confinement away from the sun, but when he lifted them out, the scraps cracked and crumbled in his hands.

'Ah.' Gwaevyr smiled. 'Behold! The brooch of the one true king!'

Nevyn sent a ray of light upon it when, with both hands, the ancient priest lifted up the huge gold ring brooch, studded with rubies and engraved in a complex braid of interlace. Its long pin was shaped like a sword blade with a ruby for a hilt.

'As the braid winds round this brooch, so must the will of the High King lace his subjects into a single whole! With the sword, must he defend them!'

The men waiting at the door caught their breath in a collective gasp. Nevyn found himself studying the brooch, worn somewhat with age. It was the authentic piece, all right – not that anyone would have believed him, if he told them that he'd seen it new.

'Are you worthy of this mark, Prince Maryn?' Gwaevyr said.

'With the help of the gods I shall become so, Your Holiness. If not, then may the gods strike me down.'

The old priest smiled, nodding.

'Well and good, then! Until the war is done and the battle over, I will keep this brooch here in safety. Once the kingdom is at peace, then return here, and by the ancient rites you shall be made High King.'

Pushed beyond the enduring of silence, Maryn's vassals cheered, their voices loud as brass bells in the temple. Gwaevyr laughed and held the brooch up with both hands as high as he could reach.

'Fight well for your prince, my lords! And then you shall see him become a king!'

The cheers rang out again, but deep in his soul, Nevyn felt a cold needle of fear. What was causing this delay?

Early in the morning, long before Maryn could wake and send for him, Nevyn returned alone to the temple of Bel. Apparently word had been left at the gates; the young priests on guard allowed him past immediately. He found Retyc, a solid man of middle years, strolling under the oaks alone. The morning sun slanted through their leaves and created long pillars of light between the trees, as if they walked in the god's own house with the sky for a ceiling. All round them birds sang.

'I guessed that you'd come up, Nevyn,' Retyc said, and he was smiling. 'Let me guess. You're wondering why we didn't declare him king last night and be done with it.'

'Just that,' Nevyn said. 'Have the omens gone sour?'

'Naught of the sort! It's a blasted strange little thing, and it irks me, but there's no way round it. The rites of kingship demand a white mare, and we can't find one.'

'What?'

'I've sent messengers all over Deverry proper, and up into Gwaentaer, too. It's this wretched war. Horses of any sort are at a premium, with so many of them killed each summer, and there's not a white mare to be found. I did hear of one old lass with a spot of grey on her forehead, but the ancient laws are absolutely unshakeable: a white mare with no blemish. And young. It's best if she's never borne a foal, though they give you a bit of leeway on that.'

'How kind of them. I trust you're still looking?'

'Of course. Unfortunately, the best horses in the kingdom all come from Cantrae. I doubt if the Boars would honour my request even if I sent a man with a bag of silver their way.'

'Imph. What a wretched circumstance!'

'Now here, don't look so distressed! We'll find one. It's a bothersome delay, truly, but white horses are sacred partly because they're so rare. And well, with this war . . .' Retyc shrugged with spread hands.

Logically, rationally Nevyn knew he was right, but dread ate at him. He felt as if this setback marked a twining-point in some band of knotwork, one that he should be able to see. But although he brooded upon it all day, the pattern hid just out of his mind's reach.

That evening Lilli dined with Peddyc and his overlord, an invitation which here in the middle of the war translated to their bringing food to her tent and sitting on the ground to eat it, while she sat in the only chair. Gwerbret Daeryc had brought her a present of a three plums wrapped in a bit of rag, which he handed her with a bow.

'My thanks, Your Grace,' Lilli said, smiling. 'Where did these come from?'

'One of men found a plum tree down in the city. Whoever owns it is long gone. No use in letting them go to waste. A bit of fresh food means a lot in a long siege like this.'

'I can well imagine, Your Grace.'

Anasyn had found mead as well, and after they ate the three men formally toasted her from chipped ceramic stoups.

'To your courage, lass!' Daeryc said.

Anasyn and Peddyc raised their mead and joined the toast. I must have done the right thing, she told herself, if they honour me for it.

'My thanks, my lords,' she said. 'I'm only grateful I can serve our Prince.'

'Our mother trained you well.' Anasyn was grinning at her. 'You know all the humble things to say, but I'll bet you're proud as proud in there.'

Lilli stuck her tongue out at him, and everyone laughed. Daeryc drained off his mead, then stood up and handed the stoup to one of Lilli's maidservants.

'We'd best be off,' Daeryc said with a nod to Peddyc. 'The Prince will be convening his council of war.'

Lilli stood at the door of the tent under the darkening sky and watched them out of sight. She felt almost giddy with happiness, yet she sensed some darker feeling under her mood; somewhere, just beyond her consciousness, terror crouched, ready to spring.

'Well, my liege,' Caradoc said. 'It seems to me that the silver daggers are the right men to open that gate for you.' He paused to glance around the assembled council of lords. 'Begging your pardon and all, my lords, but the men on this little expedition need to be absolutely loyal to the Prince, and not have kin and distant relations, like, in that dun.'

Nevyn winced. Sure enough, the noble-born began muttering among themselves. Caradoc pitched his voice above the noise.

'And what's more,' Caradoc went on. 'The men who do this can't have the slightest shred of honour. If some serving lass surprises us and starts to scream, then she'll have to die and fast. Are any of you going to do such, my lords?'

The muttering stopped. They were all perfectly capable of such murders, Nevyn knew. But they'd never admit it, not even to themselves.

'My captain speaks the truth,' Prince Maryn said. 'Although it aches my heart to condemn any man to a task like this, the silver daggers will be the ones opening the gates.'

The lords looked at one another, then nodded assent. If anything, Nevyn realized, they were relieved to be spared the job.

'So then,' Maryn went on. 'First we'll take the third wall in open assault. The army will rest afterwards, two days perhaps depending on how well the assault went. Then we'll move on the fourth wall. At night the silver daggers will go through the bolthole while we get our men ready. Once they open the gates of the fourth wall, we'll charge across and take it. Are we agreed?'

The noble-born called out their assent, nodding to the Prince and one another. Tieryn Peddyc, however, got to his feet.

'My liege,' he said. 'The silver daggers will need a man along who knows Dun Deverry. I've been riding there every summer since I was but a lad.'

'Now here!' Daeryc rose and glared at him. 'You're right about the need, but it's my place to go.'

'It's not, Your Grace. You're more valuable to the Prince outside the walls.'

Both men turned and looked at the Prince.

'I'd say it's up to Caradoc,' Maryn said. 'Which he chooses shall go.'

'I agree with the tieryn, Your Highness.' Caradoc kept his gaze on the Prince and away from Daeryc. 'His grace the gwerbret is far too valuable to risk.'

With his honour salved, Daeryc could sit down and leave the task to his vassal. Nevyn was quite willing to wager that Daeryc would have proven more hindrance than help, but he found himself wondering why Peddyc had volunteered.

When the council broke up, Nevyn caught the tieryn's attention. They walked a few steps away from the others where they could talk in reasonable privacy.

'I'm a bit surprised,' Nevyn said, 'that you're going with Caradoc's lads and not young Anasyn.'

'Anasyn is my clan's future. I'd not squander it.'

'You do know, then, how dangerous this will be.'

'Of course.' Peddyc gave him the ghost of a smile. 'But I feel like a silver dagger myself these days. I believe with all my heart that Maryn's the true king, mind. But the Rams have fought on the Cantrae side of this battle ever since the wars started, however long ago it was.'

'I see. I didn't think that you'd change allegiance lightly.'

'My thanks. Some clans are like autumn leaves. They fall whichever way the winds of victory are blowing. But it was a hard thing for me.' Peddyc paused for a long time, staring into the darkened camp. 'The Prince may have pardoned me, but I still feel like a dishonoured man.'

'For having fought against him? Or for having gone over to him?'

'Both.'

'Well, I'd count neither to your shame.'

'My thanks.' He smiled, briefly. 'It's getting late, Councillor. We'd best be getting ourselves to our rest.'

Peddyc walked off without another word. Nevyn watched him go and wondered if there was a thing he could say to the tieryn to ease this crisis of honour. He doubted very much if there were.

None of the silver daggers took part in the assault on the third ring of walls. Branoic felt ashamed at how glad he was of it, but from what Caradoc had told them, they had the hardest job of all ahead of them, anyway. When the dawn was still more a promise than first light, the assault men began readying the rams and the ladders. Caradoc gathered his men and, much to Branoic's surprise, Tieryn Peddyc and Lady Lillorigga, and led them off away from the noise.

'Now then,' Caradoc said. 'The lady has graciously deigned to tell us where this bolthole comes out, like, in the dun. And the tieryn will be coming with us when we go through to make sure we don't get ourselves lost. My lady, if you'll tell us what you know?'

Branoic was impressed with the way Lilli spoke. She described the bolthole's debouchment so well that he formed a picture of the place immediately. When other men asked, she went over the information several times, each time presenting it in a slightly different way, until at the end they all felt they knew the place. With a stick she drew a diagram in the earth, as well, which Peddyc pronounced accurate.

'I was just a lad when that section of the dun burned,' Peddyc said. 'My father told me that they weren't going to stand the expense of rebuilding, because it was deserted and held nothing of value.'

'What I wonder, my lord,' Caradoc said, 'is why no one even remembered that a bolthole existed.'

'I don't know that myself, captain, but I can guess. The kings have never trusted anyone much, and probably rightly so. I doubt if anyone knew of the bolthole but them. When my father was a lad, a king and his eldest son were killed in the same battle. I'd guess they hadn't told the younger son the family secrets yet.'

'Likely, indeed.' Caradoc turned to Lilli and bowed. 'Here, my lady, you have my humble thanks. There's no need to keep you standing around with the likes of us.'

Branoic stepped forward and made her a bow.

'I'll be glad to escort the lady to her tent,' he said.

'Indeed?' Peddyc turned and looked him over so coldly that Branoic stepped back. 'I'll take my foster-daughter back myself.'

Branoic managed a smile and faded back into the crowd of silver daggers, but not before he caught the expression on Caradoc's face – laughing at him, curse him! Fortunately, no one in the troop ragged him about it, not even when the tieryn and his foster-daughter were well out of earshot.

'I wish we could do without Peddyc's aid,' Caradoc said. 'This isn't going to be a fight for the noble-born, mucking about on foot in the dark.'

'If you think he'll get in the way,' Owaen said, 'talk to the Prince about it.'

'That's not it.' Caradoc looked around at the troop. 'Lads, listen. We're going to have find our way through a dun we've never seen, and then pray the gates aren't guarded. Do you think the gods will answer that prayer? Neither do I. Some of us are going to end up fighting a rearguard action so a few of us can win through. Do you understand what I mean?'

Branoic felt ice run down his spine. When he glanced around the troop, he saw some men smiling in a tight and twisted way, some nodding their heads, others merely grim. Very few of them were going to live through this expedition. Ah well, Branoic thought. I always knew this day would come, when I died for our prince. Maddyn stepped forward, one hand on the hilt of his dagger.

'I'm going with you when the time comes.'

'You're not,' Caradoc snapped. 'I want someone left to keep our name alive.'

From far up the hill came the call of silver horns and a sudden shouting, drifting like thunder on the wind. The silver daggers turned toward the sound and to a man they smiled. The assault on the third wall had begun.

Taking the third wall went better than could be expected, Nevyn supposed. Although the Regent had posted guards along it, still the attack seemed to come as a surprise. After a hundred years, the civil wars had become as predictable as a ritual in a temple. Everyone knew that Dun Deverry could never fall to assault; everyone knew that Dun Deverry could only be taken by siege. The exhausted leaders and their ever-smaller armies had conformed to these ritual beliefs – until Maryn.

Surprise in war is one of the seven great delights, or so the Gel da 'Thae say. By the time the Regent could muster enough men for a proper defence, the rams had started pounding at the only pair of gates in the third wall. As one ram fell back, the second rushed forward, one after the other in a constant rhythm.

'It wasn't long at all before we had our breach,' Maryn said. 'And Burcan couldn't muster enough men fast enough to keep us off the wall.'

'I see, my liege,' Nevyn said. 'Well, I'm glad it was over quickly.'

'So am I. But the next time he'll be ready. I'll pray to every god that Caradoc can get those gates open. We'll never take the fourth wall if he can't.'

A page came out of the pavilion and handed the Prince a goblet – mead, Nevyn noticed. He drank half of it straight off like water, then wiped his mouth on the back of his hand.

'But the third wall's ours now?' Nevyn said.

'Well and truly. The assault men have already stripped the old catwalks and moved the winch.' Maryn glanced at the sky, where the sun hung low in the west. 'I'd say the turning point came at noon.'

'Good. If you'll excuse me, Your Highness? Caradoc wanted a word with me.'

Nevyn met Caradoc outside his tent. The captain wasted no time in pleasantries.

'Nevyn, my lord, I've somewhat to ask you. I've been thinking about that mysterious rain that fell on Burcan's army, just before the battle of Camrydd Bridge, it would be.'

'Are you now? And I suppose you remember that I had somewhat to do with it.'

Caradoc merely grinned.

'And?' Nevyn said.

'It would be a grand thing if no one could see us silver daggers creeping through the dun from the bolthole. There's naught like a good hard rain to drive men indoors.'

'Just so. But how are the silver daggers proposing to see through a rain hard enough to hide them?'

Caradoc opened his mouth and shut it again.

'Indeed,' Nevyn said, grinning. 'Didn't think of that, did you? And before you waste the breath asking, I cannot turn men invisible.' He let the smile fade. 'Truly, if I can help you with sorcery, I will, but I need to think. Every idea I've come up with so far would hinder you more than them.'

'I see.' Caradoc reached up and rubbed the back of his head with one hand. 'Curse it all!'

On the other side of the tents, someone cheered. Distantly Nevyn heard more cheers, and then laughter, ringing out closer and louder.

'Let's just see what the lads are up to,' Caradoc said.

They walked through the tents to a sort of road, mostly an open strip of mud, that wound through the entire camp. Trotting toward them were a gaggle of men with the Cerrmor three ships blazon on their shirts. One of them carried a Boar banner, tied to a long spear. He was waving it about and laughing, while all along his route men stopped what they were doing and turned to jeer.

'It's a fine piglet now, isn't it? All ready to be roasted and sliced, isn't it?'

Others suggested a number of obscene things that the Regent could do with a boar if he were even man enough to catch one. Caradoc merely grinned with a shake of his head.

'Let them gloat,' he remarked to Nevyn. 'The gods all know they've earned it.'

Lilli was walking with Anasyn when the captured Boar pennant passed them. By then it had gathered a pack of escorts, all of them laughing and jeering, and it seemed likely that a good ration of ale had gone round among them as well. Anasyn put an arm around her shoulders and drew her off the path as the improvised parade went by. No one noticed them. Lilli felt herself tremble. Once that blazon had summed up her clan's honour, its pride, its very identity. Soon the information she'd brought the Prince would tear it down from every wall until the name itself became a word fit to jest with it.

'You're white as ghost,' Anasyn said. 'Here, do you want to go back to your tent?'

'I don't know. I feel so odd. Oh ye gods, I really am a traitor, aren't I?'

'And what did you betray? A bunch of murdering fools!' His voice cracked and growled. 'A regent who's more of a usurper. Someone who'd kill women on the roads.'

Lilli felt the tearing again, as if hands had grabbed her soul and were trying to rip it apart. The sensation suddenly became physical, as if those hands were grasping her lungs.

'Let's go back,' Anasyn said. 'Here. Lean on me.'

Panting for breath, Lilli had no choice but to let him lead her back to her tent. She sank into her chair and let her maidservants fuss over her, but in her mind the words chanted with every pound of her heart: traitor, traitor, traitor to your clan.

In the day's battle Burcan had been hit across the face with something. He neither remembered nor cared whether it was the flat of a sword, a gauntlet, or a pole. The blow had left him with a red and purple bruise marked with tiny cuts – splits in the skin, really – down the middle like a line of red embroidery. Merodda made him lie down on her bed, then brewed up a poultice of herbs at the hearth in the other room. When she came back into the bedchamber with her supplies, he'd fallen asleep, but he woke when she set the pots and cloths down on the chest under the window.

'What is that?' he said. 'It smells foul.'

'No doubt, but it'll draw any corrupted humours out of the wound.'

'It's not a wound. Just a blasted bruise.'

But he made no objection when she put the warm cloth, wrapped round damp herbs, onto his cheek. She sat down on the edge of the bed and held it in place. In a draught from the window the candle-flames danced in long shadows.

'It was a real setback today, wasn't it?' Merodda said at last.

Burcan hesitated, staring up at the ceiling.

'It was, of course, but there's some good in it. There are two rings left twixt us and them still, and now both are of a size we can hold.' He shifted uneasily. 'That blasted thing is dripping down my neck.'

Merodda took the poultice, wrung it out, and put it back. He grunted when the cloth touched him but allowed her to settle it in place.

'Tomorrow when it's light,' Burcan said, 'I'll have the villagers move inside the last wall. They're too exposed where they are now. If the demon-spawn Usurper does take that fourth wall, he'll take them with it and a lot of stored food too. We'll leave the cattle and swine out there, but the supplies and the people had best move inside.'

'Do you think he'll try for the fourth wall?'

'Why not? He's taken three of them, hasn't he? But now we're in a proper position, one we have enough men to hold. He won't be taking the fourth wall, not unless some god helps him.'

Prince Maryn rested his army for two days, and in the interval Nevyn did conceive of a way to help the silver daggers. When the chosen night came, he called upon the Great Lords of the Elements, who sent a storm over dun and camp alike to put the Regents' men off their guard. After midnight the clouds began to clear in a fitful wind; the moon would shine through, then darken again. The silver daggers would be able to see intermittently, then hide when they needed the dark – or so they could hope. As the troop made their way through the dun, Nevyn would scry them out so that the Prince would know the exact right moment to launch the attack on the fourth wall.

In the middle of the night Nevyn said farewell to Caradoc and his men down at the outermost wall, where they'd assembled with their horses to ride to the bolthole. The men had rolled their outer clothes in the mud, then rubbed earth into their hair and onto their faces for good measure. Carrying shields would have been impossible. For armour they were wearing two shirts with a hauberk between them, no sleeves or hoods for fear of noise. Tieryn Peddyc stood among them, as filthy as anyone else. Around their waists they'd coiled ropes. Although they were wearing cloaks at the moment, Caradoc remarked that they'd send those back with the horses.

'We have to move fast, my lord, and we can't have some bit of cloth getting in our way.'

'Just so. May you have the luck of the gods!'

'My thanks. We'll need it.'

They clasped hands. Although Nevyn allowed himself a wondering if he'd ever see the captain again, he received no omens. Whether they succeeded or failed, whether they lived or died – how well the silver daggers carried out their mission would answer those questions, not a Wyrd. Everything depended now on them.

When they reached the ruined dun, the silver daggers turned their horses over to servants, who would lead them back to the camp. With a lantern in one hand, Caradoc walked among his troop and made sure that each man had tied his scabbard to his leg to keep it from knocking against some wall or obstacle and sounding an alarm. Here and there he rubbed a little more dirt into someone's clothing to hide a spot of white linen. The men gathered in a loose crowd in front of the cellar door that led to the bolthole.

'All right, lads,' Caradoc said. 'Stand where you are a moment, will you?'

The troop turned his way.

'First to catch it!' Caradoc went on. 'Here.'

Caradoc tossed something above the crowd. Red-haired Trevyr reached up and plucked it from the air.

'It's a bit of cloth around a stone,' he told the others. 'We're counting out for squads.'

'Just that,' Caradoc said. 'You're number one. The man next to him, shout out two, and then the next, one again. Remember which number you draw, lads. One or two.'

Branoic ended up with number two, much to his annoyance. Whenever the troop split, Owaen always commanded the second squad, and Branoic would much rather have gone elsewhere. At the very end, Tieryn Peddyc called out 'one', but Caradoc motioned him forward.

'You go with the second squad, my lord,' he said. 'The reason will come clear later.'

'It's your command, here, not mine,' Peddyc said.

'Just that.' Caradoc smiled briefly, then turned to his men. 'Now remember, lads. Noise is the enemy. Pay careful attention to where we come out of this tunnel. If you get cut off by some mishap and you can't go forward, then retreat to the bolthole and come back here. But be blasted sure you don't give the bolthole away. We don't want the bloody little false king escaping.'

In ranks of four they entered the dark tunnel. At the head of the line Caradoc's lantern bobbed and gleamed, showing the way as they tramped along, heading downhill from the dun. Branoic had never been so aware of noise: the sound of their boots slapping on the muddy ground, their breathing, the occasional cough, the rustle of cloth on the concealed mail. He reminded himself that out in the open air the same amount of noise would sound much less.

The tunnel abruptly jogged. When Branoic reached out a hand, he touched the pillar of worked stone Lilli had mentioned. They were passing under the walls of Dun Deverry. From there the tunnel sloped up a good long hike that had Branoic sweating by the time it finally levelled out. A murmur to halt passed down the line. They had reached the door.

Branoic could see some of the men milling about at the head of line, but no one spoke. The lantern suddenly brightened, held aloft in Peddyc's hand. It seemed that Caradoc was doing something to the door itself. The candle-lantern dipped down and went out. Fresh air drifted down the passageway; the doors were opening, but in silence rather than with the shriek Lilli had mentioned. Slowly, carefully, the line began to move forward. Branoic took a deep gulp of the cleaner air and followed his troop through the cellar, then up the wet steps to the deserted ward.

Overhead the clouds were hanging thick. Branoic could only make out large shapes: the walls of the irregular ward, the broken broch behind them, a distant rise of buildings. The ground lay slick with mud and drizzle, and over everything hung the wet scent of decay. Caradoc motioned the troop back. They crowded into the cellar, then two or three at a time jogged across the ward to the wall at the far side. In the shadows they spread out and pressed back against cold stone in a ragged line one man deep. When Branoic reached the wall, he looked back across the little ward to see a distant confusion of dark towers rising against a drift of clouds. The moon broke free again and revealed the confusion as the false king's broch complex, a good safe distance away. As the light faded he saw Caradoc, running to join them. The captain slipped into place at the head of the line next to Tieryn Peddyc.

Caradoc had of course drilled them on the plan over the past few days. They would find a way out of the little ward that enclosed the bolthole, then begin looking for a place to climb over the fifth wall. With Peddyc there to guide them, the first part of the plan proved easy. They left by the same gate as Lilli had, but where she'd gone uphill toward the broch complex, they walked down a narrow space between two walls, then turned to their right and found themselves in an alley between deserted outbuildings. The fifth wall loomed beyond empty sheds – impossible to judge the distance in the murky half-light.

Slowly, moving a few men at a time and for only a few feet at a time, they crept down the alley, which debouched into a muddy open space, too narrow to be called a ward. On the other side rose the stone curve of the fifth wall. The moon broke free of the clouds. With hand signals Caradoc moved his men back among the sheds, while he remained crouching at the alley's mouth. When the moon's light faded, he dashed across and gained the shadow of the wall.

In their hiding places the silver daggers waited. To Branoic it seemed a large eternity before Caradoc appeared again, motioning them over with a wave of his arm. A few at a time, gauging the moonlight, they ran across the open space and spread themselves out along the wall. While they waited, they uncoiled the ropes from their waists. When the moonlight dimmed, Caradoc worked his way down the line.

'No guards on the fifth wall,' he whispered. 'Some on the fourth. We go over a few at a time.'

The first men up tied the ends of the ropes around merlons, but on the rough stones climbing would have been easy enough in daylight. The problem was doing it quietly while groping in the dark for handholds. Branoic was nearly to the top when he set his foot against what seemed to be a protrusion; it was only a shadow. His foot slid against wet stone. With a grab at the rope he saved himself and hung for a moment, spraddled like a target at an archery contest. His feet at last found rough stone, and he pulled himself up. At the top, he rolled onto the broad-topped wall and hid behind a merlon to catch his breath. All along the wall the other silver daggers were doing the same.

Below them, between them and the fourth wall, lay the deserted village – round houses, sheds, long barns, cattle pens, and here and there a beehive-shaped pigsty. The animals were a danger; pigs were smart enough to know an intruder when they saw one and raise a fuss. Fortunately, they could smell the pigsties a good long way off and avoid them. But if the peasants had left dogs behind to guard their houses – Branoic didn't want to think about that. In the chancy moonlight he could see Tieryn Peddyc, crouched behind a merlon, leaning a little way out to study the lie of the village while Caradoc knelt behind him.

All at once Branoic heard distant voices. Peddyc slid back behind the merlon. The voices were drifting across from the fourth wall – guards. The voices came closer, resolved at their loudest as those of two men, then faded again. So they were patrolling in pairs. For a long while the silver daggers waited, listening and judging intervals. The guards came infrequently. Nevyn's magical storm had done its work.

One man at a time, the silver daggers climbed down the far side of the wall. Branoic was half-way down when a cloud tore and exposed the moon. He froze, heard distant voices, climbed a few yards down, froze again. The moon disappeared. He clung some ten feet up from the ground while the guards walked by, arguing about some trivial thing. Once they were past, he slithered a few more feet, then let himself drop the rest. He found himself among round thatched houses. Caradoc grabbed his arm and whispered 'you blind-lucky dog.'

Once they were all down, they walked in single file, crouching as they went, pausing often to freeze and listen. Branoic had ended up near the front, just behind Owaen and Caradoc. Peddyc was doing the leading, or so Branoic supposed. In the dark, and smeared with mud as they all were, it could have been the Lord of Hell for all he knew.

Ahead loomed a big rectangular structure with its roof sagging against the backdrop of the clouds – an old barn, Branoic assumed, from the dry smell of ancient manure. Between it and the fifth wall behind them lay a gap long enough for all the silver daggers to assemble in relative safety. Caradoc walked down the line, counting heads.

'All here,' he murmured. 'Everyone rest. The worst bit's on its way.'

'My liege!' Nevyn said. 'They're over the fifth wall.'

'Has anyone spotted them?' Maryn said.

'Not so far.'

'Good. I'll go out and put the men on alert.' Maryn pulled a silver horn from his belt and handed it to Nevyn. 'Just in case. If they reach the gate, and we're not in position, step outside and blow this thing as loudly as you can.'

'I've never used a horn before.'

'A horrible squawk will do.' Maryn grinned at him. 'I don't expect music.'

With a wave the Prince ducked out of the tent. Nevyn turned back to the table and considered the bowl of water that he was using as a scrying focus. From the murky images he could tell that the silver daggers still stood between the wall and the rotting cow barn. Caradoc was making sure the Prince had time to ready the men who were waiting between the second and third walls.

Since this tent as well stood near the third wall, Nevyn could hear Maryn's voice, giving final orders to the lords outside. The gate already stood open a bare couple of feet. Just outside it, crouching at the foot of the third wall on the uphill side, were the Ram's men and a contingent of the skilled assault troop. When Caradoc's men hit the gate, these warbands would rush uphill; the gates in the third wall would be cranked wide, and men on horseback would follow.

If everything went well. If. Nevyn's stomach hurt like fire. He rubbed it and went back to his scrying.

Ah shit! Branoic thought. No more luck for us! Half-crouching, half-crawling, the silver daggers had reached a position not far from the gates in the fourth wall. By looking slantwise between two huts, he could see them clearly, some thirty yards away. It was not a pretty sight. Over the gates stood maybe twenty men, while the pairs on patrol came and went in a regular rhythm. Lantern light abounded. They had no more hope of reaching the gates unseen than a flower does of blooming in the hells.

Caradoc inched his way down the line, whispering. Branoic heard him murmuring 'first squad to me; second squad, follow Owaen,' and then he was past. The men who'd called 'one' peeled out of line and crept after the captain, who seemed to be going back the way they'd come. The second squad waited until they were safely away, then slowly and carefully closed ranks. Owaen turned and whispered to his squad as he inched past them.

'Wait for the signal. Then charge the gates.'

More cursed waiting! And what in all the hells was Caradoc up to? All at once Branoic felt his stomach turn over in a fit of cold sickness. Whether it was his omen-voice or how well he knew the captain, he realized that Caradoc and the first squad were going to make a distraction somewhere to draw the guards off. It wasn't cursed likely that any of them would be coming back, either. Inching back along Owaen confirmed it by whispering 'to the postern back there somewhere' in answer to a murmured question from someone else. Half-sick with grief, Branoic's only thought was wishing he'd paid Trevyr the five coppers he owed him – not that Trevyr would be spending them anywhere soon.

The waiting went on. The men knelt in the muddy ground and let themselves go limp and still. Up at the edge of safe shelter, Owaen knelt on one knee and every now and then risked a look around a wall at the gates. Branoic's left leg was growing numb. He shifted his weight to the right and checked his sword hilt for the hundredth time.

All at once yells cut through the night. Screams of alarum answered back from above the gates. Owaen rose, and the rest of the squad followed suit. When Branoic looked he saw half the guards running along the top of the wall and heading back toward the postern. Owaen drew his sword with his right hand and his silver dagger with his left. With the hiss of metal sliding on leather the squad did the same. Owaen raised his sword high, waited a moment, then yelled, 'Now!'

The silver daggers burst out of cover and charged for the gates. The last few of the Regent's men left froze in surprise for a moment, then began scrambling down catwalks. Someone on the wall was blowing a silver horn. Just as Branoic gained the wall, he heard horns shrieking on the far side. The Prince's forces were moving. Four of the silver daggers rushed the winch; two of them lived to claim it. Branoic swung round and saw a Boarsman running straight toward him with a drawn sword. Branoic raised his dagger, caught the blow, and swung hard from the side. His strike caught the Boarsman low; he twisted round, and on the backhand Branoic slashed – a lucky hit. His throat torn away the man fell hard, tripping the man rushing to his aid.

Owaen was screaming orders. Branoic fell back, parrying all the way, and joined the fighting around the winch. The silver daggers paired off and fought back to back, parrying more than seeking kills, desperately trying to keep the guards back while the two men at the winch swore over the handle. Over the screaming of battle, Branoic heard a sound that just might have been the gates creaking. Two Boarsmen were pressing in hard; he ducked one while he tried to see well enough in the dim light to parry the other with his blade. The silver dagger behind him grunted and went down. Branoic spun and danced just in time. A hard stab slid past him. A flat blow glanced off his left shoulder; another slit his shirt through to the hauberk underneath.

'Branno! To me!' A familiar voice, just ahead.

Branoic ducked, swung, spun again, and found himself next to Peddyc. Side by side they laid their backs against the wall and swung, parrying, ducking, dodging while they panted and cursed. Three Boarsmen plunged in. Peddyc stepped forward and took one hard blow, then stabbed the second man as he fell against him. Branoic killed the third, but in his heart he knew he was about to die. All that mattered was holding these bastards off as long as possible. Horns were shrieking. Hooves pounded.

'Silver daggers!' A voice raised, another joining in. 'To the silver daggers!'

Suddenly and seemingly from nowhere the men of the Ram came pouring through the open gates, and behind them bobbed the blue shields of Glasloc, sweeping the Boarsmen away. Branoic could see them so clearly that he looked up, and sure enough, the sky was turning grey with dawn.

Branoic flung himself down to a kneel and grabbed Peddyc by the shoulders. The tieryn opened his eyes and shut them again. Whether he lived or died Branoic didn't know. More and more of the Prince's men were pouring through the gates and spreading out in the ring, where the shouting went on and horns shrieked. Although he doubted if he could carry Peddyc, Branoic decided he'd rather be cursed than leave him to be trampled. He slipped one arm around the tieryn's shoulders.

'Branoic! Hold! I'll help!'

Young lord Anasyn broke free of the fighting and reached his father's side. Together they could lift the unconscious Peddyc and inch their way through the gates. Branoic was frantically wondering where the chirurgeons might be when he glanced around and saw Nevyn, running to meet them.

'My lord!' Branoic choked out. 'Caradoc!'

'I know.' Nevyn was shouting over the general bedlam. 'I saw him die. Come along, let's get – ah, ye gods! I'm sorry, Sanno. It's too late.'

Since neither Owaen nor Caradoc would be seeing him break orders, after the silver daggers rode out Maddyn armed. The mail felt so gruesomely heavy after his long years away from war that he realized he'd be unable to fight no matter how badly he wanted to. Cursing as only a silver dagger can, he stripped it off and threw it on the floor of his tent.

At least he'd be with the battle in spirit. Maddyn walked uphill to the third wall and climbed the catwalk to vigil the last of the night away there, out of the way of the real warriors, or so he thought it. Every time the clouds lifted enough for him to see the moon, she rode lower in the western sky. Finally, just as she was setting altogether, Maddyn heard the distant shouting that, he'd later learn, meant that Caradoc and his men were making their false attempt on the postern. Maddyn swore and started round the wall toward the sound, only to turn and rush back when the real attack hit the main gates.

Since the fourth wall stood uphill he, of course, couldn't see over, but he could watch the Ram's men leap up below him and start forward. In the false king's dun the shouting grew louder; horns blared; the Ram's men began running for the fourth wall with Glasloc close behind.

The sky turned grey. Below Maddyn the gates creaked open and horsemen thundered through. Maddyn climbed the wall to perch between two merlons and hang over the edge. When he saw Nevyn running across the ring toward the gate, Maddyn slid down to the catwalk and took the ladders down. He met the old man at the downhill side of the third wall.

'Maddo!' Nevyn yelled. 'Get some horses! There's a couple of your men at the ruined dun. They must have made it back through the bolthole.'

Maddyn turned on his heel and raced downhill to the silver daggers' camp. He commandeered a couple of servants, and together they saddled five horses. Leading two with empty saddles they set off, trotting most of the way, galloping in short spurts when the ground allowed, walking now and then to rest their mounts. The sun had hauled itself a good way up from the horizon by the time they reached the ruined dun.

Red-haired Trevyr was sitting on a bit of broken wall. Blood crusted on his face and lay thick on his muddy shirt. At his feet lay Albyn, sprawled like a sack of meal. Maddyn knew he was dead the moment he saw him. He dismounted, threw the reins of his horse to one of the servants, and hurried over. Trevyr looked up at him as if he were thinking himself delirious.

'It's me,' Maddyn said. 'Nevyn scried you out.'

'May the gods bless him! The captain's dead. We tried to get to him, but he went down in the middle of a mob.'

For a moment Maddyn could neither move nor speak. In the sky above, ravens shrieked and wheeled. Trevyr raised a hand black with blood as if to fend them off. It looked as if all his fingers had been broken by one blow, and Maddyn wondered how he could possibly move it.

'Did they get the gates?' Trevyr said.

'They did. Owaen still lives, and Branoic. Can you ride?'

Trevyr considered this question for a long moment, then tried to smile. The wound on his face cracked and oozed.

'I don't have much choice, do I?' He glanced down. 'Allo died out here. At least he made it this far.'

'Lilli!' it was Anasyn's voice, howling toward her. 'Lilli, hurry!'

Lilli rushed out of her tent. Still in his mail Anasyn stood waiting for her, and the way he stood, head back, hands clenched in fists, his mouth twisted in pain, told her what must have happened.

'Father?' she whispered.

'He's dead. Branoic and I got him free of the fighting, but it was too late.'

Lilli threw back her head and keened, a long wail that seemed to burst out of her heart. Anasyn threw his arms around her and pulled her tight. They held on like children, swaying together while he wept.

'He'll be with Bevva in the Otherlands,' Lilli said. 'They'll be together now.'

At that the tears came, and she keened in long hysterical gulps while her maidservants crept out of the tent and hovered uncertainly nearby. Anasyn stroked her hair and murmured 'here, here,' over and over again. At last she calmed herself and looked up. With his warrior's control he'd stopped weeping; his face seemed drawn on parchment like one of Brour's diagrams, all stretched tight and flat. Around them stood a circle of men, watching silently. Nevyn pushed his way through.

'Lilli, I'm so sorry,' the old man said. 'Tieryn Anasyn, the Prince has need of you.'

'I'll go to him straight away,' Anasyn said. 'Please – keep an eye on my sister?'

'I will, lad. Don't worry.'

Lilli laid a hand on Nevyn's arm and looked around dazed. Tieryn Anasyn? Of course. Anasyn was the Ram now, and it was his warband who stood watching her with such sad eyes, as if she were doing the mourning for all of them. Peddyc's captain stepped forward.

'We'll avenge him, lass. Don't you trouble your heart about that.'

Lilli tried to thank him, but the keening burst out of her mouth instead. Nevyn grabbed her arm and unceremoniously dragged her into her tent, where she could mourn with her women around her.

By noon the situation clarified. The Prince's men held the entire hill except for the crest and Dun Deverry itself. The Regent's forces held the broch complex and the inner ward around it, defended by one last towering stone ring. This left the deserted village and its patches of open ground a no-man's-land of some sixty yards wide between the Prince's men on their wall and the Regent's on theirs. The side ward that contained the bolthole belonged, however, to Maryn, as did the dun's cattle and swine.

'We can send more men through the bolthole now,' Maryn said. 'It'll be a fair bit easier to attack the King's position over that low wall.'

Nevyn was about to reply when they both heard shouting on the fourth wall – screaming, really, a berserk howl of pure rage. When the Prince took off running toward the sound, Nevyn was forced to follow. He barely restrained himself from shouting 'be careful, Your Highness!' as if the Prince were still a child. Maryn flung himself onto a ladder and climbed to the top of the wall. Nevyn scrambled after and found himself in a mob of silver daggers.

'Look, Your Highness!' Branoic snarled. 'Just look.'

Across the no-man's-land and on top of the Regent's last wall someone's head had been raised on a pike and stuck onto the wall twixt two merlons. As they watched, a couple of the Regent's men flung the headless body over. It fell spraddled into the dirt.

'It's Caradoc.' Owaen was near choking on rage. 'The piss-proud dogs!'

'You've got good eyes, lad.' Nevyn shaded his with his hand. 'But, truly, I think it is, though I'm not sure at this distance.'

'It is,' Branoic said. 'I say we go get him back.'

The silver daggers cheered, but the Prince grabbed Branoic by the arm and shook him.

'You'll do naught of the sort!' Maryn snarled. 'None of you will! Upon my direct order, do you understand me?'

The silver daggers stared for a long moment, then nodded, murmuring agreement. Branoic was the last.

'Understood, Your Highness,' he said, but he sounded near tears. 'Is it beyond my station to ask you why?'

'It's not.' Maryn softened his voice. 'When you get close to the wall, they'll kill you, that's why, with javelins if they have some or stones if that's all they have left to throw. It's a trap.'

'Oh.' Branoic flung back his head. 'I hadn't thought-'

'None of us are thinking very clearly.' Maryn paused to stare at the blasphemy on the far wall. 'I hate to leave him there, but he'd not want his men killed in vain, would he?'

'He wouldn't,' Branoic said. 'My apologies, Your Highness.'

Nevyn felt his own rage run cold rather than hot, an icy thing that left his mind perfectly clear. Caradoc's soul was beyond caring what happened to his dead body, Nevyn reminded himself. But to allow his friend's remains to be mocked as they rotted? Intolerable! He might be two hundred years old and a master of the dweomer, but he was a

Deverry man still in his heart. Nevyn turned and strode along the catwalk until he stood well away from the crowd around the Prince. He needed to concentrate.

On their far wall the Regent's men were laughing, calling out taunts incomprehensible at a distance though the tone carried across well enough. Nevyn's rage turned into fire, pure and white-hot. In his mind he called upon the Lords of Fire, who came to him as friends to share his rage. Shimmering pillars of silver light formed around him, and in each one floated a figure, vaguely man-shaped but fashioned of fire, the glowing red of embers, the golden lick of flame.

'My friend lies dead,' Nevyn thought to them. 'I would give him a pyre like a hero from the Dawntime, but I cannot reach him with wood and oil.'

In his mind he felt their answer, a rage that some mere mortal would deny their peer anything he might want. Slowly Nevyn raised his arms above his head. He paused for a moment, staring at Caradoc's body, at the pitiful severed head upon its pike, then slowly lowered his arms till his hands pointed across the ring to what was left of the captain. He called out one sacred word.

Silver light leapt down from the sky; a strange metallic flame tinged with blue fell upon Caradoc's body with a roar and gust of fire. It leapt up, reaching out long silver fingers for the severed head upon the wall. Suddenly the head flamed, too, a torch brighter than the sunlight around it. The men who'd been mocking screamed as they ran, scattering on the catwalk and suddenly disappearing as they climbed down to the ground and no doubt ran for the dun. On their wall the silver daggers stood in utter silence, staring at the magical pyre. In but a little while the flames died down, flickered on bare ground, and disappeared. All that remained of Caradoc were handfuls of pure white ash, scattering in the wind, then gone.

Maddyn had just left Trevyr with the chirurgeons when one of the Ramsmen brought him the news. He headed for the fourth wall, but by the time he reached it the Prince was leading the silver daggers downhill. Nevyn came last, looking grimly pleased with himself. When Maddyn fell into step beside him, Owaen dropped back to walk with them.

'It's over,' Owaen said. 'You missed quite a performance, bard. The Regent's men shrieked like frightened lasses, but it was a pleasant sound for all that.'

The Prince led them to his pavilion, where Oggyn, his scribe, and a pair of servants were waiting for him. When the silver daggers started to disperse, he called them back.

'I've got somewhat to say to all of you,' Maryn said. 'For the sake of the silver dagger itself I'll swear you a vow. Every man of you left alive shall have a boon from me – lands, title, horses, what little gold we have – anything at all! Ask, and I'll grant it.'

'My liege, you're too generous.' Maddyn felt his eyes well tears. 'But you have my thanks from the bottom of my heart.'

From his place behind the Prince's shoulder Nevyn was scowling. Maryn had left himself open to greed, Maddyn knew; as the new leaders of the troop, he and Owaen would need to make sure that their men asked for something reasonable.

'I only wish Caradoc had lived,' Maryn went on. 'I'd offer him the Cerrmor rhan on the spot.'

'My liege?' Maddyn said. 'There's one thing that Caradoc wanted above all else. He told me this a hundred times. He wanted us – wanted the silver daggers – to outlive him. The wars will be over soon, and maybe no one will need mercenary troops like ours, but it would gladden his heart in the Otherlands to know that silver daggers still rode in Deverry.'

'Then he shall have it!' Maryn turned to the scribe. 'Write this down: as long as my line rules this kingdom, let there be silver daggers, for as long as they wish to ride. Let it be known forever as Caradoc's Boon.'

Nevyn's scowl deepened. When the old man realized that Maddyn was watching him, he smoothed it into the bland and empty smile of a courtier.

Later Nevyn explained, as they were walking together on the outermost wall in the cool night air. Before and below them the ruins of Dun Deverry spread out. Walls of broken stone rose from the shadows or pitted the darkness, a dead black against the living night.

'Tell me,' Maddyn said. 'What have you got against us, Nevyn? When the king made that vow to Caradoc's spirit, you looked as if you'd bitten into a Bardek citron.'

'I've got naught against you. It's the men who'll come after you that trouble my heart. The silver daggers have won themselves a place in legend, truly. The kingmakers, bards call you. What's going to happen if some other man decides he wants to be king, somewhere down the long road of Time, and corrupts whoever's leading you then?'

'Oh. Oh ye gods, I hadn't thought of that! My apologies, my apologies from the bottom of my heart! I'd not have asked for such a thing if I'd thought about that.'

'No doubt. All of you lads need to do some hard thinking before you go asking for those boons. The King will honour them above any others he's granted. I know him well enough to know that. Is the point taken?'

'Very well indeed. And I'll do some hard talking to make sure we all do the hard thinking.'

'Good. I always recommend it. Thinking, that is.'

All afternoon Burcan strode through Dun Deverry with wads of bandages tied under his shirt as tight as Merodda could get them. Whenever she begged him to lie down and rest, he snarled at her. All she could do was trail along behind, ready to tend his wounds whenever he let her. He'd been struck one blow to his side that had broken several ribs and split the skin, then suffered a stab low down on his back, perhaps at the joining of his mail. Both bled, on and off, and she was afraid that the stab had gone deeper than he'd admit. At moments when no one but her could see him, he would lean against a wall or door jamb for a long moment, biting his lips against the pain.

Wherever he went, his men flocked to him. He would sometimes laugh and cheer them, at others turn solemn and tell them how much depended upon them. Although she kept out of the way, Merodda could see the change he wrought. White-faced and dispirited men slumped wearily on the ground or against walls to listen to him; men with life in their eyes jumped up to cheer him when he had finished.

'I beg you for the King's sake, and in the King's name!' To each of them Burcan said the same. 'For the King and Deverry!'

But Merodda could guess that the men were thinking the same as she, that in these moments Burcan was the King, and it would be for him that they'd fight on the morrow.

Dinner in the great hall was an agony. Since he couldn't sit without enormous pain, Burcan walked through the tables with a goblet of mead in his hand, laughing with his allies and cheering his lords on. Merodda could see him turning pale, then dead-white, then a drained, deathly grey. Finally, with one last jest, he turned and strode out of the hall. She rushed after to find him just outside, hanging on to the wall with one hand and swaying. The sunset sent a last flare of gold over the sky, but in the ward the shadows lay cold.

Burcan turned to her, started to speak, and collapsed. Merodda flung herself to the ground beside him. Through the bandages and his shirt both red blood oozed. She cradled his head in the crook of her left arm and stroked his hair and face with her other hand, while he squinted at her as if he could barely see.

'Rhodi?' he whispered. 'Do you truly love me?'

'I do. I always have.'

He smiled, seemed to be about to speak, seemed to be staring up at her face. Then she realized that he was dead. She kissed him once, then sat up and closed his eyes. His blood soaked the front of her dress; she sat there staring at it and wondering if she'd told him the truth, if she'd ever loved him at all. No matter – he'd done so much for her that she'd owed him the lie if it was one.

'My lady!' It was Lord Belryc, standing over her. 'Oh, my lady!'

'He's dead, truly.' Merodda stood up and looked around her.

Everything seemed oddly small and oddly far away, even the lord, who was holding out one hand as if offering to steady her. Men shouted, men came running from the broch to gather around.

'We should bury him somewhere in the dun,' Merodda said. 'He loved it so.'

The world spun once sharply to the left. When she woke again, she was lying on her bed with the Queen and the serving women clustered around her. Abrwnna was holding her hand and weeping. So should we all, Merodda thought. Tomorrow is the end of everything.

'Oooh, it's going to be terrible on the morrow, my lady,' Clodda said. 'I've heard all the men talking. A terrible hard battle, they say.'

'No doubt,' Lilli said. 'I don't want to think about it. I wish we were back in Cerrmor.'

'Well, I've had a longing or two that way myself.'

They were sitting just outside of Lilli's tent with a candle-lantern on the ground between them. The dapples of light from the cut tin flickered on their faces and stamped strange patterns onto the canvas of Nevyn's tent nearby. Nevyn himself was gone, off at the council of war with the Prince and the great lords, those who had lived through the day's fighting, that is.

'I feel like a murderess,' Lilli said abruptly. 'If I'd not come forward, the Prince would have had to siege the dun, and none of this ghastly slaughter would have happened.'

'What, my lady?' Clodda looked up in sincere confusion. 'But the gods want Prince Maryn to be king, and so you had to tell him.'

'But still, if I hadn't told him-'

'It was the Prince's decision to strike, my lady, not yours.'

The voice came from Branoic, standing just outside the lantern light, and he'd come up so quietly that Lilli had never heard him. With a yelp she scrambled to her feet. Although he'd washed and put on a clean shirt, he wore his mud-crusted brigga still.

'Oh ye gods!' she stammered. 'You gave me such a start!'

'Then my apologies.' He walked the last few steps to stand in front of her. 'But I'll not have you berating yourself for the fortunes of war.'

'Don't you blame me for what happened to Caradoc?'

'Not in the least, though I'm sick at heart over losing him. How can you know someone else's Wyrd? Maryn's the one who decided to attack, not siege, and Caradoc's the one who talked him into letting the silver daggers open the gates. None of that was your doing. Who knows what would have happened if we'd had to sit here all winter long? Fevers have slain many a besieging army when the snow falls and they're half-starved.'

'Well, true spoken, I suppose, but-'

'Nah nah nah, none of that supposing! Your lass is right. It's all on the knees of the gods, anyway, what a man's Wyrd may bring.'

'That eases my heart. You can't know how much. I was so afeared, thinking everyone would hate me.'

'What?' Branoic laughed at that. 'My lady, I doubt me if you could ever do anything vicious enough to make me hate you.'

He was staring at her so intensely, so sincerely, that Lilli turned tongue-tied. With a little cough, Clodda got up and curtsied.

'I'd best go inside, my lady,' Clodda said, 'and not sit here eavesdropping.'

'You can stay,' Branoic said. 'I'm not going to say anything dishonourable.' He turned back to Lilli. 'The Prince has offered all of us silver daggers a boon once the wars are over. If the gods let me live, I'm going to ask him for enough land to support a wife. And so I want to ask you to be so kind as to just keep me in mind, like. Neither of us have much of a place in the world now, but it would gladden my heart to earn one for us.'

'But I hardly know you!'

'Well, and I don't have the land yet, either.' Branoic gave her a grin. 'Just think about it.'

He bowed, then turned on his heel and hurried away before Lilli could say one thing more.

'Oooh, how exciting!' Clodda said. 'He's awfully handsome, isn't he?'

'Do you think so? He's too beefy for me.'

'Oh my lady! You're just saying that to be haughty, aren't you? I mean, ladies are supposed to be haughty to their suitors and all.'

'I'm not! I mean it.'

When Clodda giggled, so did she, covering her mouth with one hand. I certainly don't want to marry Branoic, she thought, lands or not! But she had to admit that she found it comforting that someone wanted to marry her, an exile without so much as a horse for her dowry.

Later that night, when she was falling asleep, she realized that she would worry about his safety on the morrow during the battle, that once again she would wait helplessly with nothing to do but pray that a man she cared something for would live through the fighting. She fell asleep at last to dream of Peddyc and Bevyan. She woke in tears.

Not long after dawn the attack on the last wall began. With the last of the silver daggers around him, Prince Maryn took his place on the fourth wall. The rams and the assault ladders stood in position at the fourth wall gates, and assault men stood ready to winch them open at the Prince's signal. On the fifth and last wall between the Red Wyvern and Dun Deverry, the false king's men waited in utter silence. A revulsion so physical that he felt like vomiting made Nevyn turn away long before the fighting began. He left the Prince, climbed down the catwalk, and trotted downhill until he reached the outermost wall and the refuge of the camp.

All that day Nevyn worked with the chirurgeons. The wounded men who could walk or crawl to safety kept them busy enough that he avoided thinking about the men worse off, left lying when they fell. By the time anyone could spare the effort to get them off the battlefield, most would have died. Not, of course, that there was much the chirurgeons could have done for them, anyway – Nevyn was always aware of the deadly limits of his knowledge. He had studied physic and chirurgy for nearly two hundred years, and yet he knew with a sour certainty that he lacked the keys to unlock the mysteries of wounds. Some went septic; some did not; why? The theory of humours in the books of that learnèd Greggyn, Gaelyn, never had answered this question nor the hundred others that haunted him as he worked, arms red to his elbows, washing wounds, stitching wounds, desperately trying to staunch wounds. Another mystery – why did some wounds ooze bluish blood but others pump out bright red? Those with slow bleeding he could save; few who bled fast lived to reach him.

Up the hill from the chirurgeons the battle raved in a thousand deliriums. Blended by the wind and distance, the screams and shouts, the clashing of weapons on armour drifted down to them in a meaningless babble. With the wounded came more cogent reports. The Regent's men were fighting the battle of their lives to protect the final wall into the last ward, that secret inner heart of Dun Deverry.

'We've got the ladders up,' one young lad said. 'They were trying to push them off, but we keep pulling their cursed poles away from them, and they must have run out, because they've stopped that.'

'Good,' Nevyn said. 'Now hold still. This is going to sting.'

When Nevyn poured watered mead over the gash in his face, the lad screamed and fainted. It was easier to stitch up the wound that way, but Nevyn had to wait for the next wounded man who could talk for more details of the fighting for the walls. The Boar's men on the catwalks; Maryn's men on scaling ladders: the battle hung on who would fight the longest, on whether Maryn had the men to pour over the wall like a wave and wash the Boarsmen off. Toward the middle of the afternoon the first squad gained the catwalks, only to be mobbed and killed, but in the flurry of fighting a second lot got over, and these held.

'Once we've got the place to stand, like,' a man with a broken arm said, 'then we'll have them. Ah ye gods, that hurts! It's when I try to move it, like.'

'Then don't!' Nevyn snapped. 'Hold still while I wrap this. You'll have to wait before I can try to set it.'

'There's many worse off than me, truly.' Sweat broke out on his whitening face. 'When I left, a lot of our lads were on top the wall.'

Whether they stayed there or not, the man didn't know. A few at a time, more reports filtered down to the waiting chirurgeons and through them to the camp itself. Maryn's men held a stretch of wall; Maryn's men held the wall directly over the gates. They were calling for the ram; the ram had arrived. And finally, late in the afternoon, the gates went down. That event they could hear as a massive shout on the wind, a horrendous scream of defenders and a triumph from the attackers at the walls. The stream of wounded turned into a flood, and Nevyn had no more time to worry about the battle until the sun hung low in the western sky and a messenger arrived, announcing that the Prince wanted to talk with him.

'The walls are ours, my lord, but the royal broch – well, that's another matter.'

Nevyn cleaned up by the simple expedient of dumping a couple of buckets of water over himself, clothes and all, and hurried off, still wet but cool for the first time all day. In sweaty and blood-streaked mail and helm Prince Maryn, with a tidy Oggyn in attendance, stood on the walls near the shattered gates. Nevyn climbed up a rickety seige ladder and joined them. The Prince acknowledged him with a nod.

'They hold the main broch complex and some of the side ones.' Maryn drew his sword, streaked with old blood, and pointed. 'The ward is ours, but it's nearly night. I'm not risking what we've gained by trying to finish this now.'

'Sounds wise, my liege,' Nevyn said. 'So this is the last battle-ground, is it?'

In the middle of the final ring of walls stood the central broch complex. Eight hundred years earlier it had started with a single squat tower, broader at the base than at the top. Other kings had built other brochs, some free-standing, others half-rounds joined to the first. Covered arcades and flat sheds had grown like mushrooms between and among the towers; here and there a slender tower in the new style rose from the roof of a stone building. The whole edifice covered some hundreds of yards. Off to either side, some thirty yards away, stood two smaller clusters of brochs. All three complexes flew the banner of the green wyvern, a last defiance in the gathering night.

'In the morning I'll try to parley,' Maryn said. 'I'm hoping they'll just surrender. There can't be a lot of them left.'

'True spoken, Your Highness. Well, we can hope for a surrender, though I've got my doubts that they'll take it.'

'If not, we'll have to turn into terriers and dig them out.'

Nevyn merely nodded. He was studying the complex, searching for the brochs he'd known as a child and young man, but they were too overgrown with new building for him to make them out.

'Tomorrow, my liege!' Oggyn said. 'Tomorrow you'll at last claim your birthright. Tomorrow the kingdom is yours!'

'Most likely,' Maryn said. 'I just hope it'll be worth the deaths it's cost.'

'Oh come now, Your Highness!' Oggyn barked a laugh. 'No other man in Deverry would think such a thing!'

'Just so,' Nevyn said. 'And no other man but Prince Maryn is fit to be High King.'

Trapped in the royal broch with King Olaen and his last defenders were women and children – nine women, Merodda counted, and twelve children, mostly pages, but one of the servant girls, Pavva, had a nursling, which she clutched so tightly to her chest that Merodda feared the baby would suffocate.

'Give him a little air,' she said. 'That's better, lass. We're in no danger right now.'

All of the women and children had taken refuge on the top floor of the main broch – the last place that the attackers would reach on the morrow – in an empty half-round of a storage room. Merodda had got them up there and dragooned some of the remaining male servants in the broch to haul up drinking water and food. Now there was nothing to do but wait out of the men's way until whatever Wyrd the gods had decreed swung down upon them like a scythe.

A little way off from the others the Queen sprawled on a heap of cushions. Her two maidservants had escaped from the broch in the horrible confusion earlier in the day; like the other missing women, they might have been safe or dead for all any one knew. In the lantern light Abrwnna's red hair gleamed like another fire, but her face and dress were filthy and the dress torn, as well. Merodda walked over, laid down the heavy sack she was carrying, and sat beside the Queen.

'What's in that, Rhodi?' Abrwnna said.

'Some things I saved from my chambers. A book. Some potions.'

'Do you have some poison I could eat?'

'Oh ye gods, Your Highness! I wouldn't give it to you if I did!'

'Why not? It would be better than what's going to happen to me on the morrow. I'd rather be dead when they come for me.'

Merodda merely sighed for an answer. If only the Dwarven Salts didn't deliver such a horrible death! She found herself remembering Caetha, twisting in her own vomit. From a distance it seemed she heard a woman screaming, Caetha screaming, as if her ghost had appeared to gloat over her murderer's death; then Merodda realized that the screams were real and very much present, coming from the trap-door covering the stairs down. The screams grew louder and a man's voice, angry, joined in. She leapt to her feet just as someone hoisted the trap from below.

'I can't, I can't!' A woman spoke, but her voice choked so badly that Merodda couldn't recognize it. 'I can't leave him.'

Merodda hurried over. On the steps stood Rwla, the little King's nursemaid, weeping and trembling. Behind her two soldiers were trying to force her up to the room above. Merodda leaned down and caught her hand.

'Come up,' she said. 'What's happened? Did Olaen send you away?'

'He told me maybe I could escape,' Rwla sobbed. 'As if there's any safety of any of us. Ah ye gods! Don't make me leave the poor little lad.'

'Little or not,' Merodda said, 'he's the King, and he ordered you. Now get up here!'

Still weeping Rwla allowed herself to be half-shoved, half-led up to the temporary safety. When Abrwnna slid a cushion her way, she collapsed onto it. She pulled off her black headscarf and let her grey hair spill down, then used the cloth to mop her face. Merodda tried to think of something comforting and failed utterly.

'Tell me somewhat,' she said instead. 'Have you seen any of the other women from the dun? What happened to them?'

'I've no idea. They all could be slain by now.'

Outside the daylight was fading, and shadow began to fill the room, rising from the floor like water, it seemed, and oozing out of the very walls. Merodda considered lighting candles, but the pages were already asleep, curled up together like dogs.

'Shall we try to sleep?' she asked.

Everyone agreed and began poking through the hasty armfuls of goods they'd gathered to bring to this refuge. A few at a time they found blankets or cushions and made themselves as comfortable as they could. Merodda herself fell asleep straight away, but soon after midnight she woke to lie in the dark and curse her Wyrd. So all her dweomer had come to this, that she could see her fate and not do one wretched thing to prevent it! All her scrying, all her omens and spells – nothing had saved her from this trap of a room, where queen and servant lass shared the same floor for a bed.

For comfort she had one thought: vengeance. Maryn thought himself the victor now, but he would pay for his strutting glory. If, of course, her first teacher in these dark matters had spoken the truth,

and the spell he'd wrought would live up to his claims. He had
boasted so much that she had lost her faith in him. Burcan would no
doubt lie avenged, and soon, she would no doubt join him.

Still, there was other lore, other spells she'd learned. What if it
were true, and she could take vengeance upon her enemies whether
she lived or died? For a long time she lay awake and searched her
memory for the dark things her master had taught her. If naught else
they comforted her, here at the end of everything she had ever loved,
with sweet hopes of revenge.

In the east dawn rose in a blaze of scarlet, an omen of the fighting to
come. When Nevyn tried his usual meditation, such terrible images
of death and despair flooded the astral plane that he broke off the
attempt. He had just dressed when Maddyn came running toward
him, howling his name like a banshee.

'You've got to get to the Prince!' Maddyn yelled. 'He wants to join
the final attack on the royal broch.'

'Lead me to him, lad. And hurry!'

They found the Prince at the edge of the encampment where
Maddyn had left him, circled by impassive silver daggers. Prince
Maryn was swearing and threatening them, but they kept close ranks
and ignored him. Just as Nevyn came running up, Maryn drew his
sword.

'May the gods forbid I injure one of my own men,' Maryn snarled.
'But if you don't let me through I will!'

'Here's Nevyn, my liege!' Branoic said. 'If after you talk with him
you still want to lead that charge, I'll step aside gladly.'

'Bastard!'

'You've done well, men,' Nevyn said. 'Wait for us some way away.'

The guards trotted off. When Maryn tried to follow, Nevyn stepped
in front of him. Their eyes met; the King looked away and stayed
where he was.

'In some ways,' Maryn said, 'I'm still that little lad and you my
fierce old tutor. Infuriating, but there we are.'

'My liege, my own true king, the first man through those doors is
going to die, and so will most of those who come right after him.
There's no hope for otherwise.'

'Oh spare me the clever rhetoric! How can I stand here and let
other men fight for me?'

'By keeping your two feet firmly planted on this bit of ground.'

Nevyn added a 'my liege' as an afterthought, then went on. 'If you're killed now, all the men who've died to put you on this throne will have suffered in vain. Is that what you want?'

Maryn let out his breath in a sigh that was closer to a moan and lowered his sword. From behind him Maddyn caught Nevyn's glance and mouthed silent thanks.

'What happened to the parley?' Nevyn said.

'When Gavlyn came up to the door, they emptied chamber pots on him from the windows. The message seemed clear enough.'

'So it does. It's a terrible thing, honour, when it makes a man die in a lost cause.'

Maryn shrugged and sheathed his sword with a slap of hilt against scabbard.

'I gave them their chance,' the Prince said. 'If they want to follow their false king to the Otherlands, who am I to stand in their way?'

The trapped women heard rather than saw the attack. Early on Merodda risked sidling up to a window and taking a sideways look out, but all she could see was a welter of men swarming through the ward and surrounding the towers that sheltered the king's last men. From her position the swell of the broch hid the huge iron-bound doors into the great hall, but the Cerrmor men seemed busy enough here around the side.

'They look like dogs,' Merodda called back to the others. 'A lot of dogs around a bit of dropped meat.'

The tower shook, suddenly and fiercely. The other women cried out; the shock hit again. The men outside howled, cheering someone or something on.

'That's the ram,' Merodda said.

The blows hit again and again, not hard enough to knock her from her feet, but strong ones nonetheless. It seemed she could hear the broch groan in pain – until she realized that she was hearing the King's men waiting in the great hall. With each impact they too shouted, as if begging the doors to hold. When she looked out, she saw from the floors below her a rain of stones and lit torches pounding down on the attackers, who fended them with shields. Here and there a Cerrmor man staggered and went down.

All at once the shouting both outside and in changed to shrieks and howls of rage and blood-lust.

'The doors are down,' Merodda said. 'May the Goddess help us all.'

She left the window and sat down by Abrwnna, who turned to her like a child. Merodda put an arm around her shoulders and pulled her close. A few at a time the other women joined them, huddling together in a rough semi-circle with the pages in the middle. The baby began to cry, a high endless wail that nothing would stop. From below they could hear shouting, oddly muffled and booming through the thick stone walls. At first it stayed distant, but slowly it crept closer. Cerrmor men must have cleared the hall and started up the stairs.

It went on all morning, one room, one corridor at a time, or so they could assume. They could hear the sound of fighting out in the ward, too – the screaming, the clang of metal hitting metal, dull blows and thwacks and howls of pain. None of the women spoke; no one ate, either, though once a page fetched a waterskin, and they passed that round. Toward noon the baby cried himself hoarse and fell into an exhausted sleep. That was, Merodda supposed, a small blessing and the only one they'd get. Not long after she realized that the sounds from outside were growing, swelling like a wave of noise.

'More men, it sounds like,' she said. 'The other brochs must be theirs.'

One of the pages started to weep. She got up and went back to the window. Sure enough, down below the Cerrmor army held the entire ward. She saw men with weapons sheathed casually going in and out of the other brochs in the complex.

'Everything's theirs but this tower,' Merodda said.

No one even looked her way. She wondered if she should throw herself out the window and die on her own terms, but the thought turned her body to lead. She could not force herself toward that last refuge.

All at once something whipped past the window – a rope, a grapple. The shouting below turned triumphant as another rope followed, and another. No king's men appeared at the windows below to cut the ropes.

'Oh ye gods,' Merodda said. 'They're coming for the roof.'

Abrwnna screamed, then stuffed the side of her hand into her mouth. Merodda sank down by the window and leaned against the wall. She couldn't think, she couldn't move. The baby woke and began to cry, a horrible hoarse bleat, while his mother wept and begged him to stop.

'It won't be long now,' Merodda whispered. 'That's something, I suppose.'

No one seemed to have heard her. She was aware of shadows passing over her – armed men climbing past the window. All at once she heard footsteps and a crow of laughter from the wooden roof above. The other women began to weep; Abrwnna turned so pale that Merodda feared she would faint. Some scuffling, some loud talking, though she couldn't make out the words – and then blows, the thud of axes, biting into the wood.

'Get over here!' Merodda screamed. 'Get out of the middle of the room!'

The women and boys leapt up and scurried over. They packed together, holding each other and sobbing, as axe after axe bit deep. Merodda found herself in front of her flock and decided that there was no reason to move. More men were climbing up; the axes went on beating. All at once metal flashed and a ray of sun: the first axe had broken through.

'They might not stop to harm us,' Merodda hissed. 'They have to get to the fighting below. We might escape yet.'

No one believed her, least of all herself. She heard laughter and the sound of heavy boots, trampling back and forth. Another axe broke through, then another – a whole section of roof gave way between two beams. Sunlight poured through like poisoned mead.

'We're through!' a dark voice called out. 'Get those swiving ladders over here!'

A rope ladder swung down through the hole in the roof. A man in pot helm and mail climbed half-way down, leapt the rest of the way, and made a clumsy turn as he drew his sword.

'Ye gods!' He stared at the women, then yelled up to his fellows. 'Naught here but a pack of womenfolk and their children.'

Another voice called back; another man came down the ladder, then a second. The first man down yelled again.

'I know the Prince's orders as well as you do, you hairy bastard! But how by all the shit in the hells are we supposed to get them out of here?'

In a stench of sweat and blood more men were coming down and forming up by the landing. None of them so much as looked at the women. They exchanged grim smiles, then started down the stairs a pair at a time. From below someone shrieked an alarm; then the shouting started and the dull clang of blows. Sword in hand, the fellow who'd been first down walked over to Merodda. She drew herself up to full height and looked him in the face. She had a dweomer spell ready – if they were going to rape and kill them all, she'd curse them first – but he forestalled her.

'By Prince Maryn's personal order no women are to be harmed. You'll be safest on the roof. Can you all climb up there?'

For a moment Merodda saw the room lurch and spin. Abrwnna caught her arm from behind and steadied her. Men were still climbing down the ropes and pouring down the stairs, a river of iron-clad death. Merodda found her voice at last.

'Then we throw ourselves on the Prince's mercy.'

'Cursed good idea.' He flashed her a grin. 'Now, I've been told to guard you, and I don't want no trouble. Understand? Once the squads are all down, we'll go up. You'll be safe, I swear it, but keep those pages in line. If they don't cause no trouble, they'll live to fight for the true king one sweet day.'

Tears rose and threatened to overwhelm her. Their guard turned away indifferently and watched his fellows, hurrying down to death or battle-glory.

Just after noon the last of the King's men began to surrender. From the ward Nevyn and Maryn watched them being marched out in straggling lines. Finally the Prince could stand it no longer.

'By the arses of the gods, it must be safe enough for me to go in now!'

'Most likely, my liege.' Nevyn turned to Oggyn. 'And what does my fellow councillor think?'

'I'll go look, my lord, and have a word with those guards.'

Oggyn trotted over to the broken doors of the great hall, paused briefly to talk with one of the men, then came rushing back.

'My liege, my liege,' Oggyn called out. 'They've found the false king!'

'Good!' Maryn said. 'Where is he?'

'In his chamber. I suggest you go up now. The sooner he's slain, the better.'

'I'm not going to murder him out of hand, Oggyn. He'll be judged properly in my malover.'

Oggyn bit back a reply and covered his near-discourtesy with a bow. He looked frightened, Nevyn realized, and once he saw this terrible false king, he realized why. With a handful of the King's guard they hurried up the stairs from the great hall, down a hallway where corpses lay and into a chamber littered with broken furniture. They all knew, of course, that the would-be king in Dun Deverry was but a child, but knowing and actually seeing were two different things. Little Olaen sat in the curve of the wall and clutched a wooden horse to his chest; his face was filthy with tears and snot, and he smelled of urine.

'By every god in the sky!' Maryn snapped. 'He's but a baby! I can't kill him.'

'My liege!' Oggyn howled. 'He owns a claim on your kingdom. You must kill him if there's to be any lasting peace.'

Olaen started to sob.

'Nevyn?' Maryn looked at him with one eyebrow raised.

'Oh ye gods! I don't know what to advise, my liege. It would ache my heart to slay a child, but-'

'But, my lord,' Oggyn broke in. 'I'm right, am I not? It's not the lad himself, my Prince. It's the factions that could form around him, that *will* form.'

'I know all that,' Nevyn snapped. 'But give me a day at least to consult with the priests of Bel about the law of the thing. Our liege is determined to rule by law, isn't he? Well, then, let me see what the ancient books say.'

Oggyn started to speak, but Maryn waved him silent.

'Do that, Nevyn.' The king turned to his guards. 'Take the child somewhere safe. He must have a nursemaid somewhere around here. Find her.'

It was a long while after noon before anyone remembered the captive women. By then their waterskins were long empty, and the sun beat down hard on the roof. Merodda was just considering humbling herself before their guard and begging for better shelter when another solider climbed up through the shattered roof.

'Orders from the Prince's councillor. We're to take the women down to the women's hall and let them stay there. Is the false king's nursemaid up here?'

'I am.' Rwla stepped forward. 'What have they done with my lad?'

'Naught, yet. The Prince says I'm to take you to him.'

Rwla allowed herself a sob of relief.

'Move along, all of you,' their first guard said. 'I'm sick of this duty, and it'll be cursed good to get off this cursed roof!'

Although Merodda had been hoping that they'd be left without guards, once they were back in the women's hall, two more soldiers appeared to stand outside the door. When she asked, however, they allowed two of the pages to go fetch water up, and the boys came back with a bucket full and a couple of loaves of stale bread as well. The women gathered around and gobbled shamelessly.

'This is so odd,' Abrwnna said at last. 'Why is the Prince sparing us this way?'

'I've no idea,' Merodda said. 'To make a public spectacle of us, I suppose.'

'Maybe he's truly merciful,' Pavva put in. 'Just like everyone's been saying.'

'To you he will be, lass. No doubt it's only the queen and I who have the rank to interest him.' All at once Merodda felt herself smile. 'That's true, isn't it? Here, how would you like to trade clothes with me?'

'What?' Pavva looked down at her drab dresses. 'But these are so old and dirty.'

'Just so. Would the great lady Merodda of the Boar wear such things?'

Pavva laughed.

'Very well, my lady,' she said. 'I'll trade with you and gladly when the time comes.'

'We'd best do it now. They won't be sending us a page, ever so nicely, asking us to join them at table or suchlike.' Merodda glanced at Abrwnna. 'We can do the same for you, Your Highness.'

Abrwnna shook her head, then turned and walked to her favourite chair, lying on its side in front of the dead hearth. She set it upright, then flopped into it with one of her long sighs.

'I shall die with my husband,' she announced. 'They shall find me here, defiant to the end.'

'Oh for the sake of the gods!' Merodda was about to say more, but she had run out of patience with the Queen. 'As you wish, then. Pavva, let's get our clothes changed.'

They exchanged dresses, and Pavva took her baby to sit near the Queen's feet. Abrwnna leaned back in her chair and stared at the ceiling while the others made a half-hearted attempted to convince her to try to escape. Time, however, had run out – Merodda was just tying a dirty shawl round her waist for want of a proper kirtle when the guards flung open the door. A stout man, egg-bald but with a full, brindled beard, strode into the room with other soldiers behind him.

'The one with the red hair,' the bald fellow snapped, pointing.

'That's the Queen, or so we've been told. Now come along, lass. No one will harm you. No one will harm any of you, for that matter, but I suggest you all stay here, safely away from the common-born riders. I can't vouch for their conduct. Is the Lady Merodda among you?'

'She's not.' Abrwnna rose with a toss of her hair. 'I've no idea if she lives or lies dead.'

'No doubt. Well, come along. You're going to be imprisoned elsewhere.'

With her head held high, Abrwnna strode out of the room. She's a queen at last, Merodda thought to herself – at the last, indeed.

Lilli had spent the entire day lying on top of her blankets in her tent. Since her maidservants kept badgering her, she did dress in the morning and eat some of the food they brought her, too. But forcing herself outside lay beyond her. She felt exhausted or perhaps paralysed; at times it seemed she lacked the energy or will even to sit up. Distantly she could hear the noise of the battle, and now and then one of the girls would go outside and bring back news of the fighting. At times Lilli would drift off to sleep, only to have dreams of wyverns grappling with boars that would wake her screaming.

'What is it, my lady?' Clodda would ask.

'I'm being torn in half,' Lilli would answer. 'I don't know how else to put it.'

When the sound of battle died away, Lilli finally managed to step outside her tent. The sun was setting, and up on the hill the humbled towers of Dun Deverry gleamed in the heavy light.

'Mistress?' Clodda said. 'Shall I bring out your chair?'

'If you would, please.'

Lilli sank into the chair and sat looking up at the dun. All around them swept the noise and bustle – men carrying wounded, men yelling and leaping at the victory, men weeping for dead friends. She herself felt beyond tears or hope, but Anasyn at last returned, striding across the camp, calling out to her when he drew near. Still in his mail, he was carrying his helm in one hand, swinging it the way he used to swing some toy when they'd both been children in Dun Hendyr. She rose to greet him, but she couldn't force a smile to match his.

'We've done it!' Anasyn crowed. 'The broch's ours and the false king's in Maryn's hands!'

'That gladdens my heart.' The words seemed to stick in her mouth.

Anasyn considered her, then stopped smiling. He tossed the helm to a maidservant and laid his hand on Lilli's shoulder.

'I shouldn't gloat,' he said.

'Why not? Bevva's avenged, and this rotten horrid war is over. I don't know what's wrong with me.' She turned away, afraid of tears. 'I should be happy.'

'Nah, nah, nah, no one expects that of you, little sister. You've lost the clan of your birth, and I've lost a lot of good men today, and ye gods, I've lost friends, too! It would be best for me to mourn instead of gloating.'

At the honest pain in his voice she could look at him again. They clasped hands, and he drew her close. In that moment he looked so like Peddyc that she feared she would choke on tears.

That night the last of the silver daggers gathered around a fire in front of Maddyn's tent – twenty-three out of the hundred who'd left Cerrmor in the spring, and two of those were wounded. Otho and Caudyr joined them, and Otho had loot, a whole barrel of mead.

'I reckon the cursed false king owes it to us,' Otho said, and he was actually smiling. 'I had a bit of a struggle getting it away from one of Gwerbret Daeryc's servants, but in the end I won.'

With a kindling axe Owaen broke open the top of the barrel, and they dipped mead out like ale into whatever cups they could find. Maddyn raised his high.

'To our dead!' He splashed a few drops into the fire. 'And to our captain.'

'For Caradoc,' the murmur and the libations went round. 'And all our dead.'

Everyone drank, then merely stood, looking at each other. Maddyn was remembering another time when the silver daggers had numbered so few – after the first battle he'd ever ridden with Caradoc, far away in Eldidd and a long time ago. Then they'd been dishonoured scum and taken the brunt of the fighting; now, even as honour-bound warriors, they'd taken it again.

'Otho?' he said. 'Do you remember making these knives of ours? And the battle that gave Caradoc the idea of them?'

'I do, at that. It was a feud over a bridge, wasn't it? I remember that we took it in the end, and the lord who wanted the cursed thing paid us dearly.'

'That's how I was remembering it, too.' He glanced at the younger men. 'And so Otho borrowed his lordship's blacksmith's forge and made up the first daggers.'

They nodded, smiling a little, and Branoic drew his dagger from his sheath and held it up. In the firelight the peculiar alloy gleamed as if it burned from within.

'Our honour and our curse,' Branoic said. 'To the long road that brought us here!'

Everyone drained their drink, whether it was from wooden cup or looted goblet.

'Let's fill them up again,' Maddyn said. 'Who knows what our Wyrd will bring us next, eh?'

They drank late into the night, and yet no one could think of a jest, it seemed, or start a song that didn't trail away into miserable silence. From the rest of the camp they heard laughter and singing, or ragged outbursts of cheers for no particular reason, but none of them found the heart to join in. Finally toward dawn the celebrations died into silence. One at a time the other silver daggers drifted away, leaving Maddyn alone to tend a dying fire. He put on the last few sticks of wood just for the light and poked the coals around them, then knelt in the dirt to watch the salamanders playing in the flames and the sylphs that hovered in the smoke above. His little blue sprite appeared and leaned against him while she sucked on her forefinger.

'They say the Wildfolk can travel to the Otherlands and back again,' Maddyn said. 'Go tell Caradoc that the Prince has his victory, will you?'

She looked up at him and nodded, then disappeared.

'Ye gods, Maddo lad,' Maddyn told himself. 'You're drunk, aren't you? And a cursed good thing, too.'

He dropped his face to his hands and wept.

Just at dawn Merodda wrenched herself awake from an uncomfortable sleep to find herself on the edge of screaming. Someone had come into the chamber. He was standing by the door and threatening her – except that no one was or had. The sensation lingered so strongly that she knew she'd not been having anything as ordinary as a dream. A dweomer warning, more like, and a logical one, that some of the new king's men would be searching for her.

And what would they do when they found her? She would have to plan her escape carefully, and get out of the dun as soon as possible. She got up and went to look out of the window of the women's hall.

The gates were still shut and guarded. Soon they would open, and she'd have to be ready when she saw her chance.

The soldier shoved the tent-flap aside and let the grey dawn light in with him.

'My Lord Nevyn?' He carried something in his arms, wrapped in a bit of sacking. 'Councillor Oggyn sent me to give this to you. He says it has your name written inside it.'

'Indeed?' Nevyn took the parcel, and the moment his fingers felt the smooth leather binding through the sack, he laughed.

'I'll wager it does, at that. Let me just get this off – hah! it's my book indeed, one that was stolen from me many a year ago now.'

Nevyn ran his hand down the leather and gloated. Apart from a bit of mildew, the lore-book seemed unharmed. The soldier, still in his filthy mail, smiled indulgently at the way he clucked over it.

'Where did Oggyn find this?' Nevyn said.

'He told me that one of the men brought it to him, and some other odd stuff as well, from that room where we captured the Queen and her women. Since it was a book, they reckoned he'd want it, but he opened it, and here it was yours. A weird thing, that, he said.'

'Mayhap it was Wyrd, indeed. My thanks for bringing it, and I'll give the Councillor a thousand thanks when I see him.'

Nevyn stowed the book away in his campaign chest, then left his tent. In the early morning the King's men were hard at work, digging long trenches to bury the dead from the last battle in the dun and royal broch. They would pile the earth high over them, here in the parkland outside the dun walls, in memory of the slaughter that put the true king upon his throne. When he walked through the gates, he found more dead, laid out in tidy lines to wait for burial. Beyond them stood the army's horses, tethered in close rows, with soldiers taking them a few at a time to water.

Back and forth across the innermost ward servants hurried to follow the orders of the new masters of the dun. As Nevyn was crossing the ward, he asked each servant he met if they knew the whereabouts of Lady Merodda of the Boar. None did, or at the least, none admitted to it. Nevyn was determined to find her, assuming she hadn't fled the dun, of course. He was already planning out how to question her about the curse-tablet back in Cerrmor. Unfortunately, his place during the day's events was at the Prince's side. Time to search would be hard to come by.

All that morning Maryn held an improvised malover. Although he refused to consider himself king until the priests performed the final ceremonies, no one was about to argue with his right of conquest. He was, after all, the Marked Prince of Pyrdon and Cerrmor as well as of Deverry now by default. A few at a time, stripped of all weapons and escorted by guards, the lords whom his victory had turned into rebels and traitors knelt before him to beg for his pardon and to swear fealty to him and his line forever. The lords whose lands lay to the south grovelled shamelessly; the northern lords were sullen, but they all knelt, every one of them.

The common-born in the dun and the women of all ranks were deemed beneath the King's notice – except of course for the former Queen of all Deverry. Late in the day Oggyn had her brought into the malover with a serving girl along as a protection of sorts for her honour. The Queen wore a dark green dress, stiff with embroidery at hem and sleeve, and her flame-red hair spread uncombed over her shoulders like a shawl. Nevyn noticed the men in the hall turning to appraise her as the guards hurried her forward.

'Your Highness?' said a guard. 'This is the would-be queen.'

Abrwnna knelt at the king's feet. Strands of her hair stuck to her cheeks with tears; they looked like scratches, Nevyn found himself thinking, as if this were the Dawntime and she had raked her face bloody with her own nails.

'This is the wife of the false king?' Maryn said.

'She is, my liege,' Oggyn said, 'and a pitiful sight, truly.'

'Just barely a woman, my liege,' Nevyn put in. 'And married off to an outright child. I wouldn't call her a threat to the kingdom.'

'I agree with my lord Nevyn,' Oggyn said. 'No doubt we can find her shelter in some temple of the Goddess.'

'I'd rather die.' Abrwnna's voice was a bare whisper. 'Don't lock me up. I'd rather die.'

'Now here, child!' Oggyn said. 'You'll feel differently once you've had a chance to think about things.'

Abrwnna raised her head and stared at the councillor until her rage made him turn away.

'Prince Maryn,' she said at last, 'everyone tells me you're merciful beyond belief. Then kill me and don't shut me up somewhere to moulder. I'd rather die than go mad.'

Maryn sighed, just once but sharply.

'Well, can't we make some other provision for her?' The King glanced Nevyn's way. 'She's got no claim to the throne whatsoever.'

'Just so,' Nevyn said. 'We could settle her upon one of your loyal lords. I've no doubt that she was married in name only.'

'That's true.' Hope brought a flicker of life to Abrwnna's eyes. 'I'd swear any vow you wanted me to. I'd never do anything to harm you or yours, truly I wouldn't.'

'She's not in a position to do any harm,' Oggyn broke in. 'I agree with Nevyn in *this* case.'

The stress was unmistakable. Maryn ignored it.

'Very well, then,' the Prince said. 'Who handles things like this? The priests?'

'I'll make the proper arrangements, Your Highness,' Nevyn said. 'And perhaps one of your lords will speak and take her.'

'She'll be a widow soon enough,' Oggyn muttered.

Out in the crowded hall Tieryn Anasyn leapt to his feet as fast as a grouse breaking cover and swooped down on the king. He flung himself to a kneel beside Abrwnna.

'My liege,' Anasyn said. 'I'd be honoured to stand surety for this woman and take her into my clan as my wife.'

'Done, then,' Maryn said. 'She's yours, once Nevyn works out the legalities.'

Abrwnna looked back and forth between them, seemed to be about to speak, then wept in a sudden burst of sobs, just as suddenly stifled. No doubt she could work out for herself that no one was going to ask her opinion on this matter. Anasyn rose, then helped her up. Clinging to his arm she allowed herself to be escorted out of the great hall.

When the guards started to follow, Nevyn caught their attention.

'No sign of Lady Merodda?' Nevyn asked.

'None, my lord,' one guard said.

The other shook his head and shrugged.

'I begin to wonder if she escaped,' Nevyn said. 'We know that some of the Boars did. Well, keep looking. She's cursed important.'

'I just thought of somewhat,' Branoic said. 'None of those lords who deserted the Regent ever returned.'

'True enough,' Maddyn said. 'I wonder how many of them are gathering around Lord Braemys in Cantrae?'

'No doubt we'll find out before we want to. Let's hope most of them are holed up in their duns like scared rabbits.'

The two silver daggers were standing up on the catwalk of the innermost wall. Below them the city spread out, a pool of ruins lapping around a ravaged hill.

'Think the folk will come back?' Branoic spat reflectively over the wall.

'Sooner or later. It's still the Holy City, the King's City. And the real wars are over, whether Braemys decides to rebel or not.'

'So they are. Ye gods, I never thought I'd live to see this day.'

'No more did I. I only wish we'd all-' Maddyn couldn't finish the sentence.

Branoic spat again. Maddyn looked out across the ruins, but he was seeing Caradoc, laughing as he hoisted a tankard.

'Let's go down,' Maddyn said. 'See where old Nevyn's got to, maybe.'

When they reached the ward by the main gates, they found it mobbed. Despite the new king's blanket pardon, the old king's retainers were leaving the dun – noble-born servitors and page boys, the artisans and higher rank of servant, all walking out of the gates with only what they could carry on their backs. Most of the women wept; a few of the men did, too. Maddyn wondered if it were grief for the fallen dynasty or worry at what lay ahead of them. Some of the men were pushing handcarts, piled with blankets and children.

Behind the carts a servant girl was walking – no, a woman, because despite her yellow hair and lithe body, her face in the harsh sunlight showed a fine webbing of wrinkles. Dressed in dirty brown, with an old grey shawl tied round her waist and over one hip, she plodded along, staring at the ground as if in despair. Maddyn stared, then swore softly under his breath.

'What is it?' Branoic said.

'That woman. Come with me.'

As they strode over, she looked at them with such a complete disinterest that Maddyn hesitated, wondering if he were wrong, but her hands gave her away – fine and soft with well-trimmed nails. Maddyn laid a hard hand on her shoulder.

'Lady Merodda, by the gods!'

She screamed, flailing at him with useless fists. Branoic grabbed her arms from behind and pinned her against his chest while she squealed and squirmed.

'We've got ourselves a prize,' Maddyn said. 'Merodda of the Boar, aren't you?'

'I'm not! I'm not! She's been taken by the Prince's men. Oh, don't hurt me! I'm but her maidservant.'

'Then you won't mind if the lady's daughter takes a look at you.'

'So Lilli is here.' She went limp in Branoic's hands. 'Oh ye gods, that my own daughter would turn against me!' Tears ran down her cheeks in silent lines. 'Very well, silver dagger. I am Lady Merodda, or truly, just Merodda now, an old woman like any other, since I've no kin and clan. What do you want with me? Ransom? Who's to pay it? Please let me go. I can't swing a sword to ride against you. What's my life to you?'

Branoic's grip loosened as she began to sob, but Maddyn noticed that her eyes stayed dry.

'I've got a question for you,' Maddyn said. 'Tell me, do you remember a man named Aethan? He rode for your brother a long while ago.'

'Ah Goddess!' Merodda stared at him for a long moment. 'Is he here, too?'

'He's not, but dead these long years past, and all because of you. You shamed him and stole his honour, and your brother nearly stole his life along with it when he flogged him in his ward. What you did to him is going to hang you now. Branoic, we're taking her to the King.'

Maddyn expected her to curse him, or even spit at him like a peasant woman, but she merely stared, her eyes empty of all feeling, all thought – the brazen hussy! he thought. The stinking little bitch! When Branoic gave her a little shake, she started walking and, her head held high, let them march her off to Maryn's justice.

In Dun Deverry's great hall Prince Maryn had finished with the noble-born prisoners. He was holding an impromptu court while servants poured his predecessor's mead for lord and rider alike. Although he sat at the king's old table, to honour Great Bel's dictates he'd chosen a place at the right hand of the King's chair, empty except for its pitiful cushions. With Anasyn in his dead father's place, his lords sat at table with him, and out in the hall soldiers laughed and joked as the serving lasses poured the imprisoned Olaen's mead round.

Nevyn was thinking of the child-king and how, against all odds, he might save the boy's life. The only solution the laws had turned up was almost as harsh as death – castrate or blind him, so that he'd be

unfit to rule according to ancient precedent, then turn him over to
the priests of Bel to raise as one of their own. Perhaps it would be
better to let Oggyn have his way and let the child be smothered as
painlessly as possible, so that he could begin a new incarnation in, or
so Nevyn could hope, better circumstances. But he was so young, a
bare five summers – the thought would not leave him, not even in the
comforts of victory.

In but a few moments, though, Nevyn had a distraction that in the
event he would rather have foregone. At the door someone shouted,
someone else crowed with laughter, and Maddyn and Branoic
appeared, shoving in front of them a blonde women dressed like a
servant in dirty brown and grey. She walked like one already dead, her
head high but her eyes staring at nothing as she made her way
through the jeers and mockery of Maryn's men and the former king's
servants alike. Nevyn heard a serving lass mutter, 'Good! They got the
slut, her and her poisons,' and knew then that the captive must be
Lady Merodda. At last! Soon he would be able to pry the truth out of
her. He glanced quickly around but saw Lilli nowhere.

'You!' He pointed to the serving girl. 'There's a couple of coppers
for you if you fetch Lady Lillorigga here.'

'Done, my lord!' She curtsied, then hurried off, heading for the
staircase across the great hall.

Anasyn got up and hurried after the girl, but Nevyn had no time to
wonder why. He turned back to Merodda and studied her. Would she
tell him the secret of the curse-tablet? He'd have to bribe it out of
her, most likely. Her captors were making her kneel at Maryn's feet,
while he slewed round to face her in some surprise.

'What's this, silver daggers?' Maryn said.

'My liege.' Maddyn bowed to him. 'May I present Lady Merodda
of the Boar?'

'Oh ho! A prize, then,' Maryn said. 'My thanks!'

When Maryn rose and towered over her, Merodda looked at the
floor and neither moved nor spoke. Although her face had gone pale,
she seemed perfectly composed, perfectly calm, the very picture of
someone who'd given up all hope. Maddyn, on the other hand,
brimmed with fury like a goblet about to spill. His hands clenched
into fists, he stood trembling behind her. Nevyn was alarmed enough
to rise from his chair.

'Very well, Lady Merodda,' Maryn said. 'You shall be placed under
guard in your chambers. I would suggest you begin praying to the

Goddess you women serve, because as soon as my councillors can arrange it, you'll be taken to one of her temples to live out your days.'

'My liege!' Maddyn's voice rose to a howl. 'How can you pardon her?'

Branoic grabbed him by the arm.

'My apologies, my liege,' Maddyn said and fast, 'for my discourtesy, but ye gods, if ever a woman was evil, it's her! It gripes my soul, to think of her living out her days at leisure.'

'She'll be as good as imprisoned.' Nevyn walked round the table and came to stand beside the King. 'I doubt me if such will please the lady.'

Maddyn shook his head like a wet dog trying to get dry. Out in the great hall, servants and riders alike had gathered in a circular press to watch.

'He's thinking of Aethan, my lord,' Branoic said to Nevyn. 'You'll remember how he died.'

At the name Merodda's expression changed – pain like a bird fluttered across her face, then was gone.

'I remember Aethan myself,' Prince Maryn said. 'Is this the women who-'

'It is, my liege,' Maddyn burst out. 'I swore a vow of vengeance then, and I've kept it locked in my heart ever since.'

'Well, truly it was a grievous harm she worked him.' The Prince hesitated, thinking. 'But here, good bard, what do you want me to do? She's a woman, an old woman at that, and she's never lifted a sword against me. By the gods, if I'd spare Nantyn's life, how could I not do the same for her?'

'But my liege! Everyone knows how she poisoned people and worked witchcraft.'

'Indeed? Lady Merodda, you must have some answer to these charges.'

Merodda lifted her head and looked first at the bard, then at the King.

'And will it be worth the breath to make an answer?' Her voice held steady, but it sounded curiously flat. 'Everything I ever honoured and held dear is dead and gone, Prince Maryn. Kill me if it pleases you.'

'No one's death pleases me, my lady.'

She sat back on her heels and considered him with a flicker of life in her eyes.

'I'd say that was true,' she said at last. 'And a wondrous thing in a noble-born man.'

Again Maddyn shook himself. When Nevyn reached out a hand to steady him, Maddyn knocked it away. All the colour had drained from his face, and he trembled as he stared at the women he had hated for twenty years.

'The charges against me,' Merodda went on, 'are true enough, though I only ever poisoned one woman, and I regretted it bitterly when I saw how hard it was for her to die. How many men have you slain, Prince Maryn? How many deaths lie at the feet of each and every man in this hall? Is the one death I made such a grievous thing, compared to all those slain men I saw lying in the ward and below the walls?'

Prince Maryn went tense.

'And as for the witchcraft, my prince, do you know what it means to be a woman born into a clan such as the Boar? Do you know what it feels like to be passed from one husband to the next at your brother's decree with never a thought for what you might wish? Do you know what it means to wait and wait while the man you live for rides to war, and you never knowing if he lives or dies? Do you know what it means to grovel to get a few scraps for yourself while your brothers have the feast? Do you, my prince? I think not. And so I think I could talk all day and you still would never understand why I'd turn to spells and scrying, just to have a little something of my own.'

The great hall had fallen silent to listen. Nevyn felt torn. Better than any man there he knew just how corrupt she was and how cruel, but then, indeed, were any of them better enough than she to judge her? Hadn't he used his own dweomer to put a king on his throne and to meddle in the lives of thousands of people thereby? Hadn't his omens and his spells of glamour caused the deaths of thousands in the King's cause? When Maryn looked his way for guidance, Nevyn mouthed a single word, 'mercy'.

'Your words have truth in them, my lady,' Maryn said. 'You would have made a king a splendid councillor if only you'd been born a man. You've pleaded your own case well enough, certainly, woman or no.'

'My liege!' Maddyn howled, the ringing pain of a well-trained voice.

'You!' Merodda leapt up and spun to face him. 'You were Aethan's friend, you say? Well, by the gods, I loved him. I would have run away with him, but my brother found out. Ah ye gods, I was sure he'd kill us both! I was a little stone in his game of Carnoic, a widow he could marry off to get some alliance or stop some rebellion, and here I'd dared soil myself with a common-born rider. What could I do?'

'You're lying!' Maddyn snarled. 'Aethan told me the tale, and it was a different one.'

'And how could he have known what my brother-'

'Oh hold your tongue, slut!' Maddyn spun round to face the King. 'She deserves death.'

Nevyn stepped firmly in front of Maddyn and forced him back. Back in the crowd a woman cried out, a long wail of pain. Nevyn spun around, expecting to see Lilli, but the woman who wept was someone he'd never seen before – so Merodda had had at least one friend, apparently. But where was Lilli? He turned, scanning the crowd, and finally saw her half-way up the staircase. She stood watching, her face as expressionless as her mother's, while Tieryn Anasyn stood behind, his hands tight on her shoulders.

'Does anyone speak for Lady Merodda?' Maryn said.

On the staircase Lilli started forward, but Anasyn grabbed her and hauled her back, talking all the while. Nevyn caught Maryn's attention and pointed her out.

'Tieryn Anasyn!' the prince called out. 'Let your foster-sister come forward.'

The crowd in the great hall sighed in a vast murmur as it parted to let the lady and her foster-brother through. Lilli kept her head high and her expression composed, but Nevyn could see her trembling. She curtsied to the Prince without looking at her mother. When she started to speak, Anasyn drowned her out.

'My prince,' Anasyn said. 'Merodda had my mother murdered. I add my voice to the silver dagger's.'

Lilli opened her mouth, but the Prince spoke first.

'Tieryn Anasyn, my thanks,' Maryn said. 'With all that's happened, I'd forgotten that.'

'My liege.' Nevyn decided that it was time he spoke up. 'I can understand the tieryn's desire to avenge his mother, and the bard's to avenge his friend, but I'll still ask you to spare the woman. My reasons will come clear later.'

The Prince hesitated, thinking hard. Lilli seemed to have given up trying to speak; she was leaning back against her foster-brother as if she were too exhausted to stand on her own. From behind him Nevyn heard Maddyn swear; then the bard shoved him bodily to one side and strode forward.

'My liege,' Maddyn said, 'once not so long ago you granted me a boon, that whatever I asked you for should be mine. I ask for her life, that you hang her as she deserves.'

'Maddo!' Nevyn snarled. 'Don't!'

'I will, curse it all!' Maddyn fell on his knees in front of Maryn. 'My liege, I ask you now for the boon you granted me.'

'By all the gods!' Prince Maryn said. 'I'd meant you to have somewhat glorious, not this!'

'My liege, this is the boon I ask for. And so no man will speak ill of you, let it be known that it's my demand that's caused the hanging of her. Have your scribe write it into the judgment.'

'Very well,' the Prince said. 'Lady Lillorigga, it aches my heart after all you've done for me, but I can't deny a man a boon I granted before the gods and my vassals. I hope and pray that you understand this.'

Lilli merely trembled for an answer. When Anasyn put a brotherly arm around her, she seemed not to notice. With a helpless glance Nevyn's way, the Prince shrugged, palms upward.

'So be it,' Prince Maryn went on. 'Lady Merodda of the Boar, you will hang by the neck until dead, out in the courtyard this morrow noon.' He glanced around, then gestured. 'Guards! Take her away.'

Merodda flung her arms above her head as if begging the gods, then let them fall to her sides. When the guards grabbed her by the arms, she let her eyes flick their way once. As they marched her out, she looked only straight ahead. In Anasyn's arms Lilli began sobbing – for Lady Bevyan as much as for her mother, Nevyn assumed. Maddyn got up and bowed low to the King.

'My liege, my humble thanks.' His smile was terrifying. 'I'll glorify your name forever for this.'

The Prince inclined his head. With a gesture to Branoic to follow, Maddyn bowed and left the Prince's presence. Maryn watched him as he sat down with the few remaining silver daggers, then turned to Nevyn.

'I hope to all the gods,' the Prince said, 'that I did the right thing.'

'You did the only thing you could do, my liege,' Nevyn said. 'Whatever Wyrd was born from this will fall on Maddyn's head, not yours.'

Nevyn turned on his heel and rushed out after the guards. They were marching Merodda across the ward to one of the side brochs, and it seemed that the men among the former king's servants must have hated her, because a crowd of them were jeering and calling her names. She walked proudly past, head high, eyes fixed on naught but the tower ahead of her. Nevyn trailed along behind until the guards had led her inside, then caught up with them at the foot of a winding staircase that led up. Fortunately, one of the soldiers recognized him.

'I want a word with the lady,' Nevyn said. 'Alone.'

'Of course, my lord.' He glanced around. 'Here's an empty room. We'll be right outside here should you need us.'

After the soldiers hustled the prisoner inside, Nevyn shut the heavy door and leaned against it. Smashed furniture lay across the stone floor of the narrow chamber. Merodda glanced at it, then back to him.

'Who are you, old man?'

'Brour's teacher.'

She flung up her head and took a step back.

'Indeed.' Nevyn said, smiling. 'I understand a great deal more than the prince does about this supposed "witchcraft" of yours, my lady.'

'What do you want with me?'

'The answer to a question. If you tell me what I want to know, I'll do my level best to help you escape. Your nephew Braemys escaped with some of his men. He's doubtless in Cantrae, waiting to bargain from a position of strength. You'd have somewhere to go. I can get you a good horse and plenty of provisions for the journey.'

'I see.' Life flooded back to her eyes. 'Will you swear you'll get me out of here if I tell you what you want to know?'

'I'll swear on the dweomer itself, and I'll wager that Brour told you just what that means.'

'He did. Ask your question.'

'Many years ago, when Maryn was still a prince in Pyrdon, a retainer of yours worked an evil spell. A lead tablet, it was, carved with words right out of the Dawntime. What do they mean? How do I lift it?'

'I don't know.'

'You're lying.'

'Why that?' Merodda tossed her head and looked away, her mouth working in pain. 'Why of all the things in the world must you ask that?'

'Oh here, do tell me.' Nevyn softened his voice. 'What's it to you now? The spell failed, after all.'

'Now you're the liar.' With a grimace she began pacing back and forth on a tight and narrow track. 'You wouldn't be here questioning me if you thought the dweomer spent and over with.'

'True spoken. I'll admit it.'

Merodda stopped and turned to face him.

'Not that! I'd tell you anything but that, but by the Dark Goddess herself, I'd rather die than lift that spell. Or will you put me to the torture? Do your worst! You won't break me.'

'Never would I use torture, not even for a matter this grave.'

She started to speak, her mouth half a sneer, then stopped.

'Nor would I let anyone else do such a thing.' Nevyn kept his voice quiet. 'The dweomer of Light would never allow it. Please tell me, and I'll protect you, no matter what boon the Prince granted.'

She was searching his face as if she were scrying out the truth of what he said. For a moment he thought he had her – he could see the beginning of something like trust in her eyes – but she tossed her head and stepped back.

'Your prince has his wretched victory,' Merodda said. 'The man who loved me lies dead, and even if I got away, with the Prince's judgment upon me I'd end up begging some temple for sanctuary. My clan is dead, my king's imprisoned, you and your precious prince have stripped everything from me, even my daughter.' Her voice caught, but she steadied it. 'Well, you shan't take my vengeance too! I'd rather hang than give that up.'

'Vengeance, is it?'

She swore and turned her back, her hands so tight in fists that her knuckles went white. Nevyn calmly walked around to face her.

'So, my lady, a slip on your part! I'm beginning to puzzle this out. The dead infant buried along with the tablet – the ensorcelment's meant to ruin the beginnings of things, isn't it? His victory, his reign, poisoned from the start! You've told me much already, no matter how clever you think you are.'

Merodda smiled, a narrow-eyed gloat.

'Indeed, old man?' She spat on the floor at his feet. 'Then stop it if you can!'

'Guards!' Nevyn turned away. 'Come take her!'

Nevyn unbarred the door and flung it wide. The soldiers hurried in, and as she strode over to meet them, Merodda burst out laughing.

When Nevyn returned to the great hall, the sight of the empty High King's chair next to Maryn hit him like a blow. No wonder a

white mare had proved impossible to find! Merodda's curse had
begun its work even then.

It was late in the evening before Nevyn had a chance to talk with
Maddyn. He searched for him through the dun, then went out to the
encampment on the hill side below and found where the silver
daggers had pitched their tents. Maddyn sat by a small fire under the
open sky and played his harp in a medley of songs, while all around
him the Wildfolk danced and leapt like the flames. Nevyn sat down
on a stump of log, and Maddyn let the music die away.

'Have you come to scold me? Because I had the King crush a
viper?'

'I've not,' Nevyn said. 'Because I doubt me you'd listen.'

'Well, by the gods!' Maddyn smacked his open hand on the harp
strings and made them chime a discord. 'What kind of a man would I
be if I didn't avenge my friend?'

'I don't know.'

'And then there's Lilli's foster-mother, too. Merodda had her
butchered like a hog.'

'So she did, but I doubt me if you were remembering Lady Bevyan
today.'

'Well, what of it? I want Merodda dead. Tomorrow I'm going to
stand in the crowd and laugh when the hangman shoves her off the
drop. And then Aethan will finally have peace in the Otherlands.'

Nevyn merely sighed. In the fire a log burned through and fell,
sending a long plume of flame into the dark above. And what am I
going to say? Nevyn thought. How could he explain without touching
on the great secret, that each soul lives many lives, not one? Aethan
was doubtless long reborn, and Merodda and Maddyn both would be,
but now a chain of Wyrd would link them, whether they wanted the
binding or not.

When Lilli asked, one of Maryn's pages told her where Lady Merodda
had been taken, a proper room in a side broch instead of the common
gaol as a small sign of respect to the noble-born. She'd brought coins
to bribe the guards at the door, but one of them, a stout man with
greying hair, recognized her.

'It's the lady's daughter,' he said to the others. 'I don't see any harm
in letting her say farewell to her mother.'

The others nodded; one of them lifted the heavy bar while the
second opened the door a crack and let her slip in.

By the light of a single candle Merodda was sitting on a narrow bed, little more than a straw mattress and a blanket. In the uncertain light, and, with her blonde hair down and untidy, she looked no older than her daughter. Lilli felt herself gasp for breath while Merodda considered her with shadowed eyes.

'Why are you here?' she said at last.

'I don't know,' Lilli said. 'But I had to come.'

Merodda sighed and leaned back against the wall.

'Do you want me to leave?' Lilli went on.

'I don't. I've been wondering somewhat myself. Would you have spoken for me if Anasyn had let you?'

Lilli's heart pounded once.

'It's because of Bevva,' Lilli said. 'I felt torn apart.'

'Ah. So you wouldn't have spoken.'

'I don't know. It was too late, anyway.' Lilli heard her voice choke and tremble. 'But there's Brour, too. He's dead, isn't he? You had him killed.'

'Not I, but Burcan. That was his doing.' Merodda got up to face her. 'And you're a fine one to talk, betraying your kin and clan! What did you tell your precious Prince Maryn? Where all the gates are in the dun? How many men we had? It must have been somewhat like that. I heard him talking about all you'd done for him. You traitorous little bitch!'

Lilli stepped back and found herself against the door.

'You little slut!' Merodda snarled. 'I rue the day I ever birthed you. I wish I'd smothered you with your swaddling bands. You've betrayed your own mother and your clan.'

'Oh, have I now? The Boars were never my clan!'

'Just what do you mean by that?'

'You gave me away, didn't you? Bevva was my real mother, not you. And when you killed her, you gave me away again. What do I owe to you? Just a lot of misery! And if my father had lived, I'd have been part of his clan anyway.'

'Oh, indeed?' All at once Merodda laughed, a cold little mutter under her breath. 'You're sure of that, are you?'

'It doesn't matter, anyway.' All at once Lilli realized what she had come to learn. 'Why did you have Bevva killed? Why?'

'It doesn't matter? Oh, doesn't it? You would have inherited Garedd's lands, but he wasn't your father. I've lied your whole life, my precious little daughter, lied to give you something that wasn't rightfully yours. You're a bastard, my fine Lillorigga! You can tell that to your precious prince.'

With a gasp for air Lilli leaned back against the door. Merodda laughed with a toss of her head and stepped closer.

'So how does that sit with you?' Merodda went on. 'Your ever-so-dear Bevyan had guessed the truth. So I silenced her before she could shame you and get you stripped of your inheritance.'

'She never would have. Bevva never would have hurt me.'

'Oh, are you so sure? I'm not!'

Lilli forced herself to raise her head and look at her mother, smirking in the candlelight. It can't be true, she told herself. It's not true, it's not! But a flood of memory was rising, threatening to drown her – little remarks overheard, the expression on a face when some-one mentioned her inheritance, the gossip about her mother's tarnished honour. Drop by drop the flood built.

'And who was my father, then?' Her voice shook on a whisper.

'And why should I tell you? Soon I'll be dead, and you'll never know.'

'Fair enough. No doubt I owe you that much, a little torment to get some of your own back.'

Rage bloomed on Merodda's face. So! Lilli thought. I was supposed to wheedle and beg!

'Farewell, mother,' Lilli said. 'I'll leave you now, since you can't stand the sight of me.'

Lilli turned and laid one hand on the door.

'Wait!' Merodda snapped.

Lilli turned back.

'Think about your uncle, Lilli. Surely you heard the gossip about him and me.'

'I never listened. I knew they just envied you.'

'Oh, envy me they did, but the gossip was true enough. You're twice cursed, my bastard daughter. Burcan was your father – your uncle, my brother. His love was the one good thing the gods ever gave me in life, and I would have been a fool to throw it away.'

'You're lying!'

'I'm not!' Merodda smiled, and the curve of her lips seemed to drip poison in Lilli's dweomer-touched sight. 'It's the cold truth. And when you were going to marry Braemys, didn't the old cats in the dun hiss and mutter about that? You must have heard them, wondering if I'd marry you off to your own brother. You were a Boar twice over, Lilli, as much a daughter of your clan as any woman could be.'

With a shriek Lilli spun around and slammed her fists against the door. A guard pulled it open from the other side. As she stepped out she could hear her mother laughing in a long peal of hysteria behind her.

'Well now,' the guard said, 'I don't know what she said to you, lass, but remember that she's beside herself. In a bit you'll remember the good things, eh?'

Lilli burst out sobbing and ran down the corridor, flung herself down the stairs so fast that she nearly fell and preceded her mother to the Otherlands. She fled outside and into the middle of the silent ward, stood sobbing for a moment until she could collect herself.

'It's not true. It can't be true.'

The flood of memory rose up and broke over her. Burcan defended me from Tibryn. He offered land to keep me safe.

'Bevva!' Lilli howled the name as if her grief could truly wake the dead. 'Bevva, Bevva!'

Gasping and stumbling she ran again, ran blindly, careening through the ward. She found the gate out by sheer luck and ran again until her burning lungs pulled her up. Gasping and choking, she leaned against a cold stone wall and looked around her. She'd fetched up in the main ward, and over her rose the royal broch. Torchlight spilled out the windows, and she could hear men laughing and singing.

When she slipped in, they were all too drunk to notice her. She crept upstairs, found her chamber, and collapsed onto the bed. Sleep rose up and took her.

'My lord! My lord Nevyn!' The voice came bellowing through the dark. 'Are you in there?'

Someone was shaking the tent-flap as well. Nevyn sat up and threw his blankets back.

'I am! Who is it?'

'Caudyr sent me. The little false king is dying.'

Nevyn pulled on his brigga and boots, grabbed a shirt, and ran out of the tent. The servant – little more than a boy – carried a lantern, and Nevyn followed its gleam as they hurried up the hill. At the door to the royal broch he paused and pulled the shirt over his head.

'Where are Caudyr and the lad?'

'In the false king's old chambers. Prince Maryn had him put there under guard.'

As soon as Nevyn opened the door to the royal suite he smelled vomit, and the stench had a bitter tinge. He ran into the bedroom and found it ablaze with lantern light. On his narrow bed the child-king lay, his wooden horse beside him, while Caudyr stood at a table littered with packets of herbs and medicaments. The room stank of vomit and excrement. Nevyn crossed it in two strides and flung the shutters open at the windows.

'What have you been doing for him?'

'Salt water and lots of it. He's been vomiting on his own, and I've been trying to wash his insides clean.'

Nevyn went to the bedside and laid a hand on the boy's face: clammy and cold, and his skin had a greyish tinge. At the touch he opened his eyes, then closed them again. A vomit stain lay on the blanket near his face.

'Blood,' Nevyn said. 'You can see the tinge. Let's hope it's just the straining.'

Caudyr turned and pointed to a basin on the floor. Blood and a lot of it clotted in the watery vomit. Nevyn squatted down beside the boy and touched him again. He wanted a look at the child's pupils, but this time Olaen kept his eyes shut.

'Come now, lad, look at me,' Nevyn whispered. 'We're here to help you. Open your eyes and look at me.'

Not a twitch, not a stir, not even when Nevyn gave him a gentle shake. Carefully he pried the lad's eyes open and found the pupils widely dilated even though it seemed he slept. When Nevyn swore under his breath, Caudyr came limping over.

'Is it too late?' Caudyr said.

'I fear me it is. He's slipping away from us.'

Caudyr let out his breath in a long sigh. Nevyn got up and pulled a blanket over the boy's thin shoulders – a futile gesture, but he had to do something.

'When did this happen?'

'Well, a guard fetched me some while after midnight,' Caudyr said. 'He'd looked for the regular chirurgeons but couldn't find them. Someone thought of me, and so I gathered up my supplies and got here as fast as I could.'

'He's been poisoned, of course.'

'Of course. The last person to see him was his nursemaid. The guards told me she brought him up some honey cake – a little treat, she said, from the kitchens.'

Nevyn glanced around and saw, lying broken on the floor, a pottery plate. When he picked the pieces up, he found them sticky. One trampled bit of cake lay near the table, which he scooped up with a fragment of plate. When he sniffed it, he smelled nothing unusual. With a shrug he laid it on the table.

'I want to talk with the nursemaid.'

'Through there.' Caudyr pointed at a little door in the wooden partition. 'Come to think of it, I wonder why she didn't hear the noise I've been making?'

Nevyn felt abruptly cold. He flung open the little door, stepped into the tiny chamber, and in the spill of lantern light saw what he'd feared to see, a middle-aged woman lying twisted and dead on the floor. A rumpled pallet, all stained with excrement and vomit, lay nearby. She must have lost control of herself, Nevyn supposed, and got up to get a chamber pot, only to fall and die. He knelt beside her and laid a hand on her face – barely cold. If Caudyr had only known about her, lying there helpless, he might have saved her. With a shake of his head he rose to see Caudyr in the doorway.

'Ye gods! I never heard her moan or cry out.'

'She looks frail. The poison might have killed her very quickly. No doubt she shared the little treat someone had so kindly sent the lad.'

At the sound of their voices, Olaen never moved, not even a twitch. Nevyn strode to the window and leaned out to breathe the cleaner air.

'So,' Caudyr said. 'Who did this, do you think? Councillor Oggyn?'

'It's a good guess. He feared our Maryn's talent for mercy.'

'Where do you think the old sot got the poison?'

'I don't – oh ye gods! I do know. From Lady Merodda's things, the ones the guards brought him along with my book.'

'Do we go to the Prince about this?'

'How can we? We don't have a scrap of evidence.'

'Evidence?' Caudyr looked as if he'd spit. 'Ask Oggyn outright. You can always tell when a man is lying. The Prince will take your word for it.'

'So? My word's not evidence under the laws. As much as I'd like to see this poor woman avenged, it would be a grievous thing if the Prince broke the laws to do it.'

Caudyr stared at him for a long time, then sighed.

'Sometimes,' Caudyr said, 'I think that I'll never understand you, no matter how long I know you.'

'Indeed? Well, you've had a hard life.'

Olaen never woke again but died just as the first dawn silvered the sky. Nevyn had the guards summon servants to clean up the murderous filth and lay the dead out properly, then went down to the cook house behind the dun. Although he'd hoped to find the cooks and question them, what he found was chaos. Half the high-ranking servants had fled the dun and taken their tools with them. Cleavers, iron kettles, and the like fetched a high price in the war-torn kingdom. Maryn's own servants were trying to restore order and scratch together some kind of breakfast for the prince, his noble allies, guards, councillors, and themselves while keeping a cautious eye on those who'd once served the false king. Merely from watching Nevyn realized that no one in the confusion of preparing last night's meal would have noticed Oggyn or a plate of honey cakes coming in or going out.

Nevyn also realized that he didn't even know the poison's name. How could he go to Maryn babbling of poisoners if he couldn't even name the thing out? He paused in the ward and looked up at the tower where Lady Merodda was imprisoned. That wretched fool of a bard! he thought. There's so much I could ask her if only the Prince had been able to pardon her! There's so much I need to ask her – in his mind he could see all too vividly the image of the lead tablet, scribed with evil dweomer in the ancient tongue. What did it mean? How could he turn it harmless? Merodda would never tell him now, and he couldn't even find it in his heart to blame her.

It occurred to him, however, that Lilli might know about her mother's poisons. He was heading out of the dun gates toward the encampment when he heard someone call his name and saw one of Lilli's maidservants hurrying toward him.

'My lord Nevyn!' Clodda said. 'Have you seen our lady?'

'I've not. Did she leave her tent?'

'She never came back to it last night. We've been ever so worried. I couldn't find Tieryn Anasyn or you when I went to look.'

'Well, I'm here now. Go back to the tent and wait there. I'll look for her.'

As soon as the lass was gone, Nevyn leaned against the wall and glanced at the sky – apparently just an idle look at the clouds, but he was scrying Lilli out. He saw her immediately, sitting fully dressed at the end of a bed in a chamber, up in the main dun from the look of it. But where? He went back and in the great hall he found one of the servants left over from the old regime. The girl did indeed know what suites had formerly belonged to the Boars and for a copper was glad enough to tell him.

'And Lady Lillorigga had the smallish one, right down at the end.'

When Nevyn found the chamber, he knocked, then kept knocking until Lilli let him in. He first thought she'd taken ill. Her hair hung in dull wisps around her dead-pale face, and dark circles pouched under her eyes.

'What's so wrong?' Nevyn said.

'I – I had terrible nightmares.'

Lilli sank down on a wooden chest at the room's one narrow window. When the morning sun glared on her face, she winced and got up, stood looking around her, then finally sat on the end of her bed. Nevyn took the seat in the window.

'Terrible they must have been,' he said. 'About what awaits your mother?'

'Some of that, truly. Although it gladdens my heart she's going to die.'

'Because of Lady Bevyan?'

Lilli nodded, then reached up with a trembling hand and began trying to brush her still-short hair back from her face. She would tuck a strand into place only to have another fall forward, over and over, until he felt like screaming at her to stop.

'What are you doing up here?' Nevyn said. 'Your lasses are worried about you.'

'Oh ye gods! Last night, I was just so upset. I bolted for my old chamber without thinking.'

'Lilli.' Nevyn softened his voice. 'Somewhat's gravely wrong, isn't it?'

'I went to talk with my mother last night. I'm sorry now.'

'Did she curse you?'

'She did, and she told me' a long pause 'things.'

'Things?'

Finally she stopped fussing with her hair and clasped her hands in her lap.

'Did you want to see me about somewhat?' Lilli said.

'I did.' Nevyn considered, then decided to leave his prying till later.

'The poison your mother had, do you know its name?'

'Dwarven salts. Brour called it that.'

'Not much of a name, but it will do. And how did it work?'

'You put it in someone's food or drink, and then it ate at their vitals. It was terrible, just like someone dying from eating tainted meat or spoiled milk. There was one woman, Caetha, and everyone said my mother poisoned her because-' She broke off, staring out at nothing.

'Well, your mother did confess to one poisoning.'

'Then it's true.' Lilli was whispering and mostly to herself. 'Everything points to it being true.'

'The poisoning?'

Lilli stared at him, her mouth a little slack.

'What's so wrong?' Nevyn said again. 'I can see it's somewhat truly grave, or I wouldn't be badgering you like this.'

Lilli turned her head and stared at the wall.

'Mother told me,' she said, 'she told me that I'm really a bastard, that her husband wasn't my father.'

'Ah. Well, no wonder you're so troubled! My heart goes out to you, lass, but no one need ever know. Here, Aethan wasn't your father, was he?'

'I only wish.' Lilli paused as if gathering her strength. 'She told me that my father – that my father was – well, her own brother. My uncle.'

Nevyn caught his breath in surprise. At the sound Lilli looked his way.

'I thought she was just saying it to hurt me,' she went on. 'But all kinds of things he did make sense if he was my father.'

'I see. Well, it's no crime of yours, child. You weren't there at your begetting.'

Lilli merely shrugged the comfort away. She was doubtless remembering all the things that people said about children of incest, that they were cursed by the gods and doomed to an early death. In his long experience none of this had ever held true, and he was groping for some reassuring words when she suddenly cried out, one sharp sob.

'It's almost mid-day,' Lilli whispered. 'They'll be hanging her soon.'

'They will. Don't go to watch.'

'I don't want to. Will you stay here till they're done?'

'I will. I suspect that you'll know when it's over.'

She nodded and went back to fussing with the strand of hair.

Nevyn leaned back against the window's edge and turned a little to look out. All he saw were towers and far below, a strip of cobbled ground. Wherever they would be hanging Merodda, it was mercifully out of sight. If only he could have offered her a full pardon! Perhaps she would have told him about the curse-tablet in return for her life if that life had promised freedom and rank. But Maddyn would never back down now.

'You look troubled,' Lilli said.

'I am. Your mother murdered two women who had no power to fight for their lives, and she's worked unspeakable dweomers against our prince, but still, I would rather she had been spared.'

'So would I.' Lilli's voice broke suddenly into weeping. 'Oh ye gods! So would I!'

'Well, come along!' Maddyn said. 'It's time to go.'

'Go where?' Branoic said.

'To watch Merodda hang.'

'I don't want to.'

'What? What's wrong with you?'

Branoic merely shrugged. He didn't understand himself sometimes, and this was one of them. He should want to see the Prince's executioner take Aethan's revenge for him, shouldn't he? Maddyn set his hands on his hips and glared at him.

'You go,' Branoic said. 'You can tell me about it.'

With one last shrug Maddyn turned and strode out of the great hall. Almost everyone in the dun seemed to agree with the bard about this morning's entertainment. Branoic was left alone with one serving girl, who sat weeping on the bottom step of the curving staircase. On an impulse he got up and walked over.

'What's so wrong?' he said.

'They can say what they like about Lady Merodda,' the girl snivelled. 'But she saved my life and my baby's too, when the battle was on.'

'Did she now? That's the first good thing I've heard about her.'

The girl wiped her face on her sleeve. She was wearing much better clothes than the usual wench, better enough to make him wonder if she too were a lady in disguise, until she pulled up the hem of her overdress and blew her nose upon it.

'Ah well,' Branoic said. 'At least the lady will have someone to mourn her. It would be hard thing to leave the earth knowing everyone was celebrating your going.'

She nodded and let the dress hem fall.

'That's true,' she said. 'Oh ye gods, I'd best hurry! I was supposed to bring some water upstairs, for that old man, the councillor, the one with hair.'

'Nevyn's upstairs?'

'He said there was a lady with him who'd been taken faint.'

Lilli, I'll wager! Branoic thought.

'Here, I'll take it up,' he said aloud. 'And a bit of mead, too, should help.'

With a goblet of mead in one hand and a pitcher of water in the other, Branoic trotted upstairs to find an impatient Nevyn standing out in the corridor.

'What happened to that lass?' the old man said.

'She was overcome with grief, like, my lord. Merodda had done her a good turn or two.'

Behind Nevyn stood an open door; Branoic ducked around him and carried the water inside before Nevyn could say a word against it. Sure enough, Lilli was sitting on the end of the bed, all pale and puffy-eyed – with grief, he assumed.

'My lady,' Branoic said. 'My heart aches for your loss.'

'Oh, does it really?' she snapped. 'I don't want false sympathy! I know you hated my mother.'

'Well, then, it aches because you're so sad.'

'That's better.'

'But I didn't hate her.' Branoic glanced around for a table, found none, and put the pitcher and goblet down on the windowsill instead. 'It's our Maddo who's gone daft on the subject, not me. All I cared about was the wrong she did Aethan, and by the gods, when she said she wanted to ride off with him, maybe I'm a dolt, but I believed her.'

'So did I,' Nevyn said. 'And it's a pity the gods didn't allow it. The omens would be a cursed sight better for the new kingdom if they had.'

Branoic was about to ask what he meant when from out in the ward a roar went up, a crowd of voices all raised in mockery and cheers.

'It's over,' Lilli said.

Branoic was expecting her to weep, but instead she lay down across the end of the bed and curled up like a dog in straw. Nevyn hurried round and sat next to her.

'Get out, Branoic,' the old man snapped. 'Now.'

Branoic turned and fled. He avoided angering sorcerers as a matter of principle.

Although the priests had decreed that Maryn could not become High King until the white mare had been found, they saw nothing wrong with the Prince celebrating his victory with a feast. In Dun Deverry's stores lay the best of a spring harvest, laid up for men now dead in a siege now over. All afternoon servants kept bringing food and mead, while bards sang manfully against the noise, and the laughter went round like the drink. Nevyn, however, slipped away from the feast early. While it was still light, he wanted to look in on some of the most badly wounded men. In their improvised hospital – they'd commandeered one of the barracks buildings – he found Caudyr there ahead of him.

'I just sent a page to find you,' Caudyr said.

'Well, I was coming here on my own. Is somewhat wrong?'

'Very. Come look at this.'

Caudyr took him to the bunk of a young lad whose wounds Nevyn had dressed the day before: a slice across the body that had broken several ribs and a gash from a javelin along the side of his thigh. Both wounds had bled but neither had seemed likely to kill him. Now he lay deathly still with barely the life to turn his eyes Nevyn's way. In the flickering lantern light his skin looked bluish-white. Nevyn laid a hand on the boy's face and found his skin clammy cold.

'His cuts have gone septic?' Nevyn said.

'They've not. I just changed the bandages, and everything's clean.'

Nevyn squatted down to look into the boy's eyes. The boy seemed to be about to speak, then died. One moment he was looking at Nevyn; the next he stiffened and simply stopped breathing. Nevyn swore and grabbed him by the shoulders, but his head lolled back with an unseeing stare for the ceiling. Caudyr let fly with a string of curses worthy of a silver dagger.

'It's like he didn't have the strength to live,' Caudyr said. 'But last night he ate and drank, and he was talking, too. He should have recovered.'

Nevyn rose and looked around. Most of the men in this end of the barracks were so badly wounded that they had no energy to spare for another's death; those that were awake lay staring at the ceiling or were curled up with pain. Some moaned; some wept. None would have seen – seen what? he asked himself. He glanced at the dead boy again and noticed a swollen mark on his lips, as if a bee had stung him twice, once on the upper, once on the lower.

'Here!' Nevyn said. 'That's odd! Have you seen bees in here?'

'What?' Caudyr was looking at him as if he thought Nevyn had gone daft. 'What do you mean, bees?'

'Well, I don't think a horsefly would have left that mark.'

'A sting, you mean?' Caudyr scratched his head while he thought. 'Not any bees in here that I noticed. They had kitchen gardens in the dun, so I suppose there must be a hive or two around somewhere. It seems a blasted strange thing to die off, anyway.'

'I did see it once, a child stung by a bee who went into convulsions and died. But surely someone would have noticed if this fellow had thrown fits right here in his bunk.'

'So you'd think! I'm well and truly baffled, Nevyn. I can't see any reason on earth for this lad to die like this.'

'No more can I. He wasn't important enough for anyone to poison, even.'

'Just so. Ah, that reminds me-'

Nevyn held up a hand for silence.

'Get someone to take that poor lad away and bury him,' Nevyn said. 'Then meet me in my tent.'

Nevyn had not forgotten the problem of Oggyn's possible murders. Or one murder, truly, as he remarked to Caudyr later that night.

'The young king was doomed, anyway. No one but me would hold him to account for that.'

'Just so,' Caudyr said. 'And the poor nursemaid wasn't even noble-born.'

'If I gathered enough evidence, Maryn wouldn't let that stop him. From what the servants here have told me, Rwla – that was her name, Rwla – has no living kin. If she did, it would gladden my heart to make Oggyn pay over a stiff lwdd for her. But since she doesn't, all the King can do is hang him.'

'Or send him into exile. But curse it, Oggyn's too useful. The King needs men like him. Winning a war's one thing. Restoring the kingdom's quite another.'

'That's true, and the apportioning of taxes and scrounging the coin to rebuild the city are things Oggyn will understand.'

They looked at each other, and Nevyn realized that Caudyr shared his weariness. In that moment, he knew that he would never gather the evidence against Oggyn. It's another little wound, isn't it? he told himself. Merodda's curse. It's going to be a matter of small corruptions and little faults, but in time, they'll touch the King himself – unless I can stop it.

'What's wrong?' Caudyr said sharply.

'Naught, naught. I'm just very tired.'

'No doubt. Here, I'll be going. Get some sleep. Your fellow physician commands it.'

'Very well, and I'll follow the order gladly.'

And yet, although he did lie down and try to sleep, Nevyn lay awake for many a long hour. Nothing would ever take Maryn's victory away, not the mightiest black dweomer in the world. The dweomer of light had turned the tide of history and swept back the sea of blood against all hope. In the inner planes the balance was righting itself deep within the Deverry group-mind, and there would be peace for the kingdom. But the curse-tablet and the sheer malice it represented could reach out filthy hands and infect those who had won the victory, turning all their joy into a sickness of the soul.

Finally he called upon the Light that he had served so faithfully. If he could win the battle at all, he would win it in the name of the Light and not by his own strength alone. At last then he could sleep, and for the first time in months, he slept soundly.

With the dun given over to Prince Maryn, Lilli reclaimed her old chamber. She had her maids bring her things up from the tent and add them to her own clothes in her wooden chest, which had stayed untouched. Doubtless no one had had time to worry about a traitor's pitifully few belongings. Clodda folded everything neatly, then reached in with a small laugh.

'Part of your dowry, my lady?' She held up the front of what would have been Braemys's wedding shirt.

'So it was.' Lilli took the piece from her. 'You may go now. Tell Oggyn to find you and Nalla a nice place to sleep. Tell him I'll make sure it's nice, too, so he'd better not skimp you.'

Clodda curtsied and hurried out. Lilli closed the chest, then sat down and laid the piece of shirt in her lap. Bevyan had embroidered those rows of interlace and added the Boar blazon on yoke above them. Lilli stroked the stitches, so smooth and tiny, with her finger-tips, but instead of grief, she felt only weariness.

'They hanged your murderer, Bevva,' she said aloud. 'I wish I thought you'd be pleased. You'd probably forgive her, knowing you.'

But I can't. The thought hung in her mind, too painful to voice, even to the empty air.

That night Lilli dreamt of her mother. In the dream she was a child new to Dun Deverry, and she'd got lost in the tangle of towers and wards. She looked down a long corridor and saw Bevyan standing at the end, but when she went running to meet her, the figure turned into Merodda, holding a dagger. Lilli screamed and turned to run, only to find Burcan blocking the way, and he too held a knife upraised.

She woke with a cry to find herself standing next to the bed and clutching a blanket in one hand.

At first Lilli thought herself dreaming still. The chamber stretched around her utterly silent and shadowed except for one ray of pale light that fell across the wooden chest. When she glanced around, following the beam back to its source, she found that a leather shutter had torn from its hook at the window and sagged to allow the moonlight in. The leather must have rustled as it slid, waking her. She laughed and told herself that she'd been silly, letting herself be so afraid of a dream. When she turned to climb back into bed, her mother was standing at the other side.

Dressed in a grey shift and glowing like the moonlight, Merodda stood motionless and stared at her daughter. Her mouth hung open; one hand clutched at a throat deep-furrowed and bruised. Lilli stared back across the rumpled bed until her mother's lips moved, as if she were trying to frame words.

'What is it?' Lilli whispered. 'Ah ye gods, you're dead!'

The apparition began to move toward her, but it didn't walk – rather it seemed to glide around the end of the bed. Lilli stepped back, and back again, and back, but she hit the wall behind her. The rough stone bit into her skin as she pressed against it. Merodda raised her arm and reached out a long white hand. Just as Lilli tried to scream a finger touched her lips. Like fire it was, burning on her flesh, and yet she felt as if she'd stepped outside naked on a winter's day. The cold sucked her life out; she felt herself stagger on the edge of a faint.

'Oh don't,' she whispered. 'Mother, forgive me!'

The apparition broke away and stepped back. It looked much more solid now, and Lilli could distinguish her mother's features, her mother's hair, cropped short to make the hangman's job easier. The lips moved again, still soundless, but Lilli could make out the word it mouthed over and over again: *traitor*. With a toss of its head the apparition turned and moved off, gliding back to the window.

Suddenly it was gone. Lilli took one step forward and fainted.

She woke to find herself cramped and exhausted in a shaft of daylight from the unshuttered window. Her mouth felt as if she'd been licking stone; when she touched her painful lips she found them swollen. She managed to get to her knees, then clutched the bed for support and fought her way to her feet. All she could think of was water. By leaning against the bed she managed to get to the chest on the other side, where a pitcher stood by a basin. She sat down on the floor, poured some water into the basin, then hoisted it with both hands and drank.

By the time she'd drunk half the pitcher's worth, she felt well enough to stand. Only then, looking out her window at the familiar view, a stripe of blue framed by two brochs, did she remember her visitor of the night before.

'Dream,' she whispered. 'Naught but a dream.'

But the pain in her lips belied her. She should tell Nevyn, she knew, but a sudden loathing for the man overwhelmed her. Hadn't he been the true cause behind the death of her kin and clan? Oh don't be stupid, she told herself. Of course he isn't! With that her mind suddenly cleared, and she realized that her mother had slid the thought like a thorn into her heart, deep into her heart, because all the time she dressed, she had to fight the loathing. Crossing the room to the door exhausted her. When she lifted the bar, the wood seemed to weigh as much as solid iron.

Staggering like a drunken woman, Lilli walked down the corridor. Each step seemed harder and harder; often she paused to rest, leaning against the wall, because she knew that if she sat down, she'd fall asleep. Once she'd heard a tale from a man, one of the servants at Hendyr, who'd nearly frozen to death but been rescued at the last moment. He'd described this same terrifying exhaustion and the equally terrifying lust to simply sit down and die.

At last she reached the head of the stairs, and there her legs failed her. She took a single step down and felt her body fold under her like a piece of dropped cloth. She did manage to sit rather than fall all the way down, but she settled in the shadows, huddled against the wall. All she could do was pray that someone would be coming up or down soon to find her, and that she could still talk when they did.

Down below the great hall stood nearly empty. A few servants were wiping tables; a few riders still lingered over the last of their breakfast. Even from her distance she could recognize Branoic, simply by his sheer size. If only she could call out to him, or somehow will him to look up and see her. In her mind she repeated his name, over and over – a foolish effort, she thought, but all at once he stood up. He turned around fast to peer up the stairs.

'Lilli!' he called out.

No matter how hard she tried, her mouth refuse to frame words. Branoic, however, came bounding up the stairs two at a time.

'What's wrong?' he snapped. 'I heard you calling me. Are you ill?'

When she nodded, he stooped down.

'You're white as snow! Here, Nevyn better have a look at you.'

At the mention of Nevyn, her loathing welled up strong, but fortunately Branoic misinterpreted.

'Are you going to heave?' he said. 'You look it. There's no use in you trying to walk.'

He stood, then reached down and picked her up with barely an effort. She wrapped her arms around his neck and managed to whisper 'my thanks.' Moving cautiously he carried her downstairs.

'You've got to eat more, lass,' Branoic said. 'You don't weigh much more than a hundredweight of oats. That's not good.'

Held in his arms she felt warm again and suddenly realized that she'd been shivering cold. But why? What had happened to make her so ill? Something had – she could remember that she'd woken up ill, and that perhaps she'd had a bad dream, but all the details were slipping away. Was she even remembering correctly; had there been a dream? More likely she'd merely woken to find herself ill.

'Here we are, down on the nice safe ground,' Branoic said. 'Now let's find the old man and give him a look at you.'

Lilli lifted her head from his shoulder and looked around. Someone was coming toward them, but she couldn't recognize him until he spoke.

'What's all this?' It was Maddyn the bard. 'Is the lady ill?'

'Very much so,' Branoic said. 'I'm taking her to see Nevyn.'

'Nah nah nah, take her back to her chamber and then find Nevyn. If she's ill, she shouldn't be out in the air.'

Terror slid cold hands over Lilli's back.

'Not my chamber,' she whispered.

'Why not?' Maddyn said. 'Come now, lass! You're ill and not

thinking right.'

'Not my chamber. Branoic, please, don't.'

Puzzled and insistent, Maddyn's face loomed over her. She wanted to scream at him to go away, but her voice failed her.

'What the lady wants,' Branoic said, 'is what I'll do. She doesn't want to go back, so make yourself useful, Maddo. Go on ahead of us and round up Nevyn.'

Lilli laid her face against his shoulder in a luxury of relief. With Maddyn hurrying ahead of them, Branoic walked outside to the sun and air of the ward, where, she somehow knew, she'd be safe. When he bent his head and smiled at her, she smiled back and wondered how she could have misjudged him so harshly, how she had missed seeing that indeed, he was the kind of man she could love.

After his long night's sleep, Nevyn took his time dressing. He was thinking about going up to the dun and scrounging some breakfast when he heard voices directly outside his tent.

'My lord? Are you in there?'

'I am, Maddo. What is it?'

'The lady Lillorigga's fallen ill. It's as if she's had all the life sucked out of her or somewhat.'

Nevyn grabbed the tent flap and held it up. Maddyn was standing just outside, and Branoic came right behind, carrying Lilli.

'Bring her in, lad,' Nevyn said to Branoic. 'And my thanks. Set her down on my cot.'

Even with the dim light in the tent Nevyn could see the fiery blister on her lips. Under her eyes dark marks like bruises smeared her skin.

'Maddo, Branoic, leave us,' Nevyn snapped. 'Stand guard outside or suchlike.'

Lilli watched them go, then crumpled against the pillow as if her head had become too heavy. Nevyn pulled the blankets off and bundled them up.

'Let me get these under your head, too. There, that's a good lass. Now, what's happened?'

'I don't know.' Lilli was frowning down at her hands. 'I've been trying to remember. It was some kind of dream, and I woke, and I was ill.'

Nevyn sat down on the floor cloth. When he opened his dweomer-sight, he could see that her aura, shrunken and pale, clung close to her body. Instead of a smooth ovoid, it formed a ragged cloud, as if something had torn great chunks of it away. Had the dead lad's aura looked like this? He'd died too soon for Nevyn to get a look at it. Certainly his lips bore the same mark. He brought his sight back to normal.

'A dream, was it?' Nevyn said. 'Try to think, lass. Let's start with when you woke up and try to work backwards.'

'Woke up! That's right, I woke in the night.'

'Good, good. So you woke and it was still dark in your chamber. What woke you, a noise?'

'It was. One of the hides over the windows, that's right. It slid down and rustled. And there was light in the room . . .' Lilli let her voice trail away for a long moment. 'I woke up on the floor in the morning.'

'Aha! So. Somewhat happened betwixt those two wakings. Try to cast your mind back.'

Her mouth slack, Lilli stared off into memory.

'I can't,' she said at last. 'I just can't. I do remember that I wanted to go find you, but then I felt this horrible feeling, a kind of loathing, at the very thought.'

'That's important, I'll wager.' But why? Nevyn couldn't quite tease the significance out, not yet at least. 'But in the morning, you woke on the floor.'

'And I got up and dressed, but it was ever so hard. I felt so exhausted, as if I'd been running for miles and miles.'

'No doubt. Here, let me try a little trick. Perhaps if you feel more lively, your memory will come back.'

Nevyn knelt beside the cot and laid one hand just below her ribs and above her stomach. When he called back the dweomer sight, he could see the knot in her aura just above his hand, the Sun Knot where so many energies from different parts of the body weave together and exchange their forces. In Lilli's case it glowed as dim as a cinder flung to lie too far on the hearth from the fire. Nevyn called upon the Light and felt it gather above his head like a crown. Wildfolk came rushing into manifestation all around him to watch with solemn eyes. Nevyn visualized the light, then willed it down, flowing down his spine and out of his fingertips. It poured into Lilli's aura like a spill from a full bucket into an empty one.

With a thanks to the Great Light itself, Nevyn took his hand away and sat back on his heels to watch. The golden energy wrapped

around her deosil, and all at once she laughed, stretching like a
sleeper just awakened.

'A trick you call that, my lord?' Lilli sat up and grinned at him. 'A
wondrous one!'

'You feel better then, do you?'

'I do, a thousand times over.'

'Good. I thought it would work splendidly for you, with your
dweomer gifts.'

'Well, it certainly did.' Lilli looked away, thinking hard. 'But I still
don't remember.' She caught her lower lip between her teeth, just as
so many people do when thinking, and yelped. 'Oh, that hurts!'

'No doubt. You've got quite an odd mark there, somewhat of a
blister, somewhat of a swelling like a bee sting.'

Gingerly Lilli touched the mark with one finger.

'I remember the pain,' she said. 'It was cold and hot all at the same
time. But I don't know what caused it.'

'Well, I'm putting together a few things. Somewhat got into your
chamber in the middle of the night. It touched you there, on the
mouth, and drew off enormous amounts of your life-stuff. You're
lucky you're young and healthy, lass. It would have killed an old
woman.'

'I believe you, my lord. I felt so ghastly in the morning.'

Nevyn felt the insight like a shock of lightning, running down his
spine with a crackle.

'Ghastly, indeed,' he said. 'Ye gods! Could it be? I always thought
it naught but a silly fancy!'

'What, my lord?'

'Let me think on this before I say anything more. Here, we'd best
get up to the dun. You need sustenance, and I feel hungry enough to
eat a wolf, pelt and all.'

Later that day Nevyn received proof of his peculiar theory. After
spending some long hours with the King's Council, he was walking in
the main ward when he saw a gaggle of maidservants gossiping by the
well. Something about the urgency of their talk caught his attention.
He strolled over, but before he could eavesdrop Clodda saw him and
called out.

'My Lord Nevyn, oh please, could you spare us a bit of time?'

'By all means,' Nevyn said. 'Is somewhat wrong?'

The women all turned to one of their number, much better dressed
than they, and began murmuring things like 'go on, tell him!' Finally

she got up her nerve and curtsied.

'My name's Pavva, my lord. And I – well, you'll think I'm daft but I saw Lady Merodda's spirit, walking in the dun.'

Nevyn caught his breath in a low whistle. Pavva misunderstood and blushed.

'Don't feel shamed,' Nevyn said. 'I believe you, actually. Where was this and when?'

'Just now, my lord. I went up to bring Lady Lillorigga fresh water. It's ever so dim in the halls up there and cool, but when I shut her door behind me, it was just like winter, it was, ever so cold. And all the hair on my arms stood up, like. And I saw Lady Merodda, standing in the middle of the corridor. She looked so horrible, with her throat all bruised like that, I couldn't even scream. She was trying to say somewhat to me, but I couldn't hear her. And so I told her I was so sorry she was dead, and she smiled and disappeared.'

Nevyn felt an eerie chill himself.

'How long ago was this?' he snapped.

'Not very. I came straight down and found Clodda and the lasses, and so I was just telling them.'

'Where's your lady, Clodda?'

'Up in her chambers, my lord. That's why Pavva was bringing her the water.'

Nevyn swore like a rider and took off running, leaving the lasses staring after him.

Since Nevyn's cure proved temporary, a mere trick as indeed he'd warned her, Lilli had felt exhausted again by the middle of the afternoon. She'd asked Pavva to bring her a pitcher of water, then gone to her chamber to sleep. She barely noticed when the girl came in, and by the time Pavva shut the door behind her, Lilli had dozed off – only to wake with a start some moments later.

'I didn't bar the door.' Yawning she got out of bed.

Between her and the window her mother appeared, materializing like a fall of dust in a beam of sunlight. All at once Lilli remembered everything: the dream, her mother's ghost, her mother's revenge. Her heart starting to pound.

'You've come to kill me, haven't you?' Lilli began to back away and circled toward the door as she moved. 'You want to take me with you to the Otherlands.'

The glimmering bluish-white image smiled and began to move its lips as if it spoke, but once again Lilli could hear nothing. When the apparition moved forward, Lilli stepped back, but Merodda followed, gliding a foot or so about the ground. Her lips framed the words 'my daughter, my daughter' over and over. Slowly she reached out one hand and one long pale finger, ready to pierce Lilli's aura and drain her very soul.

With a scream Lilli bolted and ran, banging out of the chamber door and into the corridor. Down at the far end a man was running straight toward her like Burcan in her dream. She screamed again, then clasped both hands over her mouth to shield her lips.

'It's just me!' Nevyn stopped running and strode up to her. 'I saw Pavva out in the ward and got here in time, and thank the gods for that!'

Lilli was shaking too hard to object when Nevyn took her arm and guided her back into the chamber. The apparition had fled. Nevyn shut the door behind them.

'Now,' he said, 'tell me what you saw.'

'My mother's spirit. She was standing at the end of the bed and looking at me. And I remember now, my lord. It was her, the other night. She came to me and touched me on the lips.'

'Well, that's what I feared, all right. It seems your mother's dweomer has true power.'

Lilli sank shaking onto her wooden chest. Nevyn glanced around the chamber, saw the pitcher and cup, and poured her water. She clasped the cool pottery cup in both hands and sipped like a child.

'Will she ever let me be?' Lilli whispered.

'Not here, not in Dun Deverry. I doubt me if she can appear anywhere else. Her dweomer's real, but she was no master of the dark craft. It takes a lifetime of practice and study to travel as a haunt. Sooner or later, she'll have to face her reckoning, but I'll wager she clings to life – if you can call it life – for as long as she can.' Nevyn considered, frowning, for a long moment. 'We'll have to find somewhere safe for you to go. As long as you're here, she'll try to prey upon you, sucking your life to feed her spirit.'

Lilli laid cold fingers on her throat.

'I'm sorry,' Nevyn said gently. 'I know these things are hard to comprehend.'

'It's not that. I felt – I was sure she was trying to kill me. Not just do what you said, but kill me.'

'Then we've got to get you out of here straightaway.' Nevyn

hesitated, thinking. 'Although it's just possible she could somehow follow you like a barnacle riding a ship, and I can't go with you. The Prince needs me here. Blast her! I'm honestly not sure what she can or cannot do. I've never heard of a haunt appearing in the middle of the day before.'

The weariness that had overwhelmed her earlier returned. Lilli felt as if she were sinking into the wood chest like water. There's no hope, she thought. She'll win the end.

'Lilli.' Nevyn's voice was a soft whisper. 'What are you thinking? Tell me what you're thinking.'

'The dark wins in the end. The dark always sucks up the light.'

Nevyn smacked his hands together hard. Lilli came to herself with a little shake of her head.

'What?' she said. 'What was that? What was I saying?'

'Naught that you need to remember. I won't lie to you. The situation's very grave.'

'If there was only somewhat I could do.'

'Oh, there is. If you're willing, you can help me win this battle. I have to tell you honestly, though, that it could be very dangerous.'

'It's dangerous already, isn't it? But what could I possibly – oh, wait, I do see. I can be bait.'

'Just so. It's a real risk, but I don't know what else to do. She could wander around here for a long time. It's a huge dun. I'd have a cursed hard time chasing her down.'

Lilli hesitated, feeling her heart pound, but she was remembering Bevyan, lying in a grave behind Lord Camlyn's dun.

'I don't care about the risk. I'll do it.'

'You're sure?'

'I am. For all I know she'll try to kill someone else once she's done with me.'

'She's already done that. Practising, I suppose. Well and good then. As much as I hate to risk you, I – wait. I can lay a double trap, now that I think of it.'

Lilli merely nodded. Her heart was pounding so loud, it seemed, that she could barely hear him. Her breath came ragged in her chest.

'I think,' Nevyn went on, 'that we'll move you to a room in another broch and put Branoic on guard at your door. I'll be hiding somewhere nearby, and we'll see if she falls into our trap.'

When Nevyn said he'd be hiding nearby, he meant of course nearby on the etheric plane. His actual body would lie some distance away. For the rest of the afternoon, he stayed with Lilli and kept her among other people where she'd be safe. Once night had fallen, and the astral tides were calm again after their change, he gave Branoic his orders.

'I'll going up to Lilli's old chamber. Give me time to get there, and then take her to the new one. You stand guard outside, but remember, lad: if you hear her scream, get into the room fast.'

'You can trust me for that, my lord,' Branoic said. 'Never fear.'

In Lilli's chamber Nevyn lay down on her bed in the darkness. He crossed his arms over his chest, each hand on the opposite shoulder, then let his breathing slow into long, measured breaths while in his mind he built up the image of his body of light, a pale blue and nearly featureless simulacrum. With an effort of trained will, he transferred his consciousness into it. Even though it hovered above him, for a moment he felt as if he were falling; then he heard a rushy click, and he slipped over to find himself floating above his body. Blue light suffused through the chamber and gleamed on black stone walls gone dead, a prison around him. Turning a little he floated up to a join of wall and ceiling. Behind him the silver cord, pulsing with life, paid out, linking him to his untenanted body below.

Curious Wildfolk appeared to hover around him. Here on their proper plane they gleamed like crystals, all angles and geometry as they trembled and flew.

'Stay away, little brothers,' Nevyn sent his thoughts to them. 'I'm laying a trap.'

They winked out and disappeared. Nevyn waited, but time is hard to measure on the etheric, and he began to fear that Merodda had gone directly after Lilli. Perhaps she could sense her daughter's presence from some distance. Yet if he left too soon and she found his unguarded body, the consequences would be grim. If she snapped the silver cord, his body would die, leaving him adrift out on the astral long before his Wyrd demanded.

Nevyn dropped down to float just above his body, but before he could transfer over he felt rather than saw another presence on the etheric nearby. Like a flushed grouse he flew up and got back into his corner just as the silvery blue form of a naked woman glided through the black wall below.

Rather than an artificially-crafted body of light, Merodda appeared in her etheric double, the matrix that had formed and interpenetrated her body during life. Faithfully it had recorded her death as well: her neck furrowed by the rope, her head flopped at an angle from its breaking. Already, however, the double was beginning to distort. Her legs seemed too long and thin; her torso, bloated and squat. Although she knew how to drain life-stuff from her victims, she seemed to lack of the knowledge of how to distribute it within her etheric form.

In this grotesque simulacrum she drifted toward the bed, then stopped, staring at the unexpected sleeper. Nevyn called upon the Light and dropped like a striking hawk. In answer to his call, light came – a vast glowing sheet of it, shifting and twisting in rainbow colours like those northern lights the Dwarven folk tell of. Nevyn caught the edge with the hands of his body of light.

Merodda looked up, saw him, and shrieked, or rather sent the thought of a wail out into the etheric where his mind heard it as a shriek. Like a fisherman throwing a net, Nevyn hurled the sheet of light at her and over her. She shrieked again, twisting back and forth as she clawed at it with both hands. He grabbed the edges and clutched them grimly, trapping her. She was beyond thinking in words; over and over she shrieked and tore and threw herself back and forth, but slowly her struggles exhausted her. She stopped moving, her shrieks turned to a thin wail of fear.

Above them both Nevyn visualized a pentagram, glowing with silver and blue, then drew round it a circle of gold. He rose, hauling Merodda with him, and flung them both through this gate into the astral plane. An indigo wind, dark as a bruise, caught them swirled them tumbled them around and around as they fell, rushing downward through a cloud of blown images – faces, beasts, star, symbols and letters in unknown scripts. The images beat against them, then flew on, borne by the indigo wind. In her net of light Merodda was screaming and twisting as she tore at the glowing strands.

'Courage!' Nevyn called out. 'You go to your redemption!'

Straight ahead in the indigo a long slash of violet appeared, then swirled and thickened into a shimmering oval of pale lavender light. Nevyn called out a Name, and they fell through, tumbling at last to rest in a field of white flowers, nodding on a breeze that barely trembled their pale white leaves. Some distance away a river gleamed silver, or was it a mist? It shifted, tenuous as moonlight. When Nevyn tugged on the last tatters of his astral net, they fell away to reveal a tiny child, formed of pale golden light.

'Call upon the Light!' Nevyn said. 'Call upon the Light and forswear the Darkness!'

The child wept, throwing tiny hands up in front of her face as if she feared a slap. Even though the astral wind blew so gently here, it caught her up and began to carry her toward the river. She drifted this way and that, bobbing on the breathless wind, but ever closer she came to the silver river.

'Go with the Light!' Nevyn called out. 'Go in peace!'

Whether she answered, he never knew. The struggle to travel on this plane in the body of light was growing too much for him. He saw his gathering weakness as a shattering of the vision: pieces of land-scape fell away, the flowers withered and vanished. Only the violet light still gleamed, and in it a rift of indigo. With a last effort he launched himself through and fell back into the wind.

Spiralling around and around, up and up it seemed, past the manic frenzy of torn images and broken snatches of strange music, he saw at last his pentacle gate of silver and blue. Soaring and struggling both at once, he reached it and slipped through, bobbing up into bluish light that glimmered on dead black walls of the chamber. Below him he saw his body, lying twisted on its side but still joined safely to his consciousness by the silver cord. Nevyn floated to a position directly over it and hovered for a moment, gathering strength for his return.

Yet someone or something shared the chamber with him. All at once he felt a presence, a trembling of life within the stone space. The presence gathered strength, glittered like crystal in a corner, swelled and grew, turned into a vaguely female form, huge and menacing. When she raised cloaked arms like huge wings he saw her long hair, streaming down black as the stone over her shoulders and down her back. Her face, shadowed by a hood, he could not see at all.

'Where is she?' The thought came to him in a silky whisper.

'She's gone to the Light, where she belongs.'

The presence considered him briefly, then vanished. Nevyn shuddered in what he could later admit was fear. He slid down the silver cord until he hovered just above his body, then let himself fall back. Another clicking sound, a long wheeze of breath, and he was back.

'It is over!' Nevyn slapped one hand hard on the mattress beside him. 'May she find the Light!'

Not so much as a crack of the Light's earthly counterpart gleamed around the hide over the window. It was late, then. He sat up, stretching his cramped muscles, wondering over the presence. A god form, perhaps? It inspired the same kind of cold awe as one of those created embodiments of raw power. And yet it seemed too personal, too individually concerned with Merodda to be a goddess. With a shrug he got up, but as he was hurrying across the ward to Lilli's refuge, he was thinking about the presence in black. The only lore he could connect with her was what Aderyn had told him about the Guardians, those strange beings attached to the elven group-soul. But what would one of them be doing in Dun Deverry? He cast that explanation aside, which in the long wheel of events proved to be most unfortunate.

By the light of a candle-lantern Branoic was standing guard, leaning against Lilli's door. At the sight of Nevyn he straightened up, all tense expectation.

'Does Lilli fare well?' Nevyn said.

'As far as I know, my lord.' Branoic spun around and pulled open the door.

Lilli nearly fell into the corridor. She managed a laugh.

'I was leaning against it,' she said. 'I wanted to stay right by it, you see, so Branoic would hear me if I screamed.'

'Very wise,' Nevyn said. 'But it's over. She's well and truly dead this time.'

Lilli let out her breath in a long raspy sigh.

'Thank the Goddess,' she whispered. 'And a thousand thanks to you, Nevyn.'

'Oddly enough, I did it for her sake as well as yours. But be that as it may, she'll never trouble you or any other soul again.'

Yet he knew that even as he spoke the truth, he was lying, that while Merodda would never trouble anyone in this life, she would have other lives in which to work her enemies harm. No doubt she would remember them all, even in her new bodies and new lives. Now that she'd learned to welcome evil, evil would seek her out. He hoped and prayed that she would renounce it when it presented itself to her, but he had no way of knowing if she would or not. One thing only he could be sure of: sooner or later in the long skein of lives, her thread would tangle round Lilli's once again.

PART III

The North Country
Winter, 1117

Sleep and Trance are Lord Death's twin sisters. A
master of the dweomer befriends all three.

The Secret Book of Cadwallon the Druid

Much to Niffa's surprise, Verrarc and Raena came to her wedding. By whining and begging and generally clamping on to the subject like a stubborn ferret, she'd talked her mother into allowing the wedding early, on the first day of the new year, which Deverry folk call 'Samaen'. During their long years of slavery, the people of the Rhiddaer had adopted the holiday and brought it with them to their new home. Although they considered the eve as ill-omened, as we do in Deverry, they judged the first day of the new year itself a splendid time for starting something new.

When the sun hung nearly to the horizon, Niffa and her family trudged up the hill to the assembly ground near the peak of Citadel. In front of the stone council hall, which sported a colonnade and a flight of shallow steps, stretched a plaza paved with bricks. The servants of the Spirit Talker were sweeping it free of snow with brooms made of twigs, while Werda herself stood beside the heaped wood of an unlit bonfire. A tall woman, thin as the twigs, she wore her long grey hair down free, a sweep of silver over her blue cloak. In the fading light her hair seemed to gleam like the moon, the home of the spirits she had mastered.

Demet's family, a veritable crowd of brothers and sisters, their wives, husbands, and children, came hurrying across the plaza, all talking and laughing except for Demet, who was smiling in tight triumph. When she saw him, Niffa felt her own blood pounding at her throat. He looked so handsome that night, blond and tall, and they had shared so many kisses and caresses. Tonight, finally –

'Niffa!' Dera's voice snapped. 'Stop smirking like that! It be unseemly.'

'I will, Mam.' Niffa wiped her smile away and tried to look composed and aloof. 'I do apologize.'

Demet and his family stood on one side of the bonfire while Niffa and hers took the other. Werda's manservant knelt and began fussing with flint and tinder box; in this cold he struggled to raise a spark, but a wedding fire had to be kindled fresh, not lit from a hearth. Niffa looked round at the crowd of guests and saw off to one side Verrarc and Raena, splendid in a blue wool cloak with a huge clasp of gold and moonstones at one shoulder.

'What be her business here?' Niffa whispered to her mother.

'Well, it were needful I invite Verro for the formality of the thing. Never did I think he'd come, but if he did, well then, his woman be welcome too.'

'No one did ask me if she be welcome.'

'Hush! And will you start your married life a miser, grudging hospitality?'

Niffa scowled down at the snow. She refused to apologize. Never would I have asked a viper to my wedding, either, she thought. Yet why was she so sure that Raena would somehow bite and poison them all? The patch of snow she so assiduously studied suddenly turned gold, and she heard the crackling of flames on kindling. She looked up to find fire blazing in the centre of the heaped-up wood and spreading gold flames along the tendrils of dry twigs. It seemed to her that she saw the doom of Cerr Cawnen in that fire, that Raena would be the spark that burnt them all.

'What troubles you?' Dera caught her arm. 'You look like death.'

'Naught, naught.' Niffa swallowed hard. 'I uh, I well, I'll be missing you, Mam, and living at home with you and the weasels.'

'Ah.' Dera patted her arm. 'It be a hard thing, to leave your mother's hearth, but truly, you'll dwell nearby, just across the lake. At least you'll not be going to some strange village. And we can spare you a ferret for a pet, like, when a litter comes.'

'If my new mother do allow.'

Demet's mother, Emla, was standing next to her son. She smiled and waved at Dera and Niffa impartially. A tall grey-haired woman with a long sharp jaw, she was beaming with excitement. At least Demet's family had whole-heartedly approved of his choice for a wife rather than spurning the ratter's girl. Since Demet's father had married a cousin, their family carried a strong stamp: like Demet they were all tall, blond, and rangy – even young Cotzi at ten summers – with angular faces that were handsome on the men if a bit unfortunate on the women. Small and dark as she was, Niffa felt like a ferret about to frolic with greyhounds. She could only hope they wouldn't bite.

The ceremony itself went fast. With a sweep of one arm Werda called Niffa and Demet up to stand next to her near the fire. The crowd stood facing the three of them.

'Before us stand a young man and a young woman who would

marry,' Werda began. 'When we fled our homeland, when our homes were stolen from us by the Slavers, our gods did travel with us to the free lands. Thanks to them we did survive, and in return, they demand of us that we grow mighty in numbers, that we may worship them always and tend their earthly homes. Demet, a man must father many sons to gain the favour of the gods. Niffa, a woman must birth many daughters to gain the favour of the goddesses.' Werda paused to look at each of them. 'Be you ready to lift up the burden of your people?'

'I am,' they answered together.

'Then the gods will bless you.' Werda paused again, this time looking over the crowd. 'Kinsfolk and friends, you have seen these young people speak out in front of you. From now on, Demet is Niffa's man, and she is his woman. It be needful for all of you to honour their marriage.' She was looking directly at Raena and Verrarc. 'It be a holy thing, marriage. Let none meddle with it, for such do shame their tribe and kin.'

Niffa could see Raena wince and look down at the ground. Verrarc's smile froze, but he kept it as he stared right back at the Spirit Talker. Silence hung over the crowd as a few at a time everyone turned to watch. At last Verrarc broke and looked away. With a little smile Werda continued.

'May the gods bless you always with health and children. May you always have enough food to feed your family, Demet, and may you, Niffa, divide it up evenly among them.'

Demet caught Niffa around the waist, pulled her close, and kissed her. The crowd broke out cheering and clapping. When she took another kiss from him, everyone laughed. She let him go and turned to wave just in time to see Verrarc and Raena slipping away into the darkness. Good! she thought. I'll not have that woman poisoning our rejoicing time!

The rest of the guests all trooped downhill to Dera and Lael's house, where Verrarc's gift of a barrel of ale stood open and ready. All the guests had brought their own tankards and some food, too, to make a resplendent feast of bread, sausages, cheese and other winter foods. Niffa and Demet stood by the door and greeted each guest in turn. While Dera heaped wood on the hearth for light, Lael placed himself by the ale barrel and started dipping it out into the wall of tankards thrust his way. The women began handing out food; everyone was laughing and talking.

'I've never been this happy before,' Niffa said. 'Not in my whole life.'

'No more I.' Demet slipped his arm around her waist and squeezed. 'I be truly glad we didn't have to wait till the dark time of the year.'

'Oh, I knew I could bring Mam round.'

He laughed and kissed her. She started to put her arms around his neck, but she saw someone coming down the side path: Verrarc, but alone.

'And a good eve to you, Mistress Niffa,' Verrarc said. 'I did think I'd stop by and have a word with your mother, if that sit well with you.'

All at once Niffa felt like that miser indeed, begrudging him and his woman when she felt so rich with happiness.

'Of course, Councilman! And where be Raena?'

'Ah well, she did feel a bit poorly and did decide to stop at home.'

'But you come in, then, man,' Demet said. 'And I thank you, too, for that barrel of ale.'

Verrarc smiled at him in an oddly grateful manner, as if Demet were the one who was rich and powerful, and slipped into the party. Niffa watched him as he stayed close to the wall and worked his way round to Dera, standing on the far side of the room.

'It mayhap were a bit sour-minded of Werda,' Demet muttered, 'to shame him and his woman that way.'

'She deserved it,' Niffa snapped. 'Sleeping twixt two pairs of blankets like that.'

'Well, it gladdens my heart to hear that you don't approve of such carrying on.'

They laughed and kissed each other.

The laughter and the talk went on until the ale barrel stood empty and the table clean of food. While Dera wiped the table down with a rag, Lael went into the other room and brought out a new wool blanket. He laid it over the table, and one thing at a time Niffa placed her dowry upon it: two dresses, a nightshirt, a long-handled cooking knife, an iron griddle of Dwarven workmanship, and four copper pieces in a leather pouch. Her cloak she kept out to wear. When Lael tied the corners of the blanket together to form a proper bundle, Niffa could see his eyes glistening with tears. Dera wept openly, snuffling into a large rag. Emla flung a long arm around her shoulders.

'I do keep thinking of our Jahdo,' Dera said. 'I do wish with all my heart that he'd be here seeing his sister marry.'

Councilman Verrarc looked abruptly at the floor and started studying the planks.

'He'll come home, sister,' Emla said. 'Come the spring we'll bring the god of the roads a sacrifice to see him safely home.'

Lael handed the bundle to Cronin, Demet's father, who took it in both long, calloused hands.

'Come along, daughter,' Cronin said. 'It be time to go home.'

Cronin and Emla led the way as Niffa, Demet, and the wedding guests left the house and her old family behind. When Niffa glanced back, she saw that Verrarc stayed, talking with Dera in the pool of firelight; then her father shut the door. Laughing and singing, the wedding procession wound its way down Citadel to the jetty at the lake shore, where much to everyone's surprise, they found the Council barge waiting, all decked out with lanterns so that it glowed in the misty night.

'Councillor Verrarc's orders,' the barge captain said. 'Congratulations, young Niffa! Now you all get in and we'll row you across.'

More laughter and a lot of cheers – Verrarc's generosity had just spared the wedding party a long drunken row across. As the barge pushed off, the men in the party began to sing, trading off verses of songs bawdy enough to make Niffa blush.

Demet's family lived in a rambling compound built partly on stilts, partly on solid ground, over by the south city gate. In the big common room a fire lay ready in the hearth. As custom demanded, Demet knelt down to light it fresh while the guests threw off cloaks and headed for the second feast of the night, spread out on a pair of tables at the far side of the room.

'Come along, daughter,' Emla said, 'and I'll bestow upon you a chamber of your own.'

Since they were the youngest married couple in the compound, they received a plank room out over the lake. Although it stood the farthest from the central hearth, the warmth from the water filtered up through cracks in the floor. Niffa could hear the lake splashing against the pilings underneath, and the room sighed like a ship in the wind. The room held a wooden chest, where Niffa unpacked her dowry goods, and a big square bed. Emla hung the candle-lantern from a long brass hook on the wall.

'There be no one to either side of you here,' she said with a wink. 'You'd best be making yourself comfortable. Demet will be finishing that fire about now.'

With another wink Emla took herself off to her guests. Niffa laid her new blanket over the old ones, then hung her cloak on another hook near the door. Since the room turned out warmer than she'd been expecting, she took off her dresses as well and tossed them into the chest. With a little shiver caused by the cold sheets she slid into bed and found a nice warm hollow in the old mattress.

Distantly she heard the singing in the common room and more immediately the water sounds. They threatened to turn into omen-voices, whispering of secrets and danger, but Demet opened the door and slipped into the room.

'You do look so beautiful in my bed like that,' he said, smiling. 'I'll treasure this night forever.'

'And so will I. Come get warm.'

He hung his cloak over hers, then stripped off his tunic and threw it into the wood chest. When he sat down on the bed to unlace his boots, she ran a hand down his bare back and felt him tremble. At last he pulled the boots off and dropped them onto the floor, then stood to strip off his leggings. She held up the blankets and let him roll into bed.

'Cold!' he whispered. 'Ah well, we'll be warm soon enough.'

He engulfed her in his embrace so fiercely that for a moment she was frightened, but his familiar kisses soothed her. In the past month or so, knowing that their marriage was arranged past breaking, they'd touched each other often, at first shyly, then more boldly when they'd discovered the pleasure it brought them. Now, when she felt his hand sliding up her thigh, she let her legs ease apart and whimpered at his touch.

'Now,' she whispered. 'Please?'

'I be afraid to hurt you.'

'If it does hurt, it'll be but that once. Do let's put that behind us.'

Yet he kissed and caressed her a while longer, so that when he finally did take her, she felt no pain at all, just a sharp thrust into her desire, and then pleasure.

It was four nights past Samaen, the turning of the new year, when the first snow fell over Cengarn, far south of the Rhiddaer. Dallandra woke one morning to the smell of snow in the air and a fanged chill in her tower room. Near her bed stood the bronze brazier, stacked ready with twigs and lumps of charcoal. She stuck a cautious arm out from under the covers and pointed, summoning Wildfolk to light the fuel, then drew her arm back in fast.

'It must be snowing,' she remarked to Rhodry.

He mumbled something foul and pulled the blankets over his head. She snuggled down next to him and watched the Wildfolk, mostly grey gnomes, who lounged at the foot of the bed like cats. The next time she woke, the air in the chamber seemed just bearable. Since she kept her clothes over the chair back and next to the brazier, they were warmer than the air, at least. She struggled into her leggings under the blankets then grabbed her tunic and, like a trout breaking water to catch a fly, sat up fast and just long enough to pull it on.

'You're determined to get up, aren't you?' Rhodry said.

'I am. I'm hungry, and the chamber-pot is almost full.'

'Ah. If you're going down to the great hall, bring me some bread back, will you?'

'Lazy sot.'

With a long martyred sigh, Dallandra sat up and grabbed her boots from the floor. Not until she had them on did she get out of bed. When she opened a shutter a crack, she could see grey light and, indeed, snow falling in long ropes let down from the heavens. At least the worst of the stinks would freeze, but she swore an oath to herself that this would be the very last winter she would spend among humans in their stone tents.

'It *is* snowing,' she said.

Rhodry had fallen asleep again.

Down in Dun Cengarn's great hall, the gwerbret's warband clustered around the lesser hearth to get warm after their night in the barracks. At the table of honour Gwerbret Cadmar was sharing a loaf of bread with his guest, Prince Daralanteriel, Carra's husband. The gwerbret had once been an imposing man, well over six feet tall, broad in the shoulders, broad in the hands, but the summer's fighting had left him exhausted and somehow shrunken. As a herb-woman and the only real physician in the dun, Dallandra frankly worried about him. His slate-grey hair was thinning, and his moustaches were turning white; he sat slumped in his chair with his twisted right leg stuck out in front of him to soak up the fire's warmth. The Prince, however, was a young man and as handsome and vital as most of his kind, with raven-dark hair but pale grey eyes, slit vertically like a cat's to reveal lavender pupils. Although his hair had grown shaggy, there was no hiding his ears, long and tightly furled like sea-shells, as elven as Dallandra's own.

At the honour hearth, where a great stone dragon embraced the fire, a clot of boys sat as near as they could get without singeing, Jahdo among them. Two of the older boys played a game of Carnoic while the others watched or fended off the dogs, who kept threatening to sweep the stones off the board with their tails. Since Jahdo was attending upon Rhodry as his page, Dallandra decided that he could take up the bread Rhodry wanted and empty the pot as well. She was just walking over when she heard first one woman scream, then another join in. She spun around in time to see Evandar walking through the dun wall some ten feet from her. The dogs leapt up and started barking.

'My pardons,' Evandar said. 'I just wanted to see little Elessi.'

'She's upstairs in the women's hall,' Dallandra said. 'And I wish you'd remember to use the door.'

With a laugh Evandar disappeared, leaving a whole gaggle of maidservants screaming and pointing while the men pretended they'd seen nothing and the boys stared goggle-eyed. Dalla kicked the nearest boar hound and bellowed at the dogs to shut up. They obeyed, lying back down with a few quiet growls.

It was later in the morning that Ylla, the lady Ocradda's maidservant, asked Dallandra to come up to the women's hall. Dalla found the gwerbret's wife sitting by the hearth in a carved chair with sewing in her lap. Dallandra sat on a footstool near her ladyship.

'Thank you for coming up,' Ocradda said. 'I trust I've not interrupted some um, er, well, important work?'

'None, my lady. What troubles your heart?'

'Well, it's the servants. They do worry so dreadfully about sorcery, and with winter here, there's not truly enough work to keep them busy.' She forced out a brittle little laugh. 'Silly of them, of course.'

'I wouldn't call it silly. They've seen enough evil dweomer to trouble anyone's heart.'

Ocradda let her forced smile disappear.

'This Evandar,' Ocradda said. 'He's little Elessi's grandfather, or so Princess Carra tells me?'

'That's true, my lady.'

'Well, then, he's welcome in our dun whenever he wants to see the child, but couldn't he ride up like an ordinary man? The way he just appears – it frightens everyone.'

'So I've noticed. I'll have a word with him the next time he comes.'

'My thanks.' Ocradda leaned back in her chair. 'We've all seen too many strange things. But ah ye gods, dweomer saved us all! I hope you don't think me ungrateful.'

'I don't. Now you know why the dweomer prefers to work in secret. Life's much easier for people if they can pretend magic simply doesn't exist.'

'So it is. I'm just so glad all that's over now.'

As she was leaving, Dallandra remembered a trifle she'd been meaning to attend to.

'My lady? Might I trouble the chamberlain for some soap?'

'Soap?' Lady Ocradda raised an eyebrow. 'At this time of year?'

'Just a little bit would do,' Dalla said. 'For the occasional wash.'

'Well, perhaps the chamberlain might be able to find you a scrap, though I doubt me it would be more than that. It's because of the siege, you see. We always make soap in the autumn, with the fats and tallow from the slaughtering, but this year every scrap of fat got itself eaten, not that there was much with the poor beasts half-starved.'

'Of course.' Dalla felt ashamed of herself. 'My apologies. I'll make do with water, then.'

'If you don't mind?' Ocradda looked faintly desperate, as if wondering whether Dallandra would set fire to the dun over its lack of soap.

'Not in the least, not at all.'

What Ocradda didn't know, and a good thing, too, was that Dallandra worked dweomer in the dun every night. For some while now she'd been placing wards around the bed she and Rhodry shared to keep Raena out of his dreams. Although she'd carved elvish runes on strips of wood for a physical focus, the true wards burned on the etheric and astral planes as images of flaming stars.

'They're working nicely, too,' Rhodry said that evening. 'I've had naught but pleasant dreams since you started doing this.'

'Good. I think it's time to spring my trap, then. By now Raena should be good and angry. I wanted to make her frustrated, you see, so she won't think clearly.'

'I think I do see. Then one night you won't put up the wards?'

'Just that, and I think I'll try it tonight. You just go to sleep as usual –'

'– knowing a crazed sorceress is out for my blood. Just a trifle. I'll not let it trouble my heart.'

'Well, you went riding with the Prince today, didn't you? You should be nice and tired.'

Involuntarily, Rhodry yawned.

'So I am,' he said. 'This cold weather takes it out of a man.'

That night when she slept, Dallandra went to the Gatelands, an 'area', if you wish to use that metaphor, at the 'edge' of the astral plane. During sleep the average person's soul drifts close enough to the astral to receive true dreams as well as the mundane images from their own minds. A dweomer master, or a strange case like Raena, can therefore track down a dreaming person and make some sort of contact with them. Conversely, another master can meet and confront the dream-meddler as well.

Long years of practice had made Dallandra adept at true dreaming; as she was drifting off to sleep she had merely to tell her mind what she wished to dream in order to dream of it. It seemed she walked through a meadow of wild grasses, strangely pale and silky against her bare legs. Overhead hung a purple moon so huge that it filled half the sky. When she glanced back over her shoulder, she saw the remains of her wards – two dull five-pointed stars on the verge of flickering out. Between them lay the dream-gate leading down to Rhodry, a mark in the grass so clear and hard that Raena must have used it often. Dallandra dreamed herself a coil of rope, then invoked pure force from the etheric and channelled it into the rope, giving it life beyond a mere image. In front of the two stars she laid a snare, hidden in the grass. She angled off a short way and sat down, hiding herself as well, with the rope's end in her lap. By parting the stalks she could see the fading wards.

Then came the waiting, and since this was the world of dream, it could have been a few moments long or several hours while the moon hung motionless in the sky. At length Dallandra heard someone rustling through the grass. When she looked, she saw Raena striding along in her dream-body. Her oily black hair hung down her back, but otherwise she was naked. At the wards she paused, smiling.

'Well-met!' Dallandra sprang from cover as fast as a lark. 'Thinking of mischief, were you?'

With a scream Raena turned to run, but Dallandra grabbed the rope and pulled. The loop tightened around Raena's legs and toppled her, flailing and shrieking. Hauling on the rope to keep it taut, Dallandra trotted over to find her prize sitting up and struggling to free the loop from her ankles. With a practised flick of her wrists,

Dallandra sent another loop spiralling around her shoulders and yanked. The rope bit before Raena could free herself.

'My people are horse-herders,' Dalla said. 'Struggle, and I'll cover you with rope burns. They'll hurt, too, even when you wake. I know a thing or two about witch bodies, you see.'

Raena glared up at her, her mouth a little open as she panted for breath.

'Leave Rhodry alone,' Dallandra went on. 'You don't truly understand what you're doing, and you could hurt yourself if you keep this up.'

Raena slumped, letting her head fall forward.

'I don't care if you want to listen or not,' Dallandra snapped. 'You don't have any proper training in dweomer. If you trust your would-be god, he'll lead you into trouble and then leave you there.'

Raena was sitting oddly still. Dallandra suddenly realized what she must be doing and leapt forward to grab her – too late. With a shimmer of blue light and a burst of silver, she disappeared in a flurry of falling rope. For a brief moment a raven hopped in the grass; then with a shriek it hurled itself into the air and flew, flapping hard, back the way Raena had come. Dallandra considered transforming into her own bird-form, but the raven had a long start. Most likely Raena could wake herself up and escape the Gatelands entirely even if Dallandra did manage to catch up to her.

Before she left, Dallandra reset the wards, pouring energy into them until they burned with red and gold. For a moment she watched them, then walked to the dream-gate and let herself drop, gliding down into her body and a normal sleep.

It was no wonder that Evandar's appearances startled the dun so badly, because he travelled by those secret routes, the mothers of all roads, that lead between the worlds. Since his country existed in no true world at all, the roads met within it. At that time, Evandar knew them better than any other being in the vast universe, but on this trip he found a surprise waiting for him. The entrance to his country lay on a small hill, and when he stepped onto it he saw a world gone strange.

Winter had settled in, the first winter this etheric land had ever known. When he'd been creating it, so many eons ago that he could no longer remember exactly how long, Evandar had chosen to keep the season always spring, and a warm and sunny one at that. In those ancient days his country had lain far beyond the physical world of elves and men, but with time and over time it seemed to have drifted closer – he could think of no other way to frame the change to himself.

Snow lay white on the long meadows. Below him at the foot of the hill, it heaped in drifts against the broken walls and dead hedges of the formal garden he'd once created for Dallandra. Trees stood leafless; dead flowers hung on blackened rose bushes. In the ruin one of his warriors was wandering around, poking at the snow with a long stick.

'Menw!' Evandar called out.

At the sound the warrior tossed the stick away and started up the hill. A tall fellow, with ash-blond hair and bright blue eyes, as he climbed he kept one broad hand on the hilt of his silver sword, as if the snow were an enemy, waiting to pounce.

'My lord!' Menw said. 'It gladdens my heart to see you. I've been waiting here, hoping you'd come back. We've all been frantic, wondering what's gone wrong.'

'A great deal,' Evandar said. 'We've swung close enough for Time to invade us.'

'Indeed, my lord? Well, so far it seems to be winning the battle.'

Evandar considered the silver river, where dead water reeds and rushes stood brown along the banks. The water still flowed, but even more sluggishly than usual.

'Where are my people?' Evandar said.

'In the pavilion, waiting for you.'

Over dead grass and snow they walked downhill to the riverbank. Some ways along it stood an enormous pavilion of cloth-of-gold, listing to one side from the weight of snow upon its roof and the drifts piled against its windward side. With cloaks over their silver armour, the men of his warband were standing outside, talking among themselves. They were a beautiful people, Evandar's folk; their illusions of bodies had been modelled on the elven race, with hair pale as moonlight or bright as the sun to set off their eyes, violet, grey, or gold, and the long delicate curled ears. For the most part they had pale skin, but some had seen the human beings of the far southern isles, and had copied their skin, as dark as fresh-ploughed earth under a rain.

'He's here!' Menw called out.

The warband cheered. As Evandar and Menw hurried over, the

women came out of the pavilion, led by the Night Princess, a dark-skinned woman whose hair was a tangle of long black curls. All the women wore dresses of silk in colours as bright as spring itself.

'What are these strange events, my lord?' she said. 'What's turned the world so cold?'

'It's called snow,' Evandar said. 'It falls during the season that men and elves call winter.'

'It's nasty stuff! Make it go away.'

Whimpering, holding out their hands, the men and women alike clustered round him. The cold was making them suffer, Evandar realized. They'd come to believe in his illusions so completely that they actually felt pain from their effects. He realized something even more important as well, that he'd learned what suffering meant, and so their unhappiness caused him pain. A strange lesson indeed! he thought. And how many more would I learn if I were born into the world of Time?

'Please, my lord, please!' They were begging him. 'Bring back the spring.'

Evandar's power stemmed from the upper astral, but eons upon eons ago he'd learned to knot and twine the stuff of the lower astral like a weaver, laying it on the loom of his will to make forms and images. To keep those forms stable he'd also learned how to call down power and ensoul them.

With a cry Evandar threw his arms over his head and saw the light swirling just beyond the grey sky. It seemed to him that he flung the images of nets out from his fingers and trapped the light, pulling it down within his reach. He grabbed huge handfuls of energy and flung them, some into the river, some into the ground, some onto his people, who laughed and caught them like children catching coins flung by a great lord. At once the air grew warmer; the snow melted; the river began to churn and flow with new power. All along the banks the reeds turned glossy green in the light of a pale sun that shone once more from the sky. Evandar drew down more light and spun around, flinging it outward. Where each glittering jewel of it fell, flowers bloomed.

The people cheered him again as they cast off their cloaks. A bard struck up a tune on his harp; others appeared and joined in. With a laugh the Night Princess called to her women.

'Dancing! We shall have dancing.'

They caught the men by the hands and dragged them off, laughing and singing, to the dance. Only Menw stayed with Evandar as they whirled off across the sunny meadows.

'My lord?' Menw said. 'Could your brother be responsible for this winter?'

'I don't know, but that's a good thought,' Evandar said. 'I think me I'll ask him. Page! Our horses!'

The boy appeared leading horses, a golden stallion for Evandar, a black gelding for Menw. They mounted and set off upriver. The water narrowed and ran faster as the land rose, dropping the river to a canyon floor below them. The light turned suddenly pale, a greenish light that thickened to mist at the far edge of the view. At a fast trot they plunged into a forest. Even though the ancient trees stood gnarled and grasping, and the bracken grew thick among thorn and vine, the horses never stumbled nor slowed, and not a single twig dared reach out and snag their clothes. In the eerie light they could just see huge stones set among the trees, and ruins that hinted of dead fortresses and lost kings. Some of this forest was Evandar's doing, but some was not, and the farther they rode the less it belonged to them.

At the very edge of Evandar's domain stood a tree, half of which grew green with summer leaves whilst the other half blazed with never-ending fire. They slowed their horses to a walk and went round it cautiously. At this beacon the roads ran into some peculiar junctions indeed.

'Did I tell you about the man named Domnall Breich?' Evandar said.

'You did, my lord.'

'I wonder how he fares? Time runs so differently in his country that I've no idea if he's a day older or twenty years.'

'Does it matter?'

'No. In the omens only his son matters, but I wish Domnall well nonetheless.'

At the very edge of this empire of images lay a barren plain. Beyond the horizon, it seemed, a great fire always raged, sending up huge plumes of smoke that turned the sun copper-coloured and the light harsh and dry. Nothing lived there, not so much as a blade of grass. Nothing broke the silence but a rumble of thunder rolling in from the endless smoke. Menw shifted uneasily in his saddle and looked around him.

'No sign of him, my lord,' Menw said.

'He'll come when I call him. I know his true name.'

'Shaetano!' Evandar tipped his head back and called as loudly as he could. 'I summon you! Shaetano!'

His words seemed to rage as loudly as the thunder and his voice carry as far. They waited while their horses danced under them and tossed their heads.

'Shaetano!' Evandar tried again. 'I call you to the battle plain!'

Once more they waited while distant lightning flashed and thunder rolled, but still Shaetano never appeared.

'I begin to remember something,' Evandar said. 'I knew Alshandra's name, too, but she evaded me quite nicely, once she had worshippers among the Horsekin.'

'I don't understand, my lord,' Menw said.

'Neither do I, not in the least. I'm merely stating it as what elven sages would call a fact. Alshandra must have drawn power from her worshippers and used it to have a life in their world apart from our country. Why shouldn't Shaetano be doing the same?'

Menw started to speak, then merely stared at him in confusion. Before I met Dallandra, Evandar thought, I wouldn't have been able to link these two events so neatly, either.

'Why don't you return to the others?' Evandar said aloud. 'Join in the feasting. I'll go on after Shaetano alone.'

'My thanks, my lord! When will you return?'

'I don't know. As soon as possible, though I've got more than a few errands to run. Shaetano may be the worst of my troubles, but he's not the only one, more's the pity.' Evandar dismounted, then threw his reins up to Menw. 'Take my horse back, too. I'll not be needing him.'

Often in the long winter darkness Raena would go up to the ruined temple to invoke Lord Havoc. Occasionally she would allow Verrarc to come with her, but more usually she would insist on going alone, no matter how much he argued against it.

'It be a frightening thing,' he said one night. 'It's the dark of the night, and there be snow all round about. What if you were to fall and hurt yourself or suchlike?'

'Then you'd come look for me, wouldn't you now, before the night was out?' She patted his arm. 'Fear you not, my love. When Lord Havoc says you may, you shall go with me and learn what I do know.'

After she left, he paced back and forth by the fire for what seemed to him half the night. Finally he decided that he'd just go to bed. Why should he give her the satisfaction of knowing he'd waited up, half-eaten away by jealousy of the secret lore she learned from her strange teachers?

Yet he'd barely fallen asleep when she returned, slipping into the bedchamber with something in her hands. He lay still, eyes half-open, and watched by the light of the glowing coals and embers in the hearth without letting her know he waked. She set the something down directly on the hearthstone – a basin filled with snow. While it melted she stripped off her dresses and hung them from the wooden peg on the back of the door. Naked and shivering, she knelt by the basin, seemed to be considering something, then began feeding tinder and scraps of wood into the dying fire. It sprang to life as she fed it and sent her shadow dancing round the room.

With a yawn Verrarc pretended to wake. He sat up, stretching.

'You're back, are you?'

'I am, and sore troubled.' Raena sat back on her heels and looked his way. 'Lord Havoc did warn me somewhat. There be someone in this town, he did say, who does have great gifts for the working of dweomer. He fears that she be a foe to him and me.'

'Did he say who this might be?'

'He did not. But I shall scry in the water and mayhap search her out.'

When she leaned over the basin, her long black hair fell forward, framing her face and gleaming in the firelight. One tendril lay snake-like between her naked breasts.

'What do you see?' Verrarc whispered.

'Naught, yet.' She frowned, waiting. 'Hah! There! I do see her now but dim, not yet her face, just her carriage. A young girl, from that walk.'

The fire crackled, sending long darts of light round the chamber. Smoke rose in a lazy drift.

'Well,' Raena said at last, 'this be a startlement, Verro. The dark young lass, the ratcatcher's daughter.'

'Niffa?'

'The very one.' Raena looked up from her scrying and sat back, crouching on her heels. 'There's a need on us to dispose of her.'

'We'll do no such thing. I won't stand for it, Rae. You mayn't harm that lass.'

'Oh indeed?' Her eyes narrowed and her voice turned lazy. 'And just why, may I ask?'

Raena got up, stretching in the fire warmth, but she kept watching him all the while, narrow-eyed and sulky. It occurred to Verrarc that she must be jealous.

'Because of her mam,' he said. 'Not for her own sake. I do owe her mam a debt, a great debt, and I'll not let anyone harm her kin.'

Raena considered, then shrugged, relaxing.

'And just what might this debt be?' she said.

'She did save me grief, and I'll not be giving her any. It were my Da. Here, you came down from the north country for the Great Market many a time when you were a lass. You did see him then, opening the fair, all smiles and bows as he did welcome merchants and men he did stand to profit by in some way. You never saw him at home. He beat my mam, he beat me, he did kill her, I'm sure of it though to this day I don't know how.' Verrarc felt his hands crush into fists, heard his voice drop. 'I were too young to know, but I do remember her face, all purple and swollen as she wept, and then the herbwoman did come, all in a flutter, and told our servant lass to take me out of the house. And when we did come home, she lay dead.'

'Ai!' Raena whispered. 'Never did I hear this tale.'

'I've kept it locked up, a poison treasure.' He forced his hands to open, took a deep breath to steady his voice. 'So then, no other woman would marry him. He had naught to soothe his rages but me, and he soothed them on my back. Here, look. He had a belt with a silver buckle, and I keep the marks of that buckle still.'

Raena sat down on the bed, slid half under the covers, and turned when he turned so that she could see his back. He could feel her fingers, soft and warm, tracing out old scars.

'I did wonder what gave you those,' she said. 'And where does Dera come into this tale?'

'Everyone in this cursed town knew what my Da did to me, and not one person would shelter me when he was in his rages nor would they speak out. Except Dera. She may be but a ratcatcher, but she does have a noble soul and the courage of one of her weasels, too. When I ran to her she took me into her house, and she would not let my father in her door, no matter how he raged and swore. And then in the public streets, whenever her path crossed his, she would denounce him, and she would point him out to all the passers-by and say what a shameful thing it was, that a man should beat a boy who was not half his size. She shamed them all into shaming him, and the beatings stopped.'

Her hands came to rest on his shoulders.

'Well, then,' she said at last. 'I'll not be harming the lass, not one hair on her head, Verro. I do promise you that. And truly, I do wonder somewhat. Mayhap I could make a friend of her, like, and then see if these gifts of hers do fit her to serve the gods.'

'My thanks.' He turned to face her, twisting around under the blankets. 'I'll not have Dera brought grief.'

'None from me, I do swear it.'

She sealed her oath with a kiss, and then another. He caught her by the shoulders and pressed her down into the bed, then took her the way she liked – roughly – while she pumped and squealed under him.

In the upper astral, what Evandar imagined became real, though it lasted but a brief span of time. Here in the physical world, what he imagined took on no existence at all.

'A riddle,' he told himself. 'One of the greatest riddles yet.'

He was standing on the top of a stone wall, crusted with moss and ivy, that was all that remained of the Palace of the Zodiac in Rinbaladelan, the City of the Moon. Over the thousand years or so since the city had fallen, the surrounding forests had moved to take it back. From his perch Evandar looked out on green: trees stood in the middle of fragments of cracked pavement, vines and mosses covered the walls, shrubs and grasses burgeoned in the courtyards. Just below him a pair of black ravens chased each other and shrieked as if they were mocking him. He could remember this part of the city clearly enough to picture it in his mind, but in his mind the picture remained, a memory only and impotent. When he tried to invoke the astral light, none came.

Dallandra had tried to explain to him the difference between the world of men and elves and his own bright country. Although her words made sense when he was listening to her, when he left her they melted away as fast as his memory-pictures. He simply did not understand what she meant by fine words such as matter or the inertia of forms. Although he'd travelled much in this world of time and stone, never had he lived here, never had he worn real flesh and felt himself bound by the passing of years.

'And I never will! Better to fade away than that!'

But for the first time in the four hundred years that he'd been mulling these questions, his proud boast sounded empty to him. What would it be like to fade away, to cease to exist, to die? Not to die and be reborn, endlessly dragging himself through the muck and pain of the world of Time, but to simply die, once and for all, to fade away like one of his memory-pictures but with no one to recall him to mind? He understood even less about this final death than he did about Dallandra's talk of things astral and material. He did know that thinking about fading away frightened him.

Evandar dropped down from the top of the wall and landed in the weed-choked courtyard below. If he remembered correctly, under the ivy covering the broken shard of wall in front of him should lie a painting of the Palace of the Sun in Bravelmelim, another city of the Westfolk that once had stood far to the north. He grabbed some of the ivy strands and began pulling them free of the wall. With the roots and stems came dust, bits of filth, dead leaves, the occasional snail, and flakes of some odd substance, faintly coloured and grainy. When he picked off a particularly large flake, as long as his little finger and a bit wider, he found upon it markings that looked like part of a character from the elven syllabary.

He felt suddenly cold when he realized that a character was exactly what he was seeing. There had been words worked into the painting. By trying to clear off the ivy, he was destroying what little was left of the art underneath. With a curse he let the flake fall. He had best not touch a thing until he learned how to go about saving the precious relics of this place he once had loved. At that thought he remembered someone who might help him, someone in fact who knew the original plan of the city almost as well as he did. First, though, he had to attend to his errant brother.

Cool with the scent of decay, the sea-breeze lifted the leaves of unpruned trees and rustled in the weeds. Evandar flung himself into the air, stepped upon the wind, and let its eddying carry him through to the Rhiddaer and, he hoped, Shaetano.

The Gel da Thae priests believe that the gods gave Cerr Cawnen to the human folk of the Rhiddaer as restitution for their sufferings at the hands of the Slavers, and at the time of which we speak, the town did seem divinely blessed. Fertile farmland surrounded the lake and yielded rich crops of oats and barley, twice what you could get for the same labour down in Arcodd. Although no one understood why, people who drank the steaming mineral waters of the lake grew strong bones and rarely lost their teeth in old age, even women who lived mostly on barley bread. The town lay at a juncture of merchant routes; Gel da Thae from the west and Dwarven traders from the far east both came to Cerr Cawnen to trade with each other as well as the Rhiddaer folk. But the greatest boon of all lay hidden in the hills nearby, veins of moonstones and volcanic crystals in a rainbow of colours.

Trading in these stones had made Verrarc's father rich, and his son knew a thing or two about merchanting himself. As a young lad he'd ridden east with the caravans and seen the life of the Dwarveholts in the northern mountains. He'd noticed that the folk raised only a few sheep and gathered little flax, either; most of their wool and linen came up from the Deverry borders, and an expensive commodity it was, too. On his own he brought one summer a few bales of fine yarns and ended up getting twelve times their value in worked jewellery. Late in the autumn Gel da Thae paid high for those trinkets, giving him the capital to buy cloth instead of yarn.

With his father long dead now, Verrarc had made his own fortune as a wool merchant, carrying gems only as a favour for long-time customers. There would come a day, he could see, when all the gems to be found had been found, but new lambs were born every spring to grow wool. Thanks to him the Weavers Guild had turned into a real power in Cerr Cawnen.

'I was ever so pleased when your da came to us about a marriage,' Emla remarked. 'Your family does have a special place in Councilman Verrarc's heart.'

'So we do,' Niffa said. 'It gladdens me that you find favour in such.'

They were hiking up the path that spiralled around Citadel. The day hung cold but clear above them; sun glittered on snow below in the meadows that surrounded the town. Although Cronin knew everything there was to know about cloth and looms, Emla was the one with the head for money and business.

'There'll be no harm in bringing you along for this bargaining,' Emla said. 'And mayhap a little good, eh? I do like all my daughters to know how to drive a good bargain, and so you'd best start learning. Mayhap one day Demet will have a shop of his own, like.'

'That would be splendid, truly.'

They stopped just below the entrance to the councilman's compound to catch their breath. Emla brought a bone comb out of her pouch, pushed back her hood, and combed her hair, then handed it to Niffa to do the same.

'A tidy appearance never hurts, either,' Emla said.

They found Verrarc's front door ajar, and when they stepped inside, they heard old Korla scolding someone at the top of her lungs while the someone snivelled and tried to make excuses. All at once Magpie came barrelling down the corridor and nearly ran into them. She looked at Niffa and Emla, burst into fresh tears, and went racing outside. Shuffling along in her floppy shoes, Korla came muttering after.

'There be a need on me to apologize, Mistress Emla,' Korla said. 'I do lack the patience to deal with that lass. Too old I be, and the cold does ache my bones something fierce, too.'

'What be wrong?' Emla said.

'Ah, she did disturb somewhat of the master's, and the woman did rebuke me.' Korla paused for a sneer. 'Such a fine lady she be. But here, you've come to see the master, no doubt, not listen to me.'

Verrarc was waiting for them in his chair before the fire in his hall. He jumped up, sat Emla down in the other chair, then pulled over a bench so that Niffa could sit in the warmth.

'Well, Niffa,' he said, 'nah nah nah, I mean Mistress Niffa now! And how do you fare?'

'Well, Councilman, and you?'

'Very well, thank you.' Yet Verrarc was looking this way and that, as if he saw trouble crouching in a corner. 'Learning the wool trade, are you?'

'Mother Emla be good enough to let me watch and learn, truly.'

'Splendid, splendid! We'd best plan now for a good trading run in the spring.'

For a long while Emla and Verrarc discussed cloth while Niffa did her best to listen. Some weaves sold well to Gel da Thae, others to the Dwarven folk, but when it came to colours, everyone wanted a bright red that would neither run nor fade.

'No doubt!' Emla said. 'Had I that secret I'd be as rich as you, Councilman. None that I know of lasts beyond a summer's sun and a few good poundings at the riverbank.'

'And a true pity it is, then. Ah well. How goes your work? How many bales will you have for me come the snow melt?'

During the long conference that followed Niffa was hard-put to stay awake. The room was warm, the voices soothing, and she and her new husband had been sleeping little these nights. Once she did nod off, but she managed to jerk herself awake before Emla noticed.

She was just wondering how soon they could go home when the door opened and Raena slipped into the room. Niffa went on guard, her sleepiness forgotten, as Raena walked in with nods to the others and sat down near Niffa on the bench. She was wearing a pair of loose grey dresses, kirtled at the waist like a proper married woman's, and her hair was neatly done up under a scarf.

'I do hope I don't intrude,' Raena said brightly.

'Not at all,' Verrarc said. 'We've told each other what we need to.'

Her lips pressed tight, Emla nodded.

'I did wish to greet our guests.' Raena turned to Niffa and smiled. 'Always it is pleasant to see you.'

'Ah well, my thanks.'

Raena was looking her full in the face. Her dark eyes seemed pools of shadow in the firelight, suddenly deep, suddenly dangerous, as if they would turn to pools of black ink that would drown her. Niffa felt as if Raena had reached out with both hands to grab her and force her to stare into those pools. With a wrench of will she broke away and stood up.

'Oh, my apologies,' Niffa said. 'But my back, it does seem cramped, what with the draughts and all.'

'That bench, it be not the best we have,' Verrarc said. 'It were better of me to have brought a chair from the other room.'

'Oh, don't trouble yourself, Councilman.' Emla rose with a nod his way. 'I'd best be getting back. We do have a dinner to prepare and all.'

'Of course.' Raena forced out a smile. 'But truly, Niffa, if you have leisure for it, these winter days, do come visit us. We might chat about things now and again.'

'My thanks.' Niffa felt like spitting at her. 'But I do have my work back at the compound. I'm learning to spin, you see, and never have I done it before.'

'It'll come to you, lass,' Emla said. 'It'll come. Well, my thanks, Councilman. I'll be telling Cronin what you did say here.'

Rather than summoning Korla, Verrarc walked them to the door himself, then on an impulse, it seemed, grabbed his cloak from its peg.

'I'll walk you down to the shore,' he said. 'If I may?'

'Of course.' Emla lifted a surprised eyebrow. 'Our pleasure, I'm sure.'

They walked in silence down the first turnings of the path, but just past the public granary, where the path widened, Verrarc paused.

'I do have a favour to ask,' he said. 'If you could find it in your heart to forgive Raena, always would I be grateful to you. She be lonely, so lonely at times it aches my heart to see. Truly, our adultery was my fault as much, nay more than hers, and yet never am I scorned and shamed by the townsfolk.'

Emla sighed, glancing Niffa's way, then back to Verrarc.

'Unjust it be, truly,' Emla said, 'but a woman's honour breaks twice as fast as a man's and takes twice the time to mend. Councilman, I hope that I speak within my bounds, but if you truly want the folk to forget and forgive, marry the poor woman, all right and proper, like. Some coins and suchlike scattered among the poor would not go amiss, either, at your wedding feast.'

Verrarc nodded, staring down at the path.

'I want to,' he said at last. 'The Spirit Talker won't bless us. I've asked.'

Emla made a snorting sound.

'Werda be a holy woman and much favoured by the gods,' Emla said. 'I do think she forgets from time to time what life gives to the rest of us. If it pleases you, Councilman, I'll have a word with her.'

'Would you?' He looked up with a grin and seemed, at that moment, no older than Demet and as much in love. 'Gratitude would fill my heart.'

'Then I'll speak with her and soon. Now, do come along, Niffa. We'd best get home before the night's cold settles down. Councilman, no need to walk with us the more.'

'If you're sure? Very well, then, and my thanks, my humble thanks!'

With a cheerful wave Verrarc started back uphill. Emla waited until he was out of earshot.

'Now listen, Niffa,' she said. 'Well do I understand why you'd not want some close friendship, like, with a slut like that Raena. But for the trading, it would be a grand thing to humour her. For the family, like. Do you see that?'

'I do.' Niffa felt a twist of disgust, deep in her stomach. 'But it's not her ways with men that gripe my soul. There be some other feeling she does give me, like stepping on a dead animal out in a field.'

'Oh, now here! You do have a colourful way of speaking sometimes, don't you? Let's get back home. We can discuss all this over dinner.'

After he left Niffa and Emla, Verrarc took the shortcut between the boulder and the militia armoury despite the frost lying heavy in the shadows. He'd taken it so many times since boyhood that he knew exactly where to put his feet. About half-way up he realized that someone was standing by the path and leaning against the trunk of an ancient pine.

'Councilman Verrarc?' The fellow stepped forward. 'A word with you, if I may.'

'Of course. I'm afraid I've forgotten your name.'

Tall and slender, wrapped in a blue cloak, the fellow looked human enough until Verrarc noticed his ears were long and pointed as well. His hair was an impossibly bright yellow and his eyes a lurid dye-pot blue. He smiled in a lazy sort of way.

'You never knew my name to forget it, actually, but I'm Lord Havoc's brother.'

Verrarc felt a chill run down his spine. Here in the shadows the fellow did indeed seem oddly weightless, as if he weren't truly standing on the ground, and around the edges his flesh seemed translucent, as if he were made of murky water, not meat and bone.

'You may call me Lord Harmony,' he went on. 'I've come with a warning for you.'

'Indeed?' Verrarc found his voice at last. 'Come from where, good sir?'

'My own fair country, and far away does it lie. But you'd best keep an eye on that woman of yours.'

'Raena? What? How do you know –'

'My brother's a great one for mischief, you see, and I try to keep a rope on his halter when I can. I've seen her worshipping him as if he were a god.'

'He's not?'

'Not in the least. No more am I. The people to the south of you call us Guardians, and that name will do. But power we have, great power for good or ill, as I've learned over the last century or so. Don't trust him, Verrarc, and you'd best put a rope on your woman's halter as well.'

Verrarc gaped, struggling for words.

'The true gods dislike it when someone pretends to their rank,' Lord Harmony went on. 'You might remind her of that nasty truth.'

'Here! Who are you, to say such things?'

The fellow laughed, a long peal like the chime of a harp, and disappeared, leaving the last few notes of his laugh ringing behind him.

In a confusion of fear and anger Verrarc hurried up the hill and stormed into his compound, practically knocking Korla aside at the door. He found Raena sitting in one of the big chairs by the hearth with her feet up on a footstool. When she saw him, she smiled so beautifully that his rage dissolved in the thought of how much he loved her. At times he felt that if she ever left him, he would wither away and die like an abandoned child.

'What be troubling you, my love?' Raena said.

Verrarc took off his cloak and tossed it onto a chest, then flopped into the chair opposite her.

'Somewhat does trouble you,' Raena repeated. 'What?'

'It does.' He stretched out his legs to savour the fire's warmth. 'Just now I did meet someone upon the road home. He said his name was Lord Harmony, and he claimed to be the brother of your Havoc.'

'Oho, so he *has* come meddling! Lord Havoc did warn me.'

'What do you mean?'

'He did tell me that he had a jealous brother who travelled where he did, spreading lies about him.'

'Indeed? I found this fellow strangely easy to believe. He did tell me that he and Havoc be not gods at all, but spirits of an ilk he did call Guardians.'

'Prattle.' Raena waved her hand as if to knock the lies buzzing around her from the air. "Tis all it is, prattle and drivel.'

'It be a grave thing, Rae, to usurp the name of the gods. If this Harmony fellow be right, then –'

'He be wrong! Verro, how can you sit there and not listen to a word I say? Lord Havoc did warn me, I tell you, about this lackwit brother of his.'

'I do believe every word you say. To hold faith in Havoc be another thing entirely. Here, if this Lord Harmony be his brother, and truly, you tell me that such is the case, well, then Harmony must be a god, too, and no lackwit or jealous spirit.'

Raena flushed scarlet, then leaned forward, her hands grabbing the ends of the chair arms.

'I tell you,' she growled, 'Lord Havoc is a god. I do feel his power upon me when I work magicks.'

'Harmony never denied that there be great power with both him and his brother.'

Raena sprang to her feet and trembled.

'I will not listen!' she snarled. 'If you think me a liar, then I will leave your house.'

'Rae!' Verrarc rose, feeling panic clutch his heart. 'Nah nah nah, I never meant –'

'How may I stand here and listen to this blasphemy?' She tossed her head. 'Better I freeze out in the winter snows!'

In two quick strides Verrarc crossed to her and flung his arms around her.

'Don't leave me! I beg you!'

'Then speak no more blasphemies and listen to none, either, from this Harmony creature.'

'Done, then. You have my word.'

At that she smiled and allowed him to kiss her. One kiss led to another, and he was about to suggest they while away the cold day in their bed, when he heard someone cough twice behind him. He let Raena go and spun round to see Korla glaring at him.

'Be you ready for the dinner, master?' she said. 'Or shall it wait at the cook's hearth?'

'We'll eat now. You may serve it at table.'

With a snort Korla shuffled off, banging the door behind her.

'I do hate that woman,' Raena hissed. 'You should turn her out and that ghastly mooncalf of her granddaughter, too.'

'And where would they go? Korla did serve my mother well, and she'll have a place here as long as she lives.'

Raena seemed about to argue, then merely shrugged and turned away.

'Let's go dine,' Verrarc said.

She hesitated, staring into the fire.

'Please, my love?' Verrarc went on. 'Let's not have the food chill with waiting.'

'Oh very well! Whatever pleases you.'

When he touched her arm, she shook him off and marched out of the room without another word. He followed, planning out apologies.

Evandar returned to his country to find winter creeping back. Although the sunlight remained warm, the trees had lost their leaves again. Great drifts of red and gold lay on the ground or scattered across the grass with each breath of cold wind. Swearing like a silver dagger, he called down the astral light yet once again and poured its energy into the Lands. He clothed the trees with green and filled the river with fresh water; he brought birds to life and scattered flowers over the green meadows. Everywhere he walked, spring returned –

but for how long? he asked himself. Would he have to stay here now to fight against the winter, like a sieged lord trapped in his dun?

He could, he supposed, go consult with Dallandra about this change in the Lands, but the thought of iron and its torments stopped him. All at once he remembered a man who must have been another dweomermaster, someone he'd met by chance during the summer's wars, when he'd been hunting Alshandra. Off at the far edge of his domain, it was, in a place that he had never created. Under an aged oak tree that grew beside the silver river, Evandar stripped off his semblance of Deverry clothes and left them in a heap on the grass. He ran naked along the riverside, stretched out his arms, and sprang into the air. As his leap carried him up, he changed into a enormous red hawk. With a screech the hawk flew high and circled to get his bearings. The Lands spread out far below in a long sweep of green meadow, divided in one direction by the boundary forest and in the other, crosswise, direction by the silver river. The landscape stretched into mist and a horizon, where, or so he suspected, other lands had sprung up following the pattern of his own, wild lands with no lord to rule them. In one of them he'd found a mysterious old man, but at the time he'd been too intent upon Alshandra to wonder who he might be.

Evandar set off, flying fast, for the edge of the mist that ran into the green meadow like feather-edged waves upon a shore. Although it hid the land below, he tucked his wings and dove, swooping down to level just under its cover. He was flying over a grey landscape stretching sullen in a grey light. Big boulders pushed up through thin soil, and a constant scour of wind blew dust in little eddies over the flat. At a distance, among a patches of green lichen and thin grass, he saw a dead tree, stripped of branches, and swooped down to land nearby.

The old man with the brown skin and ready smile still sat on the rocks where Evandar had left him. He was still cutting the apple with a blunt knife, and each time he sliced off a piece, another grew back to replace it. Yet something had changed. All around him, for a distance of some fifty feet, the barren land had turned green with the beginnings of grass. Near the dead trunk a sapling had sprouted. With a shiver of feathers Evandar changed back into elven form, then created himself a green tunic to wear as well. He sat down on the rock opposite the old man.

'An apple tree?' Evandar said. 'That's new.'

'It is.' The old man looked up and greeted him with a smile. 'You've returned.'

'I have, at that. I've come to ask you a question or two.'

'Ah, have you? Well, I may not answer unless you answer me some of my own.'

'A fair bargain, good sir. I've told you why I'm here. Why are you here?'

'To act as a canal.'

Evandar gaped.

'Haven't you ever been to Bardek?' the old man said, grinning. 'The irrigation canals bring water from where it is to where it's not.'

'And are you bringing water, then? The land's a bit greener than when last I saw it.'

'Water of a sort. But now it's my turn for the question. You came to ask questions, but why do you think I have answers?'

'Because of that apple. In my own country there's a tree that marks a borderland. One half of it is always green and in full leaf, while the other half is dead and blazes with fire. I don't know why, but the apple seems to me to be the same sort of thing.'

'Very good. You're quite right.'

'I think me that I'm a canal myself, when it comes to maintaining my lands.'

'It could well be.'

'Can you tell me how these canals work?'

'Power comes from the astral plane, meets a pattern, and fills it, like water will run down a canal and fill up a pond. Do you know what I mean by the astral plane?'

'I've heard the word before, truly. So the power runs through me to my lands?'

'I'd suppose so.' The old man suddenly laughed. 'I've never seen you at work.'

'Ah. Well, I'm the master of the green lands over there.' Evandar waved in their direction. 'I created them for my people by pulling down energy and braiding it into forms. This was all a long time ago, of course. We wandered among the stars, but we grew weary.'

'Ah, so you don't come from the world of matter.'

That word again, matter! Evandar considered it one of the three greatest riddles, along with death and time.

'I don't, good sir,' Evandar said. 'Could you be so kind as to answer me this? When I'm in residence in my lands, I can create anything I wish, just by picturing it, but the thing refuses to stay. If I don't keep bringing water down the canal, as it were, then the pond dries up. How can I stop this?'

'You can't. That's the very nature of the etheric plane at work. Nothing persists there unless you keep building it anew.'

Evandar swore with a few oaths he'd learned from Rhodry. The old man made a wry face.

'You may ask me a question now, sir,' Evandar said. 'It's your turn.'

'Oh, I don't have any more. I'll save them in case I need to ask you somewhat later.'

'Fair enough. Then I'll give you another question to hold in store. When I go to the world of men and elves, nothing I imagine gets itself born. Why?'

'That's the nature of the world of matter. It's extremely difficult to create there, but what you create takes great effort to destroy. In the etheric world, what you create with great ease fades away easily.'

Evandar sighed and considered this, while the old man kept peeling the apple and eating what he sliced away.

'I think I begin to understand,' Evandar said at last. 'Do you mean to tell me that unless I've been born, unless I've subjected myself to flesh and stench and death, that nothing I do will remain?'

'Oh, it's not quite as bad as all that. Close, but not quite. Well-loved images remain as images, though imperfect ones. In some worlds bards already sing about your country, though they have all sorts of wrong names for it.'

'So if I should lose it, it won't be completely gone?'

'Not as long as the bard songs get themselves sung and men and elves are willing to hear them. But in the end, every song falls silent.'

'Then I'm doomed to lose it for once and all.'

'Not truly. If you lose it, you'll find it again. If you hoard it, you'll lose it.'

This made no sense whatsoever, but Evandar had no time to puzzle it out. He rose and bowed.

'My thanks, good sir. If ever I can be of aid to you, I will.'

'You've got the answers you need, then?'

'I do, though I like them not.'

Evandar flung his arms into the air and leapt back in to the red hawk form. He screeched once in farewell, then flew off, fast and steadily, for his own country and the mothers of all roads.

Far, far to the south of Bardek, so far that in those days very few human beings knew they existed, lay a handful of islands, scattered across the sea by the Goddess of Fire, some say, in aeons past. Be that as it may, they'd offered a refuge to elven folk who'd fled the destruction of the Seven Cities by ship, back at the time when Deverry men first rode in Annwn. The name of the largest of them is Linalantava, the Island of Regret.

In elven form, wearing his green tunic and buckskin leggings, Evandar travelled to Linalantava. With a pair of heavy leather-bound books under his arms, he walked along a misty trail that seemed to lead nowhere. All at once he stepped off, glided down, and found himself standing among twisted, stunted pines.

A cool wind played over a barren landscape. It seemed that the very sunlight changed, turning pale while he picked his way through huge grey boulders along the crest of a hill. Below him a cliff dropped down to a long parched valley gashed by a dry river bed; far across rose high mountains, black and forbidding, peaked with snow. A wind blew steadily, whining through the coarse grass. The stunted slant of the few trees made it clear that the wind rarely stopped.

When he turned round, he saw directly behind him more of the deformed trees, scattered round a spread of low wooden buildings, long oblongs roofed with split shingles. They were covered with carvings, every inch of the walls, every window frame and door lintel, of animals, birds, flowers, words in the Elvish syllabary, all stained in subtle colours, mostly blues and reds, to pick out the designs. From round behind the complex he could hear a faint whinny of horses, and a snatch of song drifted with the swirling dust.

Evandar made his way among the huddled longhouses, some hardly better than huts, that sheltered what was left of one of the finest university systems the world has ever known, then or now. The dry air of these parched mountains protected the books that the People had brought with them into exile, the last pitiful remains of the grand libraries of Rinbaladelan and the copies that generations of scribes had made since. It was the curator of these books that he'd come to see, and he found him in the scriptorium, a long narrow building with windows all round.

Meranaldar jumped up to greet him with a low bow. Although his name meant 'demon slayer,' Meranaldar was a thin man, stooped and hollow-eyed from his long years spent tending the sacred books. His hair was as pale as Evandar's own, but his eyes were a more normal purple colour.

'My humble greetings!' Meranaldar said. 'A visit from one of the Guardians is an honour worth treasuring.'

'My thanks to you, then.' Evandar held out the books. 'I've brought these back to you.'

Meranaldar took them and laid them down on the wooden table. His long fingers, gnarled from years of holding a pen, trembled as he turned a few pages.

'Does Jill have no further need of these, then?'

It took Evandar a few moments to realize what he meant.

'I'm sorry,' Evandar said. 'But yes, she's dead.'

Meranaldar's eyes filled with tears. He wiped them away on the sleeve of his tunic.

'Well, she had the shaking fever very badly when she left us,' Meranaldar said. 'May her gods treat her well in their Otherlands, as she called them.'

Evandar considered telling him how Jill had truly died, then decided against it. Grief was grief no matter what caused the mourning, and he had no desire to tell long complex stories about dweomer and the Guardians.

'I knew she'd want you to have them back,' Evandar said instead. 'My friend, I've come with a favour to ask you. You've got a map of the city of Rinbaladelan, if I remember rightly. I should like a copy of it.'

Meranaldar stared at him for a long moment.

'Er, you do have the map, don't you?' Evandar said.

'Of course! I'm just surprised. It seems such an odd thing to ask for.'

'Ah, well, I suppose it does. I have this scheme in mind, you see, but it's not yet ripe enough for the talking about.'

'Very well. Far be it for me to argue with a Guardian.' Meranaldar paused, drumming his fingertips on the table while he thought. 'The best copy isn't here. It's down in the city. I'll have to find someone to take my place, then journey there.'

There had been a time when Evandar would have accepted all this effort as merely the tribute due to a Guardian, but recently he'd learned what effort meant to those who lived in the world of Time and Death.

'How may I repay you?' Evandar said.

'Oh, my dear Evandar! No payment needed.'

'But I want to bring you something in return. Jill told you about the

Westlands, I know, and your people left behind there. Would more news of them please you?'

Meranaldar looked up with a smile that seemed to lighten the entire room.

'Very well,' Evandar said. 'What sort of information would you like?'

'Well, I – all of us – would really like to know how they escaped the destruction of the Seven Cities. Ever since Jill was here, I've been puzzling over that. She knew very little of the actual history.'

'Excellent! Please make me my map, and in return, I'll bring back everything I can find out about the Great Burning. That's what they call those days, you see.'

'And a good and true name for them it is.' Meranaldar looked away and sighed. 'A very good name indeed.'

One sunny afternoon, though the snow lay thick over Cengarn, Dallandra went for a walk in the town, just to be out of the dun for a little while and no reason more. She was climbing the hill back when she saw Evandar, standing in the shadow of a wall, waiting for her. With a laugh she ran to him and flung herself into his arms. He held her tight and kissed her.

'Oh, it's so good to see you,' she said. 'Is it better out here, away from all the iron?'

'Somewhat, truly, but still I can't stay long. I've got an errand to run.'

'Indeed?'

'Indeed.' He smiled with a hint of teasing; he knew perfectly well that she was curious. 'Dalla, answer me one thing. In all the Westlands, is Devaberiel Silverhand still the greatest bard?'

'As far as I know, it would be hard to find a better. Why?'

But instead of answering, he disappeared, leaving her scowling after him. Apparently she wasn't the only one to receive a visit; later that day, when Rhodry joined her for a meagre supper of bread and cheese, he remarked that Evandar had come asking him questions about Devaberiel as well.

'Did he give you a chance to ask him why?' Dalla said.

'Not much of one.' Rhodry drew his silver dagger and eyed the chunk of cheese doubtfully. 'I'll pare that mould away if it's all the same to you.'

'Please do.'

'So Evandar told me that someone he knows in the Southern Isles wants to know more about the Time of Burning and the Westlands. Who? say I, and why? as well. Oh, you'll find out in good time, says he. It's a –'

'Riddle, right?'

'Just so. I expect we'll know when he tells us and not a heartbeat before.'

Dallandra made a sour face and watched him as he swept the parings of mould to one side of the board with his dagger. He wiped the blade clean on his shirt, then began to slice the cheese.

'You know, I've been thinking about the Time of Burning myself,' Dallandra said. 'When the bards recited the history of the invasions, they called the invaders meradan, demons, or maybe goblins would be a better word in the Deverry tongue. A small people they said, and ugly, too.'

'Well, I wouldn't call the Horsekin a beauty to behold, but true enough, they're taller than I am, on an average, and from what Meer told us, their women stand as high as their men.'

'It's puzzling. I wonder if maybe there were two groups of invaders, and it's the small ones who were wiped out by plague.'

'Meer never mentioned that, and the gods – his and mine – know that he'd expound upon the old days at a moment's whim.' Rhodry divided the slices up evenly and slid her share toward her. 'The only distinction he ever made was between the Gel da Thae, the ones like him, who live in cities, and then the Horsekin proper, who travel with their herds up in the far north.'

'Just so. Well, when we get back to the Westlands, we can ask the bards ourselves.'

For a moment they ate in silence.

'I'll not be going with you to the Westlands,' Rhodry said abruptly. 'I promised Jahdo that I'd take him home to Cerr Cawnen, but after that, I'll be heading back to the dwarven lands.'

'Ah.' She considered her feelings for a moment and realized that she'd been expecting just this. 'To hunt for Haen Marn?'

'To wait for it, more like – to sit in those desolate hills until I rot. But I promised Enj I'd come back when the wars were over.' He was studying her face. 'I'm sorry, but –'

'No need for an apology.' She held up one hand flat for silence. 'Haven't we both always known that my heart belongs to Evandar?'

He smiled, relaxing.

'Just so,' he said at length. 'More bread?'

'I'll have some, and my thanks.'

Out among the elves in the Westlands, winter was a thing of rain and dark skies, not snow. When the summer days became noticeably shorter, the People began driving their herds south. By the time winter had set in they were camped at the edge of the Southern Sea, where there were ravines to shelter their encampments from the wind and enough grass in the cliff-top meadows to feed their stock until spring. Riding his gold stallion Evandar went from one to the other and asked for Devaberiel Silverhand, the bard. Eventually he found him, camped with his alar far to the west of Deverry, on a day when long rains had given over to a pale sun and a damp wind.

Evandar left his horse outside the camp and made himself invisible, then walked through the circular leather tents. Their owners stood around and talked, while children and dogs chased each other, laughing and barking, from the sheer joy of being outside at last. Devaberiel was sitting in front of his leather tent on a cut log for a chair and enjoying the sunshine, it seemed. He was a tall man, Devaberiel, with moonbeam-pale hair and long elven ears, but anyone who knew Rhodry as well as Evandar did could see the resemblance between them.

When Evandar stepped back into visibility, Devaberiel leapt to his feet with a yelp, but when he spoke, his voice held steady.

'That's a rude way to introduce yourself,' the bard said. 'Although truly, I think me we've met before.'

'So we have, a very long time ago, when you'd just finished your apprenticeship. I gave you a gift.'

'The rose ring.' Devaberiel turned away and spat as if the words festered in his mouth. 'I'll never forget the cursed thing.'

'What? Now whose manners need mending? That's a fine way to treat a gift from a Guardian.'

'I don't care. You've lost me two of my sons with your poisoned trinket. Isn't that reason enough for an old man's rage, that he's lost two of his sons and him in need of them to cheer his last days?'

'Oh come now, you don't look a day over three hundred!'

Devaberiel crossed his arms over his chest and glared.

'My dear bard,' Evandar went on. 'I meant no harm when I gave you that dweomer token.'

'But harm it's brought and grief as well. Your blasted rose ring drove

Rhodry far away, back into the lands of men. Come to think of it, it was your Alshandra who chased him there!'

'Imph, well, I can't deny it, though she's no longer my wife, I assure you. But what of the other boy?'

'When he was seeking out his brother to give him the ring, Ebañy travelled to Bardek, and there he fell in love with the woman who keeps him there still, or so I heard a long while back.'

'Ah. Well, I can't deny that, either. But here, can't we lay old griefs aside and –'

'No! We most emphatically cannot. What do you want with me, anyway?'

'I need lore, and I've been told you know the lore I need. It's about the Great Burning.'

'Well, I have that lore, yes. I've collected more of it than any other bard alive, I'll wager. But I'll not be giving you one blasted scrap of it.'

'But it's for the good of your people.'

'My people are a dying race, and soon I shall die with them, alone with my grief for my missing sons.' Devaberiel turned away with a sweeping gesture and laid one hand over his eyes. 'I wish to see no more.'

Evandar felt like shaking him, but instead he considered what Dallandra would do in this circumstance. In Deverry, bards often performed for gifts – a jewel from a rich lord, or coins, or even a mere meal if they were down on their luck.

'Here, good bard,' Evandar said. 'What if I give you a gift in return for your knowledge? What would please you?'

'Surely that's perfectly clear by now.'

'Rhodry has a wyrd that I can't change, but Ebañy – now, him I can fetch home for you.'

Devaberiel let his hand fall and turned to him with a smile.

'Done, then,' the bard said. 'Bring my son home safe and sound, and I'll tell you everything I know about the Great Burning.'

'Very well, then. We have a bargain, you and I.'

Evandar held one hand up, palm up, in the ancient elven manner, and Devaberiel laid his to match it.

'A bargain,' the bard said. 'And the gods of the sky have witnessed it.'

On these winter days the sun climbed slowly and never reached zenith, as if the horizon held it on a short chain and dragged it back down before it could properly rise. Noon announced itself as a brightening behind the silver clouds; night crept over the town like silent water. Niffa would sit with her mother-in-law and practice spinning until her wrist ached from tossing the spindle. Emla would pick up her lengths of lumpy yarn, shake her head sadly, and give them to Cotzi to rework into something usable with her long thin fingers. Still, Niffa would think, it was better work than drowning rats.

It was a drowsy time, huddled by the fire with the other women, spinning and gossiping to the sounds of the men weaving in the other room. The Wildfolk would come join them, though of course Niffa was the only one who could see them, crouching near her feet and watching the spindle drop and rise, drop and rise. They were fascinated by the weaving, as well; whenever Niffa walked by the door of the shop, she would see big grey gnomes sitting at the foot of the loom and staring at the shuttle as Lark or Cronin guided it through the warp.

On the rare occasions that Demet was home and working, they would crowd round him as he wrapped the shuttles with yarn. Every now and then, Niffa saw a gnome poke one of the skeins with a long warty finger, as if wondering how well it would tangle. When it caught her watching, it would vanish, but slowly, as if creeping away in guilt.

If the weather was clear or the snowfall light, after the mid-day meal Demet would leave the house and go to his militia post. Last spring a bard of the Gel da Thae, the civilized members of the Horsekin race, had brought the town a warning that the savage Horsekin tribes to the far north were arming themselves and gathering for trouble. No more news had come their way since, but the town stayed on guard. Her brother Kyle served in the militia as well, and at times he'd stop by the weavers' compound on his way back to Citadel and home.

In the evening, Niffa would wrap Demet's supper in a bit of cloth and take it down to him on the city walls. They would have time for a few words and a kiss or two before the cold drove her back to the house to wait for him to come off watch. As she hurried back to the weavers' compound, she would look up at Citadel Isle, swimming in the steam of the lake, and wonder how her family fared. The house seemed empty, Dera told her whenever they met at market, with both her and Jahdo gone.

As the new woman in the weavers' household Niffa watched what she said and did her best to offend no one, but Lark's wife Farra had a nasty temper, flaring like oil spilled into a fire at the least wrong word. Often as they worked, Niffa would let her mind wander, wondering about her family or about what her husband might be doing, there with the other men. At times stranger thoughts came to her, as well, of things she'd glimpsed in her dreams or in the fire, where pictures came and went that only she could see. Whenever Farra caught her 'slacking,' as the older girl called it, she would turn on her with a nasty remark or two.

One particularly cold day Farra seemed in a worse mood than usual, snarling at Cotzi, sneering at Niffa, even risking a word back at Emla when she tried to restore peace at the fire.

'Well, it does gripe my very soul,' Farra said, 'seeing Niffa just sitting there looking at nothing, and us with all this wool to spin.'

'Hush, hush,' Emla said. 'It'll get itself all turned into thread sooner or later. It was needful for Niffa to learn from the beginning, like. It's not easy work for her.'

'I suppose so.' Farra looked at Niffa with a simpering smile. 'There be not much wool for the shearing off of rats, bain't?'

'Nor from bitches, either.' Niffa snapped the words out before she could stop herself. 'Or was it different in the kennel you were raised in?'

Cotzi laughed, then stuffed the side of her hand into her mouth as if to shove the sound back in. Farra flung her spindle onto the floor and leapt up, going for Niffa with an open-handed slap. In a swirl like dead leaves gnomes materialized and flung themselves at the older girl's feet. With a yelp she fell spraddled onto the floor in front of Emla's chair. The gnomes disappeared. With a long sigh Emla laid her spindle and thread down on the rush-covered floor.

'Get up, Farra,' she said. 'And do you mind your tongue from now on. Niffa, you apologize to her.'

Niffa hesitated, then decided that peace in the house would be worth it.

'I be sorry, Farra. It were a wrong thing for me to call you a bitch.'

Farra got up, smoothing her dresses down, and refused to look her way. Emla sighed again.

'If you can't be civil and take an apology –'

Farra sat down on the bench and grabbed her spindle from the floor. Emla looked at her, considering, then merely shrugged and returned to her own work.

By then it was growing dark. As Niffa struggled to twist her wool into thread, she felt her mood blackening to match the day. Farra would find a way to get back at her, and after all, they'd have to live here together for ever. All at once she felt dread like the slap of a clammy hand across her face. With a gasp for breath she let her spindle fall into her lap.

'What be wrong?' Emla said. 'You do look as pale as death.'

'Be I so? I know not, Mother. I did feel so faint, all of a sudden.'

Yet she lied. She knew what was wrong, knew what she could never tell the others, that some great evil had marked her Demet out with hate-filled eyes. She felt the danger to him like a shout, ringing in her ears. When she glanced around, she found all the women staring at her.

'May I go take Demet his bread and cheese?' Niffa said. 'It do be a bit early, but the fresh air would do me good.'

'By all means,' Emla said. 'But be you well enough?'

'That I am, truly.' Niffa managed a bright smile. 'I'll just be putting his supper together and grabbing my cloak and going.'

By the time she left the compound, the full moon was rising in a cloudless sky. With Demet's supper in one hand and a lantern in the other, Niffa made her way across the crannogs to the lake shore. In the moonlight the stone town walls rose like the shadow of death. Her heart began to pound so hard that she had to stop for a moment and gulp cold air.

'Who goes?' The voice belonged to Gart, the watch-sergeant.

'Just Niffa. I'm bringing my man's supper.'

Gart himself materialized out of the shadows at the base of the wall.

'Well, now, it be needful for you to wait a bit,' the sergeant said. 'I did send him across to Citadel.'

The shouting voices in her mind roared, deafening her. Dimly she was aware of Gart hurrying forward. He caught her elbow and steadied her.

'What be so wrong, lass?'

'Oh, the cold air and little else. Citadel? Will he be there long?'

'I've no idea. We were up on the walls, and we did see the strangest thing, so I did send him across to see what it might be. It were a light, a silvery light up on the very peak of the isle, where that fallen house or whatever it might be lies.'

'The stone ruins, then.'

'Those, indeed, and they lie too close to our armoury for me to ignore any strange goings-on among them. Here, give me that lantern, and then walk you down the shore a little ways, and see if you can see it there still. It were such a strange light I did wonder if we both were seeing some fancy, Demet and I.'

Picking her way across the dark and trampled snow, Niffa walked a fair bit away from the pool of lantern glow. When she looked up toward Citadel, she could see its crest clearly above the mists. Sure enough, a silver light shone, the strangest colour she'd ever seen burning, but no, it was too cold for a fire – more like moonlight, turned thick and brought down to earth, but touched with blue. It flickered, a mere point or glint, disappeared for a moment, reappeared, then swelled, grew brighter, spread and swelled into a huge moon that spilled silver light, washing over her and dragging her off like a great wave. She heard Gart shouting in alarm.

Silence cut the shout short, a strangely live silence that hovered on the verge of sound. She rode the silence as if it were a swell of lake water, carrying her across to Citadel, or rather, her vision did. Somewhere in the back of her mind she was aware of lying on cold snow and of Gart, kneeling beside her, but him she could not see, because her power of seeing had gone across the lake. What she did see was stone, draped by silver light like tattered cloth, clinging to the walls of a tunnel. On the ground, on a stone floor, lay a man, face down, his arms and legs all akimbo. Nearby stood a woman with long dark hair, laughing as the light faded.

Niffa screamed, and with her scream her sight returned to the lake side and the golden flickering of the candle lantern. Gart was trying to help her sit up.

'Demet!' she whispered. 'You've got to get to Demet. In the stone ruins.'

In the lantern light she could see him staring at her, puzzled at first. Suddenly he made some decision.

'Right you are,' Gart said. 'Here, let me get you to your feet and off this frozen ground.'

With his help Niffa could stagger up and retrieve the lantern. Bellowing out names, Gart ran for the guardhouse down by the main gates. She saw other lanterns bloom as men hurried out and answered him. She hesitated, wondering where she should go to wait, but Gart called to her to follow.

'You do wait in here by the fire, lass. Me and Stone will be rowing over to fetch your man.'

The men left on guard ignored her. She sat down on a stool in the corner of the tiny wooden room and watched the fire burning on the stone hearth. Smoke swirled and flew upward, sucked toward the smoke hole in the roof. For the first time it occurred to her to wonder if she could call upon her visions when she wanted them rather than waiting for them to come to her. Demet, she thought. Show me Demet, oh please, show him to me. The smoke and the flames remained naught but fire and smoke.

The wait went on and on. At a table the other guards diced for splinters of wood but said next to nothing. Were they alarmed, too, she wondered, or did they think her daft and their sergeant more so, to listen to the witch girl? Now and again someone got up to put a log on the fire, then sat back down without looking her way. In the glowing palaces of the coals she tried to see pictures, begged the pictures to come to her – nothing. Eventually she heard a voice from outside and leapt up, but it was Emla, letting herself in the door. She was muffled in a dark cloak that set off her pale face.

'Niffa!' she snapped. 'And what be you up to, sitting here? Where's Demet?'

The men all turned to look at her as she shook her head free of the cloak's hood. Niffa tried to speak but found no words.

'What be so wrong?' Emla whispered. 'Where be my son?'

'I know not, Mother.' Niffa stood up and held out her hand. 'Do come sit and I'll stand.'

Emla perched on the stool. At first she seemed to be framing some question, but the mood of the room caught her, and she stayed silent. More waiting, more smoke and flame that leapt upward without visions or hints – the men diced, speaking not at all now.

'Hola!' A shout in Stone's dark voice. 'Come out, come out!'

The men rose and grabbed cloaks, then rushed out the door. More slowly Niffa and Emla followed, carrying lanterns. Stone and Gart were hauling a coracle up onto the lake shore and straining on the rope as if they pulled a burden, not a little leather boat. Niffa screamed and went running, so fast the candle in her lantern lost its flame. She knew, then, knew with the coldness of a sliver of ice stuck into her heart even before she reached them. She grabbed the slimy-wet side of the coracle and leaned over.

Demet lay in the bottom of the boat, his arms crossed over his chest, his eyes still open, staring at nothing. Somewhere a woman was screaming, high and soundlessly, over and over. Why don't they make her stop? Niffa thought to herself. Only when Gart grabbed her shoulder did she realize that the voice was her own.

'He did see, Verro!' Raena hissed the words out. 'It were needful to silence him. He saw, I tell you. He saw Lord Havoc!'

Verrarc wanted to grab and hit her, so badly that the urge burned as strong as lust. When he took a step forward, she shrank back and threw one hand up before her face. What are you? he told himself. Your father's son indeed! He crossed his arms hard over his chest and tucked his traitorous hands into his armpits.

'What if he'd told his wife?' Raena said, and her voice shook on the edge of fear. 'Think, Verro! What if he'd told little Niffa?'

'Well, now.' He forced his voice steady. 'That would have been a worse thing, truly. But by all the gods, Rae, yours and mine both, a death in Cerr Cawnen is a grievous thing. No one will be letting this matter lie.'

'Ah, but you be the one looking into it, like, bain't? Who but you, a councilman and the powerful man that the ratters do hold as a friend?' She risked taking a few steps toward him and smiled. 'You be the man who'll be saying who did what or that naught did happen but a sudden fever. There be not a mark on him, Verro. You did see that when the sergeant fetched you.'

'So I did.'

Under the bedchamber window stood a wooden chest. He sat on it and let his arms go limp, his hands hanging between his spread knees. The cold draught from the shutters soothed him, like the touch of a hand on a fevered face.

'How did you kill him?' he said.

'What? I did never!' Raena crossed to him in two graceful strides and flung herself down in a kneel. 'Verro, Verro! How could you think it of me? It were Lord Havoc!' She caught his hands and pressed them to her chest while she leaned against his knees. 'I know not how he did slay the lad. It were dweomer, stronger than any that ever I did see before.'

'Ai! Forgive me, my love. I did think – I know not what to think, truly. Forgive me!'

He pulled her tight against him and held her, shaking against his chest. But even as he murmured soothing words, he wondered at himself, that he'd been so ready to think her a murderess, the moment that the town watch had woken him to tell him of Demet's death.

As the youngest member of the town council, Verrarc was in charge of the town watch and all matters pertaining to it. How was he going to satisfy his fellow citizens while protecting Raena? The question kept him awake for what was left of the night, even though Raena slept soundly right beside him, not waking even when he gave up the fight for sleep and left their bed.

After a few bites of breakfast he left the house and went down to the lake shore and the boat house belonging to the Council of Five. He found Admi, the town's chief speaker, waiting for him. Wrapped in the red cloaks of council members, they walked back and forth on the gravelled shore in the dark grey of a winter's morning. The lake lapped and steamed beside them.

'There be no use in our going across till proper sunrise,' Admi said.

'Just so,' Verrarc said. 'Last night by candlelight I could tell naught. If there had been a wound, though, we would have found such.'

'And what were the lad about, there in the stone ruins?'

'Sergeant Gart does tell me that they saw a light, a strange silver light, he did say.' Verrarc hesitated, thinking of lies, but Gart had doubtless told half the town by now. 'It were the strangeness of the light that did make him send a man across. I do think that they were seeing fancies, myself. It be a long and lonely job, holding the winter watch.'

'Gart be a solid man, though. If he does say he saw a light, I believe him.'

'Oh, the light be real enough! What I'm finding hard to believe is this talk of strange silver witch lights.'

'Ah.' Admi nodded, sending his prodigious jowls dancing. 'Now I do see your meaning.'

'I'll be talking with every guard who went over to the armoury. I told Gart to make sure they assembled at first light.'

'The armoury? Gart told me they did find the lad in the stone ruins.'

'Was it now? Well, that's another matter I'd best get clear.'

At the guardhouse by the gates, Gart and the other men who'd been on duty were waiting. When Verrarc opened the door, they stopped whatever they were doing and rose to greet him.

'Sit down, sit down all of you,' Verrarc said. 'I'll not be troubling you long.'

The others sat. Gart brought a stool over, which Verrarc placed at the head of the table. The guards watched him with eyes so weary he could assume they'd not slept all night.

'Very well,' Verrarc said. 'Here be the tale as I heard it. There be a need on you all to tell me if I've heard wrong.'

They nodded, glancing back and forth among themselves.

'Early in the evening watch,' Verrarc went on, 'Demet and Gart did stand upon the catwalks near the South Gate. They saw a strange silver light upon Citadel's peak, near the armoury. Demet rowed across alone and did go up the hill to see what it might be.'

The men nodded. Verrarc turned to Gart.

'You did say that Demet were a long time about it. And then his wife did come with his supper?'

'She did, Councilman,' Gart said. 'And sore upset she was, too, when she did hear where her Demet had gone. So I did take one of the lads and went over to look for him.'

'But what made you decide to go look?'

'His poor woman, that's what. Everyone knows there's a touch of the witch about Niffa. She did fall into a faint, like, and then she began talking in this strange voice, babbling of Demet lying in the stone ruins. It were like she was up on the walls and looking down, telling me what did lie below where I could not see.'

Verrarc wondered if his blood were freezing in his veins, he felt so cold and sick.

'And what else did she tell you, Sergeant?'

'Naught. Just somewhat about the silver light and Demet lying so still on the ground.'

'She saw no one there, lurking in the shadows or suchlike?'

'Naught that she told me about.'

'Ah. Very well.' Verrarc felt his blood begin to thaw. 'Well, poor Niffa's off with Demet's family, attending to his last journey. I'll not be bothering the lass today.'

As the ancient custom demanded, Demet's family took his body out to the forest to give it back to the gods who had let him wear it a little while. Niffa and Emla washed his body and laid it on a litter, then covered him with a blanket. The menfolk carried the litter out and laid it in the sledge, drawn by two heavy horses and driven by Werda, who was dressed in white fur robe, covered from head to toe in the spirit-colour. As Demet's widow, Niffa wrapped herself a white cloak and walked behind the sledge when they set out. Behind her in a ragged procession came his family and hers.

In the high snow the journey was a hard morning's trudge though a
world turned to glittering rime by a cold sun. Even though she kept to
the ruts that the sledge made, Niffa was sweating in the heavy cloak.
She welcomed the discomfort and the effort; it blocked everything
out of her mind but putting one foot after the other. Ahead of them
down the river valley the pine forest loomed closer and darker with
each mile, as if they approached the fortress of Lord Death himself.
At the forest edge Werda clucked the horses to a halt. Emla and Niffa
took the long knives she gave them and cut pine boughs to cover the
body. The blanket they left in the sledge. Demet would return naked
to the forest.

His brothers came forward. When they lifted the bier from the
sledge, his father began to weep the long sobs of a man unused to
tears.

'Why didn't they take me?' Cronin said. 'I wish I'd gone instead of
him.'

Emla caught his arm. She still looked dazed, like a woman
awakening from a hard fall.

'Don't question the gods,' Werda said. 'Or tempt them. Let us go
among the holy trees.'

Lael and Kyle took the lead to beat a path through the snow, but
the drifts lay so high among the bluish shadows of the trees that they
gave up after barely half a mile.

'We've gone far enough,' Werda said. 'Lay him down.'

The pine boughs went first, laid out to make a bed of sorts for his
naked body. Once they had him settled, Werda raised her hands high.
The fur hood slid back from her face as she looked up to the sky
through the branches.

'The gods live in the trees and the mountains. The gods live in the
springs and the earth itself. All things are holy with the life of gods.
Now Demet's body lies among holy things, though his soul has flown
far away. Let us remember him always and speak his name, for if a
man's name disappears, then his kin have lost him twice.' Werda
clapped her hands together thrice, the sound loud in the frosty air.
'So be it.'

As the procession turned to leave, Niffa stood knee-deep in snow
and looked back. On his bed of boughs Demet lay as pale as the snow
itself, a silver shadow among the dark shadows of the trees. It seemed
to her that she could see little eyes among the dead ferns, hear little
claws rustling in the drifts, ready to spring upon him as soon as the

meddling humans left. She took one step toward him, her clothes dragging through the snow, then another; she heard voices behind her, but their words had turned alien and undecipherable. Someone caught her from behind.

Even through her heavy cloak Niffa could feel her mother's fingers pressing hard into her shoulder. Her mother's voice sounded in her ear.

'That thing be not Demet no longer. Mourn him we all will, but it be needful for the wild ones to have their due. The man you loved is gone, lass, where they'll never touch him.'

The pressure from her mother's hand deepened, guiding her around to face her mother's eyes, brimming tears. Niffa took her hand, then allowed her mother to lead her away.

The walk back in twice-broken snow, following the sledge, went easier. At the very end of the procession Niffa walked with Kyle, and her brother lent an arm for her to lean upon. Even so, she felt so exhausted that they lagged a fair bit behind.

'I'll promise you this, little sister,' Kyle said at last. 'None of us will let this crime go without retribution. Me and the lads in the militia, I mean. We did talk all morning long about it, and Councillor Verrarc, too.'

'Verrarc?' Niffa turned her head and spat in the snow. 'Oh, a fine one he is, to be finding out the truth of this!'

'What?' Kyle turned to look at her. 'What do you mean?'

'In my heart of hearts I do know who killed my man, and it were that Raena creature. I saw her, plain as plain, in my faint. She were laughing over Demet's body.'

'How can you see somewhat in a faint?'

'Well, I did! On the shore of the lake. Go asking your sergeant, if you're not believing me.'

Kyle considered this for a long moment.

'The gods all know you've always been a fey one,' he said at last. 'I do remember when you were but a baby, laughing and pointing at things none of the rest of us could see.'

For a few more paces he said nothing; then he sighed with a toss of his head.

'The sergeant did tell us all you did see things that night. Well and good. If it be Raena, then true-spoken – Verrarc's the worst hound in the pack to nose out this rat.'

*

Up ahead Lael turned back, calling out, waiting for them, forcing them to hurry and catch up.

That night Niffa came back home. The ferrets danced at her feet to welcome her, unmindful of her grief.

On the battle plain Evandar sat upon his golden stallion and called his brother's name. This time Shaetano came to him, riding upon a black horse, dressed in black armour as well, though his helmet hung at the saddle peak. It seemed to Evandar that with every passing year his brother became more and more vulpine. Soft red hair grew all over his face now, though the eyes that looked out were elven, and the mouth an elven mouth. A roach of stiff red hair plumed on his head. His hands were covered in fur, and black nails tipped each finger.

'So,' Evandar said. 'You came this time when I called.'

Shaetano snarled, exposing long white teeth.

'I hear you've killed a man, back in the world of Time,' Evandar said. 'This is a grave and evil thing you've done.'

'Why?' Shaetano laughed, but the sound was oddly brittle. 'They kill each other wantonly, men do. What's one death more?'

'A very great deal to those who miss him. Why did you come here?'

'There's a question I would ask you.'

'Ask it, and I may answer, though then again I may not.'

'I'd not seen a man die before, not so close.' Shaetano was studying the reins in his hand, or was it his paw? 'Will we die as they do?'

'Oho! You've scared yourself good and proper, haven't you?'

With a snarl Shaetano wrenched the horse's head around, kicked it, and rode off at a gallop. Evandar started after, then halted. For a long while he stood watching the dust settle from his brother's hasty ride.

'Run all you want, brother,' Evandar said. 'I'll find you in the end.'

EPILOGUE

Spring, in a Far Distant Land

Three are the Mothers of All Roads, not four, not two, but three. If you would walk upon one, you must know all three as well as you know the path from your back door to the market place. For if you set out upon one, only the knowing will save you from walking all three.

The Secret Book of Cadwallon the Druid

At the turning of the year into spring, Lady Angmar gave birth to twin girls, and a close thing it was, bringing both babies through to life and health, when the only help she had was her old maidservant, Lonna. Just after sunset, when the first pain came, the two women went up to Angmar's bedchamber, where, much to the old woman's annoyance, Angmar flung open the shutters over the window. Until the pains began coming close together, she sat in the window seat and watched the full moon, hanging gravid in the sky. At dawn it set while the birds of the island sang it to sleep like bards.

The babies came when the sun had fully risen, so close together that Lonna swore the second was clutching the foot of the first. When the old woman laid them on her breast, Angmar felt more grief than joy. Both were tiny, of course, though not as small as she'd feared with twins. A good five pounds each, she thought — maybe a bit more. Would they live? Or would the gods strip her of everything that belonged to Rhodry but her memories? She held them close and listened to each tiny heart, each pair of little lungs. They were breathing cleanly, at least.

'Here comes the afterbirth,' Lonna said.

A last pain overwhelmed her, but once it passed, she could see that her daughters were still breathing, still a proper pink colour.

'They've got some good strong blood from the Mountain People in their veins,' Lonna said. 'Don't you worry now, my lady. We'll pull them through. I'm just thanking the gods in my heart that it's spring and growing warm.'

Once the babies and Angmar herself were bathed, wrapped in clean clothes, and tucked up in the big bed together for the warmth, her daughters roused themselves enough to suckle a little of her false milk. Lonna pulled up a stool and sat down with a long sigh. Angmar yawned in answer. The exhaustion was taking her over, but she wanted to stay awake for a few moments more to savour her newborns.

'The true milk feels ready to let down,' Angmar remarked. 'With both the others, I had milk soon and more than enough for two.'

'I remember, truly, and that's a good omen.'

The bigger of the two infants opened her eyes, still a cloudy blue-grey, and seemed to be staring into her mother's face. Angmar smiled; she could no more have stopped herself than she could have stopped the sun. Don't get too fond, she told herself. They could die – twins usually do – but she was too fond already, and she knew it.

'And what shall you name them, my lady?' Lonna said. 'Or will you be waiting a while?'

'One of them already has a name. Marnmara.'

The old woman's bony hands clutched at a fold of her skirts.

'Could it be?' Lonna was whispering. 'Has she come back to us?'

'I'm as sure as I can be until she begins to remember and lets us know herself. All the omens rang true. Rori saw her, you know, saw her spirit walking round Haen Marn with her maidens. She was desperate to be reborn.'

'If you can trust what he said, one of the Westfolk he was and with their chatter, too.'

'Oh, and why would he lie about somewhat such as that? Not my Rori!'

Lonna ostentatiously started to spit on the floor and just as ostentatiously stopped herself.

'If I'm right,' Angmar went on, 'she'll remember soon. That's what she told me when she lay dying, that I'd know the true Lady of Haen Marn easily and she'd know me early, once she'd learned to speak a little and could walk outside.'

'Very well, then. And what of the other?'

'Oh, she must be some ordinary soul, born in the normal way of things.' All at once Angmar laughed. 'If any child of Haen Marn could be called an ordinary soul.'

Lonna allowed herself a few of the creaky grunting sounds that did her for laughter. With another sigh she got up, stretching her back with a yawn.

'And speaking of which, I'd best be tending Avain up in her tower. The poor mite! She's not understood, of course, but she'll be worrying.'

'You're exhausted, Lonna. Send young Mic.'

The old woman considered for a moment, then nodded. 'It's a fair strange thing, how our mooncalf has taken to the boy, but he can handle her almost as well as we can, truly. I'll have him take her porridge and tell her that you've come through splendidly. The babies – will she care about them?'

'I've no idea. One never does with my poor Avain.' Angmar hesitated as a thought struck her. 'Wait a moment. Here's a name for the other one, and it's a good-omened word in our Dwarven tongue. Berwinna. For her father was Rhodry from Aberwyn, and Berwin's the North Star. She'll need something to guide her, since we're all exiles here.'

'I like it.' Lonna smiled briefly. 'But which one is which?'

'I've not the slightest idea.' Angmar studied the babies, sound asleep against the warmth of her body. 'But we'll need to call them something. I'll think on it.' All at once she yawned. 'I can't eat now. I've got to sleep.'

With a nod Lonna started for the door, then turned.

'I'll let the men know how you fare, too.'

'Do that.'

Angmar was asleep before the door closed after her.

'I'm not leaving this blasted island again!' Otho snarled. 'And that's that.'

'All right, then,' Mic sighed. 'I'll go alone, or see if one of the boatmen will come with me.'

'I don't want you going, either. What if this cursed bit of rock decides to go haring off somewhere else and leaves you behind?'

'Someone's got to go, Uncle! Here we are in this country, wherever it may be, and we've got to eat, haven't we? I'm just glad we've got those jewels to set up business with. You and Garin have taught me a fair bit about driving bargains, and so I'll have to see what I can do.'

Otho crossed his arms over his chest and glowered. Mic was stirring porridge in the big iron kettle that hung from a hook in the hearth. He used both hands to hold the long wooden spoon and scraped round the sides and bottom, turning the hot mush into the cool.

'Not done yet?' Otho snapped.

'Soon. You might call in the boatmen.'

Otho stomped out, leaving the door open to a warm spring morning. No matter what his uncle thought of his plans, soon, or so Mic was thinking, he'd be able to leave the island and explore the countryside around the lake. Maybe, just maybe, they'd find some clues as to where the dweomer had brought them. It was Mic's ruling hope that they were close enough to Dwarveholt that he could walk

home, no matter how long the walk might be. He glanced up and saw
Lady Angmar's maidservant walking over.

'There you are,' Old Lonna said. 'My lady wants you to take Avain
her breakfast.'

'As soon as I can turn this over to one of the boatmen I will. How
does Angmar fare?'

'Well, and both her daughters with her.'

'Daughters?' Mic felt his face crease in a grin. 'How splendid! And
twins, is it? Let's hope that's a good omen.'

'Huh! If they live the summer, mayhap it will be.'

'True enough.' Mic wiped the smile away. 'Well, I'll pray that
they're healthy.'

With a long sigh Lonna walked over to a wooden chest and began
bringing out bowls to feed the men. As soon as the boat crew came
stamping in, she sent Lon, her son and the head boatmen, to take
over the stirring. Mic ladled out a big serving for Avain.

'Is there any salt left?' Mic said.

'A sprinkling,' Lon said. 'Here's hoping you can barter for some.
And I wouldn't mind having some butter again.'

'There's not a lot of grain, either,' Lonna put in. 'We'd best find
some way to trade, or we'll starve.'

'You know,' Mic said, 'I have to admit that sometimes I agree with
Uncle Otho's opinion of this island. If its dweomer is so blasted
mighty, why can't it feed us as well, as you hear about in the old tales?
With a magic cauldron or suchlike.'

Lonna drew herself up to full height and glared at him.

'Don't you go questioning your betters, young Mic,' she said. 'Now
get that porridge up to little Avain.'

With a bowl of porridge and a pitcher of fresh water on a tray, Mic
left the manse and walked round to the square tower. The sun lay
warm on his back; the wind that sighed eternally across Haen Marn
felt balmy as well. The stand of trees behind the manse were putting
out pale green buds along branch and twig. Yet when he went inside
the tower, it smelled of damp stone and ancient cold.

With a careful eye on his tray, Mic hurried up the spiralling iron
staircase past a landing piled with empty sacks and firewood, then
paused half-way up the next turn.

'Avain!' he called out. 'I've come with your breakfast.'

From above he heard her giggle in answer. He climbed on and
came up into a proper room, sunny and bright from big windows,

though the walls were more of the dark stone. By the largest window
stood a table and a half-round chair. Avain herself was perched
dangerously on the windowsill, gazing out. She was plump in a soft
and puffy way, with a big round face nodding over a round body, and
a tangled mass of yellow hair curling round her face and spilling down
her back. No one, not even her mother, could coax her into allowing
her hair to be braided, just as no one could coax her into living in the
manse instead of her tower, not even in the worst of winter, when this
room had felt as cold as the snows outside.

'You'd best get out of the window now,' Mic said. 'And come eat
your porridge.'

'Avain will fly.' She spread her arms like wings and laughed. 'Avain
will fly away.'

'Oh? And where will you get porridge, then?' Mic set the tray down
on the table. 'If you don't want it, I'll eat it all up myself.'

Avain giggled and climbed down to the safety of the floor. She sat
on her chair and picked up her wooden spoon.

'Be careful now,' Mic said. 'The porridge is still very hot in the
middle.'

'Avain likes hot.'

And that was certainly true, he thought. He'd seen her eat things
hot enough to burn a man's mouth, much less a lass's. She gulped
down a few spoonsful, then looked up at him. Her eyes were the
strangest thing about her, dark green, slit by vertical yellow pupils like
those of a cat, and nearly lidless. She lacked eyebrows, too, though
she had a sharp brow ridge to mark where they should have been.

'Is the porridge good?' Mic said.

'It is.' She returned to gobbling.

'I've got news for you. Do you remember that your mother was
going to have a new baby?'

Avain nodded and held her free hand out in front of her stomach,
no doubt to indicate her mother's size.

'Well, last night she had two babies.' Mic held up two fingers. 'You
have two new sisters.'

Avain laid her spoon down, then held up two fingers in imitation
of his gesture.

'Babies,' she said. 'Avain wants to see the babies.'

'I'm afraid they're too little to come visit you yet.'

She stared uncomprehendingly. Mic held up his hands to indicate
a tiny size.

'The babies are too small,' he said. 'They are very small. They have to stay in bed.'

She smiled and nodded, started to pick up her spoon, then hesitated, her head tilted to one side.

'Avain wants to see the babies.'

'Well, can you see them in your silver basin?' Mic pointed to the big silver bowl that also sat on the table. 'Can you look into the water and see them?'

Avain frowned, considering something. Over the winter past Mic had seen her scry far-off things often enough that he no longer doubted that she was as dweomer as the island itself.

'Avain wants to really see them. Avain go downstairs.'

'All the way to the manse? Will you go all the way to the manse? That's where they are.'

'Avain go to the manse.' She stood up. 'Now.'

Getting her down the stairs and out took a fair while. She would descend a few steps, then lose her nerve, but every time that Mic suggested she go back to her room, she would shake her head and take a few more stairs. Finally they reached the tower door, where she balked one more time.

'There's the manse,' Mic said, pointing. 'The babies are in bed with your mother. Do you want to see them, or do you want to go back?'

Avain took a deep breath and stepped out into the sunlight. She yelped and put both hands over her eyes, separating her fingers just enough to peer out through them.

'Nasty,' she remarked, perhaps of the glare. 'Avain wants to see the babies.'

Mic led her inside through a back door to the manse, so they could avoid the men in the great hall. Once in the relative shade she sighed and lowered her hands. The stairs up she took willingly, giggling a little as they climbed. At the door Mic knocked; in a moment it opened a crack to reveal an irritable Lonna.

'And what do you want?' she hissed. 'I won't have any one bothering my lady — oh! Avain!'

'Avain wants to see the babies,' the lass said. 'Two babies.'

'Well, there are two, truly.' Lonna stepped back and opened the door. 'If you want to see them badly enough to come down, then see them you shall.'

Avain marched into the room, and Mic followed to keep an eye on her. Back home in Lin Serr he never would have been allowed into the presence of a woman who had just given birth – men were forbidden to impinge upon such sacred and dangerous matters – but Lonna, so long away from dwarven society, let him in. He did stay well back by the door, though, lest he pollute Angmar and the infants somehow.

Avain ran right over to her mother's bedside. Angmar woke, smiled and sat up, turning her face so Avain could kiss her cheek.

'Babies!' the lass squealed. 'Two babies!'

'Just so,' Angmar said, laughing. 'My darling Avain! How sweet of you! Here are your new sisters, right enough.'

With Lonna's help, Avain picked up the bigger infant. Mic was surprised at her gentleness; she held the baby carefully and merely gazed into its eyes. Finally with a sigh she handed it back to the maidservant.

'Pretty!' Avain announced. 'So pretty!'

'She is, isn't she?' Angmar said. 'Would you like to hold the other one?'

Avain smiled and nodded, then once again took the infant with surprising tenderness. When she bent her head to look into its eyes, she squealed in delight.

'Granmama!' Avain said. 'Avain is here, Granmama!'

With a glance at Angmar, Lonna leaned forward to take the baby. Avain planted a kiss on the baby's cheek, then surrendered her. Lonna handed her back to her mother.

'Avain?' Angmar whispered. 'Do you mean Grandmother Marnmara?'

'It is. Granmama.' Avain looked up and laughed, then spun away from the bed, spun around and around, suddenly graceful as she grabbed her dress at the seams and held it out, as if she were tugging at wings. 'Mama wants to go home, Granmama.'

In the crook of Angmar's arm the baby had fallen back asleep. Lonna came stumping over with a short bit of green thread.

'Let's just tie this around Mara's little ankle,' Lonna said. 'So we can tell her and Berwinna apart.' She glanced Mic's way. 'I'll explain later.'

'Well and good, then. If I don't die of curiosity first.'

Avain laughed, clapped her hands, and danced over to the window.

'Home,' she said. 'We all go home soon.'

Mic felt foolish for allowing himself to hope, but hope he did, that perhaps she'd been given an omen that soon Haen Marn would return to Dwarveholt. But what did 'soon' mean to her, anyway, and what, truly, would she see, staring into the future with her strange dragon's eyes?

END OF BOOK ONE OF THE DRAGON MAGE

APPENDICES

A NOTE ON DEVERRY DATING

Deverry dating begins at the founding of the Holy City, approximately year 76 C.E. The reader should remember that the old Celtic New Year falls on the day we call November 1, so that winter is the first season of a new year.

A Note on the Pronunciation of Deverry Words

The language spoken in Deverry is a member of the P-Celtic family. Although closely related to Welsh, Cornish, and Breton, it is by no means identical to any of these actual languages and should never be taken as such.

Vowels are divided by Deverry scribes into two classes: noble and common. Nobles have two pronunciations; commons, one.

A as in *father* when long; a shorter version of the same sound, as in *far*, when short.

O as in *bone* when long; as in *pot* when short.

W as the *oo* in *spook* when long; as in *roof* when short.

Y as the *i* in *machine* when long; as the *e* in *butter* when short.

E as in *pen*.

I as in *pin*.

U as in *pun*.

Vowels are generally long in stressed syllables; short in unstressed. Y is the primary exception to this rule. When it appears as the last letter of a word, it is always long whether that syllable is stressed or not.

Diphthongs generally have one consistent pronunciation.

AE as the *a* in *mane*.

AI as in *aisle*.

AU as the *ow* in *how*.

EO as a combination of *eh* and *oh*.

EW as in Welsh, a combination of *eh* and *oo*.

IE as in *pier*.

OE as the *oy* in *boy*.

UI as the North Welsh *wy*, a combination of *oo* and *ee*.

Note that OI is never a diphthong, but is two distinct sounds, as in *carnoic*, (KAR-noh-ik).

Consonants are mostly the same as in English, with these exceptions:

C is always hard as in *cat*.

G is always hard as in *get*.

DD is the voiced *th* as in *thin* or *breathe*, but the voicing is more pronounced than in English. It is opposed to TH, the unvoiced sound as in *th* or *breath*. (This is the sound that the Greeks called the Celtic tau.)

R is heavily rolled.

RH is a voiceless R, approximately pronounced as if it were spelled *hr* in Deverry proper. In Eldidd, the sound is fast becoming indistinguishable from R.

DW, GW, and TW are single sounds, as in *Gwendolen* or *twit*.

Y is never a consonant.

I before a vowel at the beginning of a word is consonantal, as it is in the plural ending *-ion*, pronounced *yawn*.

Doubled consonants are both sounded clearly, unlike in English. Note, however, that DD is a *single letter*, not a doubled consonant.

Accent is generally on the penultimate syllable, but compound words and place names are often an exception to this rule.

I have used this system of transcription for the Bardekian and Elvish alphabets as well as the Deverrian, which is, of course, based on the Greek rather than the Roman model. On the whole, it works quite well for the Bardekian, at least. As for Elvish, in a work of this sort it would be ridiculous to resort to the elaborate apparatus by which scholars attempt to transcribe that most subtle and nuanced of tongues. Since the human ear cannot even distinguish between such sound-pairings as B> and <B, I see no reason to confuse the human eye with them. I do owe many thanks to the various elven native speakers who have suggested which consonant to choose in confusing cases and who have laboured, alas often in vain, to refine my ear to the elven vowel system.

GLOSSARY

Aber (Deverrian) A river mouth, an estuary.

Alar (Elvish) A group of elves, who may or may not be blood-kin, who choose to travel together for some indefinite period of time.

Alardan (Elv.) The meeting of several alarli, usually the occasion for a drunken party.

Angwidd (Dev.) Unexplored, unknown.

Archon (translation of the Bardekian *atzenarlen*) The elected head of a city-state (Bardekian *at*).

Astral The plane of existence directly 'above' or 'within' the etheric (q.v.). In other systems of magic, often referred to as the Akashic Record or the Treasure House of Images.

Aura The field of electromagnetic energy that permeates and emanates from every living being.

Aver (Dev.) A river.

Bara (Elv.) An enclitic that indicates that the preceding adjective in an elvish agglutinated word is the name of the element following the enclitic, as can+bara+melim = Rough River. (rough+name marker+river.)

Bel (Dev.) The chief god of the Deverry pantheon.

Bel (Elv.) An enclitic, similar in function to bara, except that it indicates that a preceding verb is the name of the following element in the agglutinated term, as in Darabeldal, Flowing Lake.

Blue Light Another name for the etheric plane (q.v.).

Body of Light An artificial thought-form (q.v.) constructed by a dweomer-master to allow him or her to travel through the inner planes of existence.

Brigga (Dev.) Loose wool trousers worn by men and boys.

Broch (Dev.) A squat tower in which people live. Originally, in the home-land, these towers had one big fireplace in the centre of the ground floor and a number of booths or tiny roomlets up the sides, but by the time of our narrative, this ancient style has given way to regular floor with hearths and chimneys on either side the structure.

Cadvridoc (Dev.) A war leader. Not a general in the modern sense, the cad-vridoc is supposed to take the advice and counsel of the noble-born lords under him, but his is the right of final decision.

Captain (trans. of the Dev. *pendaely*.) The second in command, after the lord himself, of a noble's warband. An interesting point is that the word *taely* (the root or unmutated form of *-daely*,) can mean either a warband or a family depending on context.

Conaber (Elv.) A musical instrument similar to the pan-pipe but of even more limited range.

Cwm (Dev.) A valley.

Dal (Elv.) A lake.

Dun (Dev.) A fort.

Dweomer (trans. of Dev. *dwunddaevad*.) In its strict sense, a system of magic aimed at personal enlightenment through harmony with the natural universe in all its planes and manifestations; in the popular sense, magic, sorcery.

Elcyion Lacar (Dev.) The elves; literally, the 'bright spirits', or 'Bright Fey'.

Englyn (Welsh, pl. englynion.) A metrical form, consisting of a three-line stanza, each stanza having seven syllables, though an extra syllable can be added to any given line. All lines have end rhyme as well. In Deverry at the time of which we write, this form was so much the rule that its name would translate merely as 'short poem', hence my use of the corresponding Welsh term to give it some definition.

Ensorcel To produce an effect similar to hypnosis by direct manipulation of a person's aura. (True hypnosis manipulates the victim's consciousness only and thus is more easily resisted.)

Etheric The plane of existence directly 'above' the physical. With its magnetic substance and currents, it holds physical matter in an invisible matrix and is the true source of what we call 'life'.

Etheric Double The true being of a person, the electromagnetic structure that holds the body together and that is the actual seat of consciousness.

Fola (Elv.) An enclitic that shows the noun preceding it in an agglutinated Elvish word is the name of the element following the enclitic, as in Corafolamelim, Owl River.

Geis A taboo, usually a prohibition against doing something. Breaking geis results in ritual pollution and the disfavour if not active enmity of the gods. In societies that truly believe in geis, a person who breaks it usually dies fairly quickly, either of morbid depression or some unconsciously self-inflicted 'accident', unless he or she makes ritual amends.

Gerthddyn (Dev.) Literally, a 'music man', a wandering minstrel and entertainer of much lower status than a true bard.

Great Ones Spirits, once human but now disincarnate, who exist on an unknowably high plan of existence and who have dedicated themselves to the eventual enlightenment of all sentient beings. They are also known to the Buddhists, as Boddhisattvas.

Gwerbret (Dev. The name derives from the Gaulish *vergobretes*.) The highest rank of nobility below the royal family itself. Gwerbrets (Dev. *gwerbretion*) function as the chief magistrates of their regions, and even kings hesitate to override their decisions because of their many ancient prerogatives.

Hiraedd (Dev.) A peculiarly Celtic form of depression, marked by a deep, tormented longing for some unobtainable things; also and in particular, homesickness to the third power.

Javelin (trans. of Dev. *picecl*.) Since the weapon in question is only about three feet long, another possible translation would be 'war dart'. The reader should not think of it as a proper spear or as one of those enormous javelins used in the modern Olympic Games.

Lwdd (Dev.) A blood-price; differs from wergild in that the amount of lwdd is negotiable in some circumstances, rather than being irrevocably set by law.

Malover (Dev.) A full, formal court of law with both a priest of Bel and either a gwerbret or a tieryn in attendance.

Melim (Elv.) A river.

Mor (Dev.) A sea, ocean.

Pan (Elv.) An enclitic, similar to -fola- defined earlier, except that it indicates that the preceding noun is plural as well as the name of the following word, as in Corapanmelim, River of the Many Owls. Remember that Elvish always indicates pluralization by adding a semi-independent morpheme, and that this semi-independence is reflected in the various syntax-bearing enclitics.

Pecl (Dev.) Far, distant.

Rhan (Dev.) A political unit of land; thus, gwerbretrhyn, tierynrhyn, the area under the control of a given gwerbret or tieryn. The size of the various rhans (Dev. rhannau) varies widely, depending on the vagaries of inheritance and the fortunes of war rather than some legal definition.

Scrying The art of seeing distant people and places by magic.

Sigil An abstract magical figure, usually representing either a particular spirit or a particular kind of energy or power. These figures, which look a lot like geometrical scribbles, are derived by various rules from secret magical diagrams.

Taer (Dev.) Land, country.

Thought-form An image or three-dimensional form that has been fashioned out of either etheric or astral substance, usually by the action of a trained mind. If enough trained minds work together to build the same thought-form, it will exist independently for a period of time based on the amount of energy put into it. (Putting energy into such a form is known as *ensouling* the thought form.) Manifestations of gods or saints are usually thought forms picked up by the highly intuitive, such as children, or those with a touch of second sight. It is also possible for many untrained minds acting together to make fuzzy, ill-defined thought-forms that can be picked up the same way, such as UFOs and sightings of the Devil.

Tieryn (Dev.) An intermediate rank of the noble-born, below a gwerbret but above an ordinary lord (Dev. *arcloedd*.)

Wyrd (trans. of Dev. *tingedd*.) Fate, destiny; the inescapable problems carried over from a sentient being's last incarnation.

Ynis (Dev.) An island.

Table of Reincarnating Characters

THE CIVIL WARS	THE NORTHLANDS, 1116	DEVERRY, 1065
Anasyn	Kyle	
Bevyan	Dera	
Bellyra	Carramaena	
Burcan	Verrarc	Sarcyn
Branoic	(yet to appear)	Jill
Caradoc	(yet to appear)	Blaen of Cwm Pecl
Lillorigga	Niffa	
Maddyn	Rhodry	Rhodry
Merodda	Raena	Mallona
Nevyn	(yet to appear)	Nevyn
Olaen	Jahdo	
Owaen	(yet to appear)	Cullyn of Cerrmor

I must apologize to the regular readers of this series. There are errors in the incarnation chart in the back of A TIME OF OMENS. The attributions above are the correct ones.